Sebastian Barry was born in Dublin in 1955 and educated at The Catholic University School and Trinity College, Dublin, where he was later Writer Fellow in 1996. His plays include *Boss Grady's Boys* (1988), *The Steward of Christendom* (1995), *Our Lady of Sligo* (1998), and *The Pride of Parnell Street* (2007). His novels include *The Whereabouts of Eneas McNulty* (1998), *Annie Dunne* (2002), and *A Long Long Way* (2005), and he has won among other awards the Irish-America Fund Literary Award, The Christopher Ewart-Biggs Prize, the London Critics Circle Award, and The Kerry Group Irish Fiction Prize. *A Long Long Way*, which was was shortlisted for the Man Booker and the Dublin International Impac Prize, was the *Dublin: One City One Book* choice for 2007. He lives in Wicklow with his wife and three children.

The Secret Scripture

A novel

by SEBASTIAN BARRY

ff

faber and faber

First published in 2008
by Faber and Faber Limited
3 Queen Square London WC1N 3AU
This export edition first published in 2008

Typeset by Faber and Faber Limited
Printed in England by Mackays of Chatham, plc

A CIP record for this book
is available from the British Library

ISBN 978–0–571–23961–0

2 4 6 8 10 9 7 5 3 1

For Margaret Synge

'The greatest imperfection is in our inward sight, that is, to be ghosts unto our own eyes.'

Sir Thomas Browne, *Christian Morals*

'Of the numbers who study, or at least read history, how few derive any advantage from their labours! . . . Besides, there is much uncertainty even in the best authenticated ancient and modern histories; and that love of truth, which in some minds is innate and immutable, necessarily leads to a love of secret memoirs and private anecdotes.'

Maria Edgeworth, Preface to *Castle Rackrent*

PART ONE

CHAPTER ONE

Roseanne's Testimony of Herself

(Patient, Roscommon Regional Mental Hospital, 1957–)

The world begins anew with every birth, my father used to say. He forgot to say, with every death it ends. Or did not think he needed to. Because for a goodly part of his life he worked in a graveyard.

That place where I was born was a cold town. Even the mountains stood away. They were not sure, no more than me, of that dark spot, those same mountains.

There was a black river that flowed through the town, and if it had no grace for mortal beings, it did for swans, and many swans resorted there, and even rode the river like some kind of plunging animals, in floods.

The river also took the rubbish down to the sea, and bits of things that were once owned by people and pulled from the banks, and bodies too, if rarely, oh and poor babies, that were embarrassments, the odd time. The speed and depth of the river would have been a great friend to secrecy.

That is Sligo town I mean.

Sligo made me and Sligo undid me, but then I should have given up much sooner than I did being made or undone by human towns, and looked to myself alone. The terror and hurt in my story happened because when I was young I thought others were the authors of my fortune or misfortune; I did not know that a person could hold up a wall made of imaginary bricks and mortar against the horrors and cruel, dark tricks of time that assail us, and be the author therefore of themselves.

I am not there now, now I am in Roscommon. It is an old place that was one time a mansion but it is all cream paint and iron beds now, and locks on the doors. It is all Dr Grene's kingdom. Dr Grene is a man I don't understand but I am not afraid of him. What religion he is I don't know, but he looks very like to St Thomas, with his beard and balding crown.

I am completely alone, there is no one in the world that knows me now outside of this place, all my own people, the few farthings of them that once were, my little wren of a mother I suppose in chief, they are all gone now. And my persecutors are gone in the main I believe, and the reason for all this is that I am an old, old woman now, I may be as much as a hundred, though I do not know, and no one knows. I am only a thing left over, a remnant woman, and I do not even look like a human being no more, but a scraggy stretch of skin and bone in a bleak skirt and blouse, and a canvas jacket, and I sit here in my niche like a songless robin – no, like a mouse that died under the hearthstone where it was warm, and lies now like a mummy in the pyramids.

No one even knows I have a story. Next year, next week, tomorrow, I will no doubt be gone, and it will be a smallsize coffin they will need for me, and a narrow hole. There will never be a stone at my head, and no matter.

But small and narrow are all human things maybe.

It is silence all about. My hand is good and I have a beautiful biro full of blue ink, given me by my friend the doctor, because I said I liked its colour – who is not a bad man in truth, maybe even a philosopher – and I have a bundle of paper that I found in a store cupboard among other unwanted things, and I have a floorboard loosened where I hide these treasures. I write out my life on unwanted paper – surplus to requirements. I start with a clean sheet – with many clean sheets. For dearly I would love now to leave an account, some kind of brittle and honest-minded history of myself, and if God gives me the strength, I will tell this story, and imprison it under the floor-board, and then with joy enough I will go to my own rest under the Roscommon sod.

My father was the cleanest man in all the Christian world, all Sligo anyhow. He seemed to me all strapped about in his uniform – not in any manner haphazard, but regular as an account book. He was the superintendent of the graveyard, and for this work he had been given quite a resplendent uniform, or so it seemed to me as a child.

He had a barrel in the yard that gathered the rain and with that he rinsed himself every day of the year. He would turn the faces of my mother and myself to the wall of the kitchen, and stood without fear of being seen among the mosses and the lichens of the yard, stripped entirely, and laved himself mercilessly in all kinds of weather, in the deeps of winter groaning like a bull.

Carbolic soap, that would have cleaned a greasy floor, he agitated into a suit of suds, that fitted him well, and he scraped at his self with a piece of grey stone, that he stuck into the wall in a particular niche when he was done – from where it poked out like a nose. All this I saw by glimpses and quick turns of the head, because I was a dishonest daughter in that way, and couldn't obey.

No circus act could have pleased me in the same way.

My father was a singer that could not be silenced, he sang all the songs of the operettas of those days. And he loved to read the sermons of preachers long gone, because, he said, he could imagine the sermons fresh for some vanished Sunday, and the words new in the mouths of the preachers. His own father had

5

been a preacher. My father was a passionate, I might almost say celestial-minded Presbyterian man, which was not a particularly fashionable quality in Sligo. The *Sermons* of John Donne he prized above all, but his veritable gospel was *Religio Medici* by Sir Thomas Browne, a book I still possess in all the flotsam and ruckus of my life, in a little battered volume. I have it here before me on my bed, with his name in black ink inside, Joe Clear, and the date 1888, and the town Southampton, for in his extreme youth he had been a sailor, sailing into every port of Christendom before he was seventeen.

In Southampton occurred one of the kingly or main events of his life, in that he met my mother Cissy, who was a chamber maid in the sailors' boarding house he favoured.

He used to tell a curious story about Southampton, and as a child I received it as the gospel truth. It may have been true for all that.

One season coming into port he could find no bed in his favourite house and was obliged to go further along the windy wastes of terraces and signs, and found a lonely house with a vacant sign stuck out to fish in customers.

In he went and was met by a greyfaced woman in her middle years, who gave him a bed in the basement of her house.

In the middle of the night he woke, thinking he heard someone breathing in the room. Startled, and with that extreme awakeness that attends such panic, he heard a groan, and someone lay on the bed beside him in the dark.

He lit his candle from the tinderbox. There was no one to be seen. But he saw the bedclothes and mattress depressed where a heavy person lay. He leapt from the bed and called out but there was no reply. It was then he noticed also in his very entrails a terrible sense of hunger such as had not afflicted an Irishman since the dark famine. He rushed to the door but to his amazement it was locked against him. Now he was greatly outraged. 'Let me out, let me out!' he called, both terrified and

6

affronted. How dare that old hag lock him in! He banged and banged, and finally the landlady came and calmly unlocked it. She apologised and said she must have unwittingly turned the key against thieves. He told her about the disturbance but she only smiled at him and said nothing, and then went up to her own quarters. He thought he caught from her a strange smell of leaves, of underfloor and undergrowth, like she had been crawling through woodland. Then there was calm, and he snuffed out his candle and tried to sleep.

The same thing happened a little while later. He leapt up again and lit his candle and went to the door. It was locked again! Again that deep gnawing hunger in his belly. For some reason, maybe because of her extreme strangeness, he couldn't bear to call the landlady, and sweating and discommoded he spent the night in a chair.

When morning broke he awoke, and dressed, and when he went to the door it was open. He took his bags and went upstairs. It was then he noticed the decrepitude of the place, which had not been so obvious in the kinder darkness of the night. He could not raise the landlady, and with his ship due to sail, was forced to leave the house without seeing her, throwing the few shillings on the hallstand as he went out.

Outside in the street when he looked back he was greatly perturbed to see many of the windowpanes of the house were broken, and there were slates missing from the sagging roof.

He went into the shop on the corner to compose himself by talking to another human person, and asked the shopkeeper about the house. The house, said the shopkeeper, had been closed up some years ago and was uninhabited. Ideally it would be demolished except it was part of the terrace. He could not have spent the night there, said the shopkeeper. No one lived there and no one would dream of buying it, for the reason that a woman had killed her husband there, locking him in a basement room and starving him to death. The

7

woman herself had been tried and hanged for murder.

My father told me and my mother this story with the passion of a person reliving it as he spoke. The gloomy house, the grey woman, the groaning ghost swam behind his eyes.

'It's as well there was room with us the next time you were in port, then, Joe,' said my mother, in her most neutral tones.

'By God, by God, yes,' said my father.

A little human story, a sailor's story, that somehow had still bound up in it my mother's contrasting beauty, and the enormous lure she had for him then and always.

For her beauty was that darkhaired, darkskinned Spanish sort of beauty, with green eyes like American emeralds, that no man can protect himself against.

And he married her and brought her back to Sligo and there she lived her life henceforth, not bred in that darkness, but like a lost shilling on a floor of mud, glistening in some despair. A more beautiful girl Sligo never saw, she had skin as soft as feathers, and a warm, generous breast all new-baked bread and delight.

The greatest joy of my young life was issuing forth with my mother into the streets of Sligo at dusk, because she liked to meet my father on his way home from his work at the cemetery. It was only many years later when I was more grown myself that I realised, looking back, that there was a certain anxiety in that going forth, as if she did not trust time and the ordinary way of things to bring him home. For I do believe my mother suffered strangely under her halo of beauty.

He was the superintendent there, as I said to you, and wore a blue uniform and a cap with a peak as black as a blackbird's coat.

This was at a time when there was the Great War and the town was full of soldiers, as if Sligo itself were a battlefield, but of course it was not. It was but men on their furlough we saw there. But they had a great look of my own father, what with the uniforms – so that he seemed to pop up everywhere in those streets, as my mother and me were walking, myself looking out as fiercely as she for him. My joy was only completed when at last it turned out to be him, coming home from the cemetery in the dark evenings of winter, as might be, skittering along. And when he spied me he would be playing with me then, larking about like a child. And many a glance he got, and maybe such action didn't go with his dignity as superintendent of the Sligo dead. But he had that rare ability to let things ease in himself in the company of a child, and be stupid and gay in the parched light.

He was the keeper of the graves, but he was also himself, and in his peaked cap and blue uniform could guide a person to whatever plot held relative or friend with solemn dignity enough, but alone in his graveyard house, which was a little temple made of concrete, he would be heard singing wonderfully 'I Dreamt that I Dwelt in Marble Halls' from *The Bohemian Girl*, one of his favourite operettas.

And on free days he went out on his Matchless motorcycle to race along on the devious roads of Ireland. If the winning of my mother constituted a kingly event, the fact that he in one great year of fortune, around the time of my birth, raced the short course on the Isle of Man, on his lovely bike, coming in respectably in the middle of the field, and not killing himself, was the source of constant memory and joy, and I am sure consoled him in his concrete temple in the dreary stretches of an Irish winter, surrounded as he was by those sleeping souls.

My father's other 'famous' story, that is, famous in our tiny household, happened during his single days, when he was more able to get himself to the few motorcycle meetings of those times. It happened in Tullamore, and was a singularly peculiar tale.

He was going along himself at a great rate, and in front of

9

him was a long wide hill, leading down to a sharp turn where the road met a domain wall, one of those high, thick stone walls built during the Irish famine indeed, as a sort of useless labour to keep labourers alive. At any rate, the racer in front of him, tearing down the hill and picking up an enormous head of speed, instead of braking seemed even to accelerate at the opposing wall, and finally, in a horrible clutter of smoke, metal and a noise as of cannons, struck it mercilessly. My father, peering out through his dirty goggles, nearly lost his grip on his own machine, such was his horror; but then saw a sight he could not and could never explain, which was the rider rising as if on wings, and crossing the huge wall in a swift and gentle movement, like the smooth glide of a seagull in an upwind. For a moment, for a moment he thought indeed he saw a flash of wings, and never could read in his prayerbook again about angels without thinking of that extraordinary instance.

Please do not think my father was dissembling, because he was quite incapable of that. It is true that in country districts – even in the towns – people like to tell you they have seen wonders, such as my husband Tom and the two-headed dog on the road to Enniscrone. It is true also that such stories are only effective if the teller feigns absolute belief – or indeed saw such wonders truly. But my father was no magician of lies and stories.

My father managed to slow his motor-bicycle and stop, and running along the domain wall, found one of those fanciful little gates, and pushing the rusty iron, hurried in through nettles and docks to find his miraculous friend. There on the other side of the wall he lay, quite unconscious, but also, and my father swore to the truth of it, quite unharmed. Eventually the man, who happened to be an Indian gentleman who sold scarves and other items out of his suitcase all over the western seaboard, awoke, and smiled at my father. They both marvelled at this inexplicable escape, which not unnaturally was the talk of Tullamore for years after. If you ever hear that story, the teller might give it the title of 'The Indian Angel'.

Again my father's curious happiness was most clearly evident in the retelling of this story. It was as if such an event were a reward to him for being alive, a little gift of narrative that pleased him so much it conferred on himself, in dreams and waking, a sense of privilege, as if such little scraps of stories and events composed for him a ragged gospel. And if ever there were to be written an evangelical gospel of my father's life – and why should there not, as every person's life is said to be precious to God – I suppose those wings merely glimpsed on his friend the Indian's back would become more substantial, and things merely hinted at by him would become in the new telling by a second hand solid, unprovable, but raised up even higher into the realms of miracle. So that all and sundry might take comfort from it.

My father's happiness. It was a precious gift in itself, as perhaps my mother's anxiety was a perpetual spanner thrown into her works. For my mother never made miniature legends of her life, and was singularly without stories, though I am sure there were things there to tell as good as my father's.

It is funny, but it strikes me that a person without anecdotes that they nurse while they live, and that survive them, are more likely to be utterly lost not only to history but the family following them. Of course this is the fate of most souls, reducing entire lives, no matter how vivid and wonderful, to those sad black names on withering family trees, with half a date dangling after and a question mark.

My father's happiness not only redeemed him, but drove him to stories, and keeps him even now alive in me, like a second more patient and more pleasing soul within my poor soul.

Perhaps his happiness was curiously unfounded. But cannot a man make himself as happy as he can in the strange long reaches of a life? I think it is legitimate. After all the world is indeed beautiful and if we were any other creature than man we might be continuously happy in it.

The principal room in our little house, while already of narrow dimensions, we shared with two large objects, viz. the afore-mentioned motorbike which had to be kept out of the rain. It lived in our living room a quiet life as one might say, my father being able from his chair idly to run a chamois leather over the chrome when he wished. The other object which I want to mention is the little cottage upright piano, which had been bequeathed him by a grateful widower, as my father had dug a hole for this man's wife at no charge, because the circum-stances of the bereaved family had been straitened. So one summer night, soon after the burial, the piano had arrived on a donkey and cart, and was carried in with smiles and embar-rassed happiness by the widower and his two sons, and placed in our tiny room. The piano had possibly never been worth a great sum, but it had a most beautiful tone for all that, and had never been played before it reached us, in as much as one could surmise that history from the state of the keys, which were pristine. There were scenes painted on the side panels, of places which were not Sligo as such, most likely being scenes of an imaginary Italy or the like, but might have been all the same, being of mountains and rivers, with shepherds and shepherdesses standing about with their patient sheep. My father, having grown up in his own father's ministry, was able to play this lovely instrument, and his delight as I have said was in the old operettas of the previous century. He considered Balfe a genius. As there was room for me beside him on the stool I soon by grace of my love for him and my own great joy in his ability began to pick up the rudiments of playing, and slowly progressed to some real accomplishment, without in any way feeling it was an effort or a trial.

Then I could play for him as he stood out in the centre of the floor, such as it was, with his hand idly perchance on the seat of his motorbike, the other hand in his jacket like an Irish Napoleon, and sing with utmost perfection, or so it seemed to me, 'Marble Halls', or the other gems of his repertoire – and, for that matter, those little songs called Neapolitan, which of course were not as I thought in memory of Napoleon, but songs invented in the streets of Naples – songs now in exile in Sligo! His voice entered my head as a sort of honey, that lingered there potently, buzzingly, banishing all the fears of childhood. As the voice rose up, so did all of him, arms, whiskers, one foot swinging a little over the old carpet with its pattern of repeating dogs, his eyes brimming with a strange merriment. Even Napoleon might not have scorned him as a man of elevated qualities. At such moments he exhibited a most beautiful timbre in the quieter passages of songs that to this day I have never heard outmatched. Many fine singers made their way to Sligo when I was a young woman and sang in the halls under the rain, and for a few of the more popular sort I even played piano accompaniment, chopping out the notes and chords for them, more of a hindrance than a help to them perhaps. But none seemed to me to equal the strange privacy of my father's voice.

And a man who can make himself merry in the face of those coming disasters that assailed him, as disasters do so many, without grace or favour, is a true hero.

CHAPTER TWO

Dr Grene's Commonplace Book

(Senior Psychiatrist, Roscommon Regional Mental Hospital)

This building is in a terrible condition, how terrible we were not completely aware until the surveyor's report. The three brave men who climbed into the ancient roof report many timbers on the verge of collapse, as if the very head and crown of the institution were mirroring the condition of many of the poor inmates beneath. For inmates I should write patients. But as the place was constructed in the late eighteenth century as a charitable institution for the 'healthful asylum and superior correction of wounded seats of thought' the word inmate does always spring to mind. How healthful and how superior can only now be guessed. Actually in the mid nineteenth century there was a period of great enlightenment in the asylums, under the revolutionary ideas of various doctors, when strait jackets were used sparingly, a good diet was deemed wise, and plenty of exercise and stimulation of thought. Which was a great advance on the practice of Bedlam with its roaring beasts in chains on the floors. Somehow it all got worse again afterwards, and no sensitive person would choose to be the historian of the Irish asylums in the first part of the last century, with its clitoridectomies, immersions, and injections. The last century being 'my' century, since I was fifty-five when it turned, and it is difficult wholly to give one's heart and attention to a new century at that age. Or so I found. And find. Nearly sixty-five now, alas.

With the building showing its age so forcefully, we will be obliged to leave it. The department says the new building will start almost immediately, which may be true or may be cant of a sort. But how can we go till we are assured of a new building, and indeed, more philosophically, how can we prise many of the patients out of here, when their very DNA has probably melded with the mortar of the building? There are those fifty ancient women in the central block, so old that age has become something eternal, continuous, so bedridden and encrusted with sores that to move them would be a sort of violation.

I suppose I am resisting the thought of going in my mind, the way any sensible person does when a move is mooted. No doubt we will manage with all the usual mayhem and trauma.

Similarly the attendants and nurses have become as much part of the building as the bats in the roof and the rats in the cellars. Which are both legion I understand, though I am thankful to say I have only seen rats the one time, when the east wing went on fire, and I saw the dark black shapes running from the lower doors, out into the farmer's corn meadows beyond the hedges. The light from the fires threw a glare of a weird marmalade colour into their backs as they fled. I am sure when they heard the firemen give the all clear, they snuck back in in the new darkness.

So, we are to go sometime. I am obliged therefore under the new laws to assess whatever of the patients can be put back into the community (whatever that is, O Lord), and exactly what category of patient each other patient is. Many of them will be shocked even by new decor, modern plaster walls, good insulation and heating. The very moaning of the wind in the corridors, even on still days – how is that? possibly a vacuum created by heat and cold in different areas of the hospital – will be missed as the tiny background music of their dreams and 'madnesses'. I am sure. Those poor old boys in black suits made by the hospital tailor long ago, who are not so much mad as homeless and ancient, and who live along the rooms of the oldest west wing, like soldiers of some forgotten Peninsular or Indian War, will not know themselves outside this lost ground of Roscommon.

Which necessity will also bring me to a task long avoided, which is to establish what circumstances brought in some of the patients, and whether indeed, as was tragically true in some cases, they were sectioned for social rather than medical reasons. Because I am not so great a fool as to think that all the 'lunatics' in here are mad, or ever were, or were before they came here and learned a sort of viral madness. These people are perceived by the all-knowing public at large, or let us say public opinion as it is mirrored in the newspapers, as deserving of 'freedom' and 'release'. Which may be very true, but creatures so long kennelled and confined find freedom and release very problematic attainments, like those eastern European countries after communism. And similarly there is a weird reluctance in me to see anyone go. Why is that? The anxiety of the zoo keeper? Can my polar bears do as well at the pole? I suppose this is a reductive thought. Well, we will see.

In particular I will have to approach my old friend Mrs McNulty, who is not only the oldest person in this place, but in Roscommon itself, perhaps even Ireland. She was old when I got here thirty years ago, although at that time with the energy of, I don't know what, a force of nature. She is a formidable person and though long periods have gone by when I have not seen her, or only tangentially, I am always aware of her, and try to ask after her. I am afraid she is rather a touchstone for me. She has been a fixture, and not only represents the institution, but also, in a curious way, my own history, my own life. 'The star to every wandering bark,' as Shakespeare has it. My marriage troubles with poor Bet, my spirits lowering, plummeting, betimes, my feeling of not getting on, my this, my that – my companionable stupidity, I suppose. While things have ineluctably changed, she has remained the same, if grown of course weaker and slighter as the years go on. Is she a hundred now? She used to play the piano down in the recreation room, really very expert songs, jazz tunes of the twenties and thirties.

I don't know how she knew them. But she used to sit there, with her long silver hair flowing freely down her back, in one of those awful hospital gowns, but looking like a queen, and though she was seventy then, very striking in the face. Really quite beautiful still, and God knows what she must have looked like when she was young. Extraordinary, a sort of manifestation of something unusual and maybe alien in this provincial world. When a mild rheumatism – she wouldn't allow the word, she called it 'a reluctance' in her fingers – set in in later years, she stopped playing the piano. She might have played almost as well, but almost as well didn't suit her. So we lost the sound of Mrs McNulty playing jazz.

As a matter of record, that piano, assailed by woodworm, was later thrown out on a skip with an enormous unmusical clang.

So now I will have to go in and tackle her about this and that. I am unaccountably nervous about it. Why should I be nervous? I think it is because she is so senior to me, and if given to great silences, an extremely agreeable presence, like the company of an older colleague that one reveres. I think that is it. Maybe it is because I have a suspicion she likes me, just as much as I like her. Though why she does I don't know. I have harboured a curiosity about her, but I have never delved into her life, though perhaps as a professional psychiatrist that should be a black mark against me. Nevertheless, there it is, she likes me. Yet I would not trouble that liking, the condition of it I mean, for the world. So I must tread carefully.

Roseanne's Testimony of Herself

How I would like to say that I loved my father so much that I could not have lived without him, but such an avowal would be proved false in time. Those that we love, those essential beings, are removed from us at the will of the Almighty, or the devils that usurp him. It is as if a huge lump of lead were lain over the soul, such deaths, and where that soul was previously weightless, now is a secret and ruinous burden at the very heart of us.

When I was ten or so my father in a fit of educating enthusiasm brought me to the top of the long thin tower in the graveyard. It was one of those beautiful, lofty slim buildings made by monks in a time of danger and destruction. It stood in a nettled corner of the graveyard and was not much remarked on. When you had grown up in Sligo it was just there. But no doubt it was a treasure beyond compare, put up with only a murmur of mortar between the stones, each one remembering the curve of the tower, each one set in with perfect success by ancient masons. Of course it was a Catholic yard. My father had not got that job because of his religion, but because he was deeply liked in the town by all and sundry, and the Catholics did not mind their graves being dug by a Presbyterian, if it was a likeable one. Because in those days there was often much greater ease between the churches than we give credit for, and it is often forgotten that under the old penal laws in vanished days the dissenting churches were just as harried, as he often liked to point out. At any rate, there is seldom a difficulty with religion where there is friendship. And it was only later that this distinction in him made any difference. At any rate I know he was exceedingly liked by the parish priest, a little perky darting man called Father Gaunt who loomed so large later in my own story, if a small man can be said to loom large.

Those were the days just after the first war, and maybe in those ditches of history as it were, minds turn to strangenesses, quirks of education such as he was bent on that day with me. Otherwise I cannot explain why a grown man would take his child to the top of an old tower with a bag of hammers and feathers.

All of Sligo, river, churches, houses, radiated out from the foot of the tower, or so it seemed from the little window at the top. A passing bird might have seen two excited faces trying to peer out at the same time, myself heaping my weight onto my toes and bumping the underside of his chin.

'Roseanne, dearest, I shaved already this morning, and you won't shave me anyhow with the top of your golden head.'

For it was true I had soft hair like gold – like the gold of those selfsame monks. Yellow as the gleams in old books.

'Pappa,' I said, 'for the love of all things, drop the hammers and feathers and let's see what's what.'

'Oh,' he said, 'I am weary from the climb, let's just scope our eyes over Sligo before we attempt our experiment.'

He had waited and chosen a windless day for his work. He wished to prove to me the ancient premise that all things fall at the same rate, in the realm of theory.

'All things fall at the same rate,' he had said, 'in the realm of theory. And I will prove it to you. I will prove it to myself.'

We had been sitting by the spitting anthracite of our fire.

'All may fall at the same rate, as you say,' my mother piped up from her corner. 'But it's the rare thing rises.'

I do not think this was a cut at him, but just an observation. At any rate he looked over at her with the perfect neutrality she herself was mistress of and had taught him.

It is strange to me writing this here in this darkened room, scratching it all out in blue biro ink, somehow to see them in my mind's eye, or somewhere behind my eyes, in the darkened bowl of my head, still there, alive and talking, truly, as if their time was real time and mine was an illusion. And it touches my heart for the thousandth time how beautiful she is, how neat, agreeable and shining, with her Southampton accent like the pebbles on the beach there disturbed by the waves, rushing, shushing, a soft sound that sounds in my dreams. It is also true that when I was bold, when she worried that my path was veering from the path she wanted for me, even in small matters, she was wont to whip me. But in those times children were routinely hit.

So now our two faces were jostling for position, framed by the ancient frame of the monks' little look-see window. What vanished faces had peered out there, sweating in their robes, trying to see where the Vikings were that would come to kill them and take their books, their vessels, and their coins. No mason likes to leave a large window for Vikings, and that window spoke still of old nervousness and peril.

At length it was clear that his experiment was impossible with both of us there. One or other of us would miss the outcome. So he sent me back down on my own by the dank stairway of stones, and I can still feel that wet wall under my hand, and the strange fright that grew in me to be separated from him. My little breast beating as if there was an uncomfortable pigeon trapped there.

I came out from the tower and stood away from the base as he had bid me, for fear of the hammers falling and killing me dead. The tower looked enormous from there, it seemed to stretch up to the filthy grey clouds of that day. To heaven. Not a breeze stirred. The neglected graves of that section of the yard, the graves of men and women of some century where the people could only afford rough stones, and not a name writ upon them, seemed different now on my own, as if their poor skeletons might rise up against me, to devour me in their eternal hunger. Standing on the ground I was a child on a precipice, that was the feeling, like that scene in the old play *King Lear* where the king's friend imagines he is falling down a beetling cliff, where there is no cliff, so that when you read it, you also think there is a cliff, and fall with the king's friend. But

I peered up faithfully, faithfully, lovingly, lovingly. It is no crime to love your father, it is no crime to feel no criticism of him, and especially so when I knew him into my early woman-hood or nearly, when a child tends to grow disappointed in her parents. It is no crime to feel your heart beating up to him, or as much of him as I could see, his arm now stuck out the little window, and the bag held suspended in the Irish air. Now he was calling to me, and I could barely catch his words. But after a few repeats I think I heard him say:

'Are you stood back, dearest?'

'I am stood back, Pappa,' I called, I nearly screamed, such a distance the words had to rise, and such a small window to enter to reach his ears.

'Then I will let loose the bag. Watch, watch!' he called.

'Yes, Pappa, I am watching!'

He loosened the top of the bag as best he could with the fingers of one hand and shook the contents free. I had seen him place them there. It was a handful of feathers from the feather bolster on their bed, plucked out against the screeches of his wife, and two mason's hammers he kept for when he repaired the little walls and headstones of graves.

I stared and stared. Maybe I heard a curious music. The chattering of the jackdaws and the old scratchy talking of the rooks in the great beech trees there mingled like a music in my head. My neck was straining and I was bursting to see the outcome of that elegant experiment, an outcome my father had said might stand to me in my life, as the basis of a proper philosophy.

Although there was not a breath of wind, the feathers immediately drifted away, dispersing like a little explosion, even rising greyly against the grey clouds, almost impossible to see. The feathers drifted, drifted away.

My father was calling, calling, in enormous excitement in the tower, 'What do you see, what do you see?'

What did I see, what did I know? It is sometimes I think the strain of ridiculousness in a person, a ridiculousness born maybe of desperation, such as also Eneas McNulty – you do not know who that is yet – exhibited so many years later, that pierces you through with love for that person. It is all love, that not knowing, that not seeing. I am standing there, eternally, straining to see, a crick in the back of my neck, peering and straining, if for no other reason than for love of him. The feathers are drifting away, drifting, swirling away. My father is calling and calling. My heart is beating back to him. The hammers are falling still.

CHAPTER THREE

Dear reader! Dear reader, if you are gentle and good, I wish I could clasp your hand. I wish – all manner of impossible things. Although I do not have you, I have other things. There are moments when I am pierced through by an inexplicable joy, as if, in having nothing, I have the world. As if, in reaching this room, I have found the anteroom to paradise, and soon will find it opening, and walk forward like a woman rewarded for my pains, into those green fields, and folded farms. So green the grass is burning!

This morning Dr Grene came in, and I had to scramble and rush to hide these pages. For I did not want him to see, or to question me, for here contains already secrets, and my secrets are my fortune and my sanity. Luckily I could hear him coming from far off down the corridor, because he has metal on the heels of his shoes. Luckily also I suffer not a jot from rheumatism or any particular infirmity associated with my age, at least in my legs. My hands, my hands alas are not what they were, but the legs hold good. The mice that move along the skirting board are faster, but then, they were always faster. A mouse is a brilliant athlete, make no mistake, when he needs to be. But I was quick enough for Dr Grene.

He knocked on the door which is an improvement on the poor wretch that cleans out my room, John Kane, if that is how you spell his name – it is the first time I have written it down – and by the time he had the door opened I was sitting here at an empty table.

As I do not consider Dr Grene an evil man, I was smiling.

It was a morning of considerable cold and there was a rheum of frost over everything in the room. Everything was glimmering. Myself I was dressed in all my four dresses, and I was snug enough.

'Hmm, hmm,' he said. 'Roseanne. Hmm. How are you, Mrs McNulty?'

'I'm very well, Dr Grene,' I said. 'It's very kind of you to visit me.'

'It's my job to visit you,' he said. 'Has this room been cleaned today?

'It has not,' I said. 'But surely John will be here soon.'

'I suppose he will,' said Dr Grene.

Then he crossed in front of me to the window and looked out.

'This is the coldest day of the year so far,' he said.

'So far,' I said.

'And do you have everything you need?'

'I do, in the main,' I said.

Then he sat on my bed as if it were the cleanest bed in Christendom, which I daresay it is not, and stretched out his legs, and gazed down at his shoes. His long whitening beard was as sharp as an iron axe. It was very hedgelike, saintlike. On the bed beside him was a plate, still with the smeared remnants of beans from the night before.

'Pythagoras,' he said, 'believed in the transmigration of the soul, and cautioned us to be careful when we ate beans, in case we were eating the soul of our grandmother.'

'Oh,' I said.

'This we read in Horace,' he said.

'Batchelors Beans?'

'I suppose not.'

Dr Grene answered my question with his usual solemn face. The beauty of Dr Grene is that he is entirely humourless,

24

which makes him actually quite humorous. Believe me, this is a quality to be treasured in this place.

'So,' he said, 'you are quite well?'

'I am.'

'What age are you now, Roseanne?'

'I suppose I am a hundred.'

'Don't you think it very remarkable to be so well at a hundred?' he said, as if in some way he had contributed to this fact, as perhaps he had. After all, I had been under his care for thirty odd years, maybe more. He himself was growing old, but not as old as myself.

'I think it very remarkable. But, Doctor, I find so many things remarkable. I find the mice remarkable, I find the funny green sunlight that climbs in that window remarkable. I find you visiting me today remarkable.'

'I'm sorry to hear you still have mice.'

'There will always be mice here.'

'But doesn't John put down traps?'

'He does, but he won't set them delicately enough, and the mice eat the cheese with no trouble, and get away, like Jesse James and his brother Frank.'

Now Dr Grene took his eyebrows between two fingers of his right hand, and massaged them for a few moments. He rubbed his nose then and groaned. In that groan was all the years he had spent in this institution, all the mornings of his life here, all the useless talk of mice and cures and age.

'You know, Roseanne,' he said, 'as I have been obliged recently to look at the legal position of all our inmates, as this has been so much in the public discourse, I was looking back over your admittance papers, and I must confess –'

He said all this in the most easy-going voice imaginable.

'Confess?' I said, prompting him. I knew his mind had a habit of drifting off silently into a private thought.

'Oh, yes – excuse me. Hmm, yes, I was wanting to ask you,

Roseanne, if you remember by any chance the particulars of your admittance here, which would be most helpful – if you did. I will tell you why in a minute – if I have to.'

Dr Grene smiled and I had a suspicion he meant this last remark as a jest, but the humour of it escaped me, especially as, as I said, he never usually attempted humour. So I surmised something unusual was stirring here.

Then, as bad as himself, I forgot to answer him.

'You remember anything about it?'

'Coming here, you mean, Dr Grene?'

'Yes, I think that's what I mean.'

'No,' I said, a foul and utter lie being the best answer.

'Well,' he said, 'unfortunately a great swathe of our archive in the basement has been used, not surprisingly, by generations of mice for bedding, and it is all quite ruined and unreadable. Your own file such as it is has been attacked in a most interesting fashion. It would not shame an Egyptian tomb. It seems to fall apart at the touch of a hand.'

There was a long silence then. I smiled and smiled. I tried to think what I looked like to him. A face so creased and old, so lost in age.

'Of course, I know you very well. We have talked so often over the years. I wish now I had made more notes. These do not come to many pages, you will not be surprised to learn. I am a reluctant taker of notes, perhaps not admirable in my job. It is sometimes said that we do no good, that we do nothing for anyone. But I hope we have done our best for you, despite my culpable lack of notes. I do. I'm glad you say you are well. I would like to think you are happy here.'

I smiled at him my oldest old-woman smile, as if I did not quite understand.

'God knows,' he said then, with a certain elegance of mind, 'no one could be happy here.'

'I am happy,' I said.

'Do you know,' he said, 'I do believe you. I think you are the happiest person I know. But I think I will be obliged to re-assess you, Roseanne, because there has been very much an outcry in the newspapers against – such people as were incarcerated shall we say for social reasons, rather than medical – being, being . . .'

'Held?'

'Yes, yes. Held. And continuing in this day and age to be held. Of course, you have been here these many, many years, I should think maybe even fifty?'

'I do not remember, Dr Grene. It may well be so.'

'You might consider this place your home.'

'No.'

'Well. You as well as any other person have the right to be free if you are suitable for, for freedom. I suppose even at one hundred years of age you might wish to – to walk about the place and paddle in the sea in the summer, and smell the roses –'

'No!'

I did not intend to cry out, but as you will see these small actions, associated in most people's minds with the ease and happiness of life, are to me still knives in my heart to think of.

'Excuse me?'

'No, no, please, go on.'

'At any rate, if I found you to be here without true cause, without medical basis as it were, I would be obliged to try and make other arrangements. I don't wish to upset you. And I don't intend, my dear Roseanne, to throw you out into the cold. No, no, this would be a very carefully orchestrated move, and as I say, subject to an assessment by me. Questions, I would be obliged to question you – to a degree.'

I was not entirely certain of its origin, but a feeling of sweeping dread spread through me, like I imagine the poison of broken and afflicted atoms spread through people on the far margins of Hiroshima, killing them just as surely as the explosion. Dread like a sickness, a memory of a sickness, the first time in many years I had felt it.

'Are you all right, Roseanne? Please don't be agitated.'

'Of course I want freedom, Dr Grene. But it frightens me.'

'The gaining of freedom', said Dr Grene pleasantly, 'is always accomplished in an atmosphere of uncertainty. In this country at least. Perhaps in all countries.'

'Murder,' I said.

'Yes, sometimes,' he said, gently.

We stopped speaking then and I gazed at the solid rectangle of sunlight in the room. Ancient dust moiled there.

'Freedom, freedom,' he said.

Somewhere in his dusty voice there was the vague bell of longing. I know nothing of his life outside, of his family. Does he have a wife and children? Mrs Grene somewhere? I don't know. Or do I? He is a brilliant man. He looks like a ferret, but no matter. Any man that can talk about old Greeks and Romans is a man after my father's heart. I like Dr Grene despite his dusty despair because he brings to me always an echo of my father's line of talk, filleted out of Sir Thomas Browne and John Donne.

'But, we won't begin today. No, no,' he said, rising. 'Certainly not. But it is my duty to set out the facts before you.'

And he crossed again with a sort of infinite medical patience to the door.

'You deserve no less, Mrs McNulty.'

I nodded.

Mrs McNulty.

I always think of Tom's mother when I hear that name. I was once also a Mrs McNulty, but never as supremely as she. Never. As she made quite clear a hundred times. Furthermore, why did I give my name ever since as McNulty, when those great efforts were made by everybody to take the name away? I do not know.

'I was at the zoo last week,' he said suddenly, 'with a friend and his son. I was up in Dublin to collect some books for my wife. About roses. My friend's son is called William, which as you know is my name also.'

I did not know this!

'We came to the house of the giraffes. William was very pleased with them, two big, long lady giraffes they were, with soft, long legs, very, very beautiful animals. I think an animal so beautiful I have never seen.'

Then in the glimmering room I fancied I saw something strange, a tear rising from the corner of his eye, slipping to his cheek and tumbling quickly down, a sort of dark, private crying.

'So beautiful, so beautiful,' he said.

His talk had locked me in silence, I know not why. It was not opening, easy, happy talk like my father's, after all. I wanted to listen to him, but I did not want to answer now. That strange responsibility we feel towards others when they speak, to offer them the solace of any answer. Poor humans! And anyway he had not asked a question. He was merely floating there in the room, insubstantial, a living man in the midst of life, dying imperceptibly on his feet, like all of us.

CHAPTER FOUR

Later John Kane lumbered in, muttering and pushing his brush, a person I have come to accept in the way of things here, which, if they can't be changed, must be endured.

I noted with a small degree of dread that his flies were open. His trousers are decked with a series of clumsy-looking buttons. He is a little man but at the same time he is all brawn and braces. There is something wrong with his tongue, because he is obliged to swallow every few moments with strange hardship. His face has a veil of dark-blue veins in it, like a soldier's face that has been too near a cannon mouth when it exploded. In the gossip of this place he has a very poor reputation.

'I can't see how you want all them books, missus, since you have no spectacles to read them.'

Then he swallowed again, swallowed.

I can see perfectly without spectacles but I did not say this. He was referring to the three volumes in my possession, my father's copy of *Religio Medici*, *The Hounds of Hell*, and Mr Whitman's *Leaves of Grass*.

All three brown and yellow with thumbing.

But conversation with John Kane can lead anywhere, like those conversations with boys when I was a young girl of twelve or so, a gaggle of them at the corner of our road, standing in the rain indifferently, and saying things to me, in soft voices – at first in soft voices. In here, among the shadows and the distant cries, the greatest virtue is silence.

Those that feed them do not love them, those that clothe them do not fear for them.

That is a quotation from something, what or where I do not know.

Even gibberish is dangerous, silence is better.

I have been here a long time and in that time have learned the virtue of silence certainly.

Old Tom put me here. I think it was him. It was a favour to him, for he himself worked as tailor in the Sligo Lunatic Asylum. I think he put money in with me, because of this room. Or does Tom my husband pay for me? But he could not still be alive. It is not the first place I was put, the first place was –

But I am not concerned with recrimination. This is a decent place, if not home. If this were home I would go mad!

Oh, I must remind myself to be clear, and be sure I know what I am saying to you. There must be accuracy and rightness now.

This is a good place. This is a good place.

There is a town not far off, I am told. Roscommon town itself. I don't know how far, except it takes half an hour in a fire engine.

This I know because one night many years ago I was roused from my sleep by John Kane. He led me out into the hallway and hurried me down two or three flights of stairs. There was a fire in one of the wings and he was leading me to safety.

Instead of bringing me to the ground floor, he had to cut across through a long dark ward, where the doctors and other staff were also gathered. There was smoke coming up from below, but this place was deemed to be safe. The gloom gradually brightened, or my eyes adjusted to it.

There were maybe fifty beds there, a long thin room with curtains drawn everywhere. Thin ragged curtains. Old, old faces, as old as my own now. I was astonished. They had lain there not too far away from me and I did not know. Old faces that said nothing, lying in stupor, like fifty Russian icons. Who were they? Why, they were your own people. Silent, silent, sleeping towards death, crawling on bleeding knees towards our Lord.

A tribe of onetime girls. I whispered a prayer to hurry their souls to heaven. For I think they crept up there very slow.

I suppose they are all dead now or mostly. I never visited them again. The fire engine came in half an hour. I remember because one of the doctors remarked on it.

These places unlike the world, with none of the things we praise the world for. Where sisters, mothers, grandmothers, spinsters, all forgotten lie.

The human town not so far off, sleeping and waking, sleeping and waking, forgetting its lost women there, in long rows.

Half an hour. Fire brought me in to see them. Never again.

Those that feed them do not love them.

'Do you want this?' says John Kane in my ear.

'What is it?'

He was holding it in the palm of his hand. Half the shell of a bird's egg, blue like the veins in his face.

'Oh, yes, thank you,' I said. It was something I had picked up in the gardens many years before. It had sat in the window niche and he had never referred to it before. But it had lain there, blue and perfect and never ageing. Yet an old thing. Many many generations of birds ago.

'That is a robin's egg maybe,' he said.

'Maybe,' I said.

'Or a lark.'

'Yes.'

'I will put it back anyhow,' he said, swallowing again, as if his tongue were hardened at the root, his throat bulging for a moment.

'I don't know where all the dust comes from,' he said. 'I sweep it every day and there is always dust, by God there is, ancient dust. Not new dust, never new dust.'

'No,' I said, 'No. Forgive me.'

He straightened a moment and looked at me.

'What is your name?' he said.

32

'I don't know,' I said, in a sudden panic. I have known him for decades. Why was he asking me this question?

'You don't know your own name?'

'I know it. I forget it.'

'Why do you sound frightened?'

'I don't know.'

'There is no need,' he said, and taking the dust into his dustpan neatly, began to leave the room. 'Anyhow, I know your name.'

I started to cry, not like a child, but like the old old woman I am, slow, slight tears that no one sees, no one dries.

Next thing my father knew, the civil war was upon us.

I write this to stop my tears. I stab the words into the page with my biro, as if pinning myself there.

Before the civil war there was another war against the country being ruled from England but that was not much fought in Sligo.

I am quoting my husband's brother Jack when I write this, or at least I hear Jack's voice in the sentences. Jack's vanished voice. Neutral. Jack, like my mother, was master of the neutral tone, if not of neutrality. For Jack eventually donned an English uniform and fought against Hitler in that later war – I nearly said, that real war. He was a brother also of Eneas McNulty.

The three brothers, Jack, Tom and Eneas. Oh, yes.

In the west of Ireland by the way Eneas is three syllables, En-ee-as. In Cork I fear it is two, and sounds more like a person's backside than anything else.

But the civil war was definitely fought in Sligo, and all along the western seaboard, with fierce application.

The Free Staters had accepted the treaty with England. The Irregulars so-called had baulked at it like horses at a broken bridge in the darkness. Because left out of the whole matter was the North of the country, and it seemed to them that what had been accepted was an Ireland without a head, a body lopped off at the shoulders. That was Carson's crowd in the North that kept them linked to England.

It always puzzled me that one of Jack's proudest boasts was that he was a cousin of Carson. But that is by the way.

There was a lot of hatred in Ireland in those times. I was fourteen, a girl trying to bloom up into the world. Fumes of hatred all about.

Dear Fr Gaunt. I suppose I may say so. Never did so sincere and honest a man cause maiden so much distress. For I don't suppose for a moment he acted out of ill intent. Yet he moidered me, as the country people used to say. And in a time previous to that he moidered my father.

I have said he was a little man, by which I mean, the crown of his head was at an equal level to my own. Bustling, spare and neat, in his black clothes and his hair cropped tight like a condemned man.

The question breaks in on my thoughts: what does Dr Grene mean, he must assess me? So that I might go out into the world? Where is that world?

He must question me, he said. Did he not? I am sure he did, and yet it is only now I hear him properly, when he has left the room long since.

Panic in me now blacker than old tea.

I am like my father on his old motorbike, careering at speed certainly, but holding so fast to the handlebars there is a sort of safety in that.

Do not prise my fingers from the bars, Dr Grene, I beg you.

Be gone from my thoughts, good doctor.

Fr Gaunt, from the haunts of death, rush in, rush in, and take his place.

Be present, present before me as I scratch and scribble.

34

The following account may sound like one of my father's stories, part of his little gospel, but he never made a proper recitation of it, nor improved it a little in the telling, till it was rounded like a song. I give you the bare bones, which is all I have of it.

In the time of that war there were no doubt many deaths, and many deaths that were no better than murder. Of course it was my father's duty to bury some of these in his neat graveyard.

Being fourteen I had one foot in childhood still, and one foot in womanhood. At the little nuns' school I attended I was not indifferent to the boys that lurched past the school gates at the close of lessons, indeed I seem to remember thinking a sort of music rose from them, a sort of human noise that I did not understand. How I heard music arising from such rough forms I do not know at this distance. But such is the magician-ship of girls, that they can transform mere clay into large and classic ideas.

So I was paying but half heed to my father and his world. I was more concerned with my own mysteries, such as, how to get a curl into my wretched hair. I spent many hours labouring at this with a collar iron of my mother's, which she used to iron my father's Sunday shirt. It was a slim, small object that heated quickly on the fender, and if I laid out my straight yellow tresses on the table, I hoped by some alchemy to tease a curl into them. So I was preoccupied with the fears and ambitions of my age.

Nevertheless I was often in my father's temple, doing my lessons as may be, enjoying the little grate of coals he kept burning there, by grace of his fuel stipend. I learned my lessons and listened to him singing 'Marble Halls' or the like. And worried about my hair.

What I would give to have a few strands of that straight yellow hair now.

My father buried anyone that was given him to bury. In peaceful days he buried mostly the old and the sick, but in days of war he more often than not was given the corpse of a boy or nearly boy.

These caused him grief in a manner he never showed over the aged and infirm. He thought those latter deaths were simple and right, and whether the families and mourners wept or were silent at the graveside, he knew there was a sense of proper term and justice. Often he knew the old soul that was to be interred, and would share memories and anecdotes if that seemed pleasant and generous to do so. He was a sort of diplomat of grief in those instances.

But the bodies of those slain in the war grieved him mightily, differently. As a Presbyterian he might be thought to have no place in the Irish story. But he understood rebellion. In his bedroom in a drawer he kept a memorial booklet for the Rising of 1916, with photographs of the principals involved, and a calendar of battles and sorrows. The only wicked thing he thought that Rising enshrined was its peculiar Catholic nature, from which of course he felt excluded.

It was the deaths of the young that grieved him. After all it was just a few years after the slaughter of the Great War. Indeed from Sligo had gone out hundreds of men to fight in Flanders, in the years around the Rising, and since the slain of that war could not be buried at home, it might be said those dozens of men were buried in my father, in the secret graveyard of his thoughts. Now in the civil war, more deaths, and always the young. There wasn't one man of fifty in Sligo fought in the civil war anyhow.

He did not rail against these matters, he knew that there were always wars in every generation, but he gave himself to these things in a curiously professional way, since he was after all the titular custodian of the dead, as if he were a king of absences.

Fr Gaunt himself was young and might have been expected to feel a special kinship for the slain. But Fr Gaunt was so clipped and trim he had no antennae at all for grief. He was like a singer who knows the words and can sing, but cannot sing the song as conceived in the heart of the composer. Mostly he was dry. He spoke over young and old with the same dry music.

But let me not speak against him. He went everywhere in Sligo in his ministry, he walked into bleak rooms in the town where impoverished bachelors feasted on tinned beans, and lousy cabins by the river that looked like ancient starving men themselves, with rotting thatch for hair, and little staring, dull, black windows for eyes. Into those too he went, famously, and never took flea or louse out with him. For he was cleaner than the daylight moon.

And such a small, clean man when crossed was like a scything blade, the grass, the brambles and the stalks of human nature went down before him, as my father discovered.

It happened thus.

One evening as my father and myself in the temple amused ourselves before returning home to our tea, we heard a scuffling and a muttering outside the old iron door. My father looked to me, alert as a dog before it barks.

'Well, what's this now?' he said, more to himself than to me.

Three men came in carrying a fourth and, as if driven themselves by an unseen force, seemed to sweep me back from the table, and before I knew what had happened, I had the back of my school dress rubbed against the damp whitewash of the wall. They were like a little hurricane of activity. They were all young men, and the man being carried was no more I would guess than seventeen. He looked a handsome long person enough, and roughly clothed, much mud about him, and grass stains from the bog, and blood. A great deal of thin-looking blood all over his shirt. And he was obviously as dead as a stone.

The other three lads were all yappering and yammering,

hysterical maybe, which caused a hysteria to rise in me. My father however stood darkly by his fireplace, like a man making an effort to be mysterious, his face as blank as you like, but also, I thought, ready to have a thought and act on it if necessary. For the three boys were decked with old rifles and in their pockets bulged other weapons, all haphazardly gathered up as may be after a skirmish. I knew that weapons were the scarcest currency of the war.

'What are you up to, lads?' said my father. 'There's a method in all this, you know, the bringing in of bodies here, and you can't just carry in a boy out of the blue. Have mercy.'

'Mr Clear, Mr Clear,' said one of the men, a lad with a severe-looking face and hair seemingly cropped against lice, 'we'd nowhere else to be bringing him.'

'You know me?' said my father.

'I know you well enough. I know what foot you dig with anyhow, and I'm told by them that might know that you're not against us, not like many a fool here in Sligo town.'

'That's as may be,' said my father, 'but who are you? Are you Free Staters or the other lot?'

'Do we look like Free Staters, and half the mountain bog in our hair?'

'You don't. So, lads then, what do you want me to do? Who is this fellow here?'

'This poor man', said the same speaker, 'is Willie Lavelle, and he was seventeen year old, and he's after being killed up there on the mountain by a crowd of mean, unthinking vile bastards that call theyselves soldiers, but are not, and are worser to us than any Black and Tan ever was in the war just gone by. Just as evil bad anyhow. For we were so high in the mountain we were gone fierce cold and hungry and this boy surrendered to them, and us hiding in the heather all right, but nothing would do for them except to be punching and pushing him, and asking him questions. And they were laughing and one sticking his gun in

38

the lad's face, and he was the bravest lad among us, but saving your presence, girl,' he said to me, 'so frightened he pissed his ould pants, because he knew, and you always do know, you know, sir, when a man is going to shoot you, so they say, and because they thought no one was there, no one was looking and no one to see their evil, they let off three bullets into his belly. And they went off merry as you like back down the mountain. By Christ when we have Willie buried we are going to go after them, aren't we, lads? – and settle their hash for them, if we can find them.'

Then the same man did something unexpected, he burst into violent tears, and threw himself across the body of his fallen comrade, and let out a thin roar of grief that had never been heard before nor since, though it was a little temple of grief.

'Go on easy, John,' said one of the others. 'We're in the town though the bone-yard here is dark and quiet.'

But the first man continued to wail, and lay across the chest of the dead man like – I was going to say, like a girl, but hardly that.

At any rate I was up to the neck of my school blouse in horror, of course I was. My father had lost his calmness and was walking up and down quickly between the fireplace and his chair, with its few flattened old cushions of once-red cloth.

'Mister, Mister,' said the third man, a long thin boy I had never seen, who looked straight off of a mountainy holding, with trousers in no manner reaching his ankles. 'You've got to be burying him now.'

'I can't bury a man without a priest, not to mention the fact that I expect you have no plot bought here?'

'How would we be buying plots when we're fighting for the Irish Republic?' said the first man, wrenching himself from his tears. 'The whole of Ireland is our plot. You can set us down in it anywhere. Because we are Irishmen. Maybe that's something you don't know anything about?'

39

'I hope I am an Irishman too,' said my father, and I knew he was offended by the remark. Truth was, Presbyterians were not much loved in Sligo, I hardly know the reason for it. Unless it was that in the old days there was a lot of that proselytising going on, with a Presbyterian mission to the west and the like, which though it had not been a raging success, had yet gathered a number of Catholics to the fold in a time of terrible hunger and need, and thereby increased the level of fear and mistrust among the people.

'You have to be burying him,' said the third man. 'Isn't that John's little brother there on the table?'

'This is your brother?' said my father.

Suddenly the man was absolutely quiet, still.

'It is,' he said.

'That is very sad,' said my father. 'That is very sad.'

'And he has had no priest to absolve him. Would it be possible to have a priest fetched for him?'

'It is Fr Gaunt is the priest here,' said my father. 'He is a good man, and I can send Roseanne to get him, if you wished.'

'But she's not to say anything to him, just for him to come here, and she's not to speak to anyone on her way, and by no means to speak to any Free State soldier, for if she does, we will be killed here. They will kill us as easily as they killed Willie on the mountain, that's for sure. I would say to you, we will kill you if she speaks, but I am not sure if we would.'

My father looked at him surprised. And it seemed so honest and polite a thing to say, I resolved to do as he asked, and speak to no one.

'And anyhow, we have no bullets, which is why we stayed in the heather, like hares, and didn't stir. I would we had stirred, lads,' said the brother of the dead man, 'and risen up, and thrun ourselves at them, because this is no way to stand in the world, with Willie dead, and us living.'

And the young fella broke down again, pitifully weeping.

'Look it, have no heed to that,' said my father. 'I'll have Roseanne fetch Fr Gaunt. Go on you out, Roseanne, like I say, and run to the Parish House, and get Fr Gaunt, good girl.'

So I ran out into the windy, winter yard, and through the avenues of the dead, and out onto the top of the hilly road that sails down into Sligo, and hurried down there, and finally reached the house of the priest, and in his little iron gate, and up the gravel, and throwing myself against his stout door, painted as green as the leaf of an aspidistra. Now I was loosed from my father I wasn't thinking of curling irons and hair, but of his very life, because I knew those three living men had seen horrors, and those who see horrors may do horrors just as bad, that is the law of life and war.

Soon thank God Fr Gaunt showed his thin face at the door, and I gabbled at him, and begged him to come to my father, that there was a great need for him there, and would he come, would he come.

'I will come,' said Fr Gaunt, for he was not one of those people that shy away from you when you need them, like many of his brethren, too proud to taste the rain in their mouths. And indeed going back up the hill we had the rain against our faces, and soon his long black coat was glistening wet the whole front of it, and myself also, and for my part I had put on no coat, but showed only wet legs now to the world.

'What person needs me?' said the priest sceptically, when I led him in the gates of the graveyard.

'The person that needs you is dead,' I said.

'If he is dead, is all this great hurry necessary, Roseanne?'

'The other person that needs you is living. It is his brother, Father.'

'I see.'

Inside the graveyard the stones were glistening also in the wetness, and the wind was dancing about among the avenues, so you didn't know where the rain would catch you.

When we reached the little temple, and walked in, the scene had hardly changed, as if the four living persons and certainly the dead had frozen in their spots when I went out and never moved. The irregular soldiers turned their young faces on Fr Gaunt as he stepped in.

'Fr Gaunt,' said my father. 'I am sorry to call you out. These youngsters asked that you be got.'

'Are they holding you prisoner?' said the priest, affronted by the sight of guns.

'No, no, they are not.'

'I hope you will not shoot me?' said Fr Gaunt.

'There was never a priest shot yet in this war,' said the man I called the third man. 'Bad as it is. There is only this poor man shot, John's brother, Willie. He is quite dead.'

'Is he long dead?' said Fr Gaunt. 'Did anyone take his last breath?'

'I took it,' said the brother.

'Then give it back into his mouth,' said Fr Gaunt, 'and I will bless him. And let his poor soul go up to heaven.'

So the brother kissed his brother's dead mouth, returning I think the last breath that he had taken at the moment of his brother's death. And Fr Gaunt blessed him and leaned into him, and gave the sign of the cross over him.

'Can you absolve him, Father, so he will be clear to go to heaven?'

'And has he done murder, has he killed another man in this war?'

'It is not murder in a war to kill a man. It is war itself only.'

'My friend, you know very well the bishops have forbidden us to absolve you, for they have decided that your war is wrong. But I will absolve him if you tell me he has not done murder, as far as you know. I will do that.'

The three then looked at each other. There was a strange dark fear in those faces. They were young Catholic boys, and they feared this priest, and they feared to tell a lie about this matter, and they feared that they would fail in their responsibility to help their comrade to heaven, and I am sure each of them was racking his brains for an answer that would be truthful, for only the truth would get the dead man to paradise.

'Only the truth will serve you,' said the priest, making me jump that he had echoed my own thoughts. They were the simple thoughts of a simple girl, but maybe that Catholic religion is simple enough always in its intents.

'None of us seen him do anything in that way,' said the brother finally. 'If we had we'd say.'

'That's good then,' said the priest. 'And I sympathise greatly with your sorrow. And I am sorry I had to ask. Greatly sorry.'

He walked up close to the dead man and touched him with utmost gentleness.

'I absolve you from your sins in the name of the Father, the Son, and the Holy Ghost.'

And all there, my father and myself included, spake the *Amen* to that.

CHAPTER FIVE

Dr Grene's Commonplace Book

It would be a very good thing if occasionally I thought I knew what I was doing.

I have completely underestimated the Department of Health, which in honest fact I thought would never happen. I am told for a fact that work on site will begin shortly, the other side of Roscommon town, a very fine site I am assured. Just to make things not all good news, there will be a very small number of beds, whereas here we have so many. Indeed there are rooms here just with beds, not because we could not fill them, but because the rooms have gone beyond the beyonds, with the ceilings endangered, horrible swathes of dampness up the walls. Anything iron, such as bedsteads, rusts away. All the new beds in the new place will be state of the art, without rust, pristine and nice, but fewer of them, far fewer. So we will be winnowing like crazy.

I have not been able to overcome this feeling of trying to eject creatures in my charge that will not prosper away from me. It is possibly understandable, but at the same time I suspect myself. I have a really stupid habit of feeling fatherly towards my patients, even motherly. After all these years, which I know for a fact deaden the impulses and instincts of other souls working in this sector, I am jealous for the safety, the happiness, if slightly despairing of the progress, of my patients. But I am suspicious. I wonder if, having failed with my own wife, I am inclined to regard this whole place as a sort of site of marriage, where I can be sinless, unaccused, even, on a daily basis (wretched need), redeemed.

Second-hand cloth used to be called 'beyond redemption' or not. In the old days all the suits for the males and the gowns for the dames in a place like this would be stitched from charity cloth, the first by a tailor, the second by a seamstress. I am sure even that technically 'beyond redemption' was thought good enough for the poor hearts residing here. But as time goes on, as I am slowly like everyone else worn out, finding a tatter here and a tear there in the cloth of myself, I need this place more and more. The trust of those in dark need is forgiving work. Maybe I should be more frustrated by the obvious cul-de-sac nature of psychiatry, the horrible depreciation in the states of those that linger here, the impossibility of it all. But God help me, I am not. In a few years I will reach retirement age, and what then? I will be like a sparrow without a garden.

Anyway, I know these thoughts come from present necessity. For the first time I have noticed the effrontery, I think that is the word, the effrontery of my profession. The come-around-the-back-of-the-house of it, oh yes, the deviousness. And now, in a further step of stupidity, I am resolved not to be devious. I have been talking all week to particular patients here, some of them quite extraordinary persons. I feel like I am interviewing them for something, their expulsion, their ruin. That if they manifest wellness, then, they must be sent into exile in that blessed 'community'. I am very aware that this thinking is all wrong, which is why I am trying to vent it here. I must on the contrary be disinterested, as the old word goes, detached, and resist compassion at every turn, because compassion is my weakness. There was a man yesterday, a farmer from Leitrim, who used to own four hundred acres. He is mad in an absolute, pristine way. He told me his family were so old they could trace themselves back two thousand years. He himself he told me was the last of his name. He had no children, certainly no sons, and the name would die with him. The name for the record was Meel, which right enough is a very strange name, and may be from the Irish word for honey, or so he said. And he is about seventy, very dignified, unwell, and mad. Yes, he is mad. That is to say, psychotic, and I see from his file that he unfortunately was found years ago sheltering in a schoolyard, under a seat, with three dead dogs tied to his leg, which he was dragging about with him. But as I spoke to him, all I could feel was love. That was ridiculous. And I am deeply, deeply suspicious of it.

So often my patients seem to me like a crowd of ewes pouring down a hill towards the cliff edge. What I need to be is a shepherd that knows all the whistles. I know none of them. But we shall see.

'We shall see, said the rat, as he shook his wooden leg.'

A saying of Bet's. What does it mean? I don't know. Perhaps it is a phrase from a famous childhood story, yet another famous childhood Irish thing I don't know of, having spent my childhood in England. It is very stupefying to be Irish and have none of the traits or the memories or even a recognisable bloody accent. No one on this earth has ever confused me for an Irishman, and yet that is what I am, as far as I know.

Bet was silent all week in her room above me, not even playing the BBC World Service, as she usually does. My wife. It completely spooked me.

I attempted last night a rapprochement with her – if that is how you spell it. There is no doubt in my mind I do love her. Why is my so-called love then no good to her, why does it in fact imperil her? Oh, on reading over my previous entry here, where I seemed to be subtly or not so subtly flattering myself in the matter of compassion, and love – my stomach nearly turned over as I read it – I was so annoyed with myself that I went into the kitchen when I heard her making that awful stuff she drinks at night before she goes to sleep. Complan. A nightmare drink if ever there was one, that tastes of death. I mean, Life-in-Death and Death-in-Life, Coleridge, if I remember right. 'The Rime of the Ancient Mariner'. Whose sleeve do I have to grip, to tell my story to? It used to be Bet. Now, sleeveless. And I am sure I gripped her sleeve many a time too many. In my own parlance, 'feasting' on her energy, and giving nothing back. Well, maybe. We had most excellent days. We were the king and queen of coffee in the morning, in the dark of winter, in the early morning sun of summer that came right in our window, right in, to wake us. Ah, yes, small matters. Small matters, that we call sanity, or the cloth that makes sanity. Talking to her in those times made – no, God preserve me from sentimentality. Those days are over. Now we are two foreign countries and we simply have our embassies in the same house. Relations are friendly but strictly diplomatic. There is an underlying sense of rumour, of judgement, of memory, like two peoples that have once committed grave crimes against each other, but in another generation. We are a statelet of the Baltics. Except, blast her, she has never done anything to me. It is atrocity all one way.

I did not intend to write any of this here. I meant this as a professional, semi- at any rate, account of things, the last days perhaps of this unimportant, lost, essential place. The place I have been for my professional life. The queer temple of my aspirations. I know I am as afraid of having done nothing for the inmates here, of sentimentalising them and thereby failing them, I am as afraid of that as I am certain that I have ruined Bet's life. That 'life', that unwritten narrative of herself, that – I don't know. I did not set out to do it. I prided myself in all honesty on my faithfulness to her, my regard for her, my wellnigh worshipping of her. Perhaps I sentimentalised her also. Pernicious, chronic sentimentalising. Damn it, my pride in her was my pride in myself, and that was a good thing. While I had her good opinion, I had the highest opinion of myself. I lived off it, I strode out each day fuelled by it. How wonderful, how vibrant, how ridiculous. But it was a state I would give the world to retrieve. I know it's not possible. But still. When this world here is demolished so many tiny histories will go with it. It is actually frightening, maybe even terrorising.

Into the kitchen I went. How welcome a figure I can't say. Not very, probably, my sudden presence endured.

She wasn't making Complan though, she was dissolving some tablets in a glass, Disprin or the like.

'Are you all right?' I said. 'Headache?'

'I'm quite fine,' she said.

Last January twelvemonth I know she had a little scare, she fainted in the street while she was shopping, and was brought to Roscommon hospital. She was in there all day having tests, and in the evening one of the doctors innocently phoned me to come and get her. He probably thought I knew she was there. I was so alarmed. I nearly crashed the car coming out our gate, nearly hung it on the pillar, drove like a man drives his pregnant wife in the night to hospital, when the famous pains begin, not that she ever endured that, and therein maybe lies the crux of the matter.

She was staring now at the glass.

'How are the legs?' I said.

'Swollen,' she said. 'It's just water. That's what they said. I wish it would go away.'

'Yes, of course,' I said, taking some courage from the phrase 'go away', as in holiday. 'Look, I've been thinking, it might be nice, when I have everything sorted out at work, if we went away for a few days. A holiday.'

She looked at me, swilling the fizzing tablets in the glass, readying herself for the bitter taste. I am sorry to report she laughed, just a little laugh, that I suspect she would have liked not to have let loose, but here it was, a laugh, between us.

'I don't think so,' she said.

'Why not,' I said. 'Old times' sake. Do us both good.'

'Is that right, Doctor?'

'Yes, do us good. Definitely.'

It was suddenly difficult to speak, as if every word was a little lump of mud in my mouth.

'I'm sorry, William,' she said, and that was a bad sign, the full first name, no longer Will, just William, separate, 'I don't really want to. I hate to see all the children.'

'The what?'

'The people, with their children.'

'Why?'

Oh yes, depthless stupid question. Children. The thing we have none of. Infinite pains we took. Infinite. Unrewarded.

'William, you are not a stupid man.'

'We'll go somewhere where there aren't any children.'

'Where? Mars?' she said.

'Somewhere where there aren't any,' I said, lifting my face to the ceiling, as if that was a likely place. 'I don't know where that is.'

Roseanne's Testimony of Herself

It was then the horror of horrors occurred.

To this day, I swear by my God, I do not know how it happened. Someone else or others surely know, or did while they lived. And maybe the exactly how of it is not important, never was, but only, what certain people thought had happened.

Not that it matters now, maybe, because all those people are swept away by time. But maybe there is another place where everything matters eternally, the courts of heaven as may be. It would be a useful court for the living but the living will never see it.

It was persons unknown that banged on the door then, and shouted out with harsh military voices. We were like a set of hidden woodlice then inside, scattering away in different directions, myself drawing back like a tragedian in a travelling play, such as might be seen in a damp hall in the town, the three Irregulars ducking down behind the table, my father drawing Fr Gaunt near to me, as if he might hide me behind the priest and his own love. For it was clear to anyone that there would be shots now, and just as I had that thought, the iron door pushed open on its big scraping hinges.

Yes, it was lads of the new army in their awkward uniforms. It would be thought as they came in that they had bullets aplenty, at least they levelled their guns at us in their own fierce moments of concentration, and to my young eyes, looking out through my father's legs, the six or seven faces that entered the temple looked only terrified in the light of the fire.

The long thin boy from the mountain, with the trousers not quite to his ankles, jumped up from behind the table, and for mad reasons of his own, charged against the newcomers as if he was out on a proper battlefield. The brother of the dead man was right behind him, maybe in his grief demanding this of himself. It is difficult to describe the noise that guns make in a small enclosed space, but it would make the bones drop out of your flesh. My father, Fr Gaunt and I reared back against the wall as one, and the bullets that went into the two lads must have made queer tracks through them, because I saw sudden exploding pocks in the plaster of the old wall beside me. First the bullets, and then a thin falling cascade of lightest blood, over my uniform, my hands, my father, my life.

The two irregulars were not killed, but writhed now on the ground caught up in each other.

'For the love of God,' cried Fr Gaunt, 'desist – there is a young girl in here, and ordinary people.' Whatever he meant by the latter.

'Put down your guns, put down your guns,' shouted one of the new soldiers, almost a scream it was. Certainly the last man our side of the table threw down his gun, and his handgun out of his waistband, and he stood up immediately and raised his hands. He looked back at me just for a second and I thought his eyes were weeping, his eyes were doing something or other, certainly piercing into me anyhow, fiercely, fiercely, like those eyes could be used to kill, could be better than the bullets they did not have.

'Look,' said Fr Gaunt. 'I believe – I believe these men have no bullets. Just everyone do nothing for a moment!'

'No bullets?' said the commander of the men. 'Because they've put them all into our men up on the mountain. Are you the bastards were up on the mountain?'

Oh dear, oh dear, we knew they were, and yet for some reason none of us spoke a word.

'You've killed my brother,' said the man called John on the ground. He was holding the top of his thigh, and there was a great strange dark pool of blood just under him, blood as black as blackbirds. 'You killed him in cold blood. You had him captured, you had him harmless, and you shot him in the stomach, three fucking times!'

'So you wouldn't be creeping down on us and murdering us where we went!' said the commander. 'Hold these men down, and you,' he cried to him who had surrendered, 'count yourself arrested. Bring them all out to the truck, lads, and we'll sort this out. In the dark of the night we catch you, in this filthy place, gathered like rats. You, man, what's your name?'

'Joe Clear,' said my father. 'I'm the watchman here at the graveyard. This is Fr Gaunt, one of the curates in the parish. I called him, for to see to the dead boy there.'

'So you bury the likes of him in Sligo,' said the commander, with extraordinary force. And he rushed around the table and held the gun to Fr Gaunt's temple. 'What sort of a priest are you, that would be disobeying your own bishops? Are you one of those filthy renegades?'

'Are you going to shoot a priest?' said my father in astonishment.

Fr Gaunt had his eyes closed fast and was kneeling now just the same as he might in the church. He was kneeling and I don't know if he was praying soundlessly, but he wasn't saying anything.

'Jem,' said one of the other Free State soldiers, 'there was never a priest shot yet in Ireland by us. Don't shoot him.'

The commander stood back and raised his gun away from Fr Gaunt.

'Come on, lads, gather them up, we're getting out of here.'

And the soldiers raised up the two wounded gently enough and led them out through the door. Just as the third man was being arrested he turned his face full on me.

'May God forgive you for what you done but I never will.'

'But I never done nothing!' I said.

'You told them we were here.'

'I did not, I swear to God.'

'God's not here,' he said. 'Look at you, guilty as Jack.'

'No!' I said.

The man laughed then a horrible laugh like a lash of rain into your face, and the other soldiers brought him away. We could hear them cajoling the prisoners along the paths. I was shaking in all my body. The commander, when the room was clear, held out a big hand to Fr Gaunt, and helped him to his feet.

'I'm sorry, Father,' he said. 'It has been a terrible night. Murder and mayhem. Excuse me.'

He spoke so sincerely my father I'm sure was as struck by the words as I was.

'It was a blackguardly thing to do,' said Fr Gaunt, in a small voice that nevertheless had a strange taint of violence in it.

'Blackguardly. I support fully the new country. We all do, except those mad misguided boys.'

'You should heed your bishops so. And not give succour to the damned.'

'You let me have my own thoughts on that,' said Fr Gaunt, with a sort of schoolmasterish arrogance. 'What are you going to do with the body? Don't you want to take it with you?'

'What do you want to do with it?' said the soldier, now with a sudden weariness, the fall in energy that comes after great effort. They had charged into an unknown place with God knew what danger, and now it seemed the thought of lugging John's brother Willie was a feather too far. Or a hammer.

'I'll have the doctor fetched and pronounce him dead and find out who owns him, and then perhaps we can bury him somewhere in the yard, if you have no objection.'

'You will be burying a devil if you do. Better throw him in a hole outside the walls, like a criminal, or a bastard child.'

Fr Gaunt said nothing to that. The soldier went out. He never looked at me once. When his boots stopped sounding on the gravel path outside, the queerest coldest silence dreeped into the temple. My father stood silent, and the priest, and I sat silently on the cold damp floor, and John's brother Willie was most silent of all.

'I am extremely angry,' said Fr Gaunt then, in his best Sunday mass voice, 'to have been dragged into this. Extremely angry, Mr Clear.'

My father looked nonplussed. What else was he to do? My father's unmoored face scared me just as much as Willie's stiffening corpse.

'I'm sorry,' said my father. 'I'm sorry if I acted wrongly in getting Roseanne to fetch you.'

'You did wrong to do that, you did wrong, yes. I am deeply aggrieved. You may remember it was I who put you in this post. It was I, and great powers of persuasion were needed, let me tell you. I feel very poorly thanked, very poorly.'

With that, the priest went out into the dark and the rain, leaving my father and myself with the dead boy, till the doctor could arrive.

'I suppose I put his life in danger. I suppose he was frightened. But I did not intend it. By heavens, I thought priests liked to be in on everything. Indeed and I did.'

My poor father sounded frightened too, but now because of a new and different cause.

How delicately, slowly, fate undid him, I suppose.

There are things that move at a human pace before our eyes, but other things move in arcs so great they are as good as invisible. The baby sees a star winking in the dark night window, and puts out his hand to hold it. So my father struggled to grasp things that were in truth far beyond his reach, and indeed when they showed their lights were already old and done.

I think it was that my father embarrassed history.

He was neither willing nor unwilling to bury that boy Willie, and called a priest to help him in his decision. It was as if as a Presbyterian he had meddled in sacred murders, or murders so beyond gentleness and love that to be even in propinquity to them was ruinous, murderous even.

Perhaps in later years I heard versions of that night that didn't fit my own memory of it, but all the same, there was always one grand constant, that I had stopped in my path to fetch Fr Gaunt and told my tale to the Free State soldiers, either at my father's bidding or by my own instincts. The fact that I never saw the soldiers, never spoke to them, never even thought of doing so – for would that not have put my father possibly in further danger? – is in the informal history of Sligo neither here nor there. For history as far as I can see is not the arrangement of what happens, in sequence and in truth, but a fabulous arrangement of surmises and guesses held up as a banner against the assault of withering truth.

History needs to be mightily inventive about human life because bare life is an accusation against man's dominion of the earth.

My own story, anyone's own story, is always told against me, even what I myself am writing here, because I have no heroic history to offer. There is no difficulty not of my own making. The heart and the soul, so beloved of God, are both filthied up by residence here, how can we avoid it? These seem not my thoughts at all, but maybe are borrowed out of old readings of Sir Thomas Browne. But they feel as if they are mine. They sound in my head like my own belling thoughts. It is strange. I suppose therefore God is the connoisseur of filthied hearts and souls, and can see the old, first pattern in them, and cherish them for that.

He had better be in my case, or I may dwell with the devil shortly.

Our house was clean, but did not look so clean the day that Fr Gaunt came to visit us. It was Sunday morning about ten, so I may assume Fr Gaunt was between masses and had hurried from his church along the river to knock on our door. As my mother had an old mirror balanced on a yellow brick in the window of the sitting room, we could always see without showing ourselves who was at the door, and the sight of the priest sent us scurrying about. A fourteen-year-old girl is always vividly aware of her appearance, or thinks she must be, or whatever it is, but speaking of mirrors I was at that time a slave to the one in my mother's bedroom, not because I thought I looked well, but because I did not know how I looked, and laboured many a minute to adjust myself into a picture I could trust, or was content with, and never could achieve it. The gold of my hair looked like some wet grass gone wild to me, and for the life of me I did not know the soul of the person that peered back at me in my mother's mossy little mirror. Because the edges of the mirror were strangely decayed, she had actually bought some unusual enamel paint in the chemist as may be, and decorated the edges of the mirror with tiny black stems and leaves, that lent everything that appeared in that less-than-poetical mirror a funereal look, which perhaps had suited my father's profession, at least up to now. So my first action was to dash up our few little stairs to the mirror and make an assault on my fourteen-year-old sense of horror.

When I got back down to the living room my father was standing in the middle of it, looking about him like a baulking pony, his eyes lighting first on the motorcycle, then on the piano, then on the spaces in between, his hand dashing now to a cushion on the 'best' chair. When I glanced out into the tiny hall, my mother was merely lodged there, stuck there, not moving a muscle, like an actor waiting to go out on a stage, gearing up her courage. Then she lifted the latch.

As Fr Gaunt edged into our room, the first thing I noticed was how glistening he seemed, his face shaved so closely you could write on it with a pen. He looked so safe, the safest thing in Ireland in an unsafe time. Every month of that year was the worst month, my father had said, as every person killed echoed in him. But the priest looked sacrosanct, pristine, separate, as if separate from the history of Ireland itself. Not that I thought this at the time, God knows what I thought, I don't know, only that this cleanliness made me fearful.

I had never seen my father quite so fussed. He could only speak in rushes and gaps.

'Ah, but, yes, sit down there, Father, do, now,' he said, nearly advancing on the unsmiling priest, as if to knock him back into the chair. But Fr Gaunt sat down steady as a dancer.

I knew my mother was in the hallway, in that little gap of privacy and silence. I stood at my father's right side like a watchman, like a sentry against the storm of an attack. My head was filled with some unknown darkness, I couldn't think, I couldn't continue that long conversation we make in our heads, as if an angel were writing there unbeknownst.

'Hmm,' said my father. 'We'll make tea, how about that?' he said. 'Yes, we will. Cissy, Cissy, will you heat the kettle, dear, do.'

'I drink so much tea,' said the priest, 'it's a wonder my skin doesn't turn brown.'

My father laughed.

'I'm sure you do, out of a sense of duty. But no need in my house. No need. I, that owe everything in the world to you, everything in the world. Not that, not that –'

And here my father floundered, and blushed, and I blushed too I dare say, for reasons I could not understand.

The priest cleared his throat, and smiled.

'I will take a cup of tea, of course I will.'

'Ah, well, that's good, that's good,' and already we could hear my mother scraping about in the pantry down the corridor.

'It is so cold today,' said the priest, rubbing his hands suddenly, 'that I am very relieved to be near a fire, now, I am. It is so frosty along the river. Do you think', he said, drawing out a silver case, 'I might smoke?'

'Oh, fire away,' said my father.

The priest now drew his box of Swan matches from his soutane, and a funny oblong-shaped cigarette from the case, struck the match with a beautiful precision and neatness, and drew in the flame with his breath through the crisp tube. Then he exhaled and gave a little cough.

'The – the,' said the priest, 'the position in the graveyard as you can well imagine is not – tenable. Em?'

He gave another elegant pull on the cigarette, adding: 'I am afraid to say, Joe. I dislike this fact as I am sure you dislike it. But I am sure you will appreciate the – the great cloud of dust that has descended on my head, between the bishop, who believes all the renegades must be excommunicated, as was decided at the recent synod, and the mayor, who as you may be aware is very much against the treaty as it stands, and as the most influential man in Sligo carries great – influence. As you can imagine, Joe.'

'Oh,' said my father.

'Yes.'

Now the priest went a third time at the cigarette and found he already had quite an ash to deal with and in that silent dumbshow of smokers looked about for an ashtray, an item that did not exist in our house, even for visitors. My father astonished me by putting out his hand to the priest, admittedly a hard hand coarsened by digging, and Fr Gaunt astonished me by immediately flicking the ash into the offered hand, which perhaps flinched tinily for a moment when the heat hit it. My father, left with the ash, looked about almost foolishly, as if there might have been an ashtray put in the room after all, without his knowledge, and then, with horrible solemnity, pocketed it.

'Hmm,' said my father. 'Yes, I can imagine there is a difficulty to reconcile those two poles.'

He spoke the words so gently.

'I have of course looked about, especially in the town hall, for an alternative occupation, and if at first this seemed an impossible – em, possibility – then, when I was just about to give up, the mayor's secretary, Mr Dolan, told me there was a job on offer, in fact, they had been trying to fill it some time past, with some urgency, due to the veritable plague of rats that has been bedevilling the warehouses on the riverside. Finisglen as you know is a very salubrious district, the doctor himself lives there, and unfortunately the docks abut it, as of course you know, as everyone knows.'

Now I could write a little book on the nature of human silences, their uses and occasions, but the silence that my father offered to this speech was very dreadful. It was a silence like a hole with a sucking wind in it. He blushed further, which brought his face to crimson, like the victim of an attack.

At this moment my mother entered with the tea, looking like a servant among kings, you would think, afraid perhaps to look at my father, so keeping her eyes on the little tray with its painted scene of some French field of poppies. I had often gazed at that tray where it lived on the top of the dresser in the pantry, and imagined I could see a wind blowing along the flowers, and wondered what it was like in that world of heat and dark language.

'So,' said the priest, 'I am happy to offer you, in the name of the mayor Mr Salmon, em, the eh – post. Job.'

'Of?' said my father.

'Of,' said the priest.

'What?' said my mother, probably against her better intentions, the word just popping into the room.

'Rat-catcher,' said the priest.

It fell to me, I know not why, to bring the priest to the door. On the narrow pavement, with the chill gathering about him, creeping no doubt up his soutane along his bare legs, the little priest said:

'Please, tell your father, Roseanne, that all the accoutrements of the trade are at the town hall. Traps, et cetera, I suppose. That's where he'll find them.'

'Thank you,' I said.

Then he started off down the street, stopped a moment. I don't know why I stayed there watching him. He took off one of his black shoes, leaning a hand on the brick wall of our neighbour's house, then balanced on one foot, feeling the underside of his sock for whatever hindered his walk, a pebble or piece of grit. Then he unhitched the sock from its gaiter, and removed it in a smooth sweep, revealing a long white foot with the toenails rather yellow like old teeth, folding back on his toes, as if they had never been cut. Then he spotted me with my eyes still on him, and laughed, and having routed out the offending stone, put back his sock and his shoe, and stood there solidly on the pavement.

'Such a relief,' he said pleasantly. 'Good day. And,' he said, 'now I think of it, there is also a dog. A dog attached to the job. For ratting.'

When I went back into the sitting room my father had not moved. The motorbike had not moved. The piano had not moved. My father looked like he would never move again. My mother I heard scratching about in the pantry, very like a rat. Or a little dog looking for a rat.

'Do you know anything about that job, Dadda?' I said.

'Do I – oh, I suppose.'

'You won't find it so hard.'

'No, no, because I have often had to deal with such things at the cemetery. The rats do love the soft soil on the graves, and the gravestones make such good roofs for them. Yes, I have had to deal with them. I will have to study the matter. Perhaps there will be a manual in the library.'

'A rat-catcher's manual?' I said.

'Yes, don't you think, Roseanne?'

'I am sure, Dadda.'

'Oh, yes.

CHAPTER SIX

Yes, how well I remember the day my father was let go from the cemetery, a living man exiled from the dead.

That was a little murder also.

My father loved the world and his fellow humans in it, without much reservation on his part, considering as a good Presbyterian must that all souls are equally assailed, and hearing in the rough laughter of the cornerboy a kind of essential explanation of life, and thereby a redemption of it, in fact believing that since God had created everything, so everything by him must be approved, and also that the devil's own tragedy is *he* is author of nothing and architect of empty spaces. My father, by cause of all this, based his good opinion of himself on his work, that, as a person of unusual religion, he had yet been given a post to bury the Catholic people of Sligo as time claimed them one by one.

'Such pride, such pride!' he used to say, as together we locked the iron gates at evening, preparatory to going home, and his eyes fell in back through the bars to the darkening rows, the disappearing headstones that were his care. I suppose he was talking to himself, or to the graves, and probably not to me, and he might not have thought for a moment that I would have understood him. Perhaps I did not, but I think I understand him now.

The truth was, my father loved his country, he loved whatever in his mind he thought Ireland to be. Maybe if he had been born a Jamaican, he might have loved Jamaica just as much. But he was not. His ancestors had held the little sinecures available to their kind in Irish towns, inspectors of buildings and the like, and his father had even gained the eminence of a preacher. He was born in a small minister's house in Collooney, his infant heart loved Collooney, his growing heart expanding in its love to the island entire. Because his father was one of those radical thinkers, who had written pamphlets or at least preached sermons – because no pamphlets survive, but I seem to remember my father mentioning one or two – on the history of Protestantism in Ireland, my father held opinions not always favourable to himself. That is to say, he thought of the Protestant religion as an instrument as soft as a feather transformed into a hammer by the old dispensation, and used to batter the heads of those that laboured to live in Ireland, the most of them Catholics by nature. His own father loved Presbyterianism, and he did himself, but he was mortally sorry, no, he was mortally angry at the uses it had been put to, along with the religions of the Anglicans, Baptists et cetera, in Ireland.

How do I know? Because every night of my childhood, every night, the last thing he did in the house was come into my narrow bed, shoving me over with his wide hips, so that I lay half on him, my head on his whiskery face, and talked and talked and talked, while my mother went to sleep in the other room. When he heard her small snores he would leave me and join her, but in that half hour, in the darkness, as he allowed her to settle into sleep on her own, the moon first sitting on the back wall, and then floating darkly and brightly as is the manners of the moon, into the sky of unattainable stars (as I well knew), he recited to me all the intimations, suspicions and histories of his heart, not perhaps even bothering himself with the thought that I might not understand, but offering it all as a music quite as desirable to him and therefore to me as the works of Balfe and Sullivan, two of the greatest Irishmen that had ever lived, in his opinion.

And working in the graveyard, under the patronage as it were of Fr Gaunt, was in some manner to him his life perfected, made good. In some manner, made as a prayer back to his own father. It was the way he had learned to live, in Ireland, the accidental place he loved.

And to lose the job was to lose in some extraordinary fashion himself.

Now it was more difficult to be with him. It was hard for him to bring me ratting, it being such a dirty, tricky and perilous occupation.

Being a thorough man, he soon found the little book that would help him, called *A Perfect Account of Rat-Catching*, by a pseudonymous author, Rattus Rattus. This booklet recounted the adventures of a rat-catcher in the factories of Manchester, a city of heaped-up factories with infinite places for rats to live and hide. It told my father how to go about his work, itemising everything, even the sort of attention that was needed to be paid to the feet of ferrets, who it seemed were very vulnerable to foot-rot in damp cages. But my father never attained the dignity of owning ferrets. The corporation of Sligo was less ambitious. He was given a Jack Russell dog called Bob.

So began the strangest era of my childhood. I suppose also I was slowly less child than girl, less girl than woman. For the years of my father's ratting, a solemn mood of my own descended on me. Things that had delighted and pleased me as a child delighted and pleased no longer. It was as if something had been taken from the pictures and sounds of the world, or as if the greatest possession of a child is easy joy. So that I felt I was in a condition of waiting, waiting for something unknown to replace the grace of being young. Of course I was young, very young, but, as I remember it, no one is ever quite so old as a fifteen-year-old girl.

People persist with what we call ordinary life, because there is no other sort of life. My father continued to sing 'Roses of Picardy' as he shaved in the morning, the words and lines broken up, skipped here and there, as he manoeuvred the blade about his craggy face, so if I closed my eyes and listened below, I could see him in a sort of mysterious cinema at the back of my head. He continued heroically in this, and went out with his dog and his traps, and learned to make that his 'usual task', and returned from his work, not always at the old regular times, but still tried to carry the *Sligo Champion* in under his arm, and force his new life into the realm of normality.

But these days he might be reading items in the paper curiously connected to himself, or at least on one occasion, because I heard his little gasp, and looked up at him immersed in the paper. Mr Roddy was the owner of the *Champion* and very much a new government man, as they called it. So the actions of the civil war were reported in bare, plain terms, terms that also strove to suggest normalcy, solidity.

'By heavens,' said my father, 'they have shot those boys were in the graveyard that time.'

'Which boys?' I said.

'Those wild young lads brought in their murdered friend.'

'He was a brother to one of them,' I said.

'Yes, Roseanne, a brother to one. They have the names here. Lavelle was his name, isn't that a strange one? William. And the brother was John. But he got away it says here. Escaped.'

'Yes,' I said, a little uneasy, but also unexpectedly happy. It was like hearing about Jesse James or the like. You wouldn't like to meet an outlaw but you do like them to get away all the same. Of course John Lavelle we had met.

'Inishkea he is from. One of the islands. The Mullet. Very remote part of the world. Deepest Mayo. He might be safe down there among his own people.'

'I hope so.'

64

'It has been a very difficult thing for them, I am sure, shooting such men.'

My father spoke without irony. With truth. Indeed it would have been a very difficult thing. To put those boys side by side maybe, or one by one, who knew the way of these things, and shoot them – to death, as one might say. Who knows what happened on that mountain? In the dark. And now they were dead themselves, along with Willie Lavelle, from the Inishkeas.

My father spoke not another word. We were not looking at each other either, but at the same spot on the hearth, where a little hill of coals struggled.

But the silence that was on my mother was the profoundest of all. She might have been a creature underwater, or rather, when I was with her, it could have been so for both of us, because she never spoke, but moved slowly and ponderously like a swimming creature.

My father made his valiant efforts to stir her, and showed her every attention he could. His wages from his new work were small, but small as they were, he hoped they might do, especially in those hard dark years when the civil war was over, and the country was struggling to get off its knees. But I think in those days the whole world was aching with catastrophes, great wheels of history were turning not turned by man at all, but by the hand of some inexplicable agent. My father gave her what he earned, hoping she might parcel and divide the few pounds, and get us through. But something, inexplicable as the enormous forces of history, but a tiny matter since it only affected us, seemed to hold sway, and there was often almost nothing to eat in the house. My mother might bang about in the pantry at supper time, as if about to produce a meal, then come back out into the little sitting room and sit herself down, while my father, all scrubbed and ready after his work, and with a whole night ahead of him – for rats are best molested in the dark – and myself looked at her, with the realisation slowly dawning that there was nothing forthcoming. Then my father slowly shook his head, and maybe mentally tightened his belt, but hardly dared ask her what was amiss. In the face of her troubles, we were beginning to starve!

But nothing could penetrate her silence. Christmas came, and my father and myself plotted to get our hands on something that would please her. He had spotted a scarf for sale near the Café Cairo, in a little everything shop, and every week he kept back a halfpenny or so, so he could gather the necessary like a mouse hoards grain. Please remember that my mother was very beautiful, though perhaps not so beautiful now, as her silence had found an echo in some bleak thin cloth that seemed to be pulled over the skin of her face. She was like a painting with its varnish darkening, obscuring the beauty of the work. Because her lovely green eyes were dying in their lights, something of her essential self was vanishing also. But still in her general outline any artist would have been content with her I think, if Sligo had had artists, which I doubt if it had, unless it was fellas painting the faces of the Jacksons, the Middletons and the Pollexfens, who were the better people in the town.

My father was not obliged to work on Christmas eve, and it was our delight to go to the service, given by the minister Mr Ellis in his neat old church. My mother came with us silently, small like a monk in her shabby outdoor coat. I remember the scene so well, the small church lit with candles, and the Protestant people of the parish, poor and not poor and wealthy enough, gathered there, the men in their dark gaberdines, the women if they could manage it with a dash of fur about the neck, but mostly, the sombre green tones of those days. The light of the candles pierced everywhere, into the lines

66

of my father's face as he sat beside me, into the stones of the church, into the voice of the minister as he spoke his words in that mysterious and stirring English of the bible, in through my own breastbone, right into my young heart, piercing me fiercely there, so that I wanted to cry out, but cry out what I could not say. Cry out against my father's fate, my mother's silence, but also, cry out in praise of something, the beauty of my mother that was going but still there. I felt as if my mother and my father were in my care, and that it was by some action of my own that they would be rescued. For some reason this plumped me up with sudden joy, a feeling so scarce in that time, so that when the local voices began to sing some forgotten hymn, I began to flush with weird happiness, and then in the sparkling dark, to cry, long full hot tears of treacherous relief.

And I cried there, and I suppose little good it did anyone. The smell of the wet clothes all about me, the coughing of the church-goers. What would I give to put them back in that church, back in that Christmas time, put everything back that time soon took away, as time must, the shillings back in the pockets of the people, the bodies back in the long johns and the mittens, everything, everything back, so we might be balanced there, kneeling and sitting on the mahogany planks, if not eternally then again for those moments, that very inch of the material of time, the lines of my father's face accepting the glimmering light, his face slowly slowly turning to both my mother and me, and smiling, smiling in easy, ordinary kindness.

The next morning my father produced for me a beautiful segment of what I learned later was called costume jewellery. All girls going out in Sligo liked to sport a bit of 'magpie' glitter. I like other girls dreamed of the fabled magpie's nest, where brooches and bracelets and earrings would be found, a nest of lovely plunder. I took my father's gift and opened its silver-coloured pin and pinned it on my cardigan, showed it proudly to the piano and the motorbike.

Then my father handed my mother the great something wrapped in good shop paper, the sort that in older days she would have saved and folded and put in a drawer. She opened the packet quietly, and gazed on the speckled scarf folded itself within, and raised her face and asked:

'Why, Joe?'

My father had not the least idea what she meant. Was it the pattern was wrong? Had he failed in the task of buying a scarf in some manner he would not be aware of, for who would tell him, the rat-catcher, about women's fashions?

'Why? I don't know, Cissy. I don't know,' he said, valiantly. Then, suddenly, he added, as if on an inspiration: 'It's a scarf.'

'What did you say, Joe?' she said, as if lost in a mysterious deafness.

'For your head, for your neck, as you like,' he said. Beginning to churn, it was obvious to me, with that desperate feeling that grows in the belly of the giver of the wrong present. He was having to explain the obvious, always an unpleasant task.

'Oh,' she said, staring at it now in her lap. 'Oh.'

'I hope you like it,' he said, which I suppose was presenting his own neck for the axe.

'Oh,' she said, 'oh.' But what class of an *oh* it was, or what the *oh* signified, neither of us knew.

CHAPTER SEVEN

Dr Grene's Commonplace Book

Very distressed to discover, quite by accident, that Bet has decided not to attend the specialist to whom she had been referred last year (was it a year ago already, or am I dreaming? Was it this year?). By the tin of Complan last night I happened to find, temporarily forgotten, her diary. Now, of course it was wrong, unethical, wrong, wrong, but I opened it, just from the tiny passion of the husband disliked. To see what she had written in it. No, no, just to see her writing, something as intimate and private as that. Maybe not even to read the words. Just to look at the black ink of her biro for a brief moment. And there it was, just a few weeks ago, an entry bold as brass, but of course, meant only for herself: 'Rang clinic, cancelled appointments.'

Why?

This was the follow-up for her dizzy spell, I was vaguely aware, in fact when she told me she had been given the referral, I was so comforted I put the entire matter from my mind. I was in two minds. First, alarmed that she had done so, and secondly, perfectly aware that I only knew because I had violated her privacy – a further violation of herself, as I knew she would see it. And she would be right.

What to do?

So I was distracted all night. My usual solution to the problem, distraction. Possibly. But I think, with good reason.

Somewhere in the small hours I grew mysteriously furious, really really angry, with her, and wanted to storm up the stairs and have it out with her. What did she think she was doing? The bloody foolishness of it!

Thank God I did not. That would have solved nothing. But very real worries assail me. The swelling in her legs could well be due to clotting, and if the clot should climb into the lungs or the heart, she will drop dead. Is this what she wants? Now yet again I discover I do not have the language, the lingo, to talk to her about this, or about anything. We have neglected the tiny sentences of life and now the big ones are beyond our reach.

I had meant to spend the evening devising some non-devious way to question Roseanne McNulty in such a manner as to get a result. It strikes me that if I cannot speak helpfully to my own wife about her health, I have little chance with Roseanne. But maybe it is easier with a stranger, one can be the 'expert', and not the great human fool that tries to lead a life. On the plus side, I am fairly confident in my assessment of most of the other patients. They are in the main open books and their distress is self-evident. Although I cannot shed myself of the feeling of being the perpetual invader. Roseanne however confounds me.

I had wanted to consult my edition of Barthus on *Pathologies of Secrecy*, which of course is a marvellous book, if I would only find time to read it again. I suppose I could have gone into my study and looked at it, but I was trembling. I was nearly apoplectic, if that is still a real condition in the modern world. So in the upshot I neither read my Barthus nor resolved Bet's recklessness. I am exhausted.

Roseanne's Testimony of Herself

Some weeks later it must have been, I was with my father on a particular job.

Rats start to breed with a vengeance in early spring, so late winter is a good time to go get them, when they have not expanded in numbers for a while, and the weather is not too murderous to the rat-catcher. I suppose looking back it was a queer thing to bring a young girl on the trail of rodents, but I did take a great interest in it, especially after my father read me the manual, which presented the task as one highly skilled, even verging on the vocational and the magical.

He had been working a few nights already in the Protestant orphanage, a strange place in its own right, rats or no rats. It was already about two hundred years old, and my father knew old stories attached to the place, and I do not think it was a very good idea to be an orphan in centuries gone by, judging by what he said. Perhaps in those days it was a decent place enough. He intended to work from the roof down, which was the proper way to do it, ridding the place of rats floor by floor. The upper attics had been cleared, and the top floor, and there were three floors to do, where the orphan girls actually lived, about two hundred of them in their nice canvaslike pinnies, which they wore in their beds.

'They've a bed each these times, Roseanne, yes,' said my father. 'But in the times of your grandfather, or maybe it was his grandfather, but anyway, things were very different. Your grandfather, or perhaps your grandfather's grandfather, used to tell a terrible tale about this place. He came in here, inspector of buildings he was, and had been commissioned by the government in Dublin at the time, because there had been an outcry against the practices in these places, an outcry. He came in here,' and we were standing out in the ancient courtyard at the time, in a rather murky light, with two cages of rats full as you like, and Bob the dog looking very pleased with himself, having chased the rats through the very walls, which were seven or eight feet thick in places, with cavities galore, 'say maybe in one of those big rooms up there,' and he pointed up the gloomy stones of the building to the second floor, 'and there was what looked to him like an acre of beds, and on each bed was babies, maybe twenty of them, newborn or nearly, lying side by side, and he came in there with the ould nurse, as manky now as you like, as you can imagine, and he surveys the sea of babies, and he notices that there was no glass in some of the windows, not like now, and just a little fire in the huge grate, not enough to warm anything, and indeed holes in the ceiling also with the cold drear winter wind howling in, and he exclaims, "My God, woman," or however they might speak in those times, "my God, woman, but these children are not being cared for, by God," he says, "they are not even clothed," and sure enough, Roseanne, they had barely a scrap of clothing between them. And the old woman says, like it was the most reasonable and ordinary thing in the world, "But sure, Mister, aren't they lying in here to die." And he realised that these arrangements were meant, and it was a way to be rid of the sickly or surplus babies. And that was a great scandal in those days, for a while, I suppose.'

He worked away at the traps for a while, and I stood near him, the night wind moaning a little where it crept along the buildings. There was a cold cheap cankered-looking moon risen, just sitting on the roof of the orphanage. My father was dousing the rats with paraffin, preparatory to throwing them on the fire one by one, a fire he had managed to get lit in the centre of the courtyard, using smelly old boards and the like from one of the stores. This was his own method of disposing of the rats, that he had devised, working on from the manual, and he was quite proud of the method. When I think back it was perhaps a little unfortunate that the rats were still alive going into the flames, but I do not think it ever struck my father as cruel, and maybe he hoped it might serve as a warning to other rats if they were watching from the shadows. Which would be to some degree how my father's mind worked.

At any rate he was opening the traps, grabbing the rats one by one as I said and now I think of it, giving each a rap over the head before the flames, that has just popped up in my head as

72

a picture, thank God, and chatting away to me, and maybe it was because he was not able to give it his full concentration, because I was with him, but didn't one of the rats escape between the trap and the knock on the head, wriggling out of his fingers suddenly, skirting the astonished Bob, who had nary a chance to react, and was gone back towards the orphanage in a dark blaze of blackness, but with that characteristic galloping motion . . . My father cursed gently and maybe thought no more of it, thinking he would get that rat again the following day.

So he worked away at the remainder, registering no doubt the squeaking yelp that each rat gave as he dispatched it, soaked in the paraffin, and threw it onto the bonfire, a sound that I imagine he heard in his dreams. And after about an hour, he wrapped up his bits and bobs, slung his traps around his body, put Bob on his habitual string, and we passed back through the dark orphanage to the street side, where it presented a rather elaborate carved front to the town, being no doubt the result of much philanthropic cash in the vanished century of its building. It was when we were just crossing the street that we heard a roaring, and turned about and looked up.

There was a strange, full, mysterious sound coming from the building, high up on the floor where the girls were sleeping. Although not all sleeping now, because pushing up through the slates of the roof was a thick black smoke, and a grey smoke, and a white smoke, all eerily lit by nothing but the moon and the meagre illuminations of Sligo. Now we heard the glass of windows break somewhere, and suddenly a long thin arm of bright yellow flame came streaking out, seemed to hang solidly in the night air, showing up my father's upturned face, and no doubt mine, and then just as strangely retrieved itself, with a horrible roaring moan, worse than any wind. It seemed to me in my enormous fright that the fire had spoken a word: 'Death, death,' said the fire I thought.

'Jesus, Mary, and Joseph,' said my father, like a man paralysed by some awful turn in his blood and brain, and as he spoke the doors of the orphanage opened, no doubt sending up a wild fierce blow of wind through the house, and a few stunned girls, their pinnies covered in ash and dirt, came stumbling out, their faces wild like little demons. I had never seen such terror. Two or three of the attendants of the place, a woman and two men, also tumbled out, in their black clothes, and hurried out onto the cobbles to see what could be seen.

What could be seen – and now the fire engines could be heard in the distance, clanging their bells – was the floor of girls bright as day, with a foaming of flames behind the great windows, and though we were at a strict angle, the faces and arms of girls beating at the windows like moths do in daytime, or sleeping butterflies in winter when a room is suddenly heated, fatally thinking spring has come. Then some of the windows seemed to explode out, sending lethal shards and fragments of glass down towards us, making everyone run for the other side of the street. People came out of their houses, women with hands to their faces, wailing strangely, and men in their long johns from their beds, shouting and calling, and if they had never felt compassion for those parentless girls, they felt it now, calling out to them like fathers and mothers.

We could see the fire burn even fiercer behind them, offering an enormous flower of yellow and red, with such a noise as mortal never heard before hell, and indeed as hell might be thought to be in nightmares. And the girls, most of them my own age in that particular chamber, started to climb out through the windows onto the wide ledge, every one with their pinnies already burning, screaming and screaming. And when they could do no better, and had no hope of any other sort of rescue, they jumped from the ledge in little groups and single, their clothes burning and burning, the flames blown up from the pinnies till they dragged above them like veritable wings, and these burning girls fell the height of that grand old mansion, and struck the cobbles. A continuous wave of them, a wave of mere girls pouring abundantly from the windows, burning and screaming and dying before our eyes.

At the inquest which my father attended, a girl who survived offered an extraordinary explanation for the fire. She said she had been lying in her bed trying to sleep, facing the old fireplace where a little heap of coals lay smouldering, when she heard a scuffling and a squealing and a little miniature instance of mayhem. She went up on her elbows the better to see, and it was an animal she said, something thin and galloping like a rat, on fire, his fur burning with unusual venom, running about the room, and setting alight as he went the poor web-thin sheets that graced the girls' beds, falling in drapes to the bare floor. And before anyone knew what was happening, there were little fires burning in a hundred places, and the girl leaped up and called to her sister orphans and fled from the growing inferno.

When my father came home he told me this story, not lying beside me in the bed as was his usual practice, but sitting on the old stool by my bed, hunched forward. No one at the inquest could offer an explanation for the burning rat, and my father had said nothing. So bleak was his fate already he dared not say anything. One hundred and twenty-three girls had been killed, from the burning and the falling. He knew from experience, just as I knew from reading his manual, that rats liked to use the handy vertical highways of old chimney flues. A meagre little fire would be no hindrance. But if such a rat were to pass close enough to the fire and it drenched in paraffin, my father knew well the consequence.

CHAPTER EIGHT

Perhaps he should have spoken. I suppose I could have, betraying him like those children of Germans when Hitler asked them to sniff out the loyalty of their parents in that late war. But I never would have spoken.

Well, all speaking is difficult, whether peril attends it or not. Sometimes peril to the body, sometimes a more intimate, miniature, invisible peril to the soul. When to speak at all is a betrayal of something, perhaps a something not even identified, hiding inside the chambers of the body like a scared refugee in a site of war.

Which is to say, Dr Grene came back today, with his questions at the ready.

My husband Tom fished as a boy for ten years in Lough Gill for salmon. Most of that time, he stood by the lake, watching the dark waters. If he saw a salmon jumping, he went home. If you see a salmon, you will never catch one that day. But the art of not seeing a salmon is very dark too, you must stare and stare at the known sections where salmon are sometimes got, and imagine them down there, feel them there, sense them with some seventh sense. My husband Tom fished for ten years for salmon in that way. As a matter of record he never caught a salmon. So if you saw a salmon it seems you would not catch one, and if you did not see a salmon you would not catch one. So how would you catch one? By some third mystery of luck and instinct, that Tom did not have.

But that was how Dr Grene struck me today, as he sat in

silence in my little quarters, his neat form stretched out on the chair, saying nothing, not exactly watching me with his eyes, but watching me with his luck and instincts, like a fisherman beside dark water.

Oh, yes, like a salmon I felt, right enough, and stilled myself in the deep water, very conscious of him, and his rod, and his fly, and his hook.

'Well, Roseanne,' he said at last, 'hmm, I think it's true that – you came here about – how many years ago?'

'It's a long long while.'

'Yes. And you came here I believe from Sligo Mental Hospital.'

'Lunatic Asylum.'

'Yes, yes. An interesting old phrase. The second word after all quite – reassuring. The first a very old word, but its meaning a little dubious and not a nice word any more. Though, for myself, when the moon is full, I often wonder, do I feel – a little strange?'

I looked at Dr Grene and tried to imagine him altered by the moon, more whiskery, a werewolf possibly.

'Such enormous forces,' he said. 'The tides being pulled from shore to shore. Yes, the moon. A very considerable object.'

He stood up now and went to my window. It was so early in this winter day that indeed the moon was prince of all outside. Its light lay in a solemn glister on the windowpanes. Dr Grene nodded as solemnly to himself, looking out on the yard below, where John Kane and others banged the bins betimes and all the other clocklike actions of the hospital – the asylum. The lunatic asylum. The place subject to the forces of the moon.

Dr Grene is one of those men that now and then seem to stroke at phantom cravats, or some item of clothing from some other time. Certainly he might have stroked his beard, but he did not. Did he possess some fancy scarf or suchlike at his neck years ago in his youth? I think he might have. Anyway he stroked this phantom object now, running the fingers of his right hand an inch or two above his mere purple tie, the knot thick like a young rose.

'Oh,' he said, in a strange exclamation. It was a noise that spoke of utter weariness, but I do not think he was weary. It was an early-morning sound, made in my room as if he were on his own. As perhaps to all the intents and purposes of the actual world he was.

'Do you want to consider leaving here? Do you want me to make a consideration of it?'

But I could make no answer to that. Do I want freedom of that kind? Do I know what it is any more? Is this queer room my home? Whatever was the case, I felt again that creeping fear, like the frost on the plants of the summer, that blacken the leaves in that saddening way.

'I wonder how long you were in Sligo? Do you remember the year you entered there?

'No. Sometime during the war,' I said. That I knew.

'The Second World War, you mean?'

'Yes.'

'I was only a baby then,' he said.

Then there was a crisp, cold silence.

'We used to go down to one of the little Cornish bays, my father and mother and myself – this is my earliest memory, it is of no other significance. I remember the absolute chill of the water and, do you know, my nappies heavy with that water, a very vivid memory. The government allowed petrol to hardly anyone, so my father built one of those tandem bikes, welding together two different machines. He took the back position because that was where the power was needed, for those Cornish hills. Little hills, but lethal to the legs. Nice days, in the summer. My father at his ease. Tea that we boiled on the beach in a billycan, like fishermen.' Dr Grene laughed, sharing his laugh with the new light gathering outside to make the morning. 'Maybe that was just after the war.'

78

I wanted to ask him what his father's profession was, I don't know why, but it seemed too bare a question. Maybe he intended me to ask it, now I think of it. So we would begin to speak of fathers? Maybe he was casting his lure over the dark waters.

'I have not heard good accounts of the old hospital in Sligo, in that time. I am sure it was a horrendous place. I am quite sure it was.'

But I let that lie also.

'It's one of the mysteries of psychiatry that our hospitals in the early part of the century were so bad, so difficult to defend, whereas in the early part of the nineteenth century there was often quite an enlightened attitude to, to well, lunacy, as they called it. There was a sudden understanding that the incarceration, the chaining of people et cetera, was not good, and so an enormous effort was made to – alleviate matters. But I am afraid there was a reversion – something awry, eventually. Do you remember why you were changed from Sligo to here?'

He had asked that quite suddenly so that before I knew I had done so, I had spoken.

'My father-in-law arranged it,' I said.

'Your father-in-law? Who was that?'

'Old Tom, the bandman. He was also the tailor in Sligo.'

'In the town, you mean?'

'No, in the asylum itself.'

'You were in the asylum then where your father-in-law worked?'

'Yes.'

'I see.'

'I think my mother was also there, but I can't remember.'

'Working there?'

'No.'

'A patient?'

'I can't remember. I honestly can't.'

Oh, I knew he was longing then to ask me more, but to give

him his due, he did not. Too good a fisherman maybe. When you see the salmon leaping, you will not catch one. Might as well go home.

'I certainly don't want you to be fearful,' he said, a little out of the blue. 'No, no. That is not my intention. I must say, Roseanne, we hold you in some regard here, we do.'

'I don't think that is merited,' I said, blushing and suddenly ashamed. Violently ashamed. It was as if some wood and leaves were suddenly cleared from a spring, and the head of water blossomed up. Painful, painful shame.

'Oh yes,' he said, not aware I think of my distress. He was perhaps *plamasing* me, flannelling me, as my father would have said. To enter me into some subject, where he could begin. A door into whatever he needed to understand. A part of me yearned to help him. Give him welcome. But. The rats of shame bursting through the wall I have constructed with infinite care over the years and milling about in my lap, was what it felt like. That was my job to hide it then, hide those wretched rats.

Why did I feel that dark shame after all these years? Why still in me, that dark dark shame?

Well, well.

Now we had a few mysteries in our laps. But the most pressing soon became again our poverty, which my father could not fathom.

One evening of the winter returning home from school I met up with my father along the river road. It wasn't like the joyful meetings of childhood, but I would be proud to say even now that I do believe it brightened something in my father to see me. It lightened him, dark, deep dark, though that Sligo evening was. I hope that doesn't seem like boasting.

'Now, dear,' he said. 'We'll walk arm in arm home, unless you're afraid to be seen with your father.'

'No,' I said, surprised. 'I am not afraid.'

'Well,' he said. 'I know what it is to be fifteen. Like a fella out on a headland in the blazing wind.'

But I didn't really understand what he meant. It was so cold I fancied there was frost on the stuff he put in his hair to flatten it.

Then we were coming idly, easily up our street. Up along the houses in front of us, one of the doors opened, and a man stepped down onto the pavement, and raised his brown trilby hat to the mask of a face that was just visible in the door. It was my mother's face and our own door.

'Well, Jaysus,' said my father, 'there's Mr Fine himself coming out of our house. I wonder what he was looking for. I wonder does he have rats?'

Mr Fine came towards us. He was a tall, loping man, a great gentleman of the town, with a kind, soft face like a man who had been out in a sunny wind – like the man on the headland maybe.

'Good day, Mr Fine,' said my father. 'How's everything going on?'

'Just splendidly, yes, indeed,' said Mr Fine. 'How are you both? We were terrible shocked and anxious when we heard about the poor burned girls. That was a most terrible occasion, Mr Clear.'

'Jaysus, it was,' said my father, and Mr Fine pressed on past us.

'I suppose I shouldn't say Jaysus to him,' my father said.

'Why?' I said.

'Ah, just him being Jewish and all,' he said.

'Don't they have Jesus?' I said, in my deep ignorance.

'I don't know,' he said. 'Fr Gaunt I don't doubt will say the Jews killed Jesus. But, you know, Roseanne, they were troubled times.'

We were quiet then as we reached our door and my father drew out his old key and turned it in the lock and we entered the tiny hall. I knew there was something troubling him now after the speech about Jesus. I was old enough to know that people make a little speech sometimes that is not what is in their thoughts, but is a sort of message of those thoughts all the same.

It was late in the evening just before it was time to go to bed that my father finally mentioned Mr Fine.

'So,' he said, as my mother shovelled ashes over the last few bits of turf, so they would burn slowly through the night, and be beautiful eggs of red sparks in the morning when she would winnow the ashes from them again. 'We met Mr Fine this evening, coming home. We thought for a minute he might have been calling here?'

My mother straightened herself and stood there with the fire-shovel. She stayed so still and so silent she might have been posing for an artist.

'He wasn't calling here,' she said.

'It's just that we thought we saw your face in the door, and he was lifting his hat – to your face like.'

My mother's eyes looked down at the fire. She had only made half a job of the ashes but she didn't look inclined to finish the job. She burst into strange, aching tears, tears that sounded like they had come up from her body somewhere, seeped through her like an awful damp. I was so shocked my body began to tingle in a queer uncomfortable way.

'I don't know,' he said, miserably. 'Maybe we were looking at the wrong door.'

'You know well you weren't,' she said, this time quite differently. 'You know well. Oh, oh,' she said, 'that I had never allowed you to take me from my home, to this cold cruel country, to this filthy rain, this filthy people.'

My father's reaction was to blanch like a boiling potato. This was more than my mother had said for a year. This was a letter, this was a newspaper of her thoughts. For my father I think it was like reading of yet another atrocity. Worse than rebels the age of boys, worse than burning girls.

'Cissy,' he said, so gently it went almost unheard. But I heard it. 'Cissy.'

'A cheap scarf that would shame an Indian to be selling,' she said.

'What?'

'You can't blame me,' she said, nearly shouting. 'You can't blame me! I have nothing!'

My father leapt up, because my mother had inadvertently struck herself on the leg with the shovel.

'Cissy!' he cried.

She had opened a little inch of herself and there were a few jewels of dark blood glistering there.

'Oh Christ, oh Christ,' she said.

The next evening my father went to see Mr Fine in his grocery shop. When he came back his face was pallid, he looked exhausted. I was already upset because my mother, perhaps suspecting something, had gone out herself into the dark, I knew not where. She had been one minute in the scullery banging about, and the next she was gone.

'Gone out?' said my father. 'Dear me, dear me. She put on her coat in this terrible cold?'

'She did,' I said. 'Shall we go out to look for her?'

'Yes, we must, we must,' said my father, but he stayed sitting where he was. The saddle of his motorbike was just beside him, but he didn't put a hand on it. He let it be.

'What did Mr Fine say?' I asked. 'Why did you go to see him?'

'Well, Mr Fine is a very fine man, that he is. He was most concerned, apologetic. She told him it was all above board. All agreed. I wonder how she could say that. Get the words into her mouth and say them?'

'I don't understand, Dadda.'

'It's the why we've had so little to be eating,' he said. 'She's after making a purchase on Mr Fine's loan, and every week naturally he comes for his money, and every week I suppose she gives him the most of what I give her. All those rats, dark corners, all those hours of poor Bob scratching through miseries, and the days of queer hunger we have endured, all for – a clock.'

'A clock?'

'A clock.'

'But there's no new clock in the house,' I said. 'Is there, Dadda?'

'I don't know. Mr Fine says so. Not that he sold her the clock. He only sells carrots and cabbages. But she showed him the clock here one day, when you and me were out. A very nice clock, he said. Made in New York. With a Toronto chime.'

'What is that?' I said.

And as I spoke my mother appeared in the door behind my father. She was holding in her hands a square porcelain object, with its elegant dial, and around it someone, no doubt in New York, had painted little flowers.

'I don't have it ticking,' she said, in a small voice, like a fearless child, 'for fear.'

My father stood up.

'Where did you buy it, Cissy? Where did you buy such a thing?'

'In Grace's of the Weir.'

'Grace's of the Weir?' he said, incredulously. 'I have never even been into that shop. I would be afraid to go into it, in case they charged me for entering.'

She stood there, shrinking in her unhappiness.

'It is made by Ansonia,' she said, 'in New York.'

'Can we take it back, Cissy?' he said. 'Let's take it back to Grace's and see where we are then. We cannot go on making payments to Fine. They will never give you what you gave them for it, but they might give you something on it, and maybe we can close the debt with Mr Fine. I am sure he will oblige me if he can.'

'I never even heard it tick or chime,' she said.

'Well, turn the key in it and have it tick. And when it strikes the hour it will chime.'

'I can't,' she said, 'for they will find it then. They will follow the sound and find it.'

'Who, Cissy? Us, is it? I think we have done all the finding now.'

'No, no,' said my mother, 'the rats. The rats will find it.'

My mother looked up at him with an eerie glow in her face, like a conspirator.

'We will be better to smash it,' she said.

'No,' said my father as desperate as you like.

'No, it would be better. To smash it. To smash Southampton and all. And Sligo. And you. I'll raise it up now, Joe, and bring it down upon the earth like this,' and indeed she did raise it up, and indeed she did throw it down on the thin damp cake of concrete on the floor, 'there, all promises retrieved, all hurts healed, all losses restored!'

The clock lay in its porcelain pieces there, some little ratchet loosened, and for the first and last time in our house, the Ansonia clock chimed with its Toronto chime.

It was soon after this, so soon, that I have to report, my father was found dead.

To this day I don't know what killed him exactly, but I have puzzled it over these eighty years and more. I have given you the run of the thread, and where has it led me? I have lain all the facts before you.

Surely the matter of the clock was too small a thing to kill a man?

Surely the dead boys was a dark thing, but dark enough to darken my father forever?

The girls also, yes, that was a dark matter, bright though they were as they fell.

It was my father's fate to have those things befall him.

He was just as anyone else, and anything, clock or heart, he had a breaking point.

It was in the next street in a derelict cottage, where he was working to rid it of rats, at the behest of the neighbours to right and left of the empty house, that he hanged himself.

Oh, oh, oh, oh, oh, oh, oh, oh, oh.

Do you know the grief of it? I hope not. The grief that does not age, that does not go away with time, like most griefs and human matters. That is the grief that is always there, swinging a little in a derelict house, my father, my father.

I cry out for him.

CHAPTER NINE

I suppose I must add the few unpleasant things that befell my father after death, when he was no more than a big pudding of blood and past events. It is possible to love a person more than oneself, and yet as a child, or nearly woman, to have such a thought, when your father is carried into the house for the inevitable wake . . . Not that we hoped to have many to wake him.

His motorbike was put out into the little yard by Mr Pine our neighbour, a cold-eyed carpenter who yet put himself immediately to assist us. I need not tell you it was never brought in again but was left to fetch for itself as best it could in the outdoors.

In its place was set the long penny-halfpenny coffin with my father's large nose poking up. Because he had hanged himself, his face was covered in a white paint as thick as a clockface, work done by Silvester's funeral directors. The street then crowded in and if we had few pipes and pots of tea and not a drop of whiskey to offer, nevertheless I was astonished by the ease and merriment of the people there, and the obvious regret they showed for the passing of my father. The Presbyterian minister Mr Ellis came in and also Fr Gaunt, and in the way of supposed enemies or rivals in Ireland, they shared a witticism in the corner for a few moments. Then in the early morning we were left alone, and my mother and myself slept – or I slept. I wept and wept and I slept at length. But grief like that is a good grief.

When I came down in the morning from the loft where my narrow bed was kept, there was a different class of grief. I went over to my father and for a moment could not work out what

I was seeing. There was something wrong with his eyes at any rate. When I peered close I saw what it was. Someone had pierced each eyeball with a tiny black arrow. The arrows pointed upwards. I knew immediately what they were. They were the black metal hands from my mother's Ansonia clock.

I plucked them out again like thorns, like bee-stings. *A thorn to find a witch, a sting to find a love* is an old country saying. They were not tokens of love. I do not know what they were tokens of. This was the last sorrow of my father. He was buried in the small Presbyterian yard with a goodly show of his 'friends' – friends I hardly knew he had. People who he had rid of rats, or in the old high days, buried people for. Or people who cherished him for the human soul he had exhibited to the world. Who liked his ways. There were many I could not put names to. Fr Gaunt, while the Presbyterian minister of course did the ceremony, stood beside me almost as a friend and spoke a few names, as if that was what I wanted. This name and that name, that I forgot as soon as he spoke them. But there was also a man there called Joe Brady, that had taken my father's job at the cemetery at the invitation of Fr Gaunt, a queer fattish man with burning eyes. I don't know why he was there, and wasn't sure even in my grief if I wanted him there, but you can't keep anyone back from a funeral. Mourners are like Canute's sea. I was content to think he was paying his respects.

My head was aflame with the deep, dark pulse of grief, that beats like a physical pain, like a rat got into your brains, a rat on fire.

Dr Grene's Commonplace Book

Tremendously busy attending to all the arrangements at the hospital and not much time to write here. I have missed the odd intimacy of it. As I characteristically have probably a poor sense of myself, that is to say, a rather miserable sense of my own slightness as a person, as a soul, keeping this book has somehow helped me, but how I can't say. It is hardly a therapy. But it is at least a sign of ongoing inner life. Or so I hope and pray.

Perhaps with some justification. Last night coming home as weary as I have ever been, cursing everything, the dreadful potholes in these Roscommon roads, the lousy suspension in my car, the broken light in the porch that meant I banged my arm against the concrete pillar, I entered the hallway, really in a rather foul mood, prepared to curse everything there also, if given half a chance.

But Bet was standing on the landing above. I don't know if she had been there already, before I came in, maybe so, because she was at the little window, looking out across the tangle of town gardens and the haphazard premises of light industry. There was moonlight on her, and she was smiling. I think she was. Some enormous lightness got a hold of me. It was like the first time I thought I loved her, when she was young and slight as a watercolour, a mere gesture of bones and features, beautiful and perfect in my eyes, when I pledged myself to her, to make her happy, to adore her, to hold her in my arms – the strange, maybe stupid compact of all lovers. She turned about from the moonlight and looked at me, and to my astonishment she started to come down the stairs. She was wearing an ordinary print dress, a summer dress, and as she descended the stairs she brought the moonlight with her, the moonlight and other lights. And when she got to the halldoor, she leaned up and kissed me, yes, yes, fool that I am I was crying, but as quietly and with as much dignity as I could muster, wanting to match her grace for grace, even if it was beyond me. And then she brought me into the front room among all the bric-a-brac of our lives and she held me and she kissed me again, and in a passion that eventually tore the top of my head off, she pulled me against herself in a most gentle, fierce and concentrated way, kissing and kissing, and then all our little play of love we had enacted so many thousands of times in former years, and afterwards we lay there on the Axminster carpet like slain animals.

Roseanne's Testimony of Herself

I have had all my head filled with my father and hardly a word for the nuns at school.

And now I must report I must leave them to the darks of history, without itemising them, interesting women though they were. Towards us poorer girls they were savage, but we allowed that. We screamed and we wept when we were beaten, and watched the solicitous kindnesses shown towards the richer girls of the town with immaculate envy. There is a moment in the history of every beaten child when his mind parts with hopes of dignity – pushes off hope like a boat without a rower, and lets it go as it will on the stream, and resigns himself to the tally stick of pain.

This is a ferocious truth, because a child knows no better.

A child is never the author of his own history. I suppose this is well known.

But savage as they were, though they wielded sticks against us with every ounce of energy in their bodies, to drive out the devils of lust and the shoals of ignorance that teemed in us, they were interesting women enough. But I must let them go. My story hurries me on.

I think all we can offer heaven is human honesty. I mean, at the gates of St Peter. Hopefully it might be like salt to kingdoms without salt, spices to dark Northern countries. A few grams in the bag of the soul, offered as we seek entry. What heavenly honesty is like I cannot say. But I say this to steel myself to my task.

I thought once that beauty was my best possession. Perhaps in heaven it might have been. But in these earthly fields it was not.

To be alone, but to be pierced through with a kingly joy, now and then, as I believe I am, is a great possession indeed. As I sit here at this table marked and scored by a dozen generations maybe of inmates, patients, angels, whatever we are, I must report to you this sensation of some gold essence striking into me, blood deep. Not contentment, but a prayer as wild and dangerous as a lion's roar.

I tell *you* this, you.

Dear reader. God keep you, God keep you.

Or should I really go around those nuns? Perhaps I can linger a moment with such savagery and modesty mixed. No, no, I will go around them. Although many times in later years I had a dream of them coming to rescue me, like a herd of lotus blossoms with their white headdresses, pouring down Sligo Main Street, nothing of the sort of course ever happened. And I don't know why I thought there was a basis for such a dream, as I don't remember any instance of favour while I was among them. And of course, as my history would have it, I was gone from them entirely then by age sixteen.

Memories that I have of Fr Gaunt are always curiously precise and full, lit brightly, his face clear and intense. As I sit here writing away, I can actually see him behind my eyes, in this instance on the day he came to me with his own version of rescue.

I knew I had to leave school immediately on my father's death, because my mother's wits were now in an attic of her head which had neither door nor stair, or at least none that I could find. If we were to eat, I must find work of any kind.

Fr Gaunt arrived one day in his accustomed sleek soutane – I do not mean this critically – and as it was raining with that special Sligo rain that has made bogland of a thousand ancient farms, he was also covered in a sleek dark-grey coat of similar shiny material. Perhaps the skin of his face was also made of it, anciently, in his mother's womb. He carried a highly ecclesiastical umbrella, like something real and austere, that said its prayers at night in the hatstand.

I let him in and sat him in the parlour. My father's piano still remained, itself as animate as the umbrella, standing there against the wall, as if actively remembering my father somewhere in the brainways of its strings and keys.

'Thank you, Roseanne,' said Fr Gaunt, as I handed him a cup of tea I had heroically made out of a farthing of tea sadly already used three times. But I hoped it had one last squeeze of essence in it, come all the way from China after all, in Jackson's tea ship. We got our tea from the corner, not from the great emporium of Blackwood's, where the toffs shopped, so maybe it wasn't the best tea to begin with. But Fr Gaunt sipped it politely.

'Have you a drop of milk?' he said, kindly, kindly.

'No, Father.'

'No matter, no matter,' he said, regretfully enough. 'Now, Roseanne, you and I have things to talk about, things to talk about.'

'Oh, Father?'

'What will you do now, Roseanne, now that your poor father is gone?'

'I will leave school, Father, and get a job in the town.'

'Will you be advised by me?'

'Oh?' I said.

He drank his tea for a few moments and smiled his priestly smiles, a little repertoire indeed. I know even at this distance that he was trying to do his duty, to be kind, to be helpful. I know this.

'You have, Roseanne, various aspects to yourself, certain obvious gifts if I may say so, of . . .'

Just for the moment he didn't say what. I sensed that the what of this was something not completely delicate. He was looking in his arsenal of sentences for the correct sentences. He was certainly in no way being unpleasant, nor seeking to be. In fact I think he would have died before he would have offered anything unpleasant.

'Beauty,' he said.

I looked at him.

'The gift of beauty. Roseanne, I think without too much trouble I could – of course bearing in mind the opinion of your mother, and even yourself, although I must still account you almost a child, if I may so, and in grave, gravest need of advice, if I may say – but what was I saying? Oh, yes, that I think here in the town I could find you very quickly, very smartly, easily and in the nicest manner possible, a husband. Of course, there would be certain things to do first.'

Fr Gaunt was as they say warming to his theme. The more he spoke the easier the words came, all nice and milky and honey-touched. Like many a man in authority, he was sub-limely happy as long as he was presenting his ideas, and as long as his ideas were meeting with agreement.

'I don't think . . .' I said, trying to roll back this great boulder of good sense he was pushing on my head – it felt like.

'Before you say anything about this, I know you are only six-teen, and it might not be the usual thing to marry so young, but on the other hand, I have in mind a very suitable man, who I think would have a great regard for you, maybe already has, and is in steady employ, and would be in a position therefore to support you – and your mother of course.'

'I can support us,' I said, 'I am sure I can,' I said, and less sure of anything in my life I had never been.

'You may know this man already, he is Joe Brady that now holds your father's former job at the cemetery, a very steady, pleasant, kind man, who lost his own wife two years ago, and will be quite content to marry again. In life we must look for a certain symmetry of things, and as your father once held – Hmm. And he has no children and I am sure . . .'

Indeed and I knew Joe Brady, the man who had taken my father's job, and come to see him buried. Joe Brady as far as I knew or could tell was about fifty years of age.

'You'd have me marry an old man?' I said, in my innocence. Because, since he was offering such magnanimous charity, I could hardly expect a man under thirty I suppose. If I wanted a man.

'Roseanne, you are a very lovely young girl, and as such I am afraid, going about the town, a mournful temptation, not only to the boys of Sligo but also, the men, and as such and in every way conceivable, to have you married would be a boon and a rightness very complete and attractive in its – rightness.'

His eloquence had momentarily failed perhaps because he had glanced at my face. I don't know what my face was showing but it wasn't agreement.

'And naturally, I would be so pleased, so relieved and delighted to be the agent, the author as one might say, of receiving you into the fold. Which I hope you will see is a politic and indeed marvellous and magical prospect.'

'Fold?' I said.

'You will be very aware, Roseanne, of the recent upheavals in Ireland, and none of these upheavals favour any of the

Protestant sects. Of course I will be of the opinion that you are in gravest error and your mortal soul is lost if you continue where you are. Nevertheless I can say I pity you, and wish to help you. I can find you a good Catholic husband as I say, and he will not mind your origin eventually, as, as I also have said, you are graced if I may say again with so much beauty. Roseanne, you really are the most beautiful young girl we have ever seen in Sligo.'

This he said with such simplicity and transparent – I almost said innocence, but something like innocence – he spoke so nicely I smiled despite myself. It was like getting a compliment from an old lady of distinction in the Sligo Street, a Pollexfen or a Middleton or the like, in her ermine and her nice tweed clothing.

'It is stupid of me to flatter you,' he said. 'All I mean is, if you will let me take you under my wing, I can help you, and I want to help you. I must also add that I held your father in the highest regard, despite his embarrassing me, and indeed had real love for him, because he was a straightforward soul.'

'But a Presbyterian soul,' I said.

'Yes,' he said.

'My mother is Plymouth Brethren.'

'Well,' he said, for the first time with a taint of animosity, 'never mind.'

'But I must mind my mother. And I will. It is my duty as her daughter.'

'Your mother, Roseanne, is a very sick woman.'

All right, I had not heard this expressed, and it shocked me to hear it. But, yes, I knew that to be true.

'More than likely,' he said, 'you will need to commit her to the asylum, I hope I am not shocking you?'

Oh, but he was shocking me. When he spoke those fearsome words, my belly churned, my muscles ached in their slings of bones. Without knowing I was going to do it, I suddenly and inexplicably vomited onto the carpet in front of me. Fr Gaunt drew back his legs with extraordinary quickness, neatness. There on the floor was the remains of the nice toast I had made for my mother and myself for breakfast.

Fr Gaunt stood up.

'Oh. You will need to clean that up, I expect?'

'I will,' I said, and bit my tongue on the urge to apologise. I knew somehow I must never apologise to Fr Gaunt, and that from henceforth he would be a force unknown, like a calamity of weather waiting unknown and un-forecast to bedevil a landscape.

'Father, I can't do what you say. I can't do it.'

'You will think about it? In your grief you may make poor decisions. I understand this. My own father died five years ago of a cancer, it was a terrible death, and I mourn him still. Remember, Roseanne, grief is two years long. You will not make a good thought for a long time. Be advised by me, let me advise you *in loco parentis*, do you see, in place of your father let me be your father in this, as a priest ought. We have had so many dealings, he and I, and you, that you are almost in the fold already. It will save your immortal soul, and save you in this valley of sorrows and tears. It will protect you against all the foul tides and accidents of the world.'

I shook my head. I see myself, behind my eyes, shaking my head.

Fr Gaunt shook his head also, but in a different way. 'You will think about it? Think about it, Roseanne, and then we will talk again. It is a moment in your life when you are in the greatest danger. Good day to you, Roseanne. Thank you for the tea. It was lovely. And thank your mother.'

He went out into the tiny hall and into the street. When he was quite gone, long out of ear shot, and only the smell of his clothes lingered oddly in the room, I said:

'Goodbye, Father.'

CHAPTER TEN

Dr Grene today. He has shaved his beard!

I don't remember if I mentioned his beard. A beard on a man is only a way of hiding something, his face of course, but also the inner matters, like a hedge around a secret garden, or a cover over a bird cage.

I would like to say I didn't know him when he stepped in, because that is what you would expect, but I did know him.

I was sitting here writing when I heard his step in the corridor and just managed to get everything hidden in the floor before he knocked and came in, as always not an easy task for an ancient cailleach like myself. A cailleach is the old crone of stories, the wise woman and sometimes a kind of witch. My husband Tom McNulty was the master of such stories, which he told with perfect force mainly because he believed every word of them. Sometime I will tell you about the two-headed dog that he saw on the road to Enniscrone, if you like. How would I know what you like? I am getting used to thinking of you there, somewhere. This cailleach is deluded in the head! The old midwife. I am only the midwife to my own old story. It is midwifery enough.

Dr Grene was very subdued, very quiet, very shiny in the face. He might have rubbed some unguent onto his skin when he shaved it, to spare it some of the shock of the air. He wandered over to the table – I was now sitting on the bed, among the tiny landscapes of the coverlet, I think they are French scenes, there is a man carrying a donkey on his back and other things – and Dr Grene lifted from the table my father's old copy of *Religio Medici* and looked at it idly enough. I was surprised when my father died to see that the book was printed in

1869, although I knew he had it always for many years. His name, and the place Southampton, and the date 1888 were of course pencilled onto the flyleaf, but still I hoped maybe the book had been put into his youthful hands by the hands of his own father, my grandfather, a person of course whom I never met. It might have been. So that when I held it in my hands, there was as it were a history of hands surrounding the little volume, the hands of my own people. Because a lone person takes great comfort from her people, in the watches of the night, even the memory of them.

Because I knew the little book so well, I could guess what Dr Grene was looking at. It was a picture of Sir Thomas Browne, with a beard. Perhaps as he looked at the beard, a very fierce jutting object in a round engraving, he may suddenly have been regretting the loss of his own. Sampson Low, Son, and Marston were the printers. That *Son* was beautiful. The son of Sampson Low. Who was he, who was he? Did he labour under the whip of his father, or was he treated with gentleness and respect? J. W. Willis Bund supplied the notes. Names, names, all passed away, forgotten, mere birdsong in the bushes of things. If J. W. Willis Bund can pass away forgotten, how much easier for me? We share in that at least.

Son. As little I know about my own son. The son of Roseanne Clear.

'An old book,' he said.

'Yes.'

'Whose name is that, Mrs McNulty, Joe Clear?'

Dr Grene now had a perplexed look on his face, a very deep thinking look, like a young boy figuring out an arithmetic problem. If he had had a pencil he might have licked the lead.

He had shaved his beard and was no longer hiding his face, so I felt suddenly I owed him something.

'My father,' I said.

'He was an educated man then?'

'He was indeed. He was a minister's son. From Collooney.'

'Collooney,' he said. 'Collooney suffered so in the troubles in the twenties,' he said. 'I am glad somehow that one time there was a man there that read the *Religio Medici*.'

The way he said the last two words slowly I knew he had never encountered the book before.

Dr Grene opened the book further, passing by the introduction, and hunting mildly for the beginning of the book, as a person does.

'"To the reader. Certainly that man were greedy of life, who should desire to live when all the world were at an end . . ."'

Dr Grene gave a strange little laugh, not a true laugh at all, but a sort of miniature cry. Then he laid the book back where he had found it.

'I see,' he said, though I had said nothing. Perhaps he was talking to the old bearded face in the book, or to the book itself. Seventy-six, Thomas Browne was when he died, a youngster compared to me. He died on his birthday, as sometimes happens, if rarely. I suppose Dr Grene is about sixty or so. I had never seen him quite so solemn as this today. He is hardly a man for jests and jokes, but he sometimes has a curious lightness carried about with him. Compared to poor John Kane, with all his sins, his supposed rapes and wrong doing in the asylum, Dr Grene is like an angel. Perhaps compared to many, I can no longer say. If Dr Grene feels himself washed up on this terrible shore of the asylum, if he feels himself in any way yesterday's man, as the saying goes, for me he is tomorrow and tomorrow. Such were my thoughts as I looked at him, trying to untie the knot of his new mood.

Dr Grene crossed to the little chair by the window where I like to sit when the weather is a little warmer. Otherwise there is a chill that seems to penetrate the window-glass. Below the window there is the yard, the high wall, and the endless fields. Roscommon town I am told is over the horizon, and it may be.

There is a river that moves between the fields that in the summer takes the light and uses my window as a signal, signalling to what or who or where I do not know. The riverlight plays in the glass. So naturally I like to sit there. At any rate, Dr Grene put his weight into it, always a cause for slight alarm, for it is a mere dress chair, one of those nice little chairs that country women liked to have in their bedrooms for their dress, even if it was the only nice object in the house. How it got to this room God only knows, and He perhaps hardly.

'Can you remember, Mrs McNulty, what it was – I mean, the events leading up to your presence in the Sligo asylum? You remember me saying I could find no proper record of the matter? I have searched again since and certainly have found nothing further. I am afraid the history of your presence here and in Sligo is no more. But I will continue to look, and I have sent to Sligo just on the off chance they have something. Can you remember anything about the matter?'

'I don't think I remember. The Leitrim Hotel they called it. I do remember that.'

'What?'

'They called the asylum in Sligo the Leitrim Hotel.'

'Did they? I never knew that. Why so? Oh,' he said, nearly laughing, nearly, 'because – yes.'

'Half of Leitrim was said to be in it.'

'Poor Leitrim.'

'Yes.'

'That is an odd word, Leitrim. I wonder what it means? I suppose it is Irish. Of course it is.'

I smiled at him. He was like a boy that has banged his knee and now the pain was subsiding. The cheerfulness of a boy after pain and tears.

Then he sank back again somehow, blackening deeper into himself, like a mole in the earth. I answered him largely to raise him back again.

'I do remember terrible dark things, and loss, and noise, but it is like one of those terrible dark pictures that hang in churches, God knows why, because you cannot see a thing in them.'

'Mrs McNulty, that is a beautiful description of traumatic memory.'

'Is it?'

'Yes, it is.'

Then he sat there in his own version of silence for a long while. He sat so long he was almost an inmate of the room! As if he lived there himself, as if he had nowhere to go to, nothing to do, no one to attend.

He sat in the chill light. The river, drowned in its own water, and drowned a second time in the rains of February, was not in a position to throw its light. The window-glass was severely itself. Only the still grass of winter far below lent it a slight besmirch of green. His eyes, now much clearer somehow and more distinct without the beard, were looking forwards as if at an object about a yard away, that stare that faces have in portraits. I sat on the bed and without the slightest embarrassment watched him, because he wasn't watching me at all. He was looking into that strange place, the middle distance, the most mysterious, human, and rich of all distances. And from his eyes came slowly tears, immaculate human tears, before the world touches them. River, window and eyes.

'What is the matter, Dr Grene?' I said.

'Oh,' he said.

I rose and moved towards him. You would have done the same yourself. It is an ancient matter. Something propels you towards sudden grief, or perhaps also sometimes repels. You move away. I moved towards it, I couldn't help it.

'Please do not mind me if I stand near you,' I said. 'I have had my bath yesterday. I am not foul-smelling.'

'What?' he said, absolutely surprised, but minutely. 'What?'

I stood by him and held out my right hand and placed it on his shoulder, actually a little behind the shoulder on his back. I had this unbidden memory of my father sitting on his bed, holding my mother, and patting her back almost childishly. I didn't dare pat Dr Grene, but just rested my old hand there.

'What is the matter?' I said.

'Oh,' he said. 'Oh. My wife has died.'

'Your wife?'

'Yes,' he said, 'yes. Her breathing deserted her. She choked, she choked – she suffocated.'

'Oh, my poor man,' I said.

'Yes,' he said. 'Yes.'

Then I knew something about Dr Grene. I had opened my mouth to tell him something about myself, by grace of his lost beard, and out of his own mouth had issued this news, this huge information.

With infinite sadness and very quietly, he added: 'It is also my birthday.'

Now here is a story of general stupidity in me. You might not credit the level of it.

I was wanting greatly to speak to my father and my father was dead. I had been a couple of times to his grave in the Presbyterian yard, but I thought I could not find him there. Maybe his bones did not contain him, maybe his signal and his self was elsewhere.

It was the useful gloom of a December afternoon, dark by four. I knew well that the old gates up in the other cemetery would be open, but how easy it would be to slip in those gates in the dark and be there among the graves with no one to note me. I was sure, I was hoping if my father was to be found any-where, something of him might remain there, some old twist of bushes and paths and buried things that might constitute a sort of ancient radio that would carry a signal of him.

So I crept in there in my old blue dress and my coat, as thin and slight in those days as a heron, and very like a heron I am sure in that garb, with my gawky face and long neck sticking up from it, an out and out opportunity for the cold.

What calm I took from the spreading paths, the quiet stones, the familiar numbers on their iron tags stuck into the ground by each grave, that tallied I knew with the book of graves held for safety in the concrete temple. A yellow light had got stuck in the meagre forest of small trees that covered the general paths, a forest that had been made thin and poor by the very blasts of death. Now I wrapped my coat about me to the collar, and without thinking what I was really doing, without being quite in the present time, penetrated as far as the circular sweep of graves in front of the temple.

There were the pillars, the old sharp arch with its faded figures, Greek heroes and the like, of wars and times unknown, and the iron door slightly agape on its heavy hinges, and that longed-for light within of the stove and the lamp that spoke the volume of my father. Without a thought for the present moment, in other words, in great stupidity, I crept forward towards that light, thinking, my heart begging me to advance, to claim again the cherished cowl of light and warmth and talk. The door was open enough for me to go straight in.

And nothing had changed. Everything inside also spoke of my father. His kettle was on the rickety hob still beside the grate of guttering coals, his enamel cup, even my own, on the table, the few books and ledgers piled neatly there, and the same footprints on the faded slate floor. My eyes opened and opened, and my face, and I felt absolutely certain that I would soon be in his presence, soon be comforted, advised, restored.

Then I felt a sudden and shocking push from behind. I wasn't expecting such a thing in the refuge of my own father. I staggered forward a few steps, quite unbalanced, with that nasty lurching feeling in the belly from having to right myself so abruptly. I turned about and there was a strange man in the door. He had a belly on him under a gansey too small for him, that had the shape and look of the crust of a shop-bought loaf. The face was severe with odd hollow cheeks, and the bushy brows of the old, except he probably wasn't much past fifty. No, no, but I knew this man, of course I did. It was Joe Brady that had replaced my father.

Hadn't Fr Gaunt told me? So why had it gone from my mind? What in the name of God was I doing there? You will say it was a madness, an astrayness in the head. He certainly did not have the appearance of a suitor, or anything like it. He looked angry and turned about, his eyes with that unhappy burning look I had noticed in the graveyard. In my longing for my father I had simply not thought about him again since Fr Gaunt brought his request.

Hell hath no fury like a woman scorned, maybe so, but in my experience men are not any better. Terror rose in me from the cold flags of the floor, terror so severe I must confess – and forgive such honesty in an old woman remembering horrors – that I helplessly pissed in my drawers. Even in the poor light of the temple I am sure he saw that, and whether from this cause or another, he let out a laugh. It was a laugh like a dog's growl when it fears to be stepped on, a warning laugh if there is such a thing. And don't they say in books that the laugh of a human person has its origin in an ancient grimacing and growling of the face? So it looked to me that day, proof positive.

'You didn't want me,' he said, the first time in his life he had spoken to me, which amazed me, 'and you preferring to stay the Godless girl you are.'

He walked forward at me and I don't know what he intended. But as he moved I thought that indeed something ancient and irresistible was born in him. The silent temple in the silent yard, the darkness of December, and whatever was in me he wanted. It seemed as he moved forward, his intention changed, humanity cleared from his face, something private and darker than humanity, something before we were given our troublesome souls, stirred in his eyes. I think at this impossible distance that he wanted to kill me, why ever so I do not know. There was a story of this Joe Brady that I had just stepped in on, what huge plot he had plotted with Fr Gaunt I do not know. In seeking to find my father I seemed to have found my murderer. I called out with suddenly found strength of voice. I roared!

Now in behind him stepped another man. What luck I had that there was another man in that quiet place. Joe Brady by this time had completed the last step to my form, and as if it was what he greatly desired in all the things of the world, he closed his hands about my scrawny neck and pulled me to him. Then I knew somehow without knowing that he was scrabbling about at his flies to release whatever was there, God help me, I was only sixteen and though I knew about birds and bees, I hardly knew aught else, except that certain lads might stir you as you passed them, and you would not know why. At this point in my life I may have been the most innocent girl in Sligo, and I do remember even as I remember here, writing, that my first thought was that he was drawing forth a gun or a knife from his britches, because of course this was the very place I had seen guns drawn and heard them explode.

As if in very harmony with that thought, the new man behind Joe Brady indeed had a gun drawn, a big heavy-looking yoke that he brought across the back of Joe Brady's head with a movement like a man cutting a high bramble with a slash-hook. I was aware of all this even as I stood drenched in terror. Joe Brady didn't go out on the first blow, but he sank to his knees, and in utter disgust and misery I saw his swollen penis between his legs and threw my hands to my eyes. The new man gave him another swipe with his gun. I thought, does everyone in this place have a gun, am I fated always to see guns here?

Joe Brady now lay quietly on the floor. I took my hands from my face and looked at him, and then looked at the man behind him. He was a skinny youngish fella with black hair.

'Are ya all right?' he said. 'Is that your father?'

'No, it is not my father,' I said, well-nigh hysterical. 'My father is dead.'

'I see,' said the man, 'and do you not remember me? I remember you.'

'No,' I said, 'I do not remember.'

'Well,' he said, 'you knew me once. I'm going away to America and wanted to come and say goodbye to my brother Willie.'

'Who's that?' I said stupidly. 'Why would he be here?'

'Because he's buried here. Don't you remember? Aren't you the girleen brought the bloody priest for him, and that likely brought the soldiers, those very soldiers that took us off and killed the some of us, and yet me getting away back home by a miracle.'

'I do know,' I said. 'I do know you.' And his name swam into my mind, maybe only because my father had spoken it, sitting in the little room reading the paper, or was it sitting there in the temple? 'You're John Lavelle. From the islands.'

'John Lavelle from the Inishkeas. And I am going to that other place I am, far away from this stinking lousy country, with its oath of fucking allegiance and its dead betrayed.'

I stared at him. Here truly was an astonishing revenant.

'Since I did you the kindness to save you,' he said, with hostile bravery, 'a kindness you never done for me, you might tell me where my brother's grave is, for I have wandered up and down and up and down those avenues and cannot find him.'

'I don't know, I don't know.' I said. 'But, but, it will be in the book there, on the table. Is this man dead?'

'I don't know if he is dead. It is funny he is not your father, but that I have struck him down anyway. You will know your father had a sentence on his head for what he done. Or not for what he done, for what you done, bringing the soldiers. But we couldn't be shooting girls.'

'I think you could bring yourself to be shooting girls, if you tried. What do you mean, a sentence on my father?'

'While the war raged, we were obliged to send him a letter, with his death sentence in it, and he was lucky when the war was over we let it go.'

'He was lucky?' I said, the words gushing up in fury from my throat. 'The unluckiest man that ever was born in Ireland. The poor man lies dead over in the other yard! You sent him a letter? Don't you know the hard life he had of it? The dark fate of him? Oh, I knew there was another thing I did not know of. You, you, you killed him. You killed him, John Lavelle!'

Now this John Lavelle was silent. The sort of discolouring, excited look went out of his face. He spoke suddenly very normally, even nicely. For some reason I cannot fathom still, I knew my words were untrue. I am proud I could understand that much. Whatever this young man had done in his life, he had not killed my father.

'Well,' he said. 'I am sorry your father is dead. Of course I am. Don't you know they shot my comrades? They took them out without mercy and shot them, Irishmen killing their own.'

It was as if his sudden change were a sort of catching cold, and I caught it.

'I am sorry about that,' I said. Why did I suddenly feel silly and awkward? 'I am sorry about everything. I never brought in the soldiers. I never did. But I don't even care if you think I did. I don't even care if you shoot me down dead. I loved my father. And now your comrades are dead and my father is dead. I never said a word to no one but the priest, and he had no chance to speak on the way. Don't you see, the soldiers were following you? Do you think no one else saw you? This town has eyes. This town can see out secrets, no bother.'

He was staring at me then with his eyes the tainted strange colour of seaweed. The seaweed of his island was in his eyes. Maybe there was seaweed slugging about in the wombs of the women there, people half gone back to the sea, like the first little thrumming creatures in creation, if I am to believe what I read. Oh, he cleared his eyes of everything then, and he stared at me, and for the first time I saw what was also hiding in John Lavelle, a sort of kindness. How much of such kindness the war had covered over with corpses and curses I do not know.

'Will you show me my brother's grave?' he said, in the same tones as another might have said, *I love you.*

'I will, if I can find it.'

So I went over to the book in question and scanned down the names. There was my father's beautiful blue copperplate writing, the hand of a proper scribe, though he was none such. And among the Ls I found him, Willie, Willie Lavelle. Then I noted the numbers of reference, and as if I was my father himself, and not a girl of sixteen that had nearly been knocked down and raped, I walked past the still inert lump of Joe Brady, and John Lavelle, and out among the avenues, and brought John Lavelle to his brother, so that he might say goodbye.

Then maybe John Lavelle went to America for it was a long while before anyone heard anything about him.

John Lavelle went to America and I went to a place called the Café Cairo – which wasn't quite as far.

CHAPTER ELEVEN

John Kane came out today with an extraordinary statement. He said the snowdrops were early this year. You would not expect such a man to notice snowdrops. He said that in the top garden where only the workers at the asylum are allowed to go, he saw a crocus in bloom. He said all this in a very nice way, standing in the middle of the room with the mop. In fact he came in to mop the floor, told me about these miracles, and then went off, forgetting actually to mop. Distracted I must surmise by his own sudden attack of poetry. This goes to prove yet again that few people stick to the articles of their characters, and will keep breaking away from them. At the same time he has been the same stranger to the washbasin and his flies were open as is mostly the case. Some day a small animal will notice his open flies and go in and live there, like a hedgehog in the inviting damp hollow of an ash tree.

I write this calmly although at this moment I am anything but calm.

Dr Grene was here for an hour in the afternoon. I was quite shocked by his ashen face, and he was to my added astonishment wearing the dark suit of the mourner, as he had just attended his wife's removal and burial. He referred to her as Bet, which must be a shorter form of Betty, which is a short form for what name? I cannot remember. Perhaps Elisabeth. He said there were forty-four mourners, he had counted them. I had the thought that there would be fewer for me, fewer, few, or none, unless Dr Grene himself attended my interment. But what does it matter? I could see the grief in the very lines of his face and where he had shaved his beard there was a violent-looking red rash, which he kept touching gingerly. I told him there he might be better not bothering with the likes of me on such a day, but he didn't answer that.

'I have unexpectedly found some additional material,' he said. 'I don't know whether it will help us, as it pertains to matters in the long ago. As they say.'

As who say? The people he is accustomed to seeing? The old people of his youth? When was Dr Grene young? I suppose in the fifties and sixties of the last century. When Queen Elizabeth was young and England was old.

'It was a little deposition someone had made many years ago, I don't know if it belonged to this institution or in fact went back to your time in Sligo Mental Hospital, and had been transferred here with you. It has at least raised the hope in me that the original is there. This copy was in a very poor state, typed but very faint as one might expect. And a great part of it missing. Something from an Egyptian tomb indeed. It referred to your father being in the Royal Irish Constabulary, which is not a phrase I had seen for many a long year, and the circumstances of his death – of his murder as one might say. I was very distressed to read about it. I don't know, but I felt I should see you today, despite my own – challenges at the moment. It seemed so vivid, so recent, perhaps because I am just at the moment susceptible to, to grief and griefs. That might be the why. I was very upset, Roseanne. In the chief part because I did not know.'

His words hung in the room the way such words do hang.

'It must be someone else's document,' I said.

'Oh?' he said.

'Yes,' I said. 'You may have been upset unnecessarily. On my account at least.'

'This wasn't the fate of your father?'

'No.'

'He was not in the police?'

'No.'

'Oh, well, I am relieved to hear it. But it had your name attached, Roseanne McNulty.'

'You call me Mrs McNulty, but there is another story attached to that, I really should be called by my maiden name.'

'But you were married, no?'

'Yes, I was married to Tom McNulty.'

'He died?'

'No, no.'

But I wasn't able in that moment to add anything.

'The document said your father was an RIC man in Sligo during the height of the troubles in the twenties, and was tragically killed by the IRA. I must confess I am still a little musty on that whole period. It seemed to us at school so much a series of dire errors and – it is such a belligerent history. Even the Second World War seemed to us – I don't know what it seemed to us. Ancient History? And yet I was born during the war. Wasn't your father's name Joseph, Joseph Clear?'

But I was gripped by some unpleasant feeling, I don't know if you have ever had it, as if someone has stopped up your body with putty. When I closed my gums on the feeling I could have sworn I was actually biting through putty. I stared at Dr Grene in panic.

'What is the matter, Roseanne? I have upset you? I am so sorry.'

'Perhaps', I said, at last able to get words through the putty, 'that is your job, Dr Grene?'

'To upset you? No, no. My job is to help you. In this instance, to assess you. It has actually been put upon me as a duty. There is all sorts of legislation nowadays. I would be more than happy to leave you alone – I mean not alone, but be, to leave you be, and talk of other things, or talk of nothing, which I am beginning to think is the healthiest topic of all.'

'My maiden name was Clear,' I said suddenly.

'That is what I thought. I read it, didn't I, in that little book?' he said. 'That is of course a very rare name. Joe Clear. There can't have been too many of that name. There cannot be too many Clears in Ireland. I wonder is it a form of Clare, or connected to Cape Clear, or what?'

He was speaking in oddly agonised tones, with that perplexed look again as of a young boy overwhelmed at school.

'I think it is a Protestant name and maybe comes out of England long ago.'

'Do you think? Of course, McNulty is a common enough name. You might find McNultys everywhere.'

'It is an old Sligo name. My husband told me they were the last recorded cannibal tribe in Ireland. It is written somewhere that they ate their enemies.'

'Oh my.'

'Yes. Myself, I didn't eat meat at that time. The smell of meat made me feel faint, though I cooked it every day for him. So my husband liked to tell people that I was the last recorded vegetarian cannibal in Ireland.'

'He was droll, your husband.'

Oh, oh, oh, shallow rocks again. I buttoned my lip as quick as I could. I did not want to rehearse all that now.

'Well, well,' he said, stirring to go at last, 'I might bring up that document I mentioned tomorrow or the next day, it might interest you to look it over.'

'I cannot read as well as I used to. I read Thomas Browne, but then I know the writing off by heart mostly.'

'We should get you a pair of reading glasses, Mrs McNulty – or should I say Ms Clear?'

'I am as happy without them.'

'Very well.'

Then for some reason he laughed, one of those little tinkling laughs that people laugh when a private thought has amused them, and occurs before they have the power to stop it.

'Oh no,' he said, although I had said nothing, 'excuse me – nothing, nothing.'

And off he went, nodding. He raised his right hand at the door and actually waved, like I was a passenger on a ship.

Was it before or after that John Kane came in to talk about the snowdrops? I can't remember.

No, I remember. John Kane did come back in, but it was to mop the floor. He had evidently, somehow or other, realised he had not yet mopped my floor. After all, he is also now becoming elderly, the elderly fetching for the elderly. Not that he fetches. As he swept in under my bed he happened to bring out in the bristles of his brush a spoon. It was not clean but smeared with soup, and I must have knocked it from the tray. He gave me a very brief dark look, slapped my face lightly, and left.

How does good history become bad history by and by?

Dr Grene's Commonplace Book

'Certainly that man were greedy of life, who should desire to live when all the world were at an end . . .'

She is only two weeks buried. Bet. It is so difficult even to write the name. Sometimes here in the house now alone at night I hear some little banging somewhere, probably a sound I have unconsciously heard a million times, a door in the house that touches against its frame in the draught, and I don't know, I look fearfully up the dark corridor and wonder if it is Bet. It is a terrible and odd thing to be haunted by your wife.

Of course, I am not. It is one of the many strange fruits in the cornucopia of grief.

113

How difficult it is to live. I would almost say all my world *is* at an end. How often I must have listened blithely and with professional distance to some poor soul tortured by depression, a sickness that might have had its origin in just such a catastrophe as has hit me.

I feel so bereft I am almost inclined to admire any instance of simple strength of mind, all health of mind. I watched the images of Saddam Hussein, 'President of Iraq' as he still called himself, being hanged, and scoured his face for signs of suffering and pain. He looked confused but strong, almost serene. He had such contempt for his captors even as they taunted him. He did not believe maybe they had the strength to finish his term of life. To complete his story. Or he thought if he could find strength within himself, he would complete his own story with an admirable flourish. He looked so bedraggled and astray when they took him from the hidey hole months before. His jacket and shirt were always immaculate in court. Who washed them, brushed them, ironed them? What hand-maiden? What does his story look like seen with the eyes of a friend, an admirer, a fellow townsperson? I envied him the evident peace of his mind as he went to his death. They did not show mercy to Saddam, who himself had shown no mercy to his enemies. He looked serene.

It is true that for the last ten years, a whole decade, Bet removed herself to the old maid's room at the top of the house. I sit here in our old bedroom – old in a few senses, as in, for twenty years we shared it, the room has not been decorated for many years, it was where we 'formerly' slept etc., etc. – as I have sat a thousand times – how many nights in ten years, 3,560 nights – and no longer is she just above me, walking the floorboards, making her narrow bed creak as she lay on it. All is perfectly quiet and still, except for that little banging somewhere, as if she is not dead at all, but has immured herself in a cupboard and wants to get out. In the little room above, her bed is still neatly made just as she left it the last morning, I couldn't bear to touch it. Her collection of books on roses occupies the windowsill as always (when we shared a bed, it was rose books on her side, Irish history on mine), propped up by two extravagantly carved Hawaiian bookends in the shape of two shameless maidens. By the bed, her phone on a little chinoiserie table her great-aunt left her. Her great-aunt had died of Alzheimer's, but she had won the table years ago at a card game in her prime, and Bet had been thrilled and touched to get it. In the drawers are her clothes, in the cupboard are her dresses, summer and winter ones, and her shoes, among the pairs are those heeled shoes she used to wear to dinner, that I thought didn't suit her, but at least I never had the lack of grace to say so, that is not among my sins, years ago when we did such things. But it is not that woman I found in the corridor, struggling for breath as her lung collapsed, one last shout in her that brought me clattering up the little stairs, that assails me, so much as that other younger person she was when I fell in love with her, that is the person that haunts me. The perfectly desirable and neat beauty that she was, who went against her father's wishes, and insisted she must marry a penniless student studying the unknown and unpromising science of psychiatry at a hospital in England, whom she had met on a holiday to Scarborough. The sheer accidental nature of things.

There was nothing about me that her father liked, a man who had been one of the subcontractors on the great Shannon hydroelectric scheme, and as such an historical and epic man, supplying gravel from the quarries of Connaght. But she prevailed, and we had our wedding, God help her, her numerous family ranged on one side of the church, and no one on the other side but my adoptive father, enduring the warlike stares from the other side. My parents were Catholic, which might have stood in their favour, except that they were English Catholics, a people in the eyes of my inlaws more Protestant than the Protestants themselves, and at the very least, deeply deeply mysterious, like creatures from some other time, when Henry VIII was wanting to marry. They must have thought Bet was marrying a phantom.

Her greatest wish I should think was that I would remain exactly as I was, and how I regret that that was not to be. It was only for her roses that she wished for change, the strange moment of floral enchantment when the branch of a rose mutates, and shows a 'sport', something new arising from the known rose. A leap in beauty.

'I'm going out to the garden to see if there's any news,' she would say, at almost any time, because she had roses going the whole length of the year.

She was waiting for whatever God, whatever secret magician, decided things for roses to do His stuff. I am afraid I showed scant interest in all that. *Mea culpa.* I tried to, but couldn't locate that passion in me. I should have been out there with her, with the gloves and the secateurs, like someone geared for miniature battle.

Little sins of omission that loom large now. You could go mad.

Anyway for my sanity I am writing here. I am sixty-five years old. Past the Beatles song. By some accounts this is young. But when a man wakes on his fortieth birthday he may safely say he has no youth ahead of him. I suppose this is infinitely petty and ridiculous. A healthy person might be content with life as a quality in itself, and look to the passing of the years, and the gaining of age, and then great age, with interest. But I am miserable before the task. When Bet died I looked in the mirror for the first time in many years. I mean, I had glanced every morning in the mirror, trimmed my beard and the like, but had not *looked* in it at myself. I was amazed at what I saw. I did not know myself. My hair was thinning all about the crown, and was grey as a badger, whereas I had imagined myself to have retained my old colour. The lines in my face were like the folds in a bit of leather that has been outside in the rain for a long time. I was utterly dismayed, utterly shocked. I had not realised it while Bet lived, the simple fact. I was old. I didn't know what to do. So I searched out my old razor and shaved my beard.

Sixty-five. In a few years I will retire. It is not just this building is reaching its point of ultimate depreciation. Retire. To do what? Knock about Roscommon town? Yet there is Roseanne McNulty at a hundred. If she were English the queen would have sent her a letter. Does Mary McAleese send cards to the Irish centenarians? But I am sure, like the rest of the world, Mary McAleese does not know Roseanne exists.

Actually I did not mean to write anything about myself here. What I meant to write about was Roseanne.

For there is a mystery there. I suspect that somewhere in the distant past, in just such an institution as this, she suffered in some way at the hands of her 'nurses'. This would not be unusual in these old histories. Her suffering in the realm of real life, in the so-called outside world, was no doubt even greater. I have attempted a series of cautious questions, of the sort that would not scare her or drive her into silence. She is quite capable, and always has been, of playful and even fanciful talk. Myself and Bet used to be like that, years ago. At our ease – but no, let me leave all that alone. But I wonder is Bet lonely where she lies now? How odd it was at last to ring the funeral directors whose unwished-for premises I had passed in the car so many times, with the posh entrance, the yard of hearses at the back, the quiet efficient phrases, the numbers, the tea, the sandwiches, the grave documents, the service, the removal, the this and the that of death. Then just this morning the discreet bill, the things itemised, the coffin I chose in a sudden fit of meanness, and deeply regretted at the funeral. What I bought to bury my wife.

Every nuance of her, every turn of the head, every moment

117

of tenderness between us, every gift, every surprise, every joke, every outing, holidays in Bundoran and later Benidorm, every kind word, helpful sentence, it all gathered together like a sea, the sea of Bet, and rose up from the depths of our history, the seabed of all we were, in a great wave, and crashed down on the greying shore of myself, engulfed me, and would that it had washed me away for good.

Oh, dear. Again I have strayed. But this has been the pattern of the recent weeks.

Roseanne. Old lady. The cailleach of the stories. So ancient, and yet, one of those faces that is so thin she bears the look of her youth yet, what she was. Oh, she is shrunken as she must be, when the woman washes her no doubt she is skin and bone, everything that was once beautiful and fruitful about her empty and sere. Can I say, Bet was spared that? It is worthless talking about what we have been spared by death. Death grins at that I am sure. Death of all creation knows the value of life.

I would like from sheer curiosity to find an old photograph of Roseanne when she was young. She must have been a beauty in her day. But photographs there are none.

At first I could find out nothing about her. In fact it is safe to say I expected there would be little trace of her in the records, given her great age. What did I know about her? After all I had spoken with her now and then for as many as two dozen years! So few facts. That she was someone called once Mrs McNulty, that she had no known relatives still in touch with her or other contacts, no one had visited her ever in the hospital, and per-haps I had a vague sense that she had been transferred here from Sligo, but maybe forty years ago or more. How I knew this I do not know, unless I had seen once some document that said so, when I was young and came here first from England. Naturally Bet wanted to be near her family and I knew from my father that I had Irish connections, so I was more than con-tent to come here.

Accident, mere accident, everything. How surprised and pleased I had been, flattered, to receive a letter seemingly out of the blue from the then registrar here, Mr Amurdat Singh, offering me a junior post. How he had got my name I didn't know, and I was only a few months out of college, jobless, and desperate to marry Bet. And a job in Ireland, the very thing she had wanted. It was like a miracle. The Arabs say that everything is already written in the book of life, and our job is merely to fulfil the narrative already there, invisible, unknown. I thought Mr Singh had perhaps attended the same college as me, but it wasn't so, he had trained himself in Ireland, under one of the old imperial networks, still persisting long after both Irish and Indian independence, in the way of these things. I don't know if someone had given him my name, and why would they, when I must confess my degree wasn't exactly glittering, if adequate. But nonetheless the miraculous letter came, and I responded joyfully, youthfully and joyfully. I suppose you might say I had not seen Roscommon. But if it was a backwater, it was a backwater beloved by Bet. We had every chance to be happy here.

Amurdat Singh, God rest him, was a sort of saint. Perhaps because of his race he didn't flourish in Ireland as he might have. He deserved to be made Chief Psychiatrist of Ireland. His hospital while he lived was a true haven, and he had radical and exciting views. Jung and R. D. Laing were his gods, and they made a potent mix. Sadly he died a relatively young man, possibly even took his own life. I think on balance I am still glad that he sent for me, however mysteriously.

Of course when I arrived Roseanne Clear had already been here the best part of twenty years, or certainly under the care of the psychiatric services (let me not write 'so-called').

How that door bangs. As if I were five again and at home in our vanished house in Padstow, I am afraid to go and see what makes that sound. I am sure it is just a door, perhaps the door into the spare bedroom that Bet scorned, as being on the same floor as me.

I have sent to Sligo Mental Hospital to see if they have anything about her. They may not. Meantime I found here the remnant of some sort of deposition, mostly eaten away by mice and crawling with silverfish, like some ancient scroll of the desert. A little apocryphal gospel as may be. I don't know who wrote it, except that it was an educated sort of effort, though I do not think a doctor wrote it. It was faintly typed, probably from an old-fashioned carbon, that crinkly blue paper put in under the top copy in a typewriter. I am hoping that Sligo might have the original.

Meanwhile I have been talking as much as I can to Roseanne, stealing the time from my various duties, and sometimes I must confess inclined to linger longer than I should. When I am in her room it is safe to say the poison of grief is briefly lessened. Just the other day I actually broke down in her company and in a desperate attempt at professional distance blurted out that Bet had died, and far from achieving distance, it brought Mrs McNulty creeping over to me. But it was like being touched by a sort of benign lightning, something primitive, strange, and oddly clear.

Maybe a person who is never visited, stores up a sort of heat, like a power station never called on for its power – like the Shannon scheme itself in the early years, when no one had electricity in their houses.

Yes, I received few answers to my questions. At first I wondered did she know any answers, was she, in the matter of her past, truly incapable of memory, that is, in some sense, actually insane? Had she been placed in the 'care' of an asylum because she had suffered some true psychosis or breakdown of her faculties? Like some psychotics she was very certain about, and consistent in, what she seemed to know. Yet she also confessed openly to ignorance on many matters, which suggested to me she was not psychotic, but that her memory too perhaps had suffered the silverfish of age. A psychotic person often supplies answers to everything, whatever their truth. They intensely dislike not knowing, because it brings on the pain and storm of confusion.

My next thought was that she was being cagey because she feared me, or was even perhaps in dread of speaking, in case it led her back to things she would rather forget. Of course either way I know she has suffered enormously. You can see it in her eyes as plain as day. It is actually what gives her her strange grace, if I may say that. Now, that is not a thought I had before I wrote it down. So perhaps there is a certain usefulness in writing in this book.

And anyway, I would like in some way to find the heart and the thread of her story, as one might put it. Her true history or as much of it as can be salvaged. She obviously has not many years to live. I think the oldest recorded Irish person in modern times was one hundred and seven, which would give her seven years more. But I think it unlikely she will enjoy so many.

I am hoping there will be some further news from Sligo.

I regret Bet's exodus to the maid's room above all other regrets. My dalliance – oh, a quaint word chosen by my stupid inner self to hide my sin – with another, whose life I also altered for the worse, being the cause. I think it was the cause. More likely, the sudden view she got of me in the light of it. A smaller, nastier person than she had thought.

PART TWO

CHAPTER TWELVE

Roseanne's Testimony of Herself

'It don't do nothing but rain,' sang Gwen Farrar, Billy Mayerl flashing his hands about the keys. And she must have been born in Sligo, she sang so plaintively: 'I guess we were born with our raincoats on . . .'

Always the deluge of rain falling on Sligo, falling on the streets big and little, making the houses shiver and huddle like people at a football match. Falling fantastically, in enormous amounts, the contents of a hundred rivers. And the river itself, the Garravoge, swelling up, the beautiful swans taken by surprise, riding the torrent, being swept down under the bridge and reappearing the other side like unsuccessful suicides, their mysterious eyes shocked and black, their mysterious grace unassailed. How savage swans are even in their famous beauty. And the rain falling also on the pavements outside the Café Cairo, as I tugged at the boilers and the machines, and gazed out through the fuggy windows with burning eyes.

So it seems now. Who was I then? A stranger, but a stranger that hides in me still, in my bones and my blood. That hides in this wrinkled suit of skin. The girl I was.

I started to write about the Café Cairo yesterday and then was stilled by some horrible feeling. It was like my bones were turning to water, cold water. It was something Dr Grene had said in passing. The effect of his words was like a slate on top of a dry flower. I brooded in my bed all day, feeling ancient, wretched, and panicky. John Kane came in and even he was so surprised by my face he said nothing, but hurriedly scooped about the room with his awful brush. I suppose I looked quite mad. It is well known that human beings shed a rain of dead skin all the while. That brush of his must carry a little of all the hides of all the patients here. As he scrapes it about in every room. I don't know what that signifies.

I feel put away from my task. I suppose it is odd that I am trying to write out my useless life here, and resisting most of his questions. I suppose he would love to read this, if only to lighten his own task. Well, when I am dead, and if someone thinks to look under the loose board, he will find it. I don't mind him reading it as long as I don't have to be questioned closely, as no doubt he would do if it fell into his hands now. Maybe the truth is, I am writing it for him, as he is really the only person I know, in any full sense of the word. And even then it is only so recently he has been coming up here to me regularly. I do remember when I only saw him twice yearly, at Easter and Christmas, when he would come in quite briskly, ask how I was, not really listen to the answer, and go off again. But then, he has a hundred patients, I don't know, maybe more than that. I wonder indeed are there fewer people here now. Perhaps we are like those sad orders of nuns and monks, who dwindle to a handful in old nunneries. I have no way of knowing, unless I do a tour of the place myself, which is not likely now.

Down in the courtyard, now again today in deep frost, despite John Kane's snowdrops, I am sure the old apple tree is feeling the terrible cold. It must be a hundred years old, that tree. Many many moons ago I used to go down there when I was let. There is a wooden seat that circles the tree like in an old English village, something in an old English story. The village green. But it's just a narrow suntrap down there when there is sun, that warms the old tree into life in the springtime. Then come the mighty blossoms. But not yet I am sure, and if it has dared to put out a few buds, the frost will leave them blackened, and it will have to start again.

There used to be a little kitchenmaid down there that threw the crumbs from the great cuttings of bread that went on in the kitchen, out onto a makeshift bird table. That used to bring the blue-tits, the green-tits, and all the ravening finches you would think of Roscommon. I suppose she is long gone. I suppose the apple tree will outlast everyone.

That old apple tree would make a philosopher of a blackbird. Apple blossom is quieter than the cherry, but it is still overwhelming, heartening. It used to make me cry in the spring. It always came eventually, frost or no frost. I would love to see it again. The frost could only delay the old tree, never defeat it. But who would carry me down there?

> *When milk comes frozen home in pail,*
> *And Dick the shepherd blows his nail.*

Old Tom, my father-in-law, had a wonderful garden at his bungalow in Sligo. He was a mighty man for the winter vegetables. I remember him saying that frost improved the winter cabbages and lettuces. He was a demon for growing vegetables all the year round, which apparently is quite possible if you know how to do it. Like most things.

Old Tom McNulty. To this day I don't know if he was enemy or friend. To this day I am in two minds about any of them, Jack – no, no, maybe I can with justice curse Fr Gaunt, and that old woman the mother of Tom and Jack, the real Mrs McNulty as you might say. On the other hand, I don't really know. At least Mrs McNulty was always openly hostile, whereas Jack and Fr Gaunt always presented themselves as friends. Oh, it is a vexing mystery.

Now I am having a bad thought, for doesn't Dr Grene also present himself as a friend? After a manner of speaking, a professional friend maybe. Friend or enemy, no one has the monopoly on truth. Not even myself, and that is also a vexing and worrying thought.

It was very difficult to hear him say so casually that my father was in the police. I do not think he should say that. I have heard that asserted before but I do not remember where or by who. It is a lie, and not a very pretty one. Such lies in the old days could get you shot, and there was a sort of fashion of shooting one time in Ireland, for instance the famous seventy-seven that were shot by the new government. And the executed men were in the main former comrades. John Lavelle was very lucky to escape that, and not make seventy-eight. I am sure on the other hand that there were secret murders, secret shootings, that no one ever recorded or remembers. Sad, cold, wretched deaths of boys on mountainsides and the like, of the sort I saw myself, or the results of at least, as happened to John's brother Willie.

It was a true relief after all that just to wear my waitress's uniform in the Café Cairo. The café served everyone in Sligo without criticism. It was owned by a Quaker family, and we were told to turn no one from the doors. So you might see a poor lonely pensioner drinking tea, and taking from his lap, thinking he was not seen, a few morsels of cheese brought in with him in his pocket. I remember that man very well, and thinking him so old in his old brown suit. He was probably only seventy! The presence of these more unwashed characters however did not at all dissuade the dames of Sligo from coming in for a natter. Indeed they were like veritable hens in a yard, the way they sat in at the tables, the chat and gossip rising from them like dust from a desert caravan of camels. Some of them were wonderful bright women that we, I mean the platoon of waitresses, loved, and loved to see coming in every day, and who we served gladly. Some were battleaxes as you might expect. But all shades and stripes of quality came in there, it was really my university, I learned so much there, bringing the tea, and being polite, and it might have been the start of a good life, I don't know.

I suppose I might have got the job in the usual way, seen a notice in the window, gone in and somehow made it known that, unpromising as I looked, I was a Presbyterian, and so suited to the job (openhearted as the Quaker owners were, there were no Catholic girls employed there, unless it was Chrissie, who had been a Catholic, but was raised in the Charter School as a Protestant). But it came about in a different way.

After my father died, my mother, already a silent person, probably in the terms of this institution declined even further. One morning waking at home I had gone down to make her her tea, and coming back up found no one in her bed. It was a terrible shock, and I ran downstairs calling her, and looking everywhere, out in the street, everywhere. Then I happened to look out the scullery window and saw her, curled up like a sheepdog under my father's mouldering motorbike. Oh yes, I brought her back and tucked her up in bed, the sheets I am ashamed to admit grey from her lying there unwashed. I was so saddened and upset, I walked out of Sligo that day and all the way to Rosses Point, where the nicest beach was, thinking I might wander about the golf course there, with little lakes of lonely birds, and beautiful sudden views of distant mansions by the water, as if they had gone down to the water's edge to drink (of course it was the salt sea, but at any rate). And I did walk there, coming along first by the cottages of the Rosses, with Coney island across the flow of the Garravoge, and the wonderful, calming figure of the Metal Man, in his old blue iron clothes, and his black hat, pointing eternally into the deep water, to tell the ships coming up where to go. He was a statue on a rock, but so wonderful a method to indicate deep water surely had never been devised before or since. I was told once his brother is in a little park in Dalkey by the sea in Dublin, doing what task I do not know.

Beyond Coney and the Metal Man of course lies the country of Strandhill, the lesser beach, which was the scene of my own suffering later.

When I got to the strand at Rosses Point, there was that fierce little wind blowing, and although there was a number of black cars parked behind the dunes, the owners must have been sitting in them, because there was no one out on the broad strand itself. Only those buffeting cohorts of the wind. But in the distance there was one figure, a woman in a billowing white dress as I soon saw, pushing in a haphazard way a big black perambulator. As I got nearer to her I heard her calling, her words dimming and then growing just as the wind wished. Finally I reached her, and even in the chill weather of that Irish June, she was sweating.

'Oh, my dear, my dear,' she said, looking very like the rabbit in *Alice in Wonderland*, 'I cannot find her, I cannot find her.'

'Who can't you find, ma'am?' I said, deciding by her accent that she must be a toff of some kind, and likely needing to be called ma'am.

'My daughter, my little daughter,' she said, with a strange screaming tone. 'I fell asleep in the dune, in a lovely suntrap, and my little one playing about just beside me, but when I woke, she was gone. She is only two years old. Oh, my Lord, my Lord.'

'She is not in the pram?' I said, on an inspiration.

'No, she is not, she is walking. Her brother is in the pram, soundly sleeping! My daughter Winnie is walking. Winnie, Winnie!'

And she seemed suddenly to run quite away from me, as if giving up all thought I might be able to help, after my great ignorance on the topic of the perambulator.

'I will help you search,' I said, 'I will help you.' And I actually gripped her arm for a moment. It was thin under the white linen. She stopped and looked at me. Peered at me with eyes of weeping green.

Then I ran over to the dunes and took the old high path among them as I had done with my father a dozen times. The path went rushing down and up, and after a while I was back near the cars. The tide was beginning to tip against the long boots of stone the shore was there. On complete instinct I rushed towards the water, because I remembered a cave that I knew, the sort of strange deep cave that any child would love. My father told me that in the cave was found the oldest remnant of human life in Ireland, and that some of the first people, no doubt heroic, brave and terrified all at the same time, alone in a land of great forests and marshes, had sheltered there.

I came into the murk of the cave and was well rewarded for my instincts. There was a little crouched figure there, digging in the dry sand, her bottom wet as a puddle, the rest of her happy as Larry. I scooped her up, and even that did not frighten her, she maybe thinking me a creature part of her own fantasy. As I came back out into the open air, I saw the mother far off in the distance, searching among the similar rocks at the other end of the strand. It was a sort of picture of utter futility and wrongness, motherhood doomed to failure. How I wished suddenly for my own mother to seek for me so fiercely, so sweatingly, to find me again on the lost strand of the world, to rescue me, to recruit others for my rescue, to bring me again to her breast, as that distant mother so obviously ached to do with the happy creature in my arms.

But I set off nonetheless across the sand, sprinkled with those myriad razor shells, the wind ruckling up the inch of water everywhere. When I was halfway across I think the mother got a sense of me coming, her face vaguely turning to me. Even at that distance I got an immense impression of some mystery, the enormous panic of that figure, and what was almost the flame of relief leaping from it as she thought, she hoped, she spied me with her daughter in my arms. On I sped, splashety-splash across the intervening acre of sand. Now she was galloping towards me, still pushing the huge pram, and at length we were only yards apart, the mother joyfully hooting, that's what it sounded like, the pram nearly crashed into me, and the child wrenched from my arms, and only now crying, caterwauling, roaring. And it was as if I had returned the child to her from the dead, especially when I told the mother about the cave, and the advancing sea.

'I cannot describe to you, I cannot,' she said, 'the feeling of utter wretchedness when I could not see her. My head was screaming like with a thousand of these gulls. My chest was as full of pain as if you had poured hot oil into me. The whole strand was screaming back at me in its emptiness. My dear girl, my dear girl, my dear girl.'

This last was actually to me, though she held the other 'dear girl' in her grip, and gripped my own arm now.

'I thank you, I thank you, dear, dear girl.'

And that was Mrs Prunty, the wife of the owner of the Café Cairo. It did not take long for her to know my story, carefully told by me in a guise I hoped was suitable, on the drive back to Sligo in her big black car. And it was her joy to suggest I might come to the Café Cairo to work, as my schooling was finished, my father deceased, and my mother 'unwell' as I put it, at home.

I don't remember the especial moment when Tom first came into the café, but I have a vivid memory of him as if contained in a sort of photograph, gold trim around the edges, like one of those still pictures outside the cinema in Sligo, of his aura and sense of infinite wellbeing, a short, thickset, almost fat man in a sturdy and neat suit, so unlike his brother Jack, whose suits were tailoring of a higher order, and whose coat was so infinitely fine it had a soft leather collar like a film star's. They both wore extravagantly expensive hats, though they were the sons of the tailor of Sligo Lunatic Asylum, and maybe that accounted for the more brutal cut of Tom's suit – certainly not his brother's. But the fact was the father was also the bandleader of Sligo's principal danceband, Tom McNulty's Orchestra, and that meant they had more shekels than most in those predominantly shekel-less times. His father, another small man seen about the place in a straw boater in that blistering summer, and a striped jacket the like of which you would see only at the races on a Wednesday the back of the town, was called Old Tom, and Tom himself was Young Tom, a thing especially useful since he also played in that famous band, if only famous among the dunes of Strandhill and in the dreams of the Sligo people.

I must have been two years and more already in the Café Cairo when I first became aware of these McNulty brothers. Those first years there as a simple waitress were simple happy years, myself and lonesome Chrissie being fast friends and a bulwark to each other against the world. She was a petite, neat, nice person, Chrissie, for such souls do exist. It is not all knives and axes. Moreover Mrs Prunty though rarely seen was always felt by me as a secret presence behind the steaming boilers, and the beautiful many-ledged cake holders, and the river of silver knives and spoons, and those lovely forks used only for delicate cakes. Somewhere behind all that, and the elaborate carved doors, and the touches of an Egypt no one had ever seen, I was sure Mrs Prunty moved, like a Quaker angel, speaking well of me. So I imagined anyhow. I earned the few shillings, and fed and washed my mother, haunted the picture house many many evenings, saw a thousand films, newsreels, and all the rest, wonders beyond the wonders of the finest, most extravagant dreams. And somehow in those times I was content with that, rebuffed all offers to go 'steady' with anyone, dance with anyone in particular more than once or twice. We blew out, a crowd of young girls from the town, to Tom McNulty's dancehall by the sea, like a torrent of roses along the bleak roads, sometimes spilling in tremendous gaiety and simplicity out onto the strand itself, where the road came down from the village of upper Strandhill, and the bollards one after the other on the very sand itself showed the lowtide way to Coney. Maybe you would rather call us gulls, elegant white birds dipping and calling, we were always inland as it were – as if there was always a storm at sea. Oh, it is girls of seventeen and eighteen know how to live life, and love the living of it, if we are let.

No one had seen Egypt I say, but of course Jack had been a sailor in the British Merchant Navy as a lad, and had already travelled to every port of the earth – but of course I didn't know all that. The epic story of Jack – a little epic, an ordinary epic, a local epic, but epic for all that – was unknown to me. All I saw, or began to see, was two spick-and-span brothers coming in for their cups of tea, any Chinese leaf for Tom, and Earl Grey by preference for Jack.

The dark story of their brother Eneas I never knew till long after, if I ever really knew it. Just a scrap of it, a few pages torn from his raggedy book. Can you love a man you only knew – in the Biblical sense – for a night? I do not know. But there was love there, gentle, fierce, proper love. God forgive me.

Dr Grene's Commonplace Book

Mirabile dictu (my having to read Virgil at school did me some good at least, in that it has left me with that phrase), some further documentation has arrived from Sligo Mental Hospital. It is the top copy of the old deposition and their storage arrangements must be better than ours by some measure, because the sheets are quite intact. I must say her story as itemised in the document interested me greatly, offering a sort of landscape to put behind the figure I know in the bed. A sort of human vista of troubles and events, like in a painting by da Vinci or the like, the Mona Lisa itself, with its castle and hills (as I remember it – perhaps there is no castle). As she herself continues unforthcoming, I had also a great frisson of entry to read it, as if I were getting the answers I sought from her, but of this I must be very wary. The written word assumes authority but it may not have it. I must not necessarily let her silence be filled with this, although it is a great temptation, because it is a shortcut, or a way around. The sheets amount to some seventeen closely typed pages and would seem to be offering an account of the events that led up to her, I was going to say incarceration, but I mean of course her sectioning. It is in two parts, the first detailing her earlier life up to her marriage, then the reasons for the annulment of that marriage, if that is the right term of the day. It seems this was followed by a period of tremendous disarray in her life, tremendous, really rather terrible and pitiable. This is all long long ago, in the savage fairytale of life in Ireland in the twenties and thirties, mostly, though the period of her greatest difficulty seems to have occurred actually during the years of the emergency, as de Valera referred to the Second World War.

I do not in all truth and sincerity know how much of it I can present to her. Somehow I doubt, by her reaction the other day, if she will be open to its revelations, which may or may not be revelations to her. If it represents the truth, it is a dreadful and burdening truth. In a place like this we must not concern ourselves too much with moral judgement or even legal judgement. We are like prison chaplains in here, dealing with the remnant human person after the civic powers have had their say. We are trying to ready, to steady the person for what? The axe, the guillotine of sanity? For the long watches of the sentence of living death that being here really is?

The document I was interested if not a little horrified to see was signed by a Fr Aloysius Mary Gaunt, which was a name that rang a bell. I puzzled it over until I suddenly realised who that was, the man who became auxiliary bishop of Dublin in the fifties and sixties, taking from the hemming and hawing of the Irish constitution a clear statement of his powers of moral domination over the city, as did most of his brother clerics. A man who in his every utterance seemed to long for the banishment of women behind the front doors of their homes, and the elevation of manhood into a condition of sublime chastity and sporting prowess. There is something humorous about it now, there was nothing humorous about it then.

This Fr Gaunt as a young curate in Sligo seemed to be very intimate with Roseanne Clear's circumstances. She was it seems the child of a police sergeant in the Royal Irish Constabulary (which I already knew from the damaged section I had found here). De Valera, as a young leader during the war of independence, had declared that any member of the police could be shot if they in any way obstructed the aims of the revolutionary movement. So such individuals, though Irish and for the most part Catholic (Roseanne's father was Presbyterian), and their families lived under constant threat and in real danger. It is all very understandable in a revolutionary period, but I wonder if Roseanne at the age of twelve or so could have seen that. In her eyes what happened must have been genuinely tragic, genuinely bewildering and awful.

I have just looked at my watch and it is seven fifty, the very latest moment I can leave it, to make my rounds at ten past eight. I must flee.

A note to myself: the builders say six weeks and the new building will be completed. This is from the horse's mouth, because I was on site myself, asking them, like a veritable spy, the other day. But enough –

CHAPTER THIRTEEN

Roseanne's Testimony of Herself

Curious to relate, it was not in the Café Cairo that I 'met' Tom, but in quite another place. It was the sea itself.

It is along the strands of the world that the privilege of possessing children is most blatantly seen. What torment for the spinster and the childless man, to see the various sizes of little demons and angels ranged along the tide line. Like some species of migratory animal. The human animal began as a mere wriggling thing in the ancient seas, struggling out onto land with many regrets. That is what brings us so full of longing to the sea.

I am not an entirely childless person.

That story also belongs to the sea, or the strand anyway.

My child. My child went to Nazareth, that's what they told me. Or, that is what I heard them say. But I was not hearing anything very well, very properly, in that time. They might as well have said Wyoming.

Strandhill's beach is narrow, heaped, endangered, and the hill of sand itself seems to have drawn up its enormous knees to escape the goings on below. There is a long rough promenade where gigs, carts, sidecars, high traps and motorcars used to be parked, the occupants spilling out I am sure always with the same level of human anticipation, the kids barrelling away ahead, the fathers laughing, cursing, the mothers admonishing, panicking – all the to-do and turmoil of normal happiness. Kneelength bathing suits vying in eternity with those wondrous bikinis I have only seen in stray magazines. How I would like to have sported one of them.

And at first no doubt just a few brave houses built on the marsh and acres of blown sand, scotch grass, the land rising and rising until eventually touching on the realm of Knocknarea, where Queen Maeve sleeps in her stony grave. From the top of Knocknarea you can see the beach at Strandhill, but the people are only pins, and anything the size of a child is just a dust mote in your eye.

I have looked down from there, despairing and weeping.

All that country was 'my' country later. Strandhill, Strandhill, the mad woman of Strandhill.

At first, a few houses risked on that uncertain ground, then the old hotel, and then huts and more houses, and then, some time in the vanished twenties, Tom McNulty built the Plaza ballroom. A glorified corrugated-iron warehouse with a round roof, a square concrete front to the hall with an oddly modest door and a ticket window, the brightness of both beckoning, promising, oh, and a tumultuous whirlwind of dreams rising from the approaching crowd every Friday night, reaching no doubt as far as heaven, to comfort God in the doubts of his creation.

That was Tom McNulty's work, father and son, to put a ticket on those dreams. And I felt that dream in me with passionate completeness.

To sit here, writing this, my hands as old as Methuselah's. Look at these hands. No, no, you cannot. But the skin is thin as – did you ever see the shell of a razor fish? They are strewn all about Rosses Strand. Well, there is a filament of transparent stuff that covers those shells, like a drying varnish. It is strange stuff. That is my skin now. I fancy I can count my bones. The truth is my hands look like they have been buried a while and then dug up. They would give you a fright. I have not looked in a mirror for about fifteen years.

The first few feet of water at Strandhill were safe enough. In summer they were like a bath. The sea there made only the slightest effort at going in and out, it always seemed to me. Maybe the children peeing in the water had something to do with it, with the heat I mean. It was lovely though. Myself and Chrissie and the other girls from the Café Cairo . . . Mrs Prunty always tried to employ good girls for the café, but good girls that looked good, which is a different thing. I think we looked like young goddesses. Mary Thompson could have been a picture in a magazine, Winnie Jackson *was* a picture once, in the *Sligo Champion*. 'Miss Winnie Jackson Enjoys the Fine Weather at Strandhill'. Her in her beautiful one-piece bathing suit sent down to her in a box from Arnott's in Dublin, on the Dublin-to-Sligo train. There was style for you. She had a lovely plump bust and I think the lads felt only despair looking at her, that they would never even get talking to her.

Our skins going all African in the steaming heat of August. Our faces bright red sometimes in the evenings, going home across the strand, burnt off of us, and lying in bed then in the town, hardly daring to let our shoulders touch the sheets. Happy. And then the skin calmed down the next morning, and longing to get away out to the beach again, and then again, and then again. Happy. Just straightforward ordinary girls we were. We liked to bring as much despair as we could to the lads.

Who watched on the sidelines of our happiness like sharks, devouring our attributes with their eyes. Sometimes I'd get talking to a lad at the dance, lads didn't say much, and when they did talk they didn't say much worth hearing. But that was all right. There were all sorts at the dance, toffs from the town, and lads with trousers too short for them, showing their socks, or bare legs stuck into battered shoes. There were always a few donkeys tied up outside, and nags of one sort and another, and carts heeled up. The mountain spilled out its sons and daughters like a queer avalanche. Lovely humanity.

139

Fr Gaunt was always there or some such, one or other of the curates, the herons among the minnows. By God, there was some sort of Dancehall Act I seem to remember. Or maybe I imagine that. I believe they railed against dances in the church, but I wouldn't have been privy to that. There wasn't supposed to be much touching. It would be queer cold dancing without touching. It was lovely to snuggle up to a lad at the end of a dance, you sweaty and him all sweaty too, in the summer, the smell of soap and turf off him. And that stuff in their hair that time, Brilliantine, was the name I think. There'd be fellas there whose fathers and mothers probably spoke Irish in the back hills of Sligo, and who from going to pictures now and then had the idea they had obligations to look like stars of the silver screen, unless it was looking like Irish patriots they were trying to be, maybe that was it too. Michael Collins had been a strong man for the grease in his hair. Even de Valera was well slicked down.

And Tom McNulty's Band blowing up a storm. Young Tom standing there at the edge of the stage with his trumpet or clarinet raised, blasting out the sort of music we had then. You had to have the jazz for the dancing, but also the foxtrot was still danced there, and even the waltz. Tom even had a recording made, called Tom McNulty's Ragtime Band, by Jesus that sent the hall into a frenzy. There was a light shining out of Tom then. Of course at that time Tom was just the great man I had never spoken to, unless it was in the café to say 'What would you like?' To which the answer would most likely be, 'China tea and a deadfly bun. Earl Grey for the brother.' He was dead keen on the deadfly buns. I wonder if they still have them. They were like religious objects at that time, you couldn't have a café without them, what would be the point. It is funny how fixed everything was in those times. Deadfly buns, cream cakes, eclairs, cherry buns with white icing on top, it was like those things were as ancient and established as whales, dolphins, mackerel – like natural occurrences, the natural history of the café.

It mattered altogether that my father was gone, but somehow I was able to tuck that in under the pillow of my hair, to sleep on it as it were. I couldn't help the happiness, when I woke in the morning, yes, there was my mother to see to, but I was able to feed her and look after her, she never said anything or went anywhere, just kept to the house in her stripy housecoat, and there was that energy in me, like a motorcar being started with a starting handle, cranking me up, I was cranked up mysteriously every morning I woke, I was aflame with energy, it swept me out of the house, and through the streets of Sligo, and in through the glass doors of the Café Cairo, and had me kissing my friend Chrissie good morning, and laughing, and if Mrs Prunty was around, she would give me her shy smile, and I would be jubilant, jubilant.

It is always worth itemising happiness, there is so much of the other thing in a life, you had better put down the markers for happiness while you can. When I was in that state, everything looked beautiful to me, the rain slicing down looked like silver to me, everything was of interest to me, everyone seemed at ease with me, even those slit-eyed cornerboys of Sligo, with the yellow fingers from the coffin nails they smoked, the yellow stain above their lips where the fag was stuck in permanent. Accents like bottles being smashed in a back lane.

There now, and all that comes back unbidden. I sat down today to write of Tom and the sea. Rescuing me in the sea of happiness.

I plunged in. I think I knew where I was going. It is curious to me how I remember so completely the feel of that light wool bathing suit on my skin. It had three thick stripes alternating and I had saved the whole winter for it. You couldn't have found a nicer one in Sligo. A hot Irish day is such a miracle we become mad foreigners in a twinkle. The rain drives everyone indoors and history with it. There is a lovely lack of anything on a hot day, and because our world in its inner truth is so wet, the surprised greens of the fields and hills seem to burn with a sort of bewilderment, a wonderment. The land looks lovely to itself, and the girls and boys along the strand are painted into the tawny yellows and the blues and greens of the sea, also burning, burning. Or so it seemed to me. The whole town seemed to be there, everything suffering the same brushstrokes of the heat, everything joining and melding. I don't know if the Plaza existed just at that time, it must have done, because I had seen Tom McNulty playing, but if it did it would have been 1929 or after even, so I wasn't exactly a girl, but I am confused about this. It is hard to know a person's age in a bathing suit, in the riot of the sunlight, and I can't see what age I was, I am peering back with my mind's eye, and all I see is fabulous glitter.

And the undersea just as glittering, speckled, chained in miracles somehow, that wonderful half blindness the eyes have underwater, blurred because the sea itself is a huge lens, like you are wearing the sea itself before your face. So it's gone even more like a painting, a furious mad painting, there was a whole book of them in the town hall library, the fellas that painted in France and were laughed at to begin with, like they didn't know how to paint. I won't risk writing one of the names, but I do remember them, hard harsh names, and troubled lives to match, I can say them in my head as I write. But I'd be ashamed to spell them wrong. And myself in that undersea, my whole body loosened, but also sharpened, my lungs rich with air at first and then beggared, and the head lighter, lovelier, and the chiller water deeper, washing my face, asking my face who it was, what shape it was, in infinite detail. Suddenly I am longing to tell Dr Grene about this, I don't know why, I imagine he would be interested in it, it would please him, but I would also fear he would read something into it. He interprets things, which is dangerous, extremely. Oh yes, the beach at Strandhill, high tide as it was, is good for a little, then it plunges down, you are suddenly in the big water of the bay there, the big muscle, enormous, like the famous Hudson river, no, not as big as that of course, but I felt I was not so much entering as touching something vast flexing there under God's eye. And could I feel it pull me out, swiftly, deeper? I don't know. I do know I gave my heart to it, I do know I was moved by it, maybe I wept, can you weep underwater, it must be possible? How long was I swimming without coming up? A minute, two, three, like a pearl diver in the south seas, wherever they are, whatever they are? Myself and my bathing suit, and inside the suit a little pocket with two bob in it, which would be my fare back to Sligo on the old green bus, for safety's sake stuck in that pocket, like something you could keep a scapular in, if you were Catholic. And I suppose my youth, my softness, my hardness, my blue eyes, my yellow hair sleeking underwater, and maybe three hundred sharks out there, beginning to be in the neighbourhood of sharks, wonderful, wonderful, I didn't care. Become a sort of shark.

The great pull of the current beginning to take me, like a word lost in a swell of music.

Then in all that happiness, suddenly enveloped, stolen back, taken up, by human arms I knew, expert, almost devious. And this person, sleek and round and strong, raised me up through the wild glitter, and we broke the surface, and there was the roaring world again, and the heaving sea, and the sky whether up or down I didn't know. And the swimmer drew me back to the strand, with the boys and the girls, the buckets, the old cannon pointing out to sea, the houses, the Plaza, the stunned donkeys, the few motorcars, Sligo, Strandhill, my fate, my fate as woeful as my father's, my ridiculous, heartless, funny fate.

143

It couldn't have been anyone in the world fishing me out except Tom McNulty. It was always going to be him. Anyway, he was a famous swimmer, he already had a medal for saving a life given him by the mayor of Sligo himself, which was what got him into the politics, he always said. The other person he saved was an old crone that the tide plucked from the shore-line, like the joker it is – an old crone, but not as old as I am now. No.

'I know you,' he said, glistening on the sand, his nice square fat face smiling at me, and the world and its aunt gathered about us, and Jack also there now, in his sombre black bathing trunks, and his body that never really looked like flesh, but something stonier, the bones and muscles of a traveller. 'You're the lass from the Café Cairo.'

And I laughed, or tried to, the salt water spluttering in my throat.

'Oh mercy,' he said. 'You swallowed the ocean. Yes, you did. Jaysus,' he said, 'where's your blessed towel? Do you have one? You do? And your clothes? Yes, come on. Come on with me.'

So my towel was put around my shoulders and my clothes gathered for me by Jack, gingerly holding them, and the two walked me up across the burning hot road towards the Plaza, we kept to the grassy verge when we could, and across the desert of the carpark and into the ticket office with us, and Tom was laughing, very easy and relieved he probably was, to have rescued me. I can't remember if he got another medal for me, I hope he did, because he probably deserved it, all things considered.

Oh, dear, it is difficult to look back on the joy of those days, but on the other hand, it is something rare I know in a life to know such joy, and such luck.

I knew my luck, knew it as well as a sparrow when it finds a speck of bread all to itself.

It was pride too, my pride in him, with his fame and his confidence.

We'd go up the concrete steps to the pictures between those laurel hedges. We might have been a couple in Hollywood, I might have been Mary Pickford herself, though I suppose in all honesty Tom was too small to be Douglas Fairbanks.

The dark in our little world was the drinking habits of Sligo. Men like Tom and his brother would be so drunk in the small hours things would happen which not only could they not remember, but they wouldn't want to, which was no doubt a great blessing.

I would be standing down on the dancefloor, happy to be on my own, looking up at the stage where Tom's band were ranged, his little dapper father a dab hand on the clarinet, on any instrument you liked. Late in the evening Tom would play 'Remarkable Girl' with his hawk's eye peering down at me. When we were walking on the beach at Rosses Strand one time he teased me by singing 'When Lights are Low in Cairo', because I was the girl that worked in the Café Cairo. There was a singer called Cavan O'Connor that he modelled his voice on, he thought Cavan was the greatest singer that ever breathed. But Tom had grown up more or less on Jelly Roll Morton and he was cracked on Bubber Miley, like all the trumpeters were, even more than on Louis Armstrong himself. Tom said Bubber had put the jump into Duke Ellington, no question. These matters for Tom were nearly as important as the politics. But my brain left him there, once he started on that. It didn't seem as interesting at all as the music. Soon he had me sitting in with the band playing piano when the piano player proper was unwell. He was a big lad from the back of Knocknarea with TB. 'Black Bottom Stomp' was his party piece as one might say. Jack was never on stage but he liked to sing in the early part of his cups, when he was cheerful, very cheerful. Then it would be 'Roses of Picardy', 'Long Way to Tipperary', because he had been in the British Merchant Navy when he was only a boy, but I think I wrote this before. Saw every port from Cove to Cairo, but I think I wrote this. Maybe it's worth saying twice.

Jack was always about and then he'd be gone for a while. He used to go out to Africa on contracts. Oh, Tom was very proud of Jack, Jack had done two degrees at Galway at the same time, Geology and Engineering. He was just a brilliant man. I have to confess he was about three times better-looking than his brother, but that is neither here nor there. But he was, he had those smalltown filmstar looks, you'd be in the cinema watching *Broadway Melody* or some such, and when the lights would go up at the end, yes, you'd be back in bloody Sligo – except for Jack. Jack still had some halo of Hollywood about him.

But Jack kept a few feet between us, what sort of feet I don't know. He was too ironical to be friendly, he'd be jesting and joking the while, and sometimes I caught him looking at me with the wrong sort of look. I don't mean coveting me, but maybe disapproving. Long looks when he thought I couldn't see him. Sizing me up.

Jack kept a Ford car though, to go with the leather collar on his coat. We were always in that car, we saw a thousand Irish landscapes through the front screen, we washed a million tons of rain off it with that little wiper back and forth, back and forth, and gallons of whiskey they drank in it, as we went along. The big thing was to get out onto the strand by Coney island at low tide, and surge along through the shallow inch of water, roaring and at our infinite ease. There were always friends with us, the prettiest of the girls that hung after the band, and other likely lads of Sligo and Galway. The funny thing was, Jack had a girlfriend that he was actually going to marry, Mai her name was, but we never saw her, she lived in Galway with her parents, very well-to-do they were. Her father was an insurance salesman, a very impressive fact to Jack, and they lived in a house in Galway that was Something House, and that was a big fact for a man whose father was the tailor in the Sligo Lunatic Asylum. He had met her at the university, she was one of the first girls there, oh, and I'd say one of the first girls at a lot of things, looking down her nose at me being one of them. No, that isn't fair, I don't think I ever met her but the one time.

But actually I do Tom a disservice talking like this. Because his own first cousin owned the *Sligo Champion* and was a TD in what they used to call the real first Dáil, that is to say the Dáil after the Treaty. And Jack always said – I used to hear him telling a new acquaintance – that he was a cousin of that dark-hearted person Edward Carson, who opted out of the Free State like a rat leaving a sinking ship, or what he hoped and prayed was a sinking ship. Tom told me his own people had been butter importers in Sligo, or was it exporters, and had had ships, just like the Jacksons and the Pollexfens. And that the Oliver in his name, Thomas Oliver McNulty, was there because they had lost their lands in the time of Cromwell when an Oliver McNulty had refused to become a Protestant. He said this with a wary eye on me, to see how I would take it, being a Protestant myself I suppose. I was a Protestant, but maybe not the right kind of Protestant. Jack liked the big-house Protestants and he had it in his head that he was sort of Catholic gentry. I don't think he thought much of the great Presbyterian tradition in Ireland. Working-class. That was the dread phrase.

'That fella is working-class through and through,' was one of Jack's put downs. Because he had been in Africa he also had strange phrases like 'Act the white man.' And 'hamma-hamma'. Because he had seen a thousand drunken nights, another phrase was 'Keep the party clean.' If he thought someone was untrustworthy, that person was 'a casual pack of buggers'.

Red hair, auburn really, combed back. Quite severe features, very serious about the eyes. Oh yes, Clark Gable or better still Gary Cooper. Gorgeous.

I am looking for my mother in these memories, and I cannot find her. She has simply disappeared.

CHAPTER FOURTEEN

Dr Grene's Commonplace Book

Driving into work this morning I passed a previously unnoticed hillside of windmills. I may not have noticed them before because they just weren't there, but if so I certainly missed their erection, which must have taken quite a long time. They were simply suddenly there. Bet always said I did not have my mind on the world at all. One day I came in from the rain, sat on the couch, and a few minutes later, happening to touch my hair, asked, 'Why is my head wet?' Bet loved to tell that story, or used to, when there was someone to tell it to.

But there were the windmills, suddenly. It is a hill – more of a mountain I suppose, if we have such things in Ireland – called Labanacallach, and there is a wood also, called Nugent's Wood, going up to the frostline. Who Nugent was or why he planted a wood is anyone's guess, or at least there would be only old codgers who know these things. I was driving along in my Toyota, feeling quite wretched, with the same drumming recrimination going on in my stupid head, when I saw the windmills silverly turning, as one might say, and my heart lifted like a quail from the very bog. It lifted. They were so beautiful. I thought of windmills in paintings, the strange emotions still attaching even to their memory. Don Quixote maybe. How sorry I always used to feel when I saw a ruined mill long ago. Magical buildings. These modern versions of course are not quite the same thing. And of course they are strongly objected to. But they are beautiful. They made me optimistic, like I could still achieve something.

I had woken in the night with an appalling sense of shame

and disquiet. If I could itemise the attributes of my grief, and print them in a journal, I might do the world a general service. I suspect it is hard to remember grief, and it is certainly invisible. But it is a wailing of the soul nonetheless and I must never again underestimate its acidic force in others. If nothing else I will hoard this new knowledge in the hope that when it passes I may still retain its clinical anatomy.

Thank God for those windmills.

But in the small hours of the night I awoke. I think it was that mysterious knocking again, whose source I still don't know. It is Bet beseeching me to remember her. She needn't worry. I looked over what I had written about Roseanne Clear but all I saw, all that registered, was those stupid words I had written about Saddam Hussein. I suppose it is as well I am a man of no importance, which keeps my views, especially when they are inappropriate and embarrassing, private.

When the late Pope died I had also odd emotions then. I was deeply moved by the death of a man who had not been helpful to those of my patients who are religious, but also gay, or God help them, women. While he lived it seemed the apogee of existence was just what he was himself. But in his death he was magnificent, brave. In his death he became more democratic maybe, because death includes everything, likes everything human – can't get enough of it. Death be not proud. Well yes, but death *is* mighty and dreadful. The Pope made short work of it.

Too much thinking on death. Yet it is the music of our time. As the millennium passed fools like myself thought we were about to taste a century of peace. Clinton and his cigar was so much greater a man than Bush and his rifle.

The more I look at Fr Gaunt's deposition, the more I seem to believe it. It is because he writes well in a sort of classical way, no doubt taking his syntax and his skills from his training in Maynooth. He has a very Latinate style it seems to me, of the kind I remember distantly from struggling with Cicero at school in Cornwall. His desire, almost his anxiety in psychiatric terms, to tell the story illuminates it.

He is unburdening himself, as he might a sin. Certainly his text is far from sacred. But he does not flinch. He is staunch. He is fearless. Fr Gaunt conscientiously details it all.

As a rule, a policeman in Ireland was never stationed near his own home town, one presumes so that there would be no question of favour to people among whom he had grown up. Roseanne's father was actually one of the few exceptions to this rule, as he had been born and bred in Collooney, not so far, and certainly not far enough, from Sligo town itself. So he knew the district in a way that was perhaps not healthy for himself. It was possible for people to take more personally his presence in the town, in particular after the bringing in of the auxiliary police, made up of officers who had fought in World War One, and the Black and Tans, men and officers from the same site of carnage. This was in answer to the various 'outrages' of the war of independence, consisting mostly of the ambushing and shooting of soldiers and police – the crown forces as they used to say.

Her father it seems had the capacity therefore to be very aware of things happening in the town. Perhaps he was able to pick up information casually in a manner not open to a stranger. People might be more inclined to include him in gossip and rumour at the public house in the evening. Certainly her father had an enormous capacity for alcohol, being able like a docker to down fifteen pints of porter in a night and steer himself home afterwards. Apparently his daughter Roseanne would wait, anxiously no doubt, for his tread as he turned into their street, when she would gather him into the house.

Roseanne's playground was Sligo cemetery at the back of their house. She knew every alleyway and quirk of the place, and her special spot was the old ruined temple at its heart, where she liked to play hopscotch and the like in the crumbling portico. One evening, wrote Fr Gaunt, it seems she witnessed a strange burial. It was a group of men coming in with a coffin, quite without priest or ceremony, and lowering it into an open grave, and burying it there quietly in the dark, the only thing to show them the fags sparking in their mouths and the subdued chat. Roseanne, as would be natural in a daughter, ran to tell her father what she had seen. It seems she thought it was grave-robbers, though in truth the coffin was being put in not taken out, and there had not been such thefts in Ireland or anywhere else for half a century.

How Fr Gaunt knew all these details is not clear, and indeed as I read it over now I am puzzled by his omniscience, but then that was the ambition of a priest in his time.

At any rate her father had the coffin disinterred the next morning, Fr Gaunt himself in attendance, and in the coffin was found not a body but a stash of guns, items very hard to get in the war of independence and gathered with great hardship, indeed often by means of taking one from the corpse of a slain policeman. And so it turned out, many of the items in the coffin were indeed police issue, and the haul from ambushes and raids. So from Roseanne's father's point of view, he was looking at the relics and signs of murdered comrades.

The newly cut name on the gravestone was Joseph Brady, but no one of that name had died in the town.

Unbelievably, the men had also buried with the guns notes of secret meetings, including, by some foolish miracle, various names and addresses, including certain individuals wanted for murder. It was a wretched bonanza for the police. Before anyone knew what was happening, some of the names were arrested, and one of them was killed 'evading capture', a man called

Willie Lavelle, whose brother later played a part in Roseanne's life in Sligo, according to the good priest. For some reason this man Willie Lavelle was buried in the very grave where the guns had been so futilely hidden.

The recapture of the guns and documents and the killing of the man caused a subterranean furore in the circles involved in hiding them. Orders were issued no doubt for any and every possible act of reprisal against the police. But this did not happen immediately, long enough for Roseanne and her family to experience living day by day and minute by minute under this pressing tide of dread. I am sure they hoped and prayed that the insurgents would be defeated and Ireland restored to peaceable ways. Chance would be a fine thing, they might have said.

As I lay my hand on these withered sheets of Fr Gaunt, I wonder sincerely how I can use them. Can I really ask Roseanne to live through all this again? But I must remember it is not the pain of her life I am after in the first instance, but the consequence of that pain, and the true reason for her sectioning. Now I go back to the original reason for my quest, which is simply to ascertain if she was mad, and whether or not her committal was justified, and whether or not I may recommend her to be returned out into the world. I think I may decide this without her corroboration, or only with her corroboration if she wishes it. I must make a judgement about the verities that are before me, not the verities that are only intimated, or that are suggested by my own instincts.

The bells of St Thomas church in the town are ringing eight. I am as late as the rabbit in Lewis Carroll.

Roseanne's Testimony of Herself

I met the world and his wife with Tom because he was a sociable man in the extreme, but it was actually some years before I was shown to the mother. I heard about the mother of course, two brothers talking will often linger on that subject. I formed an idea of her, her small stature, her fondness for scrapbooks in which she recorded all matters pertaining to her sons, Jack's travel tickets, documents, Tom's dance notices in the *Champion*, and now, as time went on, his speaking at various times in the town, on various topics. I got the idea that she and her husband were often on poor terms, that Old Tom generally went his way in, to her, a feckless manner. But maybe she was a connoisseur of fecklessness for all that. Not on her own account. I knew she had promised her only daughter to the nuns at a young age and this girl Teasy went duly to the Sisters of Mercy, as a dowried nun. That was a mendicant order that lived in a place called Nazareth House. They had houses all over England and even America. I never knew if the mother had ambitions for her sons in the priesthood, but she must have thought it was some insurance on her immortal soul if she could offer her daughter to that life, I don't know.

There was another son called Eneas of course but he was only spoken of sideways, although once or twice it seemed he did sneak home, returning from the wide world where apparently he roamed to sleep the daylight hours in his mother's house, and only venturing forth at night. This was a small mystery in a time of great mysteries, and I don't remember me paying special heed to it.

'Why's your brother Eneas gone from home the most of the time?' I asked Tom once.

'Just a little peccadillo,' said Tom, and that's all he would say at first.

But another time we were in town together and one of his

rivals, one of the up and coming Republican men, taunted him mysteriously in the street. He was a man called Joseph Healy and by no means a blackguard.

'Ah Tom,' he said, 'the policeman's brother.'

'The what?' said Tom, not with his usual ease and bonhomie.

'Never mind, never mind. Sure we all have our skeletons in the cupboard, I am sure.'

'Do you want to make something of this, Healy, in the council elections upcoming?'

'What? No,' said Joseph Healy, almost contritely, because though they were opponents, everyone in truth liked Tom, and Healy as I say was a decent skin at heart. 'I was only teasing you, Tom.'

Then they had a hearty enough handshake. But I could see Tom's mood had changed, and all the way up the street he was quiet and darkened. In a country of cupboards, every one with a skeleton in it, especially after the civil war, no one was exempt. But I could see that Tom resented that, and bitterly. Tom after all had a plan, a road to travel, which was an admirable thing in a young man like him. But skeletons he could do without obviously.

The mother was of the same mind. She loved the glory of Jack and she loved the glory of Tom, even if Jack looked in the ransacked trunk of old decency for his clothing, and Tom was a man to wear a modern hat in the new Ireland. This I gleaned from their conversations, and I always paid heed when they spoke of her, as a spy might pay heed to chit-chat in bars, because I had a feeling that some day I would need every scrap of information I could get, if I was to survive actually meeting her.

If ever there was a cold card in that game it was the blank, dark card of my own mother.

In those strange days when if anything unexpected could happen, it probably would, Mr de Valera became head of the country.

'Now the guns are back in the Dáil,' said Tom darkly.

'How do you mean, Tom?' I asked.

'They're so afeared of being there, they're after bringing their guns into the chamber.'

Now Tom spoke with understandable disgust, as these men were the very ones his own crowd had striven to subdue, imprison, and alas execute. So how it came about that the very men against the Treaty, and who lads like Tom had wanted erased from the Irish story, were now the men in charge . . . You could almost feel a lurch in the life of Sligo. It was fellas like Joseph Healy were up now. This was hard and bitter for Tom all things considered. Myself, I wouldn't have had three thoughts about any of them, but that even in his love-talk Tom could flummox me with the politics.

We were lying up the back of the great dune that gave Strandhill its name in fact, when he uttered the above sentiment. It was a greater obstacle to his future than any he had experienced. He had never been a gunman himself, coming to maturity after all that. To give him his due, he thought the time for guns was past. He had a sort of idea that North might be joined to South at last, but with the crazy notion that it would be some man like Carson would be the first 'king of Ireland', as he jocularly put it. This was an old notion of men like Tom. There was a sort of dancing swing to his notions, like his music. Joseph Healy would've put a bullet in Carson if he could have done it quietly and gone home to his family after.

It was families and young ones mixed up in it now, it wasn't just single lads going round, and lassies maybe helping them.

Well, in spite of all that, he soon turned to kissing me again, in the quiet dunes, with the seagulls outraged but only them seeing us, and the sea bearing Tom's heroic record the other side of the sand. Strandhill's habitual breeze raged along the marram grasses minutely. It was bitter cold but kisses dealt with that.

And a few weeks later walking across the bridge by the Swan Hotel who should stop me but the fading figure of John Lavelle.

He was nearly a young man still but the fringe of something else had touched him. He looked hard beaten by his time in America, or wherever he had been, and I looked down and saw the soles of his shoes were well worn. I imagined him hopping trains like a hobo and gadding about futilely generally. He was handsome though, with his narrow grey face.

'Look at you,' he said. 'I hardly knew you.'

'Likewise,' I said. I was on my own, but wary, because Sligo was like a wretched family, everyone knew everyone and if they didn't know everything about everyone, they wanted to. I think John Lavelle noticed my furtive looking.

'What's up?' he said. 'You don't want to talk to me?'

'Ah, no,' I said. 'I do. How are you keeping? Were you away off in America then?'

'That was the idea,' he said. 'It didn't go just like that. The best laid plans.'

'Ah sure, yes,' I said.

'At least I can walk free in Ireland now,' he said.

'Oh?'

'What with Dev in now.'

'Oh, yes. Well, that's good anyhow.'

'Better than the fucking Curragh jail.'

The curse word made me jump, but I thought he had the right to use it.

'Is that where you were?'

'That's it.'

'Well, John, I'll see you around the place.'

'I'm going down home a while to the islands, but yes, you'll see me back here all right. I'm going to be working for the council.'

'You're an elected man?'

'No, no,' he said. 'On the roads. Council work. Digging and the like.'

'That's good. It's work.'

'It is work. Work's hard to find. Even in America I'm told. You working yourself?'

'Café Cairo,' I said. 'Waitress.'

'Good for you. I'll come see you when I get back to Sligo.'

'Ah, do, yeh,' I said, suddenly uneasy with myself, and embarrassed, I knew not why hardly.

John Kane brings me my soup just now.

'This bloody job will kill me,' he says. 'I'd rather be a mole-catcher in Connaght.'

All the while with his unfortunate gobbling of the throat.

'But there are no moles in Connaght,' I said.

'In none of Ireland. Isn't it the perfect job for an old man? Them bloody stairs.'

And off he went.

The mother's bungalow was nice enough but it smelt of boiling lamb – in my vivid state of alarm, I might have said sacrificial lamb. Somewhere down the back of the house you sensed pots boiling, curly kale, cabbage, from Old Tom's garden, and a lamb, boiling, boiling, spewing its distinctive mild, damp smell into the corridors. That was my impression. I was only near that bungalow twice in my whole life and both times felt like dying just to be near it. In those days, the odour of cooking meat turned my stomach. But boiling meat took the biscuit. Why, I don't know, since my mother relished all forms of meat, even offal and innards that would frighten a surgeon. She would dine quite happily on a lamb's heart.

I was brought by Tom into the front sitting room. I felt like a farm animal in there, I felt like the cow and the calf and the pig must have felt in times past, when they'd be led into a cottage at night. People and animals slept in the same house one time in Ireland. That's why many a country kitchen still has a sloping floor, sloping down from the fire and the hag's bed and the upper bedroom, so obviously the shit and the piss of the animals couldn't flow that way. Human-wards. But I felt like that, awkward, bumping into the furniture in a fashion I never would have normally. The why of it was that I shouldn't have been there. I wasn't meant to be. It even took God by surprise that I was, I'd say.

She had her few chairs and a sofa covered in a dark, dark red velvet, and they were so old and lumpy it was like things had died in them under the velvet and had become cushions of a kind. And everywhere the stench of that lamb. I don't mean to write stench, I don't mean to describe all this in a bad way. God forgive me.

She gave me a very gentle look. It surprised me. But her voice was not so nice as her look. I think, at this distance, she was probably trying to be kind, to get off on the right foot. She was a tiny woman with what they used to call a widow's peak in her hair. She was dressed entirely in black, a miniature dress of black something, that material with the suspicious shine on it, like the elbows of a priest's jacket. Indeed she had a very beautiful gold cross about her neck. I knew she was the seamstress in the asylum up the town, just as her husband Old Tom was the tailor. Yes, yes, they had met there over the cutting table.

'She looked like an angel in the window-light,' said Old Tom to me once. I don't know apropos of what, or where. Maybe in

the earlier, brighter times. His thoughts I think tended to mean-
der. He was an immensely self-satisfied man, as I suppose he had
the perfect right to be. But she didn't look like an angel now.

'You have no lap,' she said, staring now sternly at my legs.

'I have no what?' I said.

'No lap, no lap.'

'For to be sitting babies on,' said Tom helpfully, but it didn't
help me at all.

'Oh,' I said.

There was a curious skein of whiteness on her features, like
a sprinkle of halfhearted snow on a roadside. Perhaps it was a
powder she used. The sunlight that the day outside virtually
dumped into the room had betrayed it.

I must be careful to write of her fairly.

Then Old Tom sat me down on one of the lumpy chairs.
Each arm had a little mat with flowers worked into it in simple
threads. It was bare, neat work. Mrs McNulty put herself on
the couch, where beside her rose a little mound of books,
which I detected to be her scrapbooks. For the moment she left
them severely alone, like a chocolate addict torturing herself
near a chocolate bar. Old Tom pulled up a wooden chair in
front of me. He was as jolly as you would like. In his hands he
clasped a little flute or piccolo, and without further ado he
began to play an Irish tune on it, with his famous mastery.
Then he stopped, and laughed, and played another one.

'How are you on the cello?' he said. 'Do you like it?'

Of course piccolos and cellos were never played by him in
the band, and it was as if, instead of conversation, he was talking to me through these more exotic instruments. But what he
was trying to say eluded me. We had often spoken at the Plaza,
but these exchanges seemed worthless here. I might as well
have never met him in my life. It was very strange.

Mrs McNulty made a *huh* noise, and got up, and drifted
away from the room. It might have meant anything, that noise,

and I was hoping it was just a characteristic ejaculation, as the old novels used to say. Old Tom got through a little more of his repertoire, then he got up also, and left the room. Then Tom left the room. He didn't even look back at me.

So I sat in the room. It was just me and the room and the echo of Old Tom's music and the other echo that Mrs McNulty had left behind her, something quite as enigmatic as a scrap of O'Carolan.

Tom came back eventually and came over and helped me to my feet. He didn't say anything, just widened his face a moment, as if to say, *Well, there you are, what can you do.*

We walked out onto the Strandhill Road where the bungalow was just one of four or five similar properties on an acre each. There was something half-done about that road, half-finished, and something very much half-done about meeting Mrs McNulty.

'Did she not like me?' I said.

'Well, well, she is concerned about your own mother. Well, she might be said to take a professional interest in that. But it isn't the main thing. No. And I thought it might be. But no. The mother is very religious,' said Tom. 'That's the real difficulty.'

'Oh,' I said, linking his arm. He smiled at me gently enough, and we were trotting along fairly nicely, approaching all the while the older narrower streets of the town's edge.

'Ah, yes,' he said. 'She would like you to talk to Fr Gaunt, if that would be possible.'

'For what?' I said. So she was a friend of Fr Gaunt, I thought, oh God.

'You know,' he said. 'All the what's-it and to-do of these things. Yes. Decree of bloody *Ne temere*, you know, and all that. Bugger now, I couldn't care if you were a Hindu, but, you see, it's the Presbyterian angle, you know. Oh, Jesus, I don't think she ever had a Protestant before set foot in her house, that's for sure and certain. By Jesus.'

161

'But me, does she like me at all?'

'I don't know,' he said, 'she didn't say that at all. It was like a committee meeting in the scullery, formal, you know.'

Tom had not asked me to marry him or anything and yet I knew all this talk was something to do with marrying. I suddenly myself didn't want to marry him, or anyone, or be asked. I was in my early twenties and those times you were an old maid by twenty-five, you wouldn't get a hunchback to marry you then. There were far more girls than men in Ireland those times. Women were wiser and went off to America and England double-quick, before their boots were sunk and stuck for good in the mire of Ireland. America was crying out for women, we were as good an export as gold to America. Hundreds and hundreds and hundreds went, every blessed year. Lovely women, round women, small, ugly, strong, exhausted, youthful, ancient, every damn category. Freedom I suppose they were after, following their instincts. They'd rather be maids in America than old maids in bloody Ireland. I suddenly had a strong, a fervent, almost a violent wish to join them. It was the smell of that lamb was in my clothes, and only a sea-voyage across the Atlantic I thought would shift it.

Now, but you see, I loved that Tom. God help me.

CHAPTER FIFTEEN

Dr Grene's Commonplace Book

Curious and upsetting news today about John Kane. At a staff meeting we were trying to field a report from one of the wards. A relative had found one of the patients in some distress, the patient in question being quite a young Leitrim woman, by comparison with the ageing population here, early fifties I should think. She is a woman that came in only recently, having suffered a psychotic episode involving her being the new female Messiah who had failed to save the world, and must therefore scourge herself. She had used barbed wire for this purpose. All this in the setting of a perfectly ordinary Leitrim farm, and a perfectly ordinary and seemingly happy marriage. So already a tragedy. But the relative, I think her sister, had found her quite distracted in her room the other morning, with her hospital gown drawn up, and a bit of worrying blood on her legs. Not very much, just a smattering. And of course the worst was suspected, as it always is, and hence the staff meeting. All thoughts turned to John Kane because of course he has been implicated in such matters before, and let off. On the other hand he is so ancient, is he still capable? I suppose a man is always capable. But there is no proof, nothing, and we must simply all be vigilant.

I was struck again how terrified everyone always is at these staff meetings, at events in the hospital requiring any sort of outside airing. Of anything having to be mentioned to the visiting professionals in any capacity whatsoever. Even when the kitchen manages to create a mild case of food poisoning on a ward, there is exactly the same level of fear as there was this morning. The staff seems to gather together and roll itself into a ball, needles outward. I must confess I feel the same myself. Perhaps it would shock an outsider the level of things going wrong we feel we can tolerate, even of catastrophe. Nevertheless it is a profound instinct, especially I think in a mental institution, where the work is in itself often so onerous, even bizarre. Where distress can be measured to the degree of hurricane and tsunami on a daily basis. Things are best handled in-hospital. However I don't know how the relative will feel about this.

Very strange to remind oneself that soon all of this, these individuals, these very rooms, these very matters, will be dispersed to the four winds at the demise of the hospital.

Strangely enough this comes in the same week as John Kane being diagnosed with a return of his throat cancer. Not that he was told that, no. He has increasing difficulty swallowing, that's all he knows about it. This would be quite sad for him, if it wasn't for this other matter. If the other matter is true of course we must hope he will die roaring, as Irish people say. He is old enough though for such a cancer to move very slowly. How old though, I could not find out. By his own admission, he has no birth certificate, having been brought up somewhere by adoptive parents. Well, we have that in common, and hopefully little else. The reason he is still working seems to be that no one has thought to retire him, since his age has never registered. Furthermore his job is so menial it would be almost impossible to fill, as it is doubtful even a willing person from China or Bosnia or Russia would take it. John Kane himself shows no desire to lay down his brush of his own free will. And he insists on climbing the stairs to Roseanne's room, though the climb knocks the wind out of him, and he was told he could leave it to someone else. Oh no, he went into a muttering 'thunderousness' about that.

Because of Bet, I must admit I put my mind only lightly to

these matters. At least, I attempted lightness. My head is already stuffed with grief I suppose like a pomegranate with its red seeds. I can only bleed grief, having no room for more. While the registrar and the nurses spoke about the poor molested patient, if that is what happened to her, my own head was roaring. I sat there among them with a roaring head.

Then I went up to Mrs McNulty's room and sat with her a while. It seemed like the logical thing to do. Even if it is the logic of poor Mr Spock, who feels nothing. But I was feeling plenty. I didn't continue with my investigation into her presence in the hospital. I couldn't. This is a horrible admission, but there it is.

I sat there in the twilight of her room. I suppose she was watching me. But she said nothing either. I was thinking thoughts that I could not in any case, in any circumstance, have voiced out loud in her presence. Thoughts that are a savage mixture of old desire and continuously new regret.

I was trying to sort myself out, as the Yanks say. Because it was another strange night last night. I do not know what I would say to myself if I came to myself for therapy. I mean, I no longer know. There are pits of grief obviously that only the grieving know. It is a voyage to the centre of the earth, a huge heavy machine boring down into the crust of the earth. And a little man growing wild at the controls. Terrified, terrified, and no turning back.

It's that banging that has me done in. Such a little thing. But it has thrown my nerves into a sort of hyper-awareness. Nerves! Now I am sounding like a Victorian doctor. But it is something very like Victorian nerves, seances, the intimation of the living, those dying tombs in Mount Jerome cemetery, untouchable because bought in perpetuity, but mouldering, and no one alive to go and rub the brasses. Look on my works, ye mighty, et cetera.

Last night things took a step forward into the dark. I was

lying in my bed more awake than a dog. Suddenly in the pitch dark, in those un-peopled small hours, Bet's phone started to ring, I heard it going off above my head. I had got her a second line when she complained I was always on the internet and she couldn't ever make calls. She said her friends could only leave messages, and that I never gave her the messages. So yes, I got her a second line, expensive though it was. The phone sits there beside her bed. Now it was suddenly ringing, and such a jump I gave, like in a cartoon. Chemically, I suppose it was like an injection of adrenalin into the head, I don't know. But it was quite sickening, so sudden and so strange. And it rang and rang, of course it did, because there was no one to answer it. I certainly was not going to go up there into that room in the middle of the night. But then it struck me as odd that it didn't go to message, like it normally did, if Bet was out. I suppose the phone company had discontinued it. Then I had the miserable thought that hadn't I actually phoned the phone company a few weeks ago and asked for the line to be discontinued? If I had, and I couldn't really remember, it must be ringing as a result of some sort of fault. Oh, but, to lie there and hear it go on and on.

Then it stopped. I tried to calm myself, induce myself into feeling relieved. Then the terrible thing happened. Oh, Jesus, yes. I heard it so clearly, above my head, a little muffled because it had to come through the floorboards and the old plaster ceiling, but I heard it, the word 'Hello?' It was Bet's voice.

I nearly lost the grip on my bladder I was so startled. I had a vision in my head of a monster wrapping its coils about me, like an anaconda, and starting to squeeze. An anaconda kills by putting such pressure on the inner organs that the heart bursts. That one word nearly burst my heart. I missed Bet so terribly, but in all honesty I did not want to hear her voice, not like that. The living breathing woman, yes, but not that single word floating down to me, piercing down to me. But then I

166

thought, had there been some awful mistake, had I imagined her dying, or had I buried her alive, and – but I had no time for further madness of that sort, because another word followed, it was my name being called, clear as a bell, 'William!'

Oh, Jesus, I thought, it's for me. Now that in itself was a mad thought. I mean, for heaven's sake, the call could not have been answered, and therefore, how could it be for me?

My name had been called. The voice was just as it always had been, the exact same tone, carrying in it that same pulse of impatience, annoyance that I had given her number to someone, and that they were using her line.

I didn't know what to do. 'What?' I called up, without even intending to.

I couldn't just leave it at that – now here was fresh madness – I couldn't not respond. I got out of bed feeling like a dead man myself, as if I was now in the realm of the dead, or a story by M. R. James himself that Bet so loved. I went out my door with deepest reluctance and walked along the corridor on my bare feet. If she saw me like that, I thought, she would chastise me, going along without my slippers. I reached the little entry to the stairs to the attics, and went up, step by step.

I got to the landing where I had found her struggling for life, almost expecting to see her there. I flicked the switch but the bulb must have died without me noting it, because nothing happened. There was a murk of moonlight on the landing, a mere soup of light. I had left her door a little ajar so as not to impede the movement of air in the room, as a precaution against mildew. So I went to the door with slow, leaden steps, and stood there a moment.

'Bet?' I said.

Now I was all unhappiness. Whatever chemical is allied to fear – adrenalin and its sisters – was drenching my brain. My knees were literally weak, and I felt the contents of my bowels turn to water. I wanted to vomit. Years ago as a boy in the slaughter house in Padstow I had seen cows going in a queue towards the gun, and watched them pissing and shitting in terror. Now I was just the same. Part of me longed for her to be inside the room, but a far greater part dreaded that same thing, dreaded it like the living are obliged to dread the dead. It is so deep a law of life. We bury or burn the dead because we want to separate their corporeality from our love and remembrance. We do not want them after death to be still in their bedrooms, we want to hold an image of them living, in the full of life in our minds.

And yet, suddenly, equally, like the first breeze of an enormous storm, I wanted her to be there, I wanted it. I pushed open the door and stepped in, wanting Bet to be there, wanting to take her in my arms gently in a way I had not done for so many, many years, and laugh and explain to her, explain the folly of my mind, and how I thought she had been dead, and please, please now could she forgive me the stupidity of Bundoran, and could we start again, let's go on a holiday somewhere, why, to Padstow itself, to see the old house, and eat at the posh new restaurants we heard about, and have a lovely time –

Emptiness. Of course emptiness.

I think for someone to have seen me then would have been as if they were seeing a ghost – as if I were the ghost. A wild-eyed, foolish sixty-five-year-old man in his dead wife's bedroom, gone daft from grief, looking as usual for forgiveness and redemption the way normal people look for the time. The default mechanism of most every thought of her. Bet – redemption, redeem me, forgive me. When the foul truth is she should have thrown me out.

I was sitting in Roseanne's room thinking all this.

There was nothing of it I could say to her. I was in a patient's room, supposedly to assess her for release, 'back into the community'. One of the inspirations of Mrs Thatcher's regime in England, a Thatcherite fashion one might say that hasn't gone away. Roseanne was sitting up in her bed, with that white mantle thing she wears, that in the half light looks like crumpled wings, the new wings of a butterfly before the blood is pumped into them and, much to the astonishment no doubt of the creature, it can suddenly take wing and fly.

Assess her. It suddenly seemed so absurd I laughed out loud. The only person's sanity in doubt in that room was my own.

Roseanne's Testimony of Herself

We were married in Dublin, in the church at Sutton, it was the easiest thing to do. The priest there was a friend of Tom's, they had gone to college at the same time in Dublin, even if different colleges. Tom had only lasted a few months studying law at Trinity College, but long enough to make friends in the city. Tom could fashion a bosom pal out of an afternoon at the races. Whatever needed to be done, licence, banns, whatever you need to do to marry a Presbyterian woman, was done. I suppose the good people of Sutton weren't too impressed by that particular wedding, but even if it lacked tuck and thunder, there were a few of his other Dublin buddies there, and afterwards we went to Barry's Hotel for two nights, and on the second night we went to a dance at the Metropole, because Tom knew the bandleader there, and we danced together nearly for the first time. For some strange reason, we had rarely danced together in his own dancehall. I suppose that was odd, I don't know. Tom seemed quite content in every way and didn't say a word about not having any of his family there. Jack would have been there only he was in Africa, but he paid for the wedding lunch as a gift to his brother. Tom drank so much whiskey at the lunch he wasn't up to much in the hotel that night, but he made up for it the night of the dancing. He was the nicest lover. That is the truth.

We lay in the dark of the hotel room. Tom had bought a packet of these Russian oval cigarettes at College Green, just beside his old college, and he was smoking one of them. I think I was twenty-five, he was just a little older.

'Do you know,' he said. 'It's very nice up here. I wonder could I ever make a go of it in Dublin?'

'You wouldn't miss the west?'

'I suppose I would,' he said, making a swirl of Russian smoke in the gloomy room.

'Tom?' I said.

'Yes?'

'Do you love me?'

'I do, surely. Certainly I do.'

'That's good,' I said, 'because I love you.'

'Do you?' he said. 'You show very good taste. That's very wise of you, I must say. Yes.'

And then he laughed.

'Do you know,' he said. 'I really do.'

'What?' I said.

'I mean, not just talking. But I do. Love you.'

And I really think he did.

He was the decentest man, I think it is important to say that.

You could judge a lot of the effects of Mr de Valera's famous economic war that time from the window of a train. We had been married in the springtime and because there was no market for lambs now, the farmers had to kill the lambs in the fields. So as the train went through the country every now and then we saw these perishing corpses. Tom was very upset about all this. De Valera's men were in power and to him that was just the same as gunmen and murderers taking over the country, the very selfsame country they had tried to scupper after the Treaty. It all set the teeth of fellas like Tom on edge. Tom was young and coming into his own and he wanted to inherit the country I suppose, make something of it. There was a great feeling in him that de Valera, having tried to strangle the new country at birth, would now make a hames and shambles of its childhood, as it were, and ruin the place in the greater world. Anyway it broke the heart of strong farmers to have to be killing lambs, and have nowhere to send the sheep themselves, it was all a strangulation of their dreams.

'Like a fucking madhouse,' said Tom beside me, looking out on the desolation of the farms. And he knew, because of course his father and mother both worked in a madhouse. 'The whole of Ireland is just a madhouse now.'

So Tom's father was asked to cut and sew a blue shirt for Tom, and he started having little meetings and marches in Sligo, to see if they could get things going the other way. There was a man called O'Duffy had set them up, he had been in charge of the police but lost that job somehow, and now he was like one of those lads like Mussolini or Franco. Tom admired him because when he had been a minister he had tried to bring in laws to protect children in Ireland. He had failed in that, but nevertheless. Also he was a passionate man in his speeches, and Tom thought that all the great men had been killed during the troubles, Collins of course in chief. And O'Duffy had been a great ally of Collins. So it all made sense really, to Tom at any rate. I never knew a man to sweat like Tom and after a march his blue shirt would be drenched. I had to dye it a few times because it would go pale under the armpits and that didn't look right. I never saw him march but I wanted him to look smart, like a wife would naturally.

In the meantime we set up house in a small corrugated place

out in Strandhill. It was a shack really, but it was close to the dancehall and kept me out of Sligo. At the same time it was an easy jaunt for him back into the town. Our bedroom looked out on Knocknarea, we could actually see the tip of Maeve's Cairn at the top, it was funny lying there, a young married couple in the thirties, in modern times, and her up there lying in her own bed, her own *leaba* as they say, and tucked in there all of four thousand years ago. We had a nice view of Coney island from the rickety porch at the front, and although the heap of the island hid him, I knew the Metal Man was there, solid and eternal, I could imagine him in my mind's eye, faithfully and stoically pointing down into the deep water.

Flying Down to Rio. Top Hat. The man that ruled the country of the heart was not de Valera with his skinny, haunted face, but Fred Astaire, with *his* skinny, haunted face.

Even the grandees came to the pictures. If it had been a church there might have been pews for them. As it was most of the fur coats were to be found in the balcony. The rest of Sligo teemed in the stalls below. There would have been mayhem other than that Mr Clancy and his brothers had all been in the army, and marshalled the patrons like unruly recruits. Any trouble and a lad would be turfed out on his ear into the rainy dark night of Sligo, which was not desirable. Oh he didn't mind kissing, he was no parish priest, and what could he have done anyhow, when the lights were low. It wasn't the church, but it was like the church, better, far better. It was at the pictures that you could look around and see that rapt gaze on people's faces that maybe the priest or the minister dreamed of one day seeing on the faces of their parishioners. The whole of Sligo in a damp crowd, all those different people and different degrees, paupers and princes, united by their enchantment. You could have said Ireland was united and free, at the pictures anyhow. Although Tom kept me in quarantine in Strandhill, till he could get his mother to relent in her hostility to me, he wasn't so cruel as to extend my exile to Saturday nights. We roared into town in his nice little car and took our places as always, as if we feared for our souls if we did not.

There was always great joshing at the cinema, fellas freely called out insults to each other. Sometimes political affiliations were alluded to, sometimes it was all taken in good part, but just now and then things weren't so lightly taken, and bit by bit in the thirties this got worse. You could tell a lot about the state of the country from the quality of the insults at the Saturday night pictures. Of course Mr Clancy was not for any party in particular, and against politics maybe in general. You could be expelled for a nasty remark, which was more than you could say for the Dáil itself, according to Tom.

'There's things you can say with impunity in Dáil Éireann that'd get you thrun out of the Gaiety,' Tom might say.

There were always newsreels before the features and if there was stuff about the Spanish Civil War for instance, there'd be roars going up about Blueshirts and the like. Mr Clancy and his brothers would be kept real busy trying to root out the satirists.

'Crowd of bowsies,' Tom would say.

'Casual pack of buggers,' Jack would say, if he wasn't in Africa. Not that Jack followed the Blueshirts.

'I'm afraid your friend O'Duffy is a casual pack of buggers,' he might say to Tom.

But Tom always roared with laughter, he liked his brother Jack, he didn't care what he said. That was part of Tom's great charm as a friend and brother. He was easy-going in his very

173

marrow. He thought Jack was a genius too, because he had done the two degrees at Galway, Engineering and Geology, whereas he had lasted only the few months at Law School. He had a way of feasting on Jack's words that was just their ancient practice from the time they were boys together. I don't know how their other brother Eneas fitted into that. Of course I never heard much said about poor Eneas.

One night at the showing of *Top Hat* as I was going down to the ladies' toilet a familiar dark figure briefly blocked my way. It wasn't usual for a single man to engage a married woman in casual conversation, but on the other hand there was never too much casual about John Lavelle. Now that his crowd were securely in power, he seemed to be flourishing, even though he was only slashing at brambles on the roadside for the council. That was better than being on the run or eating prisoner's hash in the Curragh. He must have liked black clothes because he wore only black, and it gave him a very cowboylike look, with the white pallor of his skin and the sweep of black hair above. For a roadsweeper he certainly understood about waistcoats. Myself I was dressed in my best purple summer dress, which I must suppose was a sort of wordless remark in itself. Anyway John Lavelle didn't care too much for what a person should be doing or not be doing.

'Hello, Roseanne. You know, girl, you look really lovely.'

Now this was an enormous statement for him. For anyone. He had never offered the slightest sort of love-talk to me. After all, we only knew each other because of the direst of tragedies. Maybe he even believed still that I had brought the Free State soldiers down on his head years ago. Maybe talking like that to me was a sort of subtle revenge. Whatever it was, I didn't take it seriously, I brushed past him, and went on my way. Anyway my bladder was bursting.

'I'm out on Knocknarea most Sundays,' he said. 'Most Sundays about three you'll find me at the cairn.'

I flushed with embarrassment. There was a little mill of women and girls trying to do the same as me, but they were very quiet, because the picture was still going on behind our heads. In fact it was quite hard to make out what John Lavelle said, but nevertheless I caught it. I hoped no one else had caught it. Maybe he only meant to be friendly. Maybe he only meant, I know you're living out there, and I'm often out there myself.

I had never seen him at a dance. Mind you, I was not at the Plaza as often as in the old days when I was a single girl and could play the piano without comment. But married women never worked in those days. We were like the Muslims in those times, the men wanted to hide us away, except on occasions like that, when there was a good film to be seen.

John Lavelle wasn't just another fella. He wasn't just a bowsie in the street making a remark behind my back, he was an important person because he had known my father and things about my father. Two deaths and more linked us, you might say, the death of his brother and the death of my father. We should have been enemies but somehow we were not. I wasn't against him, even if I wasn't for him either. To this day I don't really understand it. I rarely saw him and yet he loomed in my dreams. In my dreams he was always being shot and dying, like his brother had in real waking life. I often saw him dying in dreams. Held his hand and the like. Sisterly.

I never did speak about that to Tom though. I didn't like to. How would I begin? Tom loved me, or he loved what he knew of me, what he saw of me. Now I don't want to say something untoward, but he always complimented me on my rear end. That's the truth.

'When I feel blue,' he said once, 'I think of your backside.'

Not very romantic, but in another way, very romantic. Men are not really humans at all, no, I mean, they have different priorities. Mind you, I don't know what women's priorities are either, at least, I know what they are and never did feel them. I did have a shocking desire for Tom myself. The whole lot of him. I don't know. He made me dizzy on a constant basis. There's some things you really can't get enough of. Chocolate you can get enough of. But some things. I liked his company, in all guises of company. I liked drinking cups of tea with him. I liked kissing his ears. Maybe I was never a proper woman. God forgive me. Maybe the biggest error I made was I always felt the equal of him. I felt, it was me and him, like Bonnie and Clyde, who just that time in America were going round killing people and generally what, expressing their love in curious ways.

All right, so why did I go up to Maeve's cairn that very Sunday following? I don't know. Because John Lavelle asked me? No. I know it was a wretched thing to do, a mistake. Why does the salmon go home to the Garravoge, when it has all the sea to roam over?

Dr Grene's Commonplace Book

Every year in the early days we went religiously to Bundoran for our holiday. People now laugh at Bundoran, they think it the prime example of the ancient Irish holiday, damp B&Bs, foul rain, bad food and all. But we liked all that, me and Bet. We laughed at it too, but affectionately, like you might laugh at a mad great-aunt. We loved going there – we fled there, you might say, to refresh ourselves at the altar of Bundoran.

The sunlight is a great reader of faces. Going back to the same place year after year made a sort of clock of Bet's face. Every year there was a new story, the next picture in the sequence. I should have photographed her every year in the same place at the same time. She was always growling and worried about growing old, she spotted every new line on her face just the minute it appeared, like a sleepy dog suddenly wakes when a stranger's foot is distantly heard broaching the boundaries of a property. Her only extravagance was those jars of night cream she invested in, in her war against those lines. She was a deeply intelligent person, she knew great swathes of Shakespeare from her schooldays, when one of those unsung, inspired teachers had got a hold of her, and tried to make a teacher of her too. But she wasn't looking at wrinkles with her intelligence, it was something more primal, ancient. For myself, hand on heart, those things never bothered me. It is one of the graces of married life that for some magical reason we always look the same to each other. Even our friends never seem to grow old. What a boon that is, and never suspected by me when I was young. But I suppose, otherwise, what would we do? There has never been a person in an old people's home that hasn't looked around dubiously at the other inhabitants. *They* are the old ones, they are the club that no one wants to join. But we are never old to ourselves. That is because at close of day the ship we sail in is the soul, not the body.

Oh, and I write that, the biggest agnostic in Ireland. As usual I don't have words for what I mean. I am trying to say I loved Bet, yes, soul to soul, and the lines and wrinkles were part of some other story, her own harrowing reading of her own life. Nor would I underestimate the pain it caused her. By her own estimation a plain woman, she did not wish to be a plain old woman. However I would also question her plainness. There were times when her face shimmered and flashed with its own beauty. There was the moment we stood side by side in the church, and I looked down at her face just the second before she said 'I do,' and then heard her say it, and then out of her face flew this extraordinary light, flooding up at me. It was love. You do not expect to see love like that. I did not anyhow.

So why did I have to betray her in Bundoran of all places?

I went there innocently enough, without her, but for a conference in that new hotel on the strand. It was a psychiatric gathering, right enough. Our topic as it happened was geriatric psychosis, dementia, all that. I was presenting a paper on versions of memory, the absolute fascist certainty of memory, the bullying oppression of memory. I suppose it was a sort of middle-aged nonsense, but at the time I thought it quite radical, revolutionary. It was received at the conference as a type of throwing caution to the wind. As a type of indiscretion of the mind. So perhaps it wasn't remarkable that it was followed by an indiscretion of the body.

Poor Martha. Four fine boys she had at home, and a husband who was one of the most gifted junior counsels of his generation. A remote, troubled man, but, I am sure, a worthy. It was dreadfully simple. We drank too much wine together, we wandered back to the corridor of unimpressive rooms, we had a sudden desire towards each other, I kissed her, we fumbled in the dark, she never even took her knickers off, God help us, she came under my hand, that seemed to be the end of it. It was a throwback, a surrender, a retreat to adolescence, when such fumblings seemed heroic and poetic.

Martha went home and told her good husband. I don't suppose she meant to, or wanted to. I think what she really wanted was for it not to have happened. The world is not full of betrayers, it is full of people with decent motives and a full desire to do right by those who know them and love them. This is a little-known truth, but I think it is a truth nonetheless. Empirically, from all the years of my work, I would attest to that. I know it is a miraculous conclusion, but there it is. We like to characterise humanity as savage, lustful, and basic, but that is to make strangers of everyone. We are not wolves, but lambs astonished in the margins of the fields by sunlight and summer. She lost her world, Martha. And I lost mine. No doubt it was well deserved. Whatever her husband suffered was not, and whatever Bet suffered I know for a certainty was not.

Because faithfulness is not a human question, but a divine one.

There I go again.

✤

And I wonder what Fr Gaunt would have made of that?

Fr Gaunt, so assiduous, so devoted to revealing Roseanne, her nature, her incriminating story.

The deposition is in the other room, and I am too tired to go and get it. I will see how much of it I can write down from memory. The events at the cemetery I have itemised. Then independence came, the imperial police were disbanded, increasing I must suppose the fears of Roseanne's father, then . . . I suppose, time passed. The sense of vulnerability decreased, increased? And Roseanne's father got a job in the selfsame cemetery. As this job was in the gift of the town council, it is difficult to understand why so tainted a man was given such a sinecure, unless it was a job so lowly they thought it was a just humiliation. Indeed in due course he lost this job and was given the job of rat-catcher in Sligo, surely the ultimate insult to such a man. Fr Gaunt writes with possible wryness, 'As he had hunted down his fellow countrymen like rats, it might be said he was qualified for the job.' (Or words to that effect). But memories are both long and short in Ireland, like anywhere there are such wars. The civil war that followed caused further mayhem to the kindly instincts of young men in Sligo. Eventually time was found to turn attention to Roseanne's father, and his end was curious and protracted.

One night as he came home he was abducted on the corner of his street. He was drunk as was his custom, and his daughter was waiting as was hers. And I do think, and it is really clear from Fr Gaunt's account, that Roseanne adored her curious father. At any rate he was taken by a number of men and dragged off into the cemetery. She followed. Fr Gaunt thinks the plan was to take him up to the top of the round tower there in the graveyard and fling him out of the window at the top, or some such strategy.

His mouth was stuffed with white feathers no doubt to characterise his former work, though God knows I cannot see wherein his cowardice lay, misguided though he may have been in many respects. Then alas he was beaten with hammers, and an effort made to push him out the little window at the top of the tower. Roseanne herself was below looking up. Awful noises no doubt of horror from the small room at the top. And they did get him half way out the window, except his belly was too rounded by the years of beer, and would not admit him out into the night air. The hammers had not really killed him either, and as he roared, the feathers burst from his mouth. In a desperate rage they pulled him back in, and one of the men flung the bloody hammers out the window. And the feathers flew up and the hammers fell down, striking Roseanne as she stood gazing up a blow to the head, knocking her out cold.

Their less than theatrical solution to the question of his execution was to hang him in a derelict house nearby. I do not think in the atmosphere of the times he would have been much missed. No doubt he had acted against his own people. They were young men trying to avenge a great wrong, and young men are excitable and sometimes clumsy. No, not much missed, such a man.

Except by Roseanne.

How do I put all this to her? And this is just the end of the first section, there is another part that itemises her own later history. And in it a truly miserable and even horrifying accusation against her. The sins of the father are one thing, but the sins of the mother . . . Well. I must remember, I tell myself again, why I am engaged in this assessment. Be professional.

Keep my distance. After all, having been reared in England, albeit as an Irish child of some kind, I already have distance I believe from the strange chapters of this country's bewildering story.

And aren't all our histories tangled and almost foreign to ourselves, I mean, to our imaginations? My own mother's death, how cruel that was, in every way, and the only good thing I can think of that came out of it was, it 'inspired' me to read psychiatry at Durham, almost as an act of retrospective and hopeless insurance against the thing happening.

She lived in paradise across the river from Padstow, in a house envied and admired by the summer visitors, sitting in its trees on the very strand.

Of course, not my 'real' mother, not my 'real' father either.

Every year in their retirement the two of them went to the Lake District. My father climbed a mountain one morning without her. When he reached the summit, he gazed down on the valley below, there was a lake there, and he saw a tiny figure advance into the water. He was too far away to be heard. He knew instantly who it was.

Some three years after they adopted me, having given up the hope of having a child of their own, they did have a child of their own, my brother John. He was devoted to me. When we were fishing as kids in our local stream, he would stand for hours in his shorts in the river, bending over with a jamjar to catch minnows for my hooks.

When I was fourteen, we would cycle in the morning around the estuary to get our buses, myself to the Catholic Grammar School and himself to the prep school I had once attended. The bus stops were close to each other, but on opposite sides of the road, because his school was in the other direction. It was just a little country road outside the village, and the buses were those shining, chunky vehicles of those times.

One morning – and how everything becomes a little story –

once upon a time I might as well say – having heaved our bikes behind the hedge as we always did, I saw my bus coming along the road, and his bus coming the other way almost at the same distance. John, aged about ten, gave me a kiss and a hug and started off across the road. I found I was still holding his coat with my own, and called out to him, 'Hey, young fellow!' John stopped and turned about. 'Your coat!' I said, and made to throw it, and I saw John smiling, and he came back a few steps towards me. By this time the two buses were upon us, and whatever calculation the drivers had made for the little lad crossing the road, my shout to John had done a great mischief, and my bus drove through him, myself still holding the coat out to him.

That was the cause of my mother's sorrow.

Great sorrow. Beyond imagining. Her deepest heart destroyed. And yet there is something in it that eludes me. A true understanding.

Her life was rich in other ways. She lived in paradise. Indeed she left my poor father in paradise. Was I not also angry with her? That I wasn't in any way enough? Or my father? That she didn't endure? That is so unfair, I know. But, there is such a thing as endurance, it is a quality. I suppose what I am trying to write, while not being in any way disrespectful of my mother, is that Roseanne has endured, even though her life is all farthings.

I am a bit disgusted with myself for writing this.

And why am I crying?

I am astounded to read back over what I just wrote. I have made an anecdote out of the tragic death of my brother, for which, as is clear to me from the cooled syntax, I obviously blame myself. Even when I was at Durham, and we students used to practise analysis on each other, I never discussed this. I never even think about it, I have given it no valency at all in the last fifty years. It is a scandal in the halls of myself. I see that, clearly, staring at the bare facts. But how on earth would I start to look at it now, how would I ever heal myself? It is beyond my capacity. The only man I might have talked to about this is Amurdat Singh, long in his grave. Or my father, likewise. What he must have suffered, in his lovely English privacy.

But this is beside the point. I am clearly content to be beyond help. It is disgusting. I am not only crying now, for the record, but trembling also.

Of course Roseanne's life spans everything, she is as much as we can know of our world, the last hundred years of it. She should be a place of pilgrimage and a national icon. But she lives nowhere and is nothing. She has no family and almost no nation. A Presbyterian woman. It is sometimes forgotten the effort that was made in the twenties to include all shades of opinion in the first Irish senate, but it was an effort that soon lost heart. Our first president was a Protestant which was a beautiful and poetic gesture. The fact is, we are missing so many threads in our story that the tapestry of Irish life cannot but fall apart. There is nothing to hold it together. The first breath of wind, the next huge war that touches on us, will blow us to the Azores. Roseanne is just a bit of paper blowing on the edge of the wasteland.

And I realise I have become a little too much engaged with her. Perhaps I am obsessed. Not only can I not get her story from herself, I have a version of her life that I think she would reject. I have a dozen other souls to attend to, to listen to, to see if they can be placed back in the 'community'. By God, this place is to be dismantled, dispersed, I have much to do, much to do.

But every day I feel compelled to go up to her room, often I hurry, as if there is an urgency, like at the end of that old film, *Brief Encounter*. As if, should I delay, she will not be there. As indeed she may not.

Without Bet it is impossible for me to live. Now I must learn to do that.

Perhaps I am using Roseanne as a means to that, attending someone I admire and yet at the same time have power over? I must interrogate my own motives now in everything, because I fear there has not been much in the way of justice brought to her in the past, leaving aside the seriousness of the allegation, or perhaps rumour is a better word, against her. Although she is buried here to some degree, she is not Saddam in his terrible hidey hole, she is not to be pulled from it and her teeth examined like a horse (although note to myself, her teeth should be attended to, I noticed a lot of blackness in her mouth). Her teeth examined, her body deloused, disgraced, dispatched.

CHAPTER SIXTEEN

Roseannne's Testimony of Herself

Dr Grene was in just a little while back. As he came into my room he happened to tread on the loose floorboard where I hide these pages, which gave an unmerciful squeak, just like a mouse when the bar of the mousetrap whips down, and gave me a fright. But no, Dr Grene was paying no heed to anything, even to me. He sat in my old chair and said nothing. The small light from the window barely illuminated his face. From my vantage in the bed, he was all profile. He acted really as if he were alone, now and then heaving great sighs that I don't think he was aware of. They were unselfconscious sighs. I let him be. It was nice to have him in the room, without questions. Anyway, I had my own thoughts to 'entertain' me. It is as well our thoughts are silent, closed, unread.

Why then am I writing this?

Eventually, just as I thought he was going, like those detectives in the old films, he turned about at the door and looked at me and smiled.

'Do you remember Fr Garvey?' he said.

'Fr Garvey?'

'Yes, he used to be the chaplain here. About twenty years ago.'

'Was he the little man with the hairs in his nose?'

'Well, I don't remember the hairs. I was sitting there, and I just remembered, you didn't like him coming to see you. I don't know why I suddenly remembered that. Was there any reason for that?'

'Oh,' I said. 'No. It's just that I don't like the religious.'

'The religious? You mean, people that believe?'

'No, no, priests, and nuns, and such.'

'And is there any reason for that?'

'They are so certain about things, and I am not. It's not because I am Presbyterian. I don't like holy people. He was very kind, Fr Garvey. He said he completely understood,' I said, as indeed he had.

He lingered there in the door. Was he wanting to say something else? I think so. But he didn't, he nodded his head a few times.

'You don't mind doctors, I hope?' he said.

'No,' I said. 'I don't mind doctors at all.'

And he laughed, and went out.

Fred Astaire. Not a handsome man. He said himself he couldn't sing. He was balding his whole life. He danced like a cheetah runs, with the grace of the first creation. I mean, that first week. On one of those days God created Fred Astaire. Saturday maybe, since that was the day for the pictures. When you saw Fred you felt better about everything. He was a cure. He was bottled in the films and all around the earth, from Castlebar to Cairo, he healed the halt and the blind. That's the gospel truth. St Fred. Fred the Redeemer.

I could have been praying to him that time.

At the bottom of the mountain I picked a nice smooth stone from the rainy path. It is an old custom to carry up a stone to

186

put on the cairn above. Oh but, yes, I was in a state. Not from the climb, that was going to be nothing to me that time. No, because my head was 'in a whirl' as the bodice-rippers used to say. And I can't say why exactly, only that I knew there was something amiss in what I was doing. The day was absolutely peaceful, absolutely calm, the sky ripped open by scars of blue across the expanse of clouds, but my mood belonged to some other sort of day. When the tempests poured over Knocknarea and flooded down in invisible armies and extravagant dragons onto Strandhill, having it out there between the village houses and the sea. I was bare-armed there as I stooped to pick a stone, even in my unease careful to choose a decent one, bare-armed and bare-hearted.

If my father had his fate I also had my fate I suppose.

Dear reader, I ask for your protection, because I am afraid now. My old frame is actually trembling. It is all so long ago and I am still afraid. It is all so long ago and yet I am stooping still, and feel the stone in my fingers as if it is still then. How is that? Would that I felt that same vigour now, climbing the mountain with so fierce a step. Climbing, climbing, fiercely, fiercely. Perhaps I even feel a shadow of that. My limbs with such heat in them, my skin as smooth as metal, youth unregarded and unprized in me. Why did I know so little? Why do I know so little now? Roseanne, Roseanne, if I called to you now, my own self calling to my own self, would you hear me? And if you could hear me, would you heed me?

About half way up the mountain there was a little crowd of people coming down, I could hear them laughing, and now and then a little rock came speeding down the path. Then they were upon me, all gabardine coats, Trilby hats, scarves, and more laughter. It was one of the better sets in Sligo, and I even knew one of the women, because she had often come into the Café Cairo. I even remembered her habitual order and seemingly so did she.

'Hello, hello!' she said. 'Cocoa and a cherry bun, please!'

I laughed. She certainly meant nothing demeaning by it. Her companions looked at me with mild interest, prepared to be friendly if the woman so willed it. She didn't quite introduce me. But in a quiet voice, she said:

'I hear you got married,' she said. 'To our wonderful man at the Plaza. Many congratulations.'

This was nice of her, because the marriage had not exactly been the talk of the town, or if it was, not the nice talk of the town. Let's put it that way. In fact, I am sure it caused a relatively lowscale breeze of scandal, as most things out of the way did in Sligo. It was a very small town under the rain.

'Well, it's good to see you. Have a nice climb. Cheerio.'

And with that slight Englishism she was gone, the plummeting path pulling her away, the hats and scarves sinking quickly down the mountain. And the laughter. I could hear the woman talking in her pleasant voice, maybe filling them in, maybe remarking on the fact that Tom was not with me, I don't know. But it didn't bolster me much in my task.

What was my task? I didn't know. Why was I climbing Knocknarea at the bidding of a man irregular in the recent civil war and maybe just as irregular in his life? A jailbird that was digging Sligo ditches. Who as far as I knew was unmarried and walking out with no one. I knew what it was and how it looked, but I didn't know what drove me up that mountain. It was maybe a sort of infinite curiosity rising out of my love for my father. Needing to be brought again close to his memory, or any memory of him that seemed to make him more present, even the events of that miserable night in the cemetery – both miserable nights.

At the summit there was no one at first sight, except maybe

the ancient bones of Queen Maeve under her burden of a million small stones. From far away in the lower fields, by the sea of Strandhill, her cairn looked distinctive but small. Only when I walked up to it on my tired legs did I realise what an enormous thing it was, the labour of a hundred men, gathering from the mountain long ago the strange harvest of fist-sized stone, starting maybe with the queen under a few carefully laid slabs, and slowly, like single turves added to a turf stack, like single events added to an epic story, making the great mound for her to sleep under. I say sleep, but I mean moulder, diminish, vanish into the hill, creeping down in the moisture underground, feeding little diamonds and glints of heather and moss. For a moment I thought I could hear music, a swell of old American jazz, but it was only the bleary wind staggering over the summit. And in the music I heard my name.

'Roseanne!'

I looked around and could see no one.

'Roseanne, Roseanne!'

Now the old childhood fear got a hold of me, as if I might be hearing a voice from the next world, as if the banshee herself might be sitting atop the cairn with her last strands of dusty hair and her hollow cheeks, wanting to add me to the underworld. No, but it wasn't a woman's voice, but a man's, and now as I looked a figure rose from a little enclosure of stones, in black clothes, black hair and a whitened face.

'There you are,' said John Lavelle.

I had taken the time from the clock in the everything shop down in Strandhill village, but I still thought it an unlikely success to have met him here on the barest of information. Sunday at three. If it had been a great necessity, if it had been contingents of an army meeting to overwhelm the enemy by stealth, it might not have worked out so neatly. But fate it would seem is a perfect strategist and will work miracles of timing to assist our destruction.

I walked down to him where he stood. I think I had a great sympathy for him, I think that was it, he having lost his brother in such a terrible fashion. He was like a piece of the history of my childhood that I could not sever myself from. He had an importance whose nature I could not really fathom. It was a sort of dire respect, for him who was only a ditch-digger maybe, but nevertheless for me had an heroic aspect, the prince in beggar's clothing.

He was standing in what looked like a little bare bed of stones. One time it might have been roofed with a slab that had long ago fallen or been pulled sideways.

'I was lying in here,' he said. 'It makes a lovely suntrap. Feel my shirt.'

And he held out the black front of his shirt. When I put a hand on it briefly it was quite warm.

'That's what the sunlight will do in Ireland,' he said, 'given half a chance.'

Then we had nothing to say it seemed for a few moments. My heart was pounding under my ribs, I was afraid he would hear it. Oh, it wasn't love for him. It was love of my poor father. To be close to a man who was close to my father. The awful, dangerous, inexplicable stupidity of it.

I suddenly saw it. I suddenly thought, Tom has married a mad woman. It is a thought that haunted me many many times since. But I am nearly proud to say that it was I myself first had that thought.

I could not resist the lure of the river. The open sea could not keep me. The salmon lays her eggs on the shingle of the last narrow reaches of her home river, where the water first trickles from the earth. Mysterious world, mysteries upon mysteries, queens in stones, rivers gathering underground.

'Do you know what it is, Roseanne?' he said, after a while. 'You are the very spit of my wife.'

'Your wife, John Lavelle?' I said, suddenly angry.

'My wife, yes. You look like her, or maybe your face has taken the place of hers in my memory.'

'And where is your wife then?'

'She's on the North Island of the Inishkeas. In '21 a few of the island lads burned down the police barracks. I don't know why, because there was no polis in it. So the Black and Tans came out in a boat to see what they could see by way of revenge. My twins were only new born that time. My wife Kitty was standing at the door of our house, holding the two boys, one in each arm, to "air" them as we say in Irish. The Tans who were a good way off decided to take a few pot shots at her. She was shot through the head, and another bullet killed Michael a'Bhilli, and Seanín fell from his mother's arm, and struck his head on the threshold stone.'

He was speaking very quietly and as if fearfully now. I gripped his sleeve.

'I'm sorry,' I said.

'Well, I have Seanín still, he's fifteen now. He's not just right in the head, you know, after his fall. A little bit strange. He's a fellow that likes to stand out on the margin of things, looking in quietly. His mother's people are rearing him, and so he has his mother's name, you know the fine old island name of Keane. But he likes to talk to me. I told him the last time I was home about you, and he asked me a hundred questions. And I said to him if anything happened to me, he was to look out for you, and he said he would, although I don't think he understood the half of what I was saying, nor even knows where Sligo is.'

'Why would you tell him to do that, John Lavelle?' I said.

'I don't know. Only that . . .'

'Only that what?'

'That I don't know what's going to happen to me now. I think I must go for the gun again. I haven't taken much to the road digging. That's one reason, and it frightens me to death.

The other reason might be, that I never saw anyone as lovely as you only except Kitty.'

'You're nearly a stranger. There's nothing of normal things in this.'

'There it is,' he said. 'A stranger. It's a country composed entirely of strangers then. You are right. But all the same what do people say when they feel like I do? *I love you*, they say, I suppose.'

We had been there a good while and now I heard other voices, new voices coming up from below. I gathered my self and my wits, and almost bolted for the path. There was no way down the mountain except by that course, though my first thought was to strike out across the heather and scree eastwards, but at the same time I knew there was a great cliff below Knocknarea, and I might be many hours trying to get round it, and onto a road. So many hours that Tom might finally wonder what was amiss with me, and even raise the country to find me. Such were my thoughts as the wind, stiffened now as it came on towards teatime, threw my hair forward across my face, and the little group came into view below.

It was a group of men in black coats and cassocks. A little party of priests out on a Sunday walk. Wasn't there a touch of blasphemy in that? Would that their piety and their prayers and their rules had kept them close in the town. But here they were, with their different laughter, and their murmuring voices. I looked back wildly to see where John Lavelle might be. Oh, he was standing right behind me, like a component of the wind itself.

'Go back away!' I said. 'Can't you hide yourself? I can't be seen up here with you!'

'Why not?' he said.

'Why not? Are you mad? Are you as mad as me? Go and hide yourself in those rocks.'

But it was too late. Of course it was. The gaggle of holy men was upon us, all smiles and good days, and raising of the hats. Except for one face, whipped red by the exertion and the wind, which looked at me with a blank, heart-hurting look. It was Fr Gaunt.

When I got back down to our little house in Strandhill, Tom was not there because he had gone into Sligo to greet 'the General' at the station, in preparation for a parade along Wine Street, to highlight as Tom put it the great enthusiasm for General O'Duffy's movement in the town. He had begged me to put on a blue blouse that Old Tom had been inveigled into stitching up for me, but the truth was that part of Tom frightened me. I suppose in the original Café Cairo, in Cairo itself – and I do not think nice Mrs Prunty was ever there – there was a lot of use of the hubble bubble, not to mention the famous hootchie cootchie girls doing their belly dance. I had never seen a man with opium in him, but I wondered was it something like the almost oriental glow in Tom's face when he spoke of the General, and Corporatism (whatever that was, I'm not sure he really knew himself), and getting back at the 'traitor de Valera', and the 'true start of Ireland's glory', and all the rest of the jangling song of those times. When they had marched in Sligo, they were all coming out to Strandhill for a rally in the Plaza. Not the least of my residual dread after meeting John Lavelle was the obvious fact that a man like him was in effect the 'enemy' of the General's movement. I don't know why that bothered me so much, but it did. I stood in our little sitting room, bare as a tenement but clean and nice, and shivered in my summer dress. I shivered, and shivered all the more when I heard the sound of engines in the distance, a little roaring noise that grew and grew, till I ran to the window and looked out and saw the stream of Fords and the like going by, Tom at the front driving his own vehicle, with a very important-looking creature altogether in the seat beside him, in one of those folding caps and a hooked nose not unlike Tom's brother Jack's. There were dozens and dozens of surging motors, all with their metallic music, the white dust of the narrow seaside road rising from the wheels like the Sahara itself. And all the faces, men and women, alight above the blue blouses and shirts, with that strange glow, just a few fields east of happiness – the picture of impossible optimism, like advertisements in the odd American magazine that reached us in that far-off world of Sligo, sent to relatives wrapped up with the coveted Yankee dollars.

And I had the curious sensation of looking out on someone else's world, someone else's Tom, someone else's Sligo. Like I wasn't going to be there very long, and had not been there long enough, or even had never been there. Like a ghost to myself and certainly not for the first time.

I went to bed and lay in the cool sheets and tried to be calm. I tried to be myself, and yet could not really locate that person. Roseanne. She was maybe slipping away from me. Perhaps had done so long ago. In the war of independence it wasn't just soldiers and policemen had to be killed, even those stupid fellas that had gone out to the Great War without thinking what they were doing, but also tinkers and tramps and the like. People that were dirtying up the edges of things, those people that stood at the edges of photographs of nice places and in certain people's eyes were starting to stink them up. When there were bombs dropped on Belfast by the Germans in that coming war, tens of thousands of people fled out into the countryside, thousands of them from the Belfast slums, and no one wanted them in their houses, because they were a forgotten race of savages, so poor they had never seen a lavatory, and would eat nothing but tea and bread. They pissed on the floors of decent houses. It was all the people that were hidden till the Germans bombed them out of it, burned them out. Like my father's poor rats. I was lying in a bed of clean sheets, but I felt like them. Like them, I wasn't grateful enough, and had fouled my own nest. I knew that in the eyes of Tom's friends outside, gathered in the Plaza, if they knew everything about me, they would want to – I don't know, extinguish me, judge me, put me outside the frame of the photographs of life. The delightful landscapes of ordinary life. Of course I knew nothing of Germans then, except the General was a man like they had in Italy, in Germany, in Finland those times, mighty noisy men that wanted to fire everyone up and have them all clean and fit and pure, so that they could go out in a great horde and extinguish the lousy, the ragged, the morally unsound. Somewhere in my heart, in the passport of my heart, if you opened it, you would see my real face – unwashed, seared by fire, terrified, ungrateful, diseased, and dumb.

I awoke in the small hours, nudged into wakefulness by little sounds of Tom in the room. There was a huge moon over Knocknarea, the cairn visible as if in the very sunlight. I was still caught in a dream, and just for a moment thought I saw a figure atop the cairn, in black clothes, with a great fold of bright wings behind him. But of course it was far too far away for that.

'Are you awake, pet?' said Tom, and when I looked at him, he was struggling out of his braces.

'You have blood on your face,' I said, sitting up.

'I have blood all over my blessed shirt,' he said, 'although you can barely see, what with the blue.'

'My God,' I said, 'whatever happened, Tom?'

'Nothing at all. We had a bit of resistance from the guards in Sligo. We were marching as good as gold, when out from Quay Street comes a fierce little muster of lads, fellas brought in from Collooney I suppose, because they were not regular Sligo guards. And one of them gave me such a swipe with a stick, I tell you, it hurt like the bejaysus. And the General starts roaring at them, and the guards roaring back, "You have no permit to march in Sligo!" And the General the head of the same guards only a few years ago. Well. There was such shouting and frothing about generally. So we were very glad to get out to the hall, let me tell you. And didn't we have a great time then. Such a crowd you never saw.'

By this time he had his nice striped pyjamas on and then he went to the washstand basin and vigorously flung water at his face, and wiped it off in the towel, and then threw himself into the bed beside me.

'What did you do?' he said. 'You ought to have come. It was great.'

'I went walking,' I said.

'Oh ho,' he said, 'did you? And why not?'

Then he put his left arm under my hand and held me close to him, and after a while, between the blood and moonlight, we went to sleep.

Dr Grene's Commonplace Book

There was absolute panic in the building yesterday. I must say I was almost encouraged by the level of response, because so often in the past there has been what felt like a cloud of inaction hanging over these old roofs. But the young lady who had been found upset and bloodstained had then disappeared. The ward nurse was terrified, because her sister had just been in, and given her a gift of a nice new dressing-gown. Nurse had noted the belt made of the same light material as the gown, but had not had the heart to remove it straight away. So she was tearing about the wards, asking everyone had they seen the poor unfortunate woman, and generally making the ancient patients stir for the first time in many years. In the end it was discovered not that she had hanged herself, but that she had gone down to front office in her dressing-gown, and signed herself out, as she has the perfect right to do under the new legislation. And had gone down to the main road and hitched a lift to the town, and from there boarded a bus to Leitrim, all of this still in the gown. It was like a magic coat, carrying her back to Leitrim. Her husband rang last night to tell us, and he was a very angry voice at the other end of the phone. He said the hospital was supposed to be a place of refuge. The head nurse spoke to him, and was very submissive, not in the style of the old matrons we used to have here. I don't know what resolution this will have, but it struck me as having all the qualities of a rescue. I wish the poor woman well and I am sorry we were of so little use to her, quite the opposite. And I am very glad the nurse's panic was unfounded.

This morning I went up to Mrs McNulty's – no, no, Roseanne's – room quite light-hearted. Of course, the position of the young woman is still perilous, but I am old enough now to put a premium on mere life.

The room had a little bit of sideways spring sunlight, that seemed to have crept in through the window-glass with an almost apologetic delicacy. A little square beam of it sat across Roseanne's face. Yes, she is very old. Sunlight as always the most brutal measurer of age, but also, the most faithful painter. I thought of the line from T. S. Eliot that we learned at school in England,

> My life is like a feather on the back of my hand,
> Waiting for the death wind.

It is spoken by Simeon, the man who wished to live long enough to see the newborn Messiah. I do not think Roseanne is waiting for that. I thought also of those self-portraits of Rembrandt van Rijn, so faithfully faithless to the idea of our own looks that we carry as an antidote against remorse. How we decide not to allow the fact that our skin is dropping down our jaws and coming away underneath our chins like plaster detaching from its laths in an old-fashioned ceiling.

Her skin is so thin you can see the veins and whatnot, like roads, rivers, towns, and monuments on a map. Something stretched for purposes of writing on it. No monk however would have risked the nib of a pen on such thin parchment. And again I thought, how beautiful she must have been, if she is so oddly beautiful now at one hundred years old. Good bones, as my father used to say, as if, growing old himself and those he knew growing old around him, he knew the value of them.

She has a rash on one side of her face though, quite red and 'angry' as they say, and I thought her tongue was rather in the way of her talking in some way, like it was a little swollen at the root. I must get the medical doctor Mr Wynn to have a look at her. She may well need an antibiotic.

Whether she caught my mood or what, I don't know, she was very responsive, even revealing. She was at her ease in a curious way. Maybe it was happiness. I know she absolutely delights in the improvement of the weather, in the turning of the year. She puts a lot of faith in those daffodils along the avenue, planted there by some old grandee when this place was a great house and estate, in those old vanished days. With fearful delicacy on my own part, trying to take my cue from the sunlight, I finally broached the subject of her child. I say 'finally' as if I have successfully broached a thousand other subjects, or have been leading up to the child. But I had not. But the whole matter has been much on my mind, because of course, if what Fr Gaunt wrote is true, then the whole question of her state of mind and her long presence here and in Sligo is decidedly and probably permanently vexed. Speaking of Sligo, I have written again to ask if I may visit there sometime soon, and talk to the administrator, who it turns out is an old acquaintance, a man called Percival Quinn, I think the only Percy I have ever heard of in the present era, let alone met. It was he apparently who made the extra effort to dig out Fr Gaunt's deposition, and there may well be other files there that even Percy feels can't be communicated, but I don't know. We are like MI5 sometimes in this our profession of psychiatry. All information becomes sensitive, worrying, and vulnerable, even sometimes I think the mere time of day. However, I will follow my instincts.

Tonight there is total calm in the house. It is almost as eerie as the knocking was. But I am grateful. Human, alone, ageing, and grateful. Would it be out of place to write here, to write here directly to you, Bet, to say, I love you still, and am grateful?

Roseanne was so vulnerable, so admirable, so open in my meeting with her, I knew I could have asked her anything, pursued any topic, and probably got the truth, or what she believes is the truth. Well I knew it, my advantage, and if I had pressed it, I would have gained a great deal but, maybe, lost something. Today was the day she might have told me everything, and today was the day I opted myself for her silence, her privacy. Because it strikes me there is something greater than judgement. I think it is called mercy.

Roseanne's Testimony of Herself

Dr Grene came in, very upbeat, drew up his chair like he certainly meant business. I was so taken aback that I actually engaged in a certain amount of conversation.

'It is a lovely spring day,' he said, 'and I am emboldened to ask you again some of these wearying old questions that I am sure you wish I would stop asking. But I do feel there may be some gain in doing so. Just yesterday I heard something that makes me feel that nothing is impossible. That things that at first sight seem dark and intractable may actually be able to admit some light, some unexpected light.'

He talked like that for a while and finally reached the question. It was again about my father and I was content enough, for the second time, to tell him that my father was never in the police. I told him though that there was a police connection in the McNulty family.

'My husband's brother called Eneas was in the police. He joined them in about 1919, which was not a good time to seek employment there,' I said, or words to that effect.

'Ah,' said Dr Grene, 'so you think that may be how the police connection was – was mooted?'

'I don't know,' I said. 'Are the daffodils out yet on the old avenue?'

'They are nearly out, they are threatening to come out,' he said. 'They may be fearful of a last frost.'

'The frost is nothing to the daffodils,' I said. 'Like the heather, they can bloom in the snow.'

'Yes,' he said, 'I believe you are right. Now, Roseanne, the second topic I thought I might raise with you is the topic of the child. I am reading in the little deposition I mentioned that there was a child. At some point.'

'Yes, yes, there was a child.'

Then I said nothing because what could I say. I am afraid I started to cry as quietly as I could.

'I don't mean to upset you,' he said, with great softness.

'I don't think you do,' I said. 'It is just that – looking back, it is all so –'

'Tragic?' he said.

'That is a big word. Very sad anyhow, it seems to me.'

He reached into his jacket pocket and pulled out a little folded paper handkerchief.

'Don't worry,' he said, 'I haven't used it.'

I took the useless little object gratefully. Why wouldn't he have used it, him with his own troubles so recently? I tried to imagine him sitting somewhere in his house, a place of course unknown to me. With his wife gone from him. Death as ruthless as any other lover, taking her away.

And I dabbed at my tears. I felt like Barbara Stanwyck in a stupid weepie, or at least Barbara Stanwyck when she was a hundred years old. Dr Grene was gazing at me with a face so miserable I laughed. Then he perked up at this and laughed too. Then the two of us were laughing, but very softly and quietly, like we didn't want anyone else to hear.

I must admit there are 'memories' in my head that are curious even to me. I would not like to have to say this to Dr Grene. Memory, I must suppose, if it is neglected becomes like a box room, or a lumber room in an old house, the contents jumbled about, maybe not only from neglect but also from too much haphazard searching in them, and things to boot thrown in that don't belong there. I certainly suspect – well, I don't know what I certainly suspect. It makes me a little dizzy to contemplate the possibility that everything I remember may not be – may not be *real*, I suppose. There was so much turmoil at that time that – that what? I took refuge in other impossible histories, in dreams, in fantasies? I don't know.

But if I put my faith in certain memories, perhaps they will serve as stepping stones, and I will cross the torrent of 'times past', without being plunged entirely into it.

They say the old at least have their memories. I am not so sure this is always a good thing. I am trying to be faithful to what is in my head. I hope it is trying also to be as faithful to me.

It was the simplest thing in the world. He just never came home. For a whole day I waited. I cooked the hash as I had promised him in the morning, because he had a weakness for foods mashed up and reheated, even though it was his brother Jack was the navy man. It is a great favourite with sailors and soldiers, as my own father might attest. But the food cooled again under its cover. Night closed over Knocknarea, over Sligo Bay, over Ben Bulben, where John Lavelle's brother Willie had been murdered. On the upper slopes, in the privacy of the thinner air and the heather. Shot in the heart, was it, or the head, after surrendering. John Lavelle saw that from his hiding place. His own brother. The brothers of Ireland. John and Willie, Jack and Tom and Eneas.

I knew immediately something was terribly wrong, but you can know that and not allow the thought in your head, at the front of your head. It dances around at the back, where it can't be controlled. But the front of the head is where the pain begins.

I sat there I must confess in a swelter of love for my husband. It was his strange efficiency, even his purposeful stride along the pavements of Sligo. His waistcoats, his gaberdine, or his trenchcoat with the four linings, his boots with the patented double sole, that would never need mending (of course they did). His beaming face and the ruddy signs of health in his cheeks, and his cigarette on the loll in his mouth, the same brand his brother smoked, 'Army Club Sandhurst'. And his musicality and his confidence, the way he was always up in the world, and ready for it. And that he was not only ready for it, he was going to conquer it, conquer Sligo and all points west and east, 'from Portugal to the Sea' as the old saying went, although in truth that is a nonsensical saying. Tom McNulty, a man that had every right to life because he honoured it so in the enjoyment of it.

Oh dear, oh dear, I sat there. I am sitting there still.

I am old enough to know that time passing is just a trick, a convenience. Everything is always there, still unfolding, still happening. The past, the present, and the future, in the noggin eternally, like brushes, combs and ribbons in a handbag.

He just didn't come back.

Out there in Strandhill, on nights there were no dances, when only the odd car was heard coming into the village above, there was an owl that used to call. I think it lived on the backland under Knocknarea, where the land falls and becomes a sort of valley to the sea. The owl lived close enough for his one repeated note to come clearly over the scrubby fields and the wastelands. Calling and calling, as if to say what I don't know. Do creatures that wake and hunt in the night, call to their possible mate in the night? I suppose they must.

My own heart was also calling, signalling out into that difficult human world. For Tom to come home, to *come home*.

CHAPTER SEVENTEEN

Two nights later I think I must have been still sitting there. Although this is hardly possible. Had I not eaten, gone out to the toilet at the back of the hut, stretched my legs? I can't remember. Or rather, I only remember the sitting there, and then, just as the twilight came down on Strandhill, calming everything, even the colours of the grass, that night breeze hurrying in from the bay, making my roses rustle at the window-glass, or at least the new buds, tap tap tap, like Gene Krupa himself starting a little something on the drums. And then, as if on cue, I heard coming up the road and around the corner and in the door the strains of 'Honeysuckle Rose', just a few notes at first, and then I heard Harry B. hit the drums, and then the clarinet going, which I supposed was Tom, and some-one on the piano, obviously not myself, and by the rusty stabs he was making I guessed it was maybe Old Tom himself, and that was probably Dixie Kielty on the rhythm guitar he loved like a child, oh, and they were unfolding it, stem by stem and bloom by bloom, just like honeysuckle itself, though that was a bloom for later in the year in those parts.

Of course then I knew it was Saturday. That was something to get my bearings from.

By Jiminy though that is a great song for the guitar solo.

'Honeysuckle Rose'. Whap whap whap go the drums and up and down and round the clock go the chords of the guitar. You can drive even the hill boys of Sligo half mad with that song. A dead man would dance to it. A dumb man would cheer the solos.

It was said, at least Tom told me, that Benny Goodman would give a good twenty minutes to that song, at dances. I could well believe it. You could play it all day and still have things to say with it. That was it, you see, it was a speaking song. Even without someone singing the words.

So.

So, I went over there. It was the strangest darkest feeling to do that. To put on what I had of finery there, my best dress, hurriedly dab on some 'slap', comb my hair, fix it, shove on my stage shoes, and all the while breathing in and out a little heavily, then stepping out into the breeze, feeling the chill in it, so that my breast seemed to shrug minutely. But I didn't care about that.

Because I thought it was still possible everything was all right. Why did I think that? Because I had not heard otherwise. I was in the middle of a mystery.

It was early for the dance but there were cars coming out from Sligo already, their big beams like big shovels shovelling the rutted road. Expectant faces in the cars, and lads standing on the running boards now and then. It was a happy sight, the happiest sight in Sligo.

I was feeling more and more like a ghost the nearer I came to the Plaza. Now the Plaza used to be just a holiday house, and they built the hall on at the back, so the front looked just like an ordinary dwelling, except concreted over, erased somehow. There was a nice flag fluttering above the roof, with P-L-A-Z-A written on it. There wasn't much in the way of lights, but who needed lights, when the building was the Mecca of everyone's weekday dreams and thoughts. You could slave all week in a rotten job in the town, but as long as you had the Plaza . . . It was bigger than religion, I can tell you, the dancing. It was a religion. To be denied the dancing would have been like what's-it, excommunication, to be not allowed the sacraments, like the IRA men in the civil war.

Boys like John Lavelle of course.

'Honeysuckle Rose'. Now the band let that be and began to play 'The Man I Love', which as the world and his brother knows is a slower tune, and I was thinking it wasn't such a good choice for so early in the night. Ever the band member. Every tune is right in the right moment. Some tunes only rarely find their moment, like some ould Christmas song, or slushy old ballads in the deeps of winter when everyone wants to be melancholy. 'The Man I Love' is for the second last dance, or thereabouts, when everyone is weary but happy, and there is a shine on everything, faces, arms, instruments, hearts.

When I entered the hall there were only a few souls dancing. I had been right, it was much too early for that song. But the band all the same had a late-night look to them. Old Tom was playing the solo bit near the start, and then his son was cutting in with the clarinet. It was actually shocking. Maybe the people there noticed also that Tom, my Tom, seemed a little drunk. He was certainly swaying a bit, but he held the music just fine, until suddenly he seemed to stall, and took the beak out of his mouth. The band played the song to the nearest ending, and stopped as well. Their faces looked round at Tom, to see what he wanted to do. Tom placed his instrument down with his usual care, stepped down off the stage, and swayed away backstage, to where our dressing room was. I didn't know whether he had even seen me.

I was going to go in there too. There was only the dancefloor between me and the old curtains that hung across the door. I stepped forward, full of intent, but suddenly there was Jack at my side, his face very stern in the turning shadows.

'What do you want, Roseanne?' he said, the coldest I had ever heard him, and he could be an arctic man.

'What do I want?'

It was funny, I had been so silent for two or three days that my voice almost cracked when I spoke, gghh, like a needle dropped on a record.

I don't suppose anyone was looking at me. We must have seemed like two old friends chatting, as a thousand old friends did there on a Saturday night. What would friendship have done without the Plaza, let alone love?

My stomach was probably empty, but that didn't stop my body from trying to throw up. It was a reaction to the ice in Jack's words. It told me more than any little speech of his could, no doubt the little speech I was about to hear. It wasn't the voice of the executioner, like that Englishman Pierrepoint the Free State government brought over in the forties to hang IRA men, but it was the voice of the judge, announcing my execution. How many murderers and felons already know by the very look on the judge's face, never mind the black cloth shortly put on his head, their fate, even though every fibre of their being cries out against the knowledge, and hope is brought right to the very brink of irrevocable words. The patient staring up into the face of the surgeon. Death sentence. What Eneas McNulty got for his being in the police. Death sentence.

'What do you want, Roseanne?'

'What do I want?'

Then that dry retching. Then people were looking at me. Probably thought I had downed a half bottle of gin too quick, or the like, like nervous dancers did, or dodgy customers as Tom called them. There was nothing to show for my retching, but that didn't stop my grievous embarrassment. Close on the heels of which was a deep deep feeling of something, maybe remorse, maybe self-horror, that bored down into me.

Jack hung back from me as if indeed I were a cliff, or something dangerous that might crumble at the edge, and send him plummeting to his death. The cliffs of Mohar, Dun Aengus.

'Jack, Jack,' I said, but meaning what, I didn't know.

'What's going on with you?' he said. 'What's going on with you?'

'Me? I don't know. I feel sick.'

'No, not now, not fucking now, Roseanne. What have ya been up to?'

'Why, what's they saying I was up to?'

Now, that didn't even sound like English to me. What's they saying. Like some old Black song from the Southern States.

But Jack didn't say.

'Can I go back and see Tom?' I said.

'Tom doesn't want to see you.'

'Of course he does, Jack, he's my husband.'

'Well, Roseanne, we'll have to see about that.'

'What do you mean, Jack?'

Then suddenly he wasn't icy any more. Maybe he remembered other days, I don't know. Maybe he remembered I was always friendly to him, and respectful of his achievements. I liked Jack, God knows. I liked his sternness and his queer quick gaiety now and then, when he would suddenly shake out his legs, and do what he called an African dance. At a party as may be, just all of a sudden, no warning, an enormous gaiety that would seem to get a hold of him and sweep him all the way to Nigeria. I liked him, with his nice coats and his even nicer hats, his thin gold watchchain, his car that was always the best car in Sligo, bar the big saloons of the toffs.

'Lookit, Roseanne,' he said. 'It's all very complicated. There's a book opened for you up at the shop in Strandhill. You won't starve.'

'What?'

'You won't starve,' he said.

'Look,' I said, 'there's no reason for me not talking to Tom. Just to have a word. This is what I came down to do. I don't expect to – to play in the band, for God's sake.'

This was not very logical, and I do believe I shouted the last few words. This was not a good move with Jack, who was so extremely selfconscious, and hated a scene above all else. I don't suppose his precious Galway girl ever made a scene. Nevertheless Jack kept his cool, and came a few inches closer to me.

'Roseanne, I've always been a friend to you. Trust me now, and go back to the house. I'll be in touch. This whole thing may blow over yet. Just calm down and go back to the house. Go on, Roseanne. The mother has spoken on this matter and there's no going against the mother.'

'The mother?'

'Yes, yes, the mother.'

'And what in the name of God does she say?'

'Roseanne,' he said, fiercely, quietly, 'there's things about the mother you don't understand. There's things about her I don't understand. She's had her own vicissitudes when she was a child. The result is, she knows her own mind.'

'Vicissitudes? What vicissitudes?'

He was almost hissing now when he spoke, seemingly in a ferment not to be heard, but also, to impress something on me that was maybe impossible to impress.

'Old stuff. She's determined that Tom will make good, because, because – ould reasons, ould reasons.'

'You're talking like a lunatic,' I shouted. I might have burned him with a burning stick.

'But look, but look, the whole thing may blow over,' he said.

Somehow in my heart of hearts I knew if I turned about and left that dancehall that 'the whole thing' would most certainly not blow over. There is a moment to speak to a topic, just like there is a moment for every song, no matter how rare. This was a rare moment in a life and I knew that if I could just see Tom, or rather, just let him see me, the woman he loved so greatly, desired, revered and loved, everything would be all right, eventually.

But Jack was barring my way. No doubt about it. He was standing just a little sideways to me, like a salmon fisherman about to cast out across the stream, leaning his weight on his left foot.

Jack wasn't a bastard, he wasn't a cruel man. But in that instance he was a brother, not a brother-in-law.

He was also a mighty big obstacle. I tried to surge forward, to go past him by mere force of will, a substance much softer than he was trying to go through him. He was hardened by his sojourns in Africa, it was like hitting a tree, he put his arms around me as I tried to break away down the hall, and I was screaming, screaming for Tom, for mercy, for God. His arms closed around my waist, closed tight tight around, hamma-hamma tight, to use the words he had learned in Africa, the pidgin English he liked to mimic and mock, he drew me to him, so that my bottom was fastened into his lap, docked there, held tight, fast, impossible to get away, like a weird love embrace.

'Roseanne, Roseanne,' he said. 'Will you whisht, woman, whisht.'

Myself roaring and caterwauling.

That's how much I loved Tom and my life with Tom. That's how much I baulked at and hated the future.

Back in the corrugated-iron hut I didn't know what to do with myself. I went to bed to sleep but there was no sleep. A cold creeping feeling came into my brain, lending a physical pain, as if someone were opening the back of my grey matter with the sharp sharp blade of a tin opener. Hamma-hamma sharp.

There are some sufferings that we seem as a creature to forget, or we would never survive as a creature among all the other creatures. The pain of childbirth is said to be one, but I cannot agree there. And the pain of whatever had happened to me is certainly not one either. Even as a sere old crone in this room I can still remember it. Still feel a shadow of it. It is a pain that removes all other things except itself, so that the young woman lying there in her marriage bed was just all pain, all suffering. I was drenched in a strange sweat. The chief part of the pain was caused by the enormous panic that nothing would ever arrive, no circus, Yankee cavalry, human agency, to relieve it. That I would always be sweltering in it.

And yet I suppose it was of no importance. In that I was of no account in the world, in a time of dark suffering much greater than mine, if the ordinary history of the world is to be believed. This comforts me to think of now, curiously enough, but not then. What would have comforted that writhing woman in a lost bed in the lost land of Strandhill I do not know. If I were a horse they would have shot me out of mercy.

It is no small thing to shoot a person, yet in those days it seemed to be considered a thing of small account. Generally, in the world. I know Tom was gone shortly with the General out to Spain to fight for Franco, and there was a lot of shooting there. They drove men and women to the edges of scenic abysses and shot them, and let them fall away into those fathomless places. The abyss really was both history and the future. They shot people into the ruin of their country, into the moil and the ruin, just like in Ireland. In the civil war we shot enough of each other to murder the new country in its cradle. Enough and more.

I am speaking for myself, as I see things now. I didn't know much about such things then. I had seen murder though, with my very eyes. And I had seen how murder could travel sideways and take other lives all unbeknownst. The very cleverness and spreadingness of murder.

Next morning it was an absurdly beautiful day. A sparrow had got into the house and was very dismayed and alarmed to see me when I came into the empty sitting room from the bedroom. I walked it into a corner, took its wild beating self into my hands, like a flying heart it seemed, brought it to the door which I had forgotten to close in my strange grief the night before, and walked out onto the porch, raised my arms, and released the little useless grey bird back into the sunshine.

As I did this, Jack McNulty and Fr Gaunt were coming up the road towards me.

✤

As priests felt in those times that they owned the new country, I suppose Fr Gaunt felt he also owned the iron hut, and at any rate he walked straight in, and chose a rickety chair, not speaking a word yet, Jack striding in after him, and myself nearly backing into a corner like the sparrow. But I did not think somehow they would gather me in their hands and let me go.

'Roseanne,' said Fr Gaunt.

'Yes, Father.'

'It's been a little while since we spoke last,' he said.

'Yes, a little while.'

'You've been through a few changes since, I suppose that is true to say. And how is your mother, I haven't seen her either this long time?'

Well, I didn't think that needed answering, it was him had wanted to commit her to the asylum, and anyway I couldn't have answered it even if I had wanted to. I didn't know how my mother was. I suppose that was evil of me not to know. But I didn't. I hoped she was all right, but I didn't know if she was. I thought I knew where she was, but I didn't know how she was.

My poor beautiful mad ruined mother.

And of course I started to cry. Not for myself strangely enough, though I am sure I could have, with capital and interest, but no, not for myself. For my mother? Who can really itemise the cause of our human tears?

But Fr Gaunt wasn't interested in my stupid crying.

'Em, Jack here wishes to represent a certain family angle on things, isn't that correct, Jack?'

'Well,' said Jack. 'We want to keep the party clean. We want to act the white man here. Everything has a solution, no matter

212

how knotted it has become. I believe this to be true. Often in Nigeria there have been problems that seemed insurmountable, but with a certain flair of application . . . Bridges over rivers that change their course every year. That sort of thing. Engineering has to meet all these problems.'

I stood there patiently enough and listened to Jack. Actually it probably qualified as the longest speech he had ever made to me, or at least in my presence, or my vague direction anyhow. He was looking very shaven, spruce, clean, his leather collar up, his hat set at a perfect angle. I knew from Tom that he had been drinking spectacularly for a few weeks past, but he didn't look at all unwell. He was engaged to be married to his Galway girl, and that, said Tom, had put him in a bit of a manly panic. He was going to marry her and bring her out to Africa with him. Tom had shown me pictures of Jack's bungalow in Nigeria, and Jack with groups of men, both white and black. Indeed I had been intrigued, enchanted maybe was the word, to see Jack in his nice open shirt and white trousers, with a cane, and in one picture there was a black man, maybe an official also, though not in an open shirt, but a full black suit, with waistcoat, and stiff collar and tie, in what degree of heat I did not know, but looking quite cool and confident. Then there was a picture of Jack with a crowd of nearly naked men, dark dark dark black, the lads maybe that had dug the canals there that Jack was building, long straight canals Tom had said, going off upcountry to bring the longed-for water to distant farms. Jack, the saviour of Nigeria, the bringer of water, the builder of bridges.

'Yes,' said Fr Gaunt. 'I am sure it is all fixable. I am sure it is. If we put our heads together.'

I had a not very relaxed vision of my head put near Fr Gaunt's severely cropped head and Jack's elegantly hatted head, but it dissolved in the floating motes of the sunlight that pierced the room.

'I love my husband,' I said, so suddenly it nearly made me jump. Why I said it to those two emissaries of the future puzzles me even now. Two men less likely to say it to, with any good result, I could not think of. It was like shaking the hands of the two poor soldiers requisitioned to attend to my execution. That was how it felt as soon as the words were out.

'Well,' said Fr Gaunt, almost eagerly, now that the subject was broached. 'That is all history now.'

I made a few little grunts then of consonants and vowels, my brain not really sure what words to use, but then got out the word:

'What?'

'I need some time in which to find the boundaries of this problem,' said Fr Gaunt. 'In that time I want you, Roseanne, to remain where you are, here in this hut, and when I am able to bring things to a resolution, I will be better able to inform you of your position, and then make arrangements for the future.'

'Tom has put the matter in Fr Gaunt's hands, Roseanne,' said Jack. 'He has the authority to speak in the matter.'

'Yes,' said Fr Gaunt. 'That is so.'

'I want to be with my husband,' I said, since it was true, and the only thing I could say without anger. Because rising up greater than the feeling of abject grief was a new anger, a sort of hungry wild anger, like a wolf in a fold of sheep.

'You should have thought of that before,' said Fr Gaunt, with a matching succinctness. 'A married woman –'

But he stopped. He either did not know what to say next, or did and chose not to, or did not want to, or could not bring himself to say the words. Jack actually cleared his throat like he was in a film at the Gaiety cinema, and shook his head, as if his hair were wet and needed shaking. Fr Gaunt looked suddenly grievously, gravely embarrassed, just as he had that night long ago when Willie Lavelle's body lay so barely, so ruined, in my father's temple. I suspected what he was thinking. This was the second time I had brought him into a situation that caused him what? Displeasure, disquiet. Displeasure and disquiet at the nature of woman? Who knows? But suddenly I was looking at him with eyes of unexpected contempt. If my gaze had been made of flames it would have turned him to cinders. I knew his power, which in that situation was absolute, and it seemed to me in that moment that I knew his nature. Small, self-believing to every border, north, south, east, and west, and lethal.

'Well,' said Fr Gaunt, 'I think we have done our business here, Jack. You must stay where you are, Roseanne, get your groceries from the shop every week, and be content with your own company. You have nothing to fear, except your own self.'

I stood there. I am content to say that caught as I was, without rescuers as I was in that moment, there was a fierce, dark fury moving through me, wave upon wave, like the sea itself, that was bizarrely a comfort. My face maybe showing only a shadow of it, as faces will.

The two dark-suited men went out into the sunlight. Dark suits, dark coats, dark hats trying to lighten in the flood of seaside blues, yellows, greens.

Rage, dark rage, lightened by nothing.

But a raging woman all alone in a tin hut is a small thing, as I said before.

The real comfort is that the history of the world contains so much grief that my small griefs are edged out, and are only cinders at the borders of the fire. I am saying this again because I want it to be true.

Though one mind at a pitch of suffering seems also to fill the world. But this is an illusion.

I had seen, with my own eyes, much worse things than had befallen me. With my own eyes. And yet that night, alone and unfathomably angry, I screamed and screamed in the hut as if I was the only hurting dog in the whole world, no doubt causing horror and disquiet to any passing person. I screamed and I squawked. I beat my breast till there were bruises there the next morning so that my breast looked like a map of hell, a map of nowhere, or as if the words of Jack McNulty and Fr Gaunt had actually burned me.

And whatever my life had been up to that day, it was another life after that. And that is the gospel truth.

PART THREE

CHAPTER EIGHTEEN

Unfathomable. Fathoms. I wonder is that the difficulty, that my memories and my imaginings are lying deeply in the same place? Or one on top of the other like layers of shells and sand in a piece of limestone, so that they have both become the same element, and I cannot distinguish one from the other with any ease, unless it is from close, close looking?

Which is why I am so afraid to speak to Dr Grene, lest I give him only imaginings.

Imaginings. A nice sort of a word for catastrophe and delusion.

Years and years they left me there, because it takes years to sort out what they were trying to sort out, Jack and Fr Gaunt and no doubt others, for the saving of Tom McNulty. Was it as much as six, seven, even eight? I cannot remember.

When I wrote those words a few minutes ago, I put down my biro and placed my forehead in my hands, and thought a while, trying to fathom those years. Difficult, difficult. What was true, what was not true? What road did I take, what road refuse? Poor ground, false ground. I think an account before God must, must contain only truth. There is no human agency I need to bamboozle. God knows the true story before I write it, so can easily catch me out in falsehood. I must carefully winnow out one from the other. If I have a soul remaining, and perhaps I do not, it will depend on it. I think it must be possible that souls are rescinded in hard cases, cancelled at some office in the halls of heaven. That you arrive at the gates of heaven already at the wrong address, before St Peter says a word.

But it is all so dark, so difficult. I am only frightened because I don't know how to proceed. Roseanne, you must leap a few ditches now. You must find the strength in your old corpse to leap.

Is it possible I spent all those years in that hut without event, collecting my groceries every week, saying nothing to no one? I think it is. I am trying to be certain. Without event, I say, and yet I knew that war had begun in Europe, just like those days when I was a little girl. And yet I saw no army uniforms now. The hut was like the centre of a huge clock, the turning of the year in Strandhill, the roaring of the cars going by on Saturday night, the kids with their buckets, the starlings all winter, the darkening and brightening mountain, the heather with its snow of tiny flowers, what a comfort, and myself trying to do my bit with the roses on the front porch, tending them, clipping them back ready for the off, and watching them day by day in the strengthening year plump out their bulbs; 'Souvenir de St Anne's' they were, now I think of it, a rose bred in a Dublin garden out of that famous rose bred by Josephine in memory of Napoleon's love for her, 'Souvenir de Malmaison'.

Now, dear reader, I am calling you God for a moment, and God, dear dear God, I am trying to remember. Forgive me, forgive me if I am not remembering right.

I would rather remember aright than just to remember things so they will stand in my favour. That luxury is not allowed to me.

When Fr Gaunt finally came back to me, he did so alone. I suppose a priest is always alone in some sense. Never a creature to lie at his side. And he looked older suddenly, less the bright prospect, I could see he was losing his hair just at the temples, it was drifting back, a little tide that would not be coming in again.

It was high summer and he looked very hot in his woollen clothes. He ordered his clothes from the clerical outfitters in Marlborough Street in Dublin – how I knew that I do not know now. These clothes were quite new, oddly stylish, the soutane like something a woman might wear at a pinch to a formal dance, if in another colour, and shorter. I was tending to my roses as he came in the little gate, surprising me, giving me a fright really, because no one for a long, long time had made that noise on the latch except myself, creeping out late at night to walk on the dunes and the marshy ground, which was now dry and springy from a few weeks of comparative heat. I think I was presentable, unlike later, I had a scissors to cut my own hair in front of Tom's little shaving mirror, and my dress was clean, with that lovely stiffness in the cotton from being dried on a bush.

He carried a little leather case with him, scuffed and dented here and there from long and assiduous use. Really this man might have qualified as an old friend, I had known and had dealings with him so long. He was certainly qualified to write quite an intimate history of my life, since he had been witness to certain curious parts of it.

'Roseanne,' he began, with just exactly the same tone as he had used those years before, indeed as if this was a mere continuance of that conversation. There was no hello, how are you, or hesitancy. In fact he had the demeanour of a doctor with serious news to impart, not even the friendly alertness of Dr Grene when he has to make yet another gentle assault on my 'secrets'. Can I say I disliked him? I don't think so. Nor though did I understand him. What gave him pleasure in life, what sustained him. He did give my roses a glance as he went up the little steps and on into the dark hut.

I wiped my fingers on the wood of the steps, just to get the green juice off them, and followed him in.

Was it not an extraordinary meekness in me to stay in that hut at his bidding? I am almost ashamed to think it might be so. Should I not have raged at him that time before, rushed at his throat and the throat of Jack, got my teeth on his jutting Adam's apple and ripped out his voice? Berated them, shouted at them? But to what end? Only rage, useless rage expending itself on the white dust of a Strandhill road.

'I haven't anything to offer you, Father,' I said. 'Unless you will take a glass of Beecham's powders?'

'Why would I drink a glass of stomach powders, Roseanne?'

'Well, it says on the packet, a refreshing summer drink. That's why I bought it.'

'It is for those who have overindulged,' he said. 'But thank you.'

'Well, you are welcome, Father.'

Then he sat down just where he had sat before and indeed I had not seen any reason to move the chair from where it stood. The sunlight had followed us both into the room and lay about us in dusty bushels.

'I see you are keeping well,' he said.

'Oh, yes.'

'Of course, I have had my spies keep an eye on you.' He said this without any trace of guilt. Spies.

'Oh,' I said. 'I did not notice them.'

'Well, naturally,' he said.

Then he opened the case on his lap, the lid obscuring the contents. He took out a sheaf of papers, very neat and clean, the top one containing I could see a very impressive-looking design or seal.

'I have been successful,' he said, 'in my efforts to free Tom.'

'Excuse me?' I said.

'If you had followed my advice, Roseanne, some years ago, and put your faith in the true religion, if you had behaved with the beautiful decorum of a Catholic wife, you would not be facing these difficulties. But I do appreciate that you are not entirely responsible. Nymphomania is of course by definition a madness. An affliction possibly, but primarily a madness, with its roots possibly in a physical cause. Rome has agreed with this estimate, in fact the department of the Curia that deals with these thankfully rare cases not only agreed, but also posited the same theory. So you may rest assured that your case was seen to with all the thoroughness and fairness of minds well-informed, disinterested, and with no bad intention of any kind.'

I looked at him. Neat, black, clean, strange. Another human creature in the lair of a human creature. His words sombre, measured, at ease. No trace of excitement, victory, nothing only his usual careful, measured tones.

'I don't understand,' I said, nor did I, though I think I *knew*, all the same.

'Your marriage is deemed null, Roseanne.'

As I did not speak, after a full half minute, he said, 'It never happened. It does not exist. Tom is free to marry another, as if he had never been married. Which as I say he never was.'

'This is what you have been doing these last years?'

'Yes, yes,' he said, with some impatience. 'It is a monumentally complex undertaking. Something like this is never granted lightly. Deep deep thought at Rome, and my own bishop of course. Weighing everything, sifting through everything, my own deposition, Tom's own words, the elder Mrs McNulty who of course has experience of the troubles of women, in her work. Jack of course is away in India at the war, or else he might have made his contribution. The courts sit in careful judgement. No stone unturned.'

I was still staring at him.

'You may rest assured every possibility of justice has been afforded to you.'

'I want my husband to come here.'

'You have no husband, Roseanne. You are not in a state of matrimony.'

'I am divorced?'

'It is not a divorce,' he said, suddenly with vehemence, as if he found the word disgusting in my mouth. 'There is no divorce in the Catholic church. The marriage never existed. By reason of insanity at the time of the contract.'

'Insanity?'

'Yes.'

'How do you reckon that?' I asked after a moment, and with difficulty, words now becoming awkward and thick in my mouth.

'We do not believe your indiscretions are confined to one instance, an instance you will remember I was witness to with my own eyes. It was not thought probable that that instance did not have a history, given of course your own position vis-à-vis your early years, not to mention of course the condition of your mother, which we may assume was hereditary. Madness, Roseanne, has many flowers, rising from the same stem. The blooms of madness, from the same root, may be variously displayed. In your mother's case an extreme retreat into herself, in your case, a pernicious and chronic nymphomania.'

'I don't know what that word means.'

'It means,' he said, and yes, with a trace of fright now in his eyes, because he had used the word once and maybe thought I had accepted it. But he knew I spoke the truth and he was suddenly afraid now. 'It means a madness manifest in the desire to have irregular relations with others.'

'What?' I said. The explanation was as mystifying as the word.

'You know what it is.'

'I don't,' I said, and I did not.

I had shouted the last words, and indeed he had shouted his. He put the papers swiftly back into the case, closed it with a snap, and stood up. For some reason I noticed how polished his shoes were, with that little skirt of road dust on them from when he had no doubt reluctantly left his car and approached my house.

'I will not explain it to you further,' he said, almost in a paroxysm of annoyance and anger. 'I have tried to make your position clear. I believe I have done so. You understand your position?'

'What is that word you used?' I shouted.

'Relations!' he shouted, 'Relations! Congress, sexual congress!'

'But,' I said, and before God this was the truth, 'I never had relations with another besides Tom.'

'Of course, you may take refuge in an atrocious lie, if you choose that.'

'You may ask John Lavelle. He will not fail me.'

'You do not keep up with your paramours,' he said, quite nastily. 'John Lavelle is dead.'

'How can he be dead?'

'He went back into the fold of the IRA, thinking we would be weakened by this German war, shot a policeman, and was justly hanged. The Irish government brought Albert Pierrepoint himself over from England to do the work, so you can be sure it was done well.'

Oh, John, John, foolish John Lavelle. God rest and forgive him. I will admit I had often wondered about him, where he was, what he was doing. Had he gone back to America? To be a cowboy, a train-robber, a Jesse James? He had shot a policeman. An Irish policeman in an Irish state. That was a terrible act. And yet he had done me the great grace of keeping away,

225

he had not haunted me again as I had feared he might, he had kept himself away, he had not sought to trouble me again, having no doubt a true understanding of the trouble he had brought me on Knocknarea. That had been his promise, and he had kept it. After the priests had gone, he had gripped my hand, and promised me. He had honoured his promise. Honour. I did not think this other man in front of me now had as much.

Fr Gaunt wanted to move past me now, to get to the narrow door and out and away. For a moment I blocked his path. I blocked it. I knew I would have the strength if I willed it to kill him, I felt it in that moment. I knew I could snatch at something, a chair or anything close to hand, and bring it down on his head. And as true as my declaration to him was, this was also true. I would have if not happily, at least gladly, openheartedly, fiercely, finely, murdered him. I don't know why I did not.

'You are menacing me, Roseanne. Step back away from the door, there's a good woman.'

'A good woman? You say that?'

'It is an expression,' he said.

But I stepped out of his way. I knew, I knew any proper, decent life was over. The word of a man like that was like a death sentence. I felt all about me the whole hinterland of Strandhill speaking against me, the whole town of Sligo murmuring against me. I had known it all along, but it is a very different matter to know your sentence, and then to hear it spoken by your judge. Perhaps they would come out and burn me in my hut for a witch. Truest of all things, there was no one to help me, no one to stand at my side.

Fr Gaunt removed himself neatly from the dreaded house. The fallen woman. The mad woman. Freedom for Tom, my lovely Tom. And what for me?

Dr Grene's Commonplace Book

Absolute stillness again in the house last night. It is as if, having called out to me one last time, she will never need to call out to me again. This thought brought me out of fear, and into quite a different state. A sort of pride that after all I had love in me, buried in the mess. And that maybe she also. I listened again not out of fear, but a sort of sombre longing. But knowing nothing again would be asked or answered. A strange state. Happiness I suppose. It didn't last, but like I would a vulnerable patient in the throes of grief, I asked myself to note it, remember it, give it passionate credence when other darker feelings assail me again. It is very difficult to be a hero without an audience, although, in a sense, we are each the hero of a peculiar, half-ruined film called our life. Now there is a remark that will not bear much scrutiny, I fear.

What is that passage in the bible about the angel that sits inside us? Something similar. I can't remember. I think it is only the angel, the part of us unbesmirched maybe, that is such a connoisseur of happiness. He would want to be, because he tastes little enough of it. And yet . . . Enough.

Angels. A sorry subject for a psychiatrist. But now I am old, and have tasted grief that in the first days I thought might murder me, flay me, hang me, so I say, if only in the privacy of this book, why not? I am mortally sick of the rational mind. What creature does that look like? The celestial pedant?

I have been reading through Fr Gaunt's deposition again. I wonder if such all-knowing, stern-minded, and entirely unforgiving priests still exist? I suppose they do, but in private as it were. Maybe it was because de Valera's parentage was so insecure or mysterious that he took especial comfort in the confidence of the clergy. He certainly enshrined them in his constitution, but it is also true that he resisted the final demand of the archbishop of that day actually to make the Catholic church an established church. Thank God he didn't go so far, but he went far enough, far further than perhaps he ought. He was a leader wrestling with angels and demons, sometimes in the same body. Having been in the IRA in the war of independence, then the IRA as it was represented by the anti-Treaty forces, and indeed imprisoned after the civil war, he found when he came to power in the thirties that his erstwhile comrades, who rejected both the Treaty and him for good measure, needed to be suppressed with the utmost force. This must have caused him enormous grief, and troubled his dreams, as it would anyone's. Fr Gaunt itemises the fate of a man called John Lavelle, who figured in Roseanne's life, who in the end was hanged by de Valera at the outbreak of World War Two, quite without mercy. Others of his comrades were flogged, and I did not know there was judicial flogging in Ireland, not to mention hanging. Fr Gaunt says it was thirty-six lashes of a cat-o'-nine-tails, but that sounds much too harsh. But for de Valera it must have been like whipping and hanging his sons, or the sons or heirs of the companions of his youth. Which must have constituted another sort of disruption in him. It is a wonder the country ever recovered from these early miseries and traumas, and de Valera is to be greatly pitied that he was met with these necessary horrors. Perhaps here we can also trace the origin of the strange criminality of the last generation of politicians in Ireland, not to mention so many priests being found to have moved across the innocence of our children with the harrows and ploughshares of abuse. The absolute power of such as Fr Gaunt leading as day does to night to absolute corruption.

I had the unworthy thought that maybe de Valera's great desire to avoid the Second World War was not because he feared the enemy within, feared to split his new country, but that it actually constituted a further effort to expunge sexuality. A sort of extension of the intentions of the clergy. In that instance, if this is not too obvious and crude, male sexuality.

I am so tired at this moment that I do not know whether what I am writing is banal. Later I can tear it out.

This man Lavelle, for all that he may have shared a prison yard with Dev long ago, and was hanged on Dev's watch, as you might say, was no angel. According to Fr Gaunt, he brought his captive policeman into the hills behind Sligo, put a hood over his head, and held a gun to his temple. He kept spinning the barrel and pulling the trigger. I should think the poor garda was soon in a state of terror. Lavelle was trying to find out when the wages were brought into the barracks, because he had a desire to rob the very pay of the police. It seems an esoteric crime. But the garda for whatever reason, courage or ignorance, would not or could not answer. Lavelle clicked away with the gun. Some of his accomplices had also kidnapped the garda's wife and daughter, and were holding them in a derelict house in the town, and Lavelle kept telling him that they would be killed if he did not answer. But truth to tell the poor man mustn't have known too much. Eventually Lavelle shot him. This all came out because one of his companions turned State's evidence, and got away with the above-mentioned flogging. But the war had begun and de Valera was terrified the IRA would become strong again and he knew that they were already in contact with the Germans. And if Dev had a second religion its name was neutrality, he defended that to the last ounce of his sense. So he could not spare Lavelle. In all honesty I cannot say he was any great loss.

I write this as if I were a holy man in a beehive hut on Skellig. Of course I am not. It behoves us I suppose to admit we are all brother and sister to these modern sins. And civil war is an evil that befalls all souls equally.

Although there was nothing in my training that allowed me to talk of sins.

Fr Gaunt tells all this in his document in I think a sort of massive Ciceronian effort to implicate, no, perhaps that's not the right word, somehow to wrap Roseanne in some of the same knotted wool, to catch her up in it. Fr Gaunt spared no ink in that direction. It really is a remarkable piece of work, clerical, thorough, and convincing. It is like a forest fire, burning away all traces of her, traversing her narrative and turning everything to ashes and cinders. A tiny, obscure, forgotten Hiroshima. There is a sort of anxiety throughout the document, an anxiety that expresses itself sometimes in excessive, or I should say unexpected, detail. Fr Gaunt is almost clinical in his anatomising of Roseanne's sexuality. It is exceedingly strange of course to read about this Roseanne of old, when the bearer of the same name is one hundred years old and in my care. I don't know if really it is privileged information. It feels sometimes highly voyeuristic, morally questionable to read it. Partly because Fr Gaunt's own morality is of an old-fashioned kind. He betrays at every stroke an intense hatred if not of women, then of the sexuality of women, or sexuality in general. For him it is the devil's cloak and hood, whereas for me, it is a sort of saving grace of being alive. I am no enemy of Mr Sigmund Freud. It is also crystal clear that he regards her Protestantism as a simple, primal evil in itself. His anger that she would not let herself be made a Catholic at his request is absolute, long before she married her Catholic husband, and likewise remained what she was. This in itself for Fr Gaunt is a real perversion.

So he believes from very early on that she is, if not evil, then stubborn, difficult, perhaps mysterious. He does not ever pretend to understand her, but he certainly claims a hold on her history. She has laid herself open to the eyes of the town, she has flaunted her beauty by, it must be said, merely being beautiful. It is as if she has tempted all of male Sligo, and then, having snared this Tom McNulty, a rising man in the new country, she chooses to abase herself before a wild creature like John Lavelle, whom Fr Gaunt describes as a 'savage man from the darkest corner of Mayo'.

Then, having done such a thing, and having been duly offered assistance by Fr Gaunt, this assistance is rejected. You can feel his new fury here. Fury. She is put to live in an iron hut in Strandhill, where again she is like a magnet to the lusts of Sligo. Most terrible of all, Fr Gaunt having secured from Rome an annulment of her marriage, Roseanne then becomes mysteriously pregnant, and bears a child. Bears a child, says Fr Gaunt, and in a savage line of his own, containing only three words, he writes: 'And kills it.'

If I had read those words years ago, with the authority of a priest behind them, I would myself have been obliged to commit her.

CHAPTER NINETEEN

Roseanne's Testimony of Herself

John Kane is becoming more mysterious by the minute. He does not speak at all now, but this morning offered what I think was a smile. It was certainly an odd, broken-sided effort. The left side of his face seems to have fallen a little. When he was going out he managed to give the loose floorboard another whack with his shoes. I wonder does he do it to signal to me that he knows there's something there. He can't think it is of any value anyhow, or it is not in his nature to look under floorboards. I was trying to remember as I stood by the window watching him how long I have known him. It seems like my acquaintance with him stretches into the very ashy distant times of childhood, but that is not correct. It is a long long time anyway. He has been wearing the same blue denim coat for about thirty years I should say. Which is a match for my own threadbare wardrobe. My dressing-gown shamed me in the windowlight, because there I could see how splashed and blotched the front of it is. My instinct was to retreat from the light, but having got so far from the bed, I couldn't give up my advantage. I wanted to ask him about the progress of the spring outside, now that he has revealed himself a botanist, or the nearest thing I have to it. White, yellow, blue is the sequence. Snowdrops, daffodils and bluebells, and as the daffodils come on the snowdrops are beginning to die away. I wonder why that is. I wonder why anything is.

Then I became quite dizzy at the window and felt a sort of lurching in my limbs, like my joints wanted to fold me over. I lifted my arms and tried to balance myself against the wall. To give John Kane his due, he was not yet out into the corridor, and came back in and helped me into bed, though it is not his task. He was quite gentle and was still smiling. I looked up into his face. He has hair on his face not quite a beard, more like the patchy heather on bogland. His eyes are quite blue. Then I realised he wasn't truly smiling, but that his mouth is caught somehow, he can't seem to move it easily. I wanted to ask him about it, but didn't want to embarrass or upset him. I suppose that was stupid of me.

It was not so long after Fr Gaunt's 'visit' that I was wandering over the further dunes of Strandhill beach on a crisp, moonlit night. Since he had come to see me I had felt very confined in the iron hut, as if his presence were somehow still in the room. I waited with no trace of patience every night for darkness, which at least gave me the liberty of the dunes and the marsh-land.

I had no desire to be seen by anyone, or talk to anyone. Sometimes out walking I would be in such a peculiar state of mind that I would rush home at the merest hint of another person. Indeed, there were times I used to fancy I actually saw people that possibly weren't there, little tricks of the marram grass or whatnot, the rise of a marsh bird – in particular I seemed to be 'haunted' by a figure that sometimes appeared, seemed to appear, at the far edges of where I was, in what might have been a black suit, and what might have been a brown hat, but even when I gathered my courage and walked towards him, the few times I thought I saw him, he instantly disappeared. But such matters were the nature of those days.

I remember this night in particular because it is probably the single most peculiar thing I ever witnessed, having seen a few peculiar things in my time.

I have to be very careful with these 'memories' because I realise there are a few vivid remembrances from this troubled time that I know in my heart cannot have happened. But I don't think this night is one of them, improbable though it was.

It is a measure of my shame that instead of climbing to the top of the hill of sand itself, which I had previously loved to do, though it was at the risk of bumping into, even stumbling over, the courting couples, I had walked out right to the edge of everything, where a deep narrow river poured into the sea, and in the daytime was a sort of luncheonette for seabirds.

I stood on the sand. The tide was out a way, and it was all perfectly quiet. Far off to the right of Knocknarea, some twisting little road entertained the lights of an unseen motorcar, appearing and disappearing. But it was too far away to hear it.

There was no wind and the sky was enormous and that enamel blue the moonlight makes. It was very easy to suppose that one human creature was the least important element there. The sea stood off in acre after acre of private, dreamy water.

Then in the distance, that tiny growling. I actually looked behind me, thinking there might be a rabid dog or some such on the beach. But no, the sound was coming from far off to the right of me. I looked towards it, all along the empty beach, to the small lights of the few buildings on the strand about an eighth of a mile away. There I saw a sort of line of piercing yellow light begin to grow on the horizon, a horizon half land and half sea.

I thought God was coming to cancel me out just as surely as Fr Gaunt had. I don't know why I thought that, except, I felt that guilty.

The thin glimmering line grew and grew. The noise also increased, and under my bare feet I thought I felt the sand tremble, tremble deep under me, as if something were rising up through the ground. The lights widened and grew taller, and then it was roaring, gathering and gathering, and then it was what looked like the edge of a flying carpet of monsters, and then that noise had grown into the noise of an enormous waterfall, and I was looking up, indeed like a mad woman, certainly feeling as mad as a hatter, and fuller and fuller, bigger and bigger, came the noise and the lights, till I could see the round bellies of individual parts of it, and metal noses, and gigantic whirrings, and it was airplanes, dozens of them, maybe hundreds, all animal-like in the moonlight, but bizarrely, with the little thin windows visible at the front, and perhaps it was really madness, but I thought I could see little heads and faces, and it was all in formation as they say, grim, catastrophic, like something at the end of the world. And because the airplanes were all together, their noise was increased truly to biblical proportions, something out of Revelation, and the sky was filled with it over my head, metal, light and ruckus, and they poured over me, flying so close to the water that the power of the engines sucked up the water, tore the water up in torn sheets, that fell back to the surface with a swishing of snakes, and I could feel the airplanes pull at me, pull at the beach, trying to tear us from our places, trying to pull the brains out of my skull, the eyes out of my sockets, and then they were pouring over me, line after line, were there fifty, a hundred, a hundred and fifty? – for full minutes pouring over, and then beginning to draw away further, leaving a huge vacuum it seemed in the sky, leaving a silence almost more painful than the noise, as if those mysterious airplanes had taken the oxygen out of the Sligo air. And off they went, rattling and ravelling the Irish coast.

Some days later I was out on my porch, fussing over my roses. It was an activity that even in my distress brought a tincture of comfort. But then it is clear to me that any effort at gardening, even a haphazard, stop-go one such as mine was, is an effort to drag to earth the colours and the importances of heaven. It was cold that day and there were goosebumps raised along my bare arms. The very existences of the roses, not yet seen, furled so tightly and mysteriously in their green buds, was making me almost dizzy.

I looked back over my right shoulder because I heard someone moving along the road. Someone or something, it might have been an old donkey scuffling along, to judge by the noises. I didn't really want to be seen by man nor beast, even though there was such comfort in my roses. Maybe this year there would be a new look to them, not quite 'St Anne's' or 'Malmaison', but becoming slowly Sligo, 'Souvenir de Sligo', a memory of Sligo. But it wasn't a donkey, it was a man, a very strange man, I thought, because his hair was cut tight to his head in a sort of frizz, like a Negro jazzman, and his suit of clothes was a strange dark ashen colour. No, it wasn't a suit of clothes, more of a uniform of some kind. Even his face looked queerly blue. And to my astonishment I saw that it was Jack. Of course, that would explain the uniform, and him off in India wasn't it, fighting in the king's name – but if he was off in India what in the world was he doing in Strandhill, No-Man's-Land that it was?

And then it seemed suddenly colder than the mere cold of the treacherous Irish seaside day, and there seemed to be goosebumps added to my goosebumps. Wasn't this odd apparition my enemy now?

'Jack?' I called out anyhow, throwing caution to the wind. I had the mad thought that he might have come to help me. But what had happened to him? Now he was closer and even odder, if I didn't know better I would say he was *singed*, he was veritably *singed*.

The man stopped on the path, maybe astonished I had spoken to him. In fact he looked frightened.

'Jack McNulty?' I said, as if that might be helpful. Surely he knew his own name. Now I'm sure I looked as uncertain as he did.

He spoke like a man who has not spoken for a few days, the words stumbling out of his lip.

'What?' he said. 'What, what?'

He looked so solemnly scared I went down the path to the gate and stood nearer to him. I thought he might bolt away down the road, like a donkey after all. But I was just a small woman in a cotton dress.

'You're not Jack McNulty, are you?' I said. 'You certainly look like him.'

'Who are you?' he said, and gazed back towards the sea like he feared an ambush.

'I'm no one,' I said, meaning no one for him to fear. 'I'm Roseanne, Tom's wife – as was maybe.'

'Oh, I heard about you,' he said, but without the expected censure. He suddenly seemed very glad to be talking to me, to be meeting me. He raised his right hand a moment as if he meant to shake one of mine, but he let it drop. 'Yes.'

I was so relieved, I was so delighted he had taken this tone with me that I wanted to joke with him, to be pleasant with him, to tell him all the things that had happened, just little things, like the two rats the night before that I had caught in the act of carrying away one of my eggs through a hole in the hut wall, a hole so small one rat had put the egg up on his belly and let the other rat pull him away through the gap! Ridiculous. But it was the friendliness in his voice that did it, the mere simple friendliness, a thing I hadn't heard for so long, and didn't even know I missed.

'I'm Eneas,' he said, 'Tom's brother.'

'Eneas?' I said. 'What are you doing here?'

'I'm not really here,' he said. 'I shouldn't be here, and I should be gone shortly.'

'What's the stuff all over you?'

'What stuff?' he said.

'You're all black,' I said, 'And grey, like ashes.'

'Jesus, so I am,' he said. 'I was in Belfast. I was going back to France, you know. I'm a soldier.'

'Like Jack,' I said.

'Like Jack, only he's an officer. I was in Belfast, Roseanne, waiting for my ship, sleeping in a little hotel, when the few poor lousy sirens they have there went off, and in a few minutes they came in, the bombers, dozens and dozens and dozens, dropping their bombs at will, not a puff in the sky of an antiaircraft gun, not a puff, and all around me the houses and streets erupted. How did I get out, I ran like a demon along the ways, screaming I do not doubt, and saying wild prayers for the people of Belfast, and soon there were hundreds in the streets, all doing the same as me, people in their nightdresses and people naked as babes, running and screaming, and at the edge of the city we just kept going, and the waves of planes had come in behind us, all the while without mercy letting go the bombs, and an hour later, or maybe more, I cannot say, I was perched on the edge of a huge dark mountain, and looked back, and Belfast was a huge lake of fire, burning, burning, the flames leaping like red creatures, tigers and such, high high into the sky, and those that had run with me were also looking, and weeping, and giving out sounds like the lamentations of the bible. And I thought of the bit of the bible they like to give out in the seamen's missions, where I used to frequent before the war, being just a wandering man, *They who are not written in the book of life will be cast into the lake of fire*, and I trembled trembled to see the anger of the Lord, excepting it wasn't the Lord, but those Germans away up nearer the stars, looking down on their work and I should think marvelling, marvelling as much as us.'

This man Eneas stopped. He was trembling again now. He

was in a bad state. The reflection of that lake of fire was still burning in his eyes.

'Come in,' I said, 'just for a minute, and rest.' Whether this was a maternal instinct or a sisterly I cannot say. But suddenly an enormous rush of tenderness went from me to him. I thought, he is like me, a little. He has been cast out from his world, this world of Sligo. And I cannot say he looked like a villain. I cannot say he looked like a murdering policeman of old, of his legend – not that I knew his legend then. Indeed and indeed, how little I knew about him, how rarely his brothers had spoken of him – only with heavy sighs and meaningful looks.

'No, I cannot,' he said. 'You don't know me. I am not a man you want in your house. I'll bring trouble to you. Didn't they tell you, I have a death sentence on my head? I shouldn't even be here in Sligo. I have walked out of Belfast, and through Enniskillen, and just sort of came here, like a pigeon flying home and cannot help it.'

'Come in,' I said, 'and never mind any of that. I am your sister-in-law after all. Come in.'

So in he came. As he walked, little tumbles of black dust fell from him. He had walked all the way from Belfast, a long long way indeed, returning to Sligo like a pigeon – like a salmon looking for the mouth of the Garravoge. He seemed to me the saddest man I had ever met.

When I got him in the hut, I indicated to him without much ceremony to remove his uniform. The first thing he needed was a cup of water to drink, which he drank with a miniature ferocity, like he had a fire also in his insides that needed putting out. I had an old tin bath for my own use, and filled it with a few visits to the well, trying to keep the water clean, while my kettle came to boiling on the fire. Then I was able to take the chill off the bath with the boiled water, but no more than that. All this while the small ashen man stood in the centre of the floor in his long johns, and the cleanliness of that garment surprised me. He was a neat-boned, well-constructed man, not in the slightest plump like Tom, no, not a pick on him.

'I'll go out to the scullery now and put some cheese in a sandwich,' I said.

So for modesty's sake, I left him to it, and I could hear him stumble about a little as he took off his long johns, and stood into the tub, and gave himself a wash. I suppose an army man like him was used to cold washing, I hoped so. Anyway, there wasn't a squeak out of him. When I deemed it right, I came back in. He had suds-ed himself rightly, the tub was a boil of ash-streaked soap, and now was standing again in the centre of the floor, doing up the buttons of his long johns. His hair I now could see was a sort of russet red, even burned so close to his scalp. His skin was darkly marked by the sun, and his hands were rough and thick-fingered. I nodded to him as if to say, *Are you all right?* and he nodded back, as if to say, *I am.* I handed him the thick slice of bread and cheese, and he wolfed it down gently where he stood.

'Well,' he said then, smiling, 'it's nice to have family.'

And I laughed.

'I know what you mean,' I said.

Outside it was falling dark and my old companion the owl was starting up his motor. Now I didn't know what to do with him. I seemed to know him so well, at least the makeup of his body and his face, and of course didn't know him from Adam. And yet so gentle and strange a man I never had encountered. He was standing with absolute stillness like a deer on the mountain when he hears a twig snap.

'I thank you,' he said, with complete simplicity and sincerity. I was so affected to be thanked by another human being. I was so affected by hearing another human speak to me with grace and respect. I was standing still also now, staring at him, almost astounded.

240

'I can take the uniform outside and beat it,' I said, 'otherwise it would never be dry on the morrow.'

'No,' he said, 'leave it alone. I'm not supposed to wear it in the Free State. It'll do as it is, all covered over like that. I'll make my way to Dublin and try to rejoin my unit from there. The sergeant will be very worried about me.'

'I'm sure he will,' I said.

'I'm a good soldier, you know,' he said.

'I'm sure you are,' I said.

'Not the deserting type,' he said, unnecessarily. I could tell he wasn't.

'Do you know,' he said, 'I don't mean anything by this, I mean, me standing here in my long johns, and you a stranger, but, the reason I came to Strandhill was because I used to have a girl, and she and me used to come down here, for the dancing of course, and her name was Viv, and she was warned off of me, you know, and I don't see her. But I wanted to stand on the beach where we used to stand, looking out on the bay. You know, a simple thing like that. And Viv was a lovely-looking girl, she was indeed. And I wanted to say, and not meaning anything by it, but you are also the most beautiful-looking person I ever saw, you and she both.'

Well, that was a lovely speech. And he didn't mean anything by it, unless it was to speak the truth. I was suddenly flushed with a sort of pride, that I hadn't felt for a long time. This man, and he didn't know, spoke like my father when my father wished to say something important. There was a sort of strange old flounce to it, like out of a book, the very book I still guarded and cherished, old Thomas Browne's *Religio Medici*. And he was a boy from the seventeenth century, so I don't know how that lingo had crept into Eneas McNulty.

'I know you're a married woman,' he said, 'so please forgive me, and you married to my brother.'

'No,' I said, also in the interests of truth, and before I could

241

think better of it, 'I am not a married woman. Or so I'm told.'

'Oh?' he said.

'No,' I said. 'You see, I have had my own death sentence spoke against me.'

Then he was standing there and I was standing there. And I went over to him like a mouse, quietly, quietly, in case I would scare him, and took one of those calloused hands of his, and led him into the room behind, where the owl was better heard, and Knocknarea more easily seen, from the poor feather bed.

Then after that later, we were lying there like two stone figures on a tomb, quite as happy as any moment of childhood.

'I think Jack told me your father was in the Merchant Navy,' he said after a little.

'Oh, yes, he was,' I said.

'Like myself – and Jack too, you know.'

'Oh, yes?'

'Oh, yes. And he said your father was in the old police then, wasn't that it?'

'Jack said that?' I said.

'I think he did. And I was interested to hear that of course, since I was in myself. Which of course cost me dear in the end. But sure, we didn't know. We seem to like to be signing up to things, the McNulty boys. There's Jack now in the Royal Engineers. And even young Tom himself going off to Spain with that Duffy character, hah?'

'O'Duffy. Did he? I didn't know that.'

'O'Duffy, that's right. I should know because he was head of the new police after. Yes, Tom went off, so I'm told.'

'And how did he get on?'

'Jack said he was back in two weeks. Jack didn't think much of Tom going off giving support to Franco now. No. Anyhow, Tom came back. Disgusted he was. Broke with O'Duffy then entirely. He had them stuck in trenches with rats eating their toes, and O'Duffy himself off somewhere, Salamanca I don't doubt. Living it up. Ah well, sure.'

'Poor Tom,' I said. 'That lovely uniform, gone to waste.'

'Oh, indeed,' said Eneas. 'So he wasn't in the police then, your father?' he said, innocently enough, chatting in the moonlight.

'What sort of love-talk is this?' I said, not wanting to offend so innocent a man. He laughed anyhow.

'Irish love-talk,' he said. 'Battles, and who you're for, and all that.'

And he laughed again.

'When was all that anyhow, going to Spain and everything?' I said.

'Oh, '37, I suppose. It's a long while back, isn't it? Seems like.'

'And do you hear any other more recent news of Tom?'

'Oh, just that he's thriving, you know. The coming man and all that, you know.'

And he looked at me then, maybe fearing he was upsetting me. But he wasn't really. It was nice to have him there. His leg was very warm against my leg. No, I didn't mind him.

The medical doctor was in to me a while ago. He didn't like the rash on my face, and indeed he found it on my back also. Truth to tell I have been feeling a little tired, and I told him so. It was strange, because usually as the spring got going outside I perked up in myself. I could see in my mind's eye the daffodils ablaze along the avenue and I longed to go out and see them, give them a raise of the old hand in greeting. Such long lurking under the cold wet earth, and then, all their resplendent joy. So that was strange, and I told him so.

He said he didn't like my breathing either, and I said I liked it well enough, and he laughed, and said, 'No, I mean, I don't like that odd little rattle in your chest, I think I will give you some antibiotics.'

Then he gave me real news. He said the whole main body of the hospital had been cleared out, and the two wings up my end were the only ones still going. I asked him if the old dames had been cleared out and he said they had. He said it was a terrible job, because of the bed sores, and the pain. He said I was very wise to keep moving about, and not have the bed sores. I said I had had them when I first went into Sligo and hadn't liked them much. He said, 'I know.'

'Does Dr Grene know of these changes?' I said.

'Oh, yes,' he said, 'he has masterminded the whole thing.'

'And what will happen to the old place now?'

'It will be demolished in due course,' he said. 'And of course you will be put in a nice new place.'

'Oh,' I said.

I was suddenly frantic, because I was thinking of these pages under the floor. How would I gather them and keep them secret if I was to be moved? And where would I be moved to? I was in turmoil now, like that blow hole in the cliff the back of Sligo Bay, when the tide comes in and forces the water into the rock.

'I thought Dr Grene had mentioned all this, or I wouldn't have said anything. You're not to worry.'

'What will happen to the tree below, and the daffodils?

'What?' he said. 'Oh, I don't know. Look, I'll have Dr Grene discuss all this with you. You know. That's his department and I am afraid I have strayed into it, Mrs McNulty.'

I was then too weary to explain yet again, for the millionth time in sixty years and more, that I wasn't Mrs McNulty. That I wasn't anybody, wasn't in fact anybody's wife. I was just Roseanne Clear.

CHAPTER TWENTY

Dr Grene's Commonplace Book

Catastrophe. The medical doctor Mr Wynn, having gone up to attend Roseanne at my request, has inadvertently let the cat out of the bag vis-à-vis the hospital. I mean, I think I thought she knew, that someone would have told her. If they did, the information flew out of her head. I should have been wiser and prepared her. Mind you, I don't know how I would have broached this, without a similar result. She seemed most distressed that the bedbound old ladies are gone. Actually I feel we have all been moved on much quicker than we wanted, but the new facility in Roscommon town will be ready in a while, and there were complaints in the paper that it might be lying unused. So we bestirred ourselves in a final push. Now all that remain are the people here in Roseanne's block and the men's wing to the west. They are mostly old codgers of one sort and another, in their black hospital clothes. They are also very unhappy to hear of imminent plans, and actually what delays everything now is that there is nowhere for them to go. We cannot put them out on the road, and say, right, lads, off you go. They gather about me like rooks, when I talk to them in the yard where they do a bit of walking about and smoking. These are some of the fellows that were so helpful the night there was a fire in the hospital, many of them carrying old ladies on their backs, down the long stairs, quite amazing, and afterwards making jokes about it being a long time since they went with a girl, and wasn't it nice to do the foxtrot again, and related jests. They are certainly not mentally ill the most of them, they are just the 'detritus' of the system, as I once heard them referred to. One of them that I know well fought in the Congo with the Irish army. A good few of them in fact are ex-army men. I suppose we lack a place like Chelsea barracks, or Les Invalides in Paris. Who would be an old soldier in Ireland?

Roseanne was actually sweating in her bed when I went in to her. It may be a reaction to the antibiotics, but I fancy it is simple fear. This may be a terrible place in a terrible condition, but she is a human creature like the rest of us, and this is her home, God help her. I was surprised to find John Kane there, with his gobble-gobble voice like a turkey, the poor man, and though I was suspicious of him, he actually seemed concerned, old rogue that he may be, and worse.

Truth to tell I am not so sanguine about all this myself, and feel very much hurried and harried, but all the same it must be a good thing to be getting new premises, and ones not streaked with rainwater in some of the rooms, and gashes in the slates of the roof that we could get no one to risk fixing, because I am assured the timbers themselves are going. Yes, yes, it is a death-trap, the whole building, but at the same time the element of depreciation has been scandalously ignored and never funded, and what could have been maintained has been let go to hell. And a species of hell it most likely appears to the untutored eye. Not Roseanne's eye.

Roseanne did perk up when she saw me, and asked me to go to her table and find a book for her. It was a book called *Religio Medici* in that very old battered copy I have often noticed as I passed. She said it was her father's favourite book, had she ever told me that, and I said, yes, I thought so. I said I thought she might even have showed me her father's name in it once, yes.

'I am a hundred years old,' she said then, 'and I want you to do something for me.'

'What is it?' I said, wondering at her now, coming back so courageously from her panic, if panic it was, and her voice

246

steady again now, even if her old features were aflame still from the damn rash. She looks like she has jumped through a bonfire and dipped her face to the heat.

'I want you to give this to my child,' she said. 'To my son.'

'Your son?' I said. 'And Roseanne, where is your son?'

'I do not know,' she said, her eyes abruptly clouding, almost fainting away, and then she seemed to shake her mind clear again. 'I do not know. Nazareth.'

'Nazareth is a long way,' I said, humouring her.

'Dr Grene, will you do it?'

'I will, I will,' I said, absolutely certain I would not, would not be able to, considering what I knew from Fr Gaunt's blunt statement in his document. And anyhow, all the sea of time between. Her child would be also an old person now surely, even if living? I suppose I might have asked her, Did you kill your child? I suppose I might have asked her that, if I had been so mad myself. No, that wasn't a question that could be posed nicely, even I think professionally. And anyway, she had given me answers to nothing really. Nothing that could alter my opinion of her status, medically speaking.

Oh, and I was suddenly weary, weary, as if I were all her years and more. Weary, because I could not lift her back into 'life'. I could not do it. I could not even lift myself.

'I think you will,' she said, looking at me acutely. 'I hope so anyhow.'

Then rather incongruously she took the book from my hands and then put it back into them, and nodded her head, as if to say, be sure that you do do it.

Roseanne's Testimony of Herself

I am not very well, it seems, I am poorly, but I need to keep going at this because I am coming to the part that I need to be telling you.

Dear Reader, God, Dr Grene, whoever you may be.

Whoever you are, I pledge you again my love.

Being an angel now. I am joking.

Flapping my heavy wings in heaven.

Maybe. Do you think so?

Terrible, dreepy, dark February weather I remember, and the worst, most frightened days of my life.

Maybe seven months I was at that time. But I could not mark it for sure.

I was growing so heavy that my old coat could not hide my 'condition' at the shop in Strandhill, though I chose only the last hours of darkness in the working day ever to go there, and in that way winter was a mercy, dark by four.

When I looked at myself in the mirror of the wardrobe I saw a whitened phantom woman with a strangely lengthened face, as if the weight of my belly was drawing me down everywhere, like a melting statue. My belly button was pushed out like a little nose and the hair under my belly seemed to have grown to twice its length.

I had something in me, like the river had something in it when the salmon were running. If there were still salmon in the poor Garravoge. Sometimes the talk in the shop was of the river, and how it was silting up because of the war, because the wharves and harbour upriver in the town itself were closed for the duration, and the dredgers no longer hauled up the great buckets of mud and sand. They talked about submarines out in the bay of Sligo, and the shortages, the scarcity of tea and the odd abundance of things like Beecham's powders. They might also have mentioned the scarcity of mercy. There were next to no cars on the roads and my hut was silent most nights, though bicycles and walkers and pony-and-traps did make their way out for the dance. Someone in Sligo had got up a charabanc and it would come crawling over the sand with its cargo of revellers like a stray vehicle from another century. The Plaza sent out a few points of light which might have been a beacon to any German airplanes in the sky, the like of which I had seen returning from their work in Belfast, but nothing rained down on those dancers except time.

I was only the observer of these matters. I wonder what my fame was in those days, the woman in the corrugated-iron hut, the fallen woman, the witch, the creature 'gone over the edge'. Like there was a waterfall at the edge of their world that a woman could be washed over, like an invisible Niagara in daily life. A vast high wall of boiling, misty water.

A nice-looking woman in an ermine-collared coat looked at me one day as she passed. She was very well-to-do, with black polished boots, and brown hair whose style was the result of many hours in the hairdressers. There was an old house with a high wall across the road from my hut, and she was going there, and there was the sound of a party somewhere, a gramophone playing that song Greta Garbo used to sing. I thought I knew her, so that I had stopped uncharacteristically on the road, without meaning to, as if it were some other days. Much to my astonishment, when I glanced in the gates, I saw Jack McNulty, in the most tremendous coat as usual, but I must say also with a haunted, exhausted face. Or maybe I saw everything in those terms in those days. I wondered therefore if this was the famous Mai, the grand girl of Galway that he had married. I supposed it was. She was my sister-in-law, I suppose – as was.

She seemed suddenly angry and bothered. I am sure I looked a sight, in my wretched coat that had never been much to write home about, and my brown shoes that had turned into clogs of a sort because I had no laces for them, they needed delicate, long laces that such a shop as Strandhill boasted did not stock. Yes, maybe my lower legs showed I had no stockings, which I know was a crime, and as for the swelling stomach under the coat . . .

'Gone over the deep end, have we?' she said, and that's all she said. She went on then through the gates. I looked after her, marvelling at the words, but also, wondering how she meant it, cruelly, despairingly, factually? It was impossible for me to know. The couple went on together into the house, not looking back, in case I suppose Mai were to be turned to a pillar of salt, glancing back at Sodom.

The weather was worsening and I was growing sick. It wasn't just the sickness in the morning, going out the back of the hut onto the marram grass and heather to retch into the wind. It was another sort of sickness, something that seemed to boil in my legs, and hurt my stomach. I was getting so heavy that it was starting to be difficult to rise from my chair, and I had a great fear of being suddenly stuck there, stranded, and my greatest fear was for the child. I could see sometimes little elbows and knees poking out under my skin, and who could want to bring danger to such a thing? I did not know the number of months, and I was so terrified I would start to birth the baby, far from anyone who would help me. I wished time and again I had spoken to Mai, or called out to Jack, and I don't know why I did not, except that my state was visible and plain to them, and they had not thought to help me. I knew that wild women on the plains of America went into the scrubland alone to give birth to their children, but I did not want Strandhill to be my America, and have to attempt something so lonesome, so full of danger. While it had been just myself, I had learned a little strategy of secrecy and survival, but now I was drifting well beyond that. I did pray to God that He might help me, I said the Our Father a thousand thousand times, if not on my knees, then by necessity in my chair. I knew I must do something, not for myself, as it was clear I was beyond help and sympathy, but for the baby.

It was somewhere in those days of February that I set out on the road to Sligo town. I had spent an hour or two washing myself. The night before I had washed my dress, and tried to dry it all night before the dying fire. It was a little damp when I put it on. I stood before the mirror and combed my hair again and again with my fingers, because for the life of me I couldn't find my brush. I had one last spark of red lipstick in a surviving tube, just one last smudge for the lips. I wished I had some pancake for my skin, and all I could do was take some old plaster off the part of the hut that was the fireplace, built of solid stone, crumble it in my hands, and try to smear it on evenly. I was going into the town itself and I would have, to some degree, to be respectable. I worked away at myself like Michelangelo on his ceiling. There was nothing I could do about my coat, but I tore a strip off the sheet on my bed, and wound it round my throat for a scarf. I did not have a hat, but anyway, the wind was so fierce it wouldn't last long. Then off I went, pushing further up the hill than I had been for a long time, passing the Church of Ireland church at the corner, and onto the Strandhill road. I wished I could hitch a lift from the underbelly of one of those German planes I had seen, because the road stretched long and forbidding before me. The mountain reared up at my right, and I wondered at myself that I had ever walked up there so readily, so easily. It was as if a hundred years had elapsed.

I don't know how many hours' walking it was, but it was a long, hard walk. The sickness, though, seemed to pass from my body as I went along, as if there was no room for it in my present emergency. I started to become strangely buoyant and hopeful, as if my mission might be blessed after all. I started to tell myself, she will help me, of course she will help me, she is a woman also, and I was married to her son. Or might have been if it hadn't been crossed out in Rome. I thought, cold though she had been those years ago, when first I appeared in her bungalow, surely her long experience of the world would oblige her to cast aside her dislike and – and so on.

Round and round and round in my head it went, mile after mile, my feet plodding on, with that kind of splayed-out motion because of my big belly, not a pretty sight you may be sure, and me convincing myself of this certainty.

Dr Grene's Commonplace Book

We have a demolition date now, of all things, not that far off. I must keep reminding myself. It is somehow very difficult to imagine this eventuality, although everywhere in the hospital are items standing boxed up and ready, every day vans and lorries come and bring stuff away, great reams of correspondence and records have been put in store, dozens of patients have been moved out, places suddenly, unexpectedly, in the daft way of these things, found even for my poor black-coated men, and some even tentatively put back among – among the living I almost said. Sheltered housing is the official phrase, for once a decent, human phrase. At my assessment, such as it is. A core group at the end will go to the new facility. Oh, but, I feel mightily desirous to reach a conclusion about Roseanne.

Nice letter from Percy Quinn in Sligo saying to come over

any time I liked. So I must set my mind to doing that. He sounded so friendly that in writing back I asked him if he knew where old Royal Irish Constabulary records were kept in Sligo, and if he could find out, he might look for the name of Joseph Clear among them, of his kindness. The civil war years were so disruptive, destructive, I don't even know if such arcana survive, or if anyone would have bothered to protect them if they had. The Free State army, trying to bomb the Irregulars out of the Four Courts in Dublin, burned almost every civil record to ashes, births, deaths, marriages, and other documents beyond price, wiping out the records of the very nation they were trying to give new life to, actually burning memory in its boxes. With guns given or lent to them if I remember rightly by the exiting British, trying no doubt to be helpful to the new government, with that appealing, large-hearted characteristic of the British, as opposed to their con-comitant murderousness. Not that I said any of this to Percy. I remembered suddenly as I replied to his letter that he had been at that fateful conference in Bundoran, but he certainly hadn't said anything about that, and I certainly didn't refer to it.

Yesterday afternoon, coming in early and weary, I went up rather fearlessly I thought to Bet's room. I think I may have moved beyond the stage of self-recrimination and guilt. After all, when all is said and done, I am on my own now, and our story is over. I lay on her bed trying to get close to her. I smelled the faint smell of her perfume, Eau de Rochas, that I used to look for at airport duty-frees when they still had such things. I just felt rather light and strange, but not unhappy. I was asking her absence to be there as a sort of bizarre inverted comfort. Just for a few minutes I felt I was her, lying there, and that I, the real other I, was downstairs in the old bedroom, and I won-dered what I thought about myself. An inadequate, traitorous, unloving man? A presence oddly necessary, even with a floor and ceiling between? I didn't know. Even as Bet I didn't know

Bet. But just for a few minutes also I had something of her strength, her niceness, her integrity. What a wonderful feeling.

My eye fell on her choice library of rose books, and I took one up and started to read. I have to say it was very interesting, even poetic. I gathered myself up then, and carefully put my hands each side of the collection, and lifted them as one, and turned them on their sides so I could carry them downstairs, like booty, like something stolen. I lay down on my own bed and continued reading, long into the night. It was as if I were reading a letter from her, or was privileged to enter a subject that probably lined her mind like wallpaper. *Rosa Gallica*, a plain little rose like the one you see carved on medieval buildings as *Rosa Mundi*, was the first. The late roses are the huge tea roses that look in gardens like dancers' bottoms in frilly knickers. What a creature we are, bringing a simple bloom to that over the centuries, and turning those mangy scavenging animals at the edge of our ancient camp fires into Borzois and poodles. The thing itself, the first thing, will never do us alone, we must be elaborating, improving, poeticising. 'To palliate the shortness of our lives,' I suppose, as Thomas Browne wrote in the book that Roseanne has given me to give to her son. Between *Religio Medici* and the Royal Horticultural Society's *Roses* I have pitched a tent of sorts. And that Bet needed and wanted to know all these things about roses suddenly filled me with happiness, and pride. And curiously enough, this feeling didn't give way to regret and guilt. No, it opened room upon room, rose upon rose, to further happiness. That was not only the best day I have had since she died, but one of the best days of my life. It was as if she had dipped something of her essence down from heaven and helped me. I was so bloody grateful to her.

Oh, and I forgot to say (but to whom am I saying it?) that while putting Roseanne's book carefully aside, so I could concentrate on Bet's volumes, a letter almost fell out of it. It was a very curious letter, in that the envelope seemed not to have been opened, unless the damp of her room had somehow resealed it. Furthermore the postmark was from May 1987, fully twenty years ago. So I didn't know what to make of it, or quite what to do with it. My father always taught me that post was somehow sacred, and not only was it an actual crime to open another person's letter, as I believe it is, but a grave moral lapse also. I am afraid I am sorely tempted into such a moral lapse. On the other hand, maybe I should return it. Or burn it? No, hardly. Or leave it?

Roseanne's Testimony of Herself

The edges of the town received me coldly. I suppose I looked like something very wild blown in from the bog. A little girl sitting with her doll in the window of her house, trapped indoors by the storm, gave me a wave, with the mercy of little girls. I was thankful I did not have to go into the town proper. The hard pavement seemed to send bangs into my stomach, but I soldiered on. Then I was at the gates of Mrs McNulty's bungalow.

Old Tom's garden was an acre of beauty just withheld. I could see all his beds of well-prepared plants and flowers trying to bud, with bamboos holding everything against the wind. It was going to be a wonderful show in a few weeks right enough. In the top corner of the field there was an indistinct man digging, who might have been Old Tom. Digging, unperturbed by the twisting gusts and the sleeting rain, in a big coat and a solemn sou'wester. I thought to go over to him but I didn't know who was my enemy. Or I thought, by Jack's bleak stare at the gates across the road from my hut, they were all enemies. I decided not to approach him. I decided to take my chance at the door. I do remember at this point that the muscles in my stomach felt like they had highwire artists using them for swings.

I suppose I was muddy and drenched, I suppose I was. All my efforts to look well had no doubt been entirely undone by the journey. I had no mirror to check myself, except the dark windows each side of the door, and when I looked in there I saw only a ghoul with outlandish hair. That wasn't going to help me. But what could I do? Go back the way I came, in silence, defeated? I was frightened, I was terrified of this house, but I was more frightened of what would happen if I did not press the bell.

I sit here dry and old with measly shins writing this. It is not like long ago, it is not like a story, it is not like it is over and done. It is all to do. It is something like the gates of St Peter, banging on the gates, asking for entrance to heaven, and in my heavy heart knowing, too many sins, too many sins. But perhaps mercy!

I pushed in the thick Bakelite bell. It made no sound going in, but on withdrawing, I heard its petulant rattle inside the hall. Nothing happened for long time. I could hear my own distressed breathing in the close porch. I thought I heard my heartbeat. I thought I could hear my infant's heartbeat, willing me on. I pushed in the fat button again. Would that I were anyone else ringing there, a butcher's boy, a travelling salesman, and not this heavy, panting embarrassment of a creature. I had a vision of Mrs McNulty's miniature form, her neatness, her face as white as the flower honesty, and just as I did, I heard a scuffling the other side of the door, and the door pulled open, and herself in the gap.

She gazed out at me. I don't know if she knew immediately who it was. She might have thought me a beggerwoman, or a tinker, or something escaped from the madhouse where she worked. Indeed I was a sort of beggarwoman, begging another woman to understand my plight. Forsaken, forsaken was the word that began to ring in my head.

'What do you want?' she said, understandably, probably eventually realising it was me, the undesirable woman her son had married and not married. I supposed she had plotted against me years before, but that did not concern me now. I didn't know how many weeks I was. I was almost afraid I would start to bring forth the baby on her doorstep. Maybe better for the baby if I had.

I didn't know what to say to her. I had never known anyone in my situation. I did not know what my situation was. I needed – I desperately needed someone to . . .

'What do you want?' she said again, as if inclined to shut the door if I didn't speak.

'I'm in trouble,' I said.

'I see that, child,' she said.

I tried to peer into her face. Child. That sounded there in the porch with the force of a beautiful word.

'I am in desperate trouble,' I said.

'You're nothing to do with us any more,' she said. 'Nothing.'

'I know that,' I said. 'But I've nowhere else to go. Nowhere.'

'Nothing and nowhere,' she said.

'Mrs McNulty, I am begging you to help me.'

'There's nothing I can do. What could I do for you? I am frightened of you.'

This suddenly gave me pause. I had not considered that. Frightened of me.

'I'm not to be frightened of, Mrs McNulty. I need help. I'm, I'm –'

I was trying to say pregnant, but it didn't seem a word that could be said. I knew in her ears if I said the word it would have the same meaning as whore, prostitute. Or she would hear those shadowing words in the word pregnant. It felt like there was wood in my mouth, the exact shape of my mouth. A big heave of wind came up the path behind me and tried to bundle me into the door. I think she thought I was trying to force my way in. But I was so weak on my legs suddenly, I thought I was going to collapse.

'I know you have had your own troubles in the past,' I said, desperately trying to remember what Jack had said at the Plaza. But had he said anything? Whatever you say, say nothing.

'Vicissitudes, he said. In the long ago?'

'Don't!' she shouted. And then she shouted, 'Tom!'

Then she whispered, as woundable as a wounded bird.

'What did he tell you, what did Jack tell you?'

'Nothing. Vicissitudes.'

'Filthy gossip,' she said. 'All it was.'

I don't know how Old Tom had heard her, maybe by long attention to her voice, but in a few moments he appeared around the house in his coat and hat, looking like a half-drowned mariner.

'Jesus, Mary and Joseph,' he said. 'Roseanne.'

'You have to get her to go away,' said Mrs McNulty.

'Come on, Roseanne,' said Old Tom, 'come on, come back out the gate.'

I did obediently as I was told. His voice was friendly. He was nodding his head as he drove me backwards.

'Go on,' he said, 'go on,' like I was a calf in the wrong part of the field.

'Go on.'

Then I was out on the pavement again. The wind drove along the street like a gang of invisible lorries, roaring and piercing.

'Go on,' said Old Tom.

'Where?' I said, with utmost desperation.

'Go back,' he said. 'Go back.'

'I need you to help me.'

'There's no one to help you.'

'Ask Tom to help me, please.'

'Tom can't help you, girl. Tom's getting married. You know? Tom can't help you.'

Married? My God.

'But what will I do?'

'Go back the road,' he said. 'Go on.'

I didn't go back the road at his bidding but because I had no other choice.

My thought was, if I could reach the hut again, I could dry myself, and rest, and think of another plan. But only to get out of the rain and the wind, and be able to think.

Tom marrying again. No, not again, for the first time.

If I had had him in front of me then, I might have killed him with whatever implement I could find. I might have torn a stone from a wall, a stick from a fence, and battered him, and killed him.

For bringing me with love into such wretched danger.

I don't think I was walking then but sort of heaving myself along. The little girl was still behind the window-glass as I passed, still with her doll, still waiting for the storm to abate, so she could go outside and play. This time for some reason she didn't wave.

They say that we come from apes and maybe it is the residing animal in us that knows things deep down that we almost don't realise we know. There was something, some clock or engine, beginning to stir in me, and my whole instinct was to hurry my steps, to hurry my steps, and find somewhere quiet and sheltered where I could try and understand that engine. There was an urgency in it, and a smell to it, some strange noise rose from me, and was whipped away by the wind. Now I was out on the tarmacadam road to Strandhill, green fields and stone walls around me, and the visible rain striking the surface of the road and leaping about with a sort of anger. It was like I had music in my belly, strong driving drumming music, the 'Black Bottom Stomp' gone over the edge, the piano player going wilder and wilder at the keys.

The road took a slow turn and then the bay began to be visible below. Who did I have to help me? No one. Where was the world? How was it I had managed to live in the world with no one? How was it that the inhabitants of the few houses along the way didn't rush out to me, to hurry me into their houses, to hold me in their arms? A savage sense entered me, of being of such small account in the world that I wasn't to be helped, that priest and woman and man had put out an edict that I wasn't to be helped, I was to be left to the elements, just as I was, a walking animal, forsaken.

Maybe it was then that some part of me leapt away from myself, something fled from my brain, I don't know.

Refuge. A forlorn being seeks refuge. I had the fire covered in ashes in my hut, and all it would need would be the ashes knocked off the turves, and more turves added, and soon I would have a decent fire. And I could peel off my old coat and my dress and my slip and my shoes and dry myself exultant in the dry room, laughing, victorious, having gained a victory over storms and families. I had a simple stew in a covered pot and I would eat that, and then when I was dry and fed, into the bed with me, and I would lie there looking out on Knocknarea, poor old Queen Maeve above in her own stone bed, feeling maybe the worst of the storm so high up, and I would look at my belly as I liked to do, and see the elbows and the knees poking out and disappearing as my baby stretched and stirred. I had about six miles to go before I reached this longed-for safety. I could see from the cut of the land that if I went out on the beach as the motorcars used to do at low tide, I would take a good two miles from the journey. I noted even in my distress that the tide was at its lowest ebb, though it was hard to make this out with the armies and legions of rain that lashed across it. So I cut down from the high road along a steep boreen, not minding the rough stones too much, contented in my mind I was shortening my way, and indeed so numb in my feet and legs I think I no longer felt much pain there. The pain was all in my stomach, the pain was all about my child, and I was fearsomely anxious to gain my advantage.

Beautiful once, but beauty ended.

Down on the sand all was like a dance, as if the Plaza itself had expanded to fill Sligo Bay. The rain was like huge skirts, swirling and lifting, with hammering pillars of legs driving down, the whole of the strand and the sea between Strandhill and Rosses blanked out by a million brushstrokes of grey and grey. I thought then that it was not so sensible to have taken to the sand, or at least, I was cursed by a change in the gear of the weather, an infinite swelling and belling of the storm, tearing at me and my stomach, my little creature of elbows and knees.

Then I was starting to slosh through shallow runs of water and knew I was not on a proper course. The sand that the cars favoured as they roared out to the dance sat higher than the rest, and on a summer's night was dry. I feared I was heading towards the channel of the Garravoge, a disaster unimaginable, and now I didn't know which way to turn. Where was the mountain, where was the bulge of the land? Where was Strandhill and where was Coney?

Suddenly in front of me loomed a monster – no, it wasn't a monster, it was a cone of carved stones, it was one of the bollards that were set up in a line to show the way to the island, along the best sand, the last sand to be covered as the tide came in. A thing the tide was beginning to do, I knew, because I could hear, inside the roaring of the storm, the other galloping sound of the sea, as it rushed in eagerly to take the empty places in its arms. But I reached the bollard and held onto its stones for a few moments, trying to calm myself, at least a mite encouraged to have found it. Unless I had turned myself around completely, I judged the river would be over to my right, and Strandhill somewhere to my left. At the top of the bollard was a rusty metal arrow, pointing to the island.

Fearsomely in the storm the Metal Man would be standing on his rock, pointing to deep water, pointing, pointing. He would have no time to help the likes of me.

I knew I had to keep going, if I stayed where I was the tide would simply gather in, cover the sand at my feet, and slowly slowly rise up the bollard. I did not dare go back towards the shore, where there might be a rising flood. But at high tide most of the bollards were covered, and there would be no safety here. It would be the realm of currents and fishes. I put the bollard at my back, taking a course from the arrow, and stepped forward into the storm, praying I could keep enough of a straight line from that compass, and reach Coney.

A swathe of blue angry light was cut into the storm, like a slice of mad cake, and suddenly I saw the great prow of Ben Bulben looming, like a liner that was going to run me down. No, no, it was miles away. But it was also where I had supposed it to be, and then I was able to gain the next bollard. Oh, I sent my heart to the Metal Man in gratitude. Now I could see indistinctly but distinctly enough the mound of Coney island ahead. I forged on towards it. As I moved from the next bollard I felt that water gush from me and briefly warm my legs. With another hundred aching strides I had reached the first rocks, and the black seaweed, and drove myself up the sloping path. Without that break in the storm I don't know what I would have done, except drowned in the hurrying sea. Because now the storm closed about me again like a room of utter madness, walls of water and ceiling of banging fire, it seemed, and I lay in a nest of boulders, panting, and half expired.

I awoke. The storm was still howling roundabout. I hardly knew who I was. I remember searching in my mind even for words. In my sleep or whatever state it was, I had heaved my back up against a mossy rock, I don't know why. The storm was howling, with enormous drenching drifts of rain. I was lying so still I had the mad thought that I was dead. But I was far from dead. Every so often, minutes or hours I couldn't tell, something took a hold of me, like I was being squeezed from the crown of my head to my toes. It was so painful it seemed to have crept beyond pain, I don't know how other to describe it. I pulled myself onto all fours, again not exactly deciding to, but responding to a will unknown. Looking now wildly forwards, I thought in the cascading sheets of rain I saw a person standing, watching me. Then the storm seemed to blot the figure out. I screamed out to whoever it was, screamed and screamed. Then another shock of pain gripped me, as if someone had cleaved my backbone with an axe. Who was it watching me in the rain? Not someone who was going to approach and help. More hours passed. I felt the tide recede again from the island, felt it in my veins. The storm burned down from the heavens. Or rather, I was on fire in all that wetness. My stomach was like a bread oven, gathering in heat. No, no, it could not have been. The time of human clocks flew away, the coming and going of the pain was the new marker of time. Did the pain come closer and closer now? Less time between? Had night fallen secretly to darken the storm? Was I blind? Now there was suddenness, arrival, blood. I looked down between my legs. I felt I had my arms outstretched like wings, ready to catch something falling from the sky. But it wasn't falling from the sky, it was falling down through me. My blood fell on the soaking heather and cried out to God to help me, His striving animal. The voice of my blood cried out. No, no, that was only madness, madness. Between my legs was only coals, a ring of coals burning so redly nothing could live if it passed through it. In that second of madness then was the crown of a little head, and in another second a shoulder, all smeared in skin and blood. There was a face, there was a breast, there was a belly and two legs, and even the storm seemed to draw its breath in silence, there was a silence, I looked, I took up the little creature, it drew out after it a vivid cord, I lifted the baby to my face and, again without real thought, bit the cord, the storm swelled up and howled and howled, and my child also swelled, seemed to form himself in the lashing dark, gathered his first diamond of air, and howled out in miniature, called out tinily, to the island, to Sligo, to me, to me.

When I awoke again, the storm had cleared away like a savage dress sweeping out of the room of Sligo. Where was the little creature? There was the blood and the skin and cord and the placenta. I started to my feet. I was as dizzy and weak as a new-born foal myself. Where was my baby? Such a wild feeling of panic and loss poured into me. I looked about with the frantic longing and fiery head of any mother, human or animal. I parted the low sprigs and plants of heather, I searched about me in circles. I called out for help. The sky was big and blue all the way to heaven.

How long had the storm been gone? I didn't know.

I fell back down, striking a hip against the rock. There was still a steady twine of blood coming out of me, dark blood, warm and dark. I lay there, staring out at the world like a woman who had been shot in the head, the peaceful beach, the sandbirds dipping and striking with their long beaks along the receding tideline. 'Please help me,' I kept saying, but there seemed to be no one to hear me except those birds. Weren't there a few houses on the island, hiding here and there from the wind? Could someone not come and help me find my baby? Could someone not come?

As I lay there a strange sharp hurting feeling came into my breast, it was the milk coming into them, I thought. I had the milk now, ready. Where, where was my baby to drink it?

Then down the winding road to the strand I saw a white van moving. I knew immediately it was an ambulance, because even so far away I could hear its siren in the stillness. It reached the sand and surged forward, taking its course, just as I had in the storm, from bollard to bollard. I stood again and waved my arms, like the shipwrecked sailor does when at last he sees the far-off ship to rescue him. But it wasn't me that needed rescue, it was that tiny person vanished from the space he should have occupied. When the men came up to me with their stretcher, I asked them to tell me where my baby was, I begged them.

'We don't know, ma'am,' one said, with perfect manners. 'What are you doing out here on Coney having a baby? It's no place to have a baby, now, that's for sure.'

'But where is it, where is my baby?'

'Was the tide in high, ma'am, and washed it away, God bless the poor mite?'

'No, no, I had him in my arms, and slept, and kept him close, and warm. I knew he could be warm beside me. Look, I had him here, in my breast, look, the buttons are undone, I had him safe and warm.'

'All right,' said another. 'All right. Do calm yourself. There's still bleeding,' he said to his colleague. 'We'll have to try and stop that.'

'You mightn't stop it,' said the man.

'We'll get her to Sligo quick.'

And they loaded me into the back. But were we abandoning my child? I didn't know. I scrabbled at the door when it closed.

'Look everywhere,' I said. 'There was a child. There was.'

Oh, then when they started the engine, it was like falling through floors, I swooned away.

Now I begin to encounter difficulties. Now the roads seem to take two courses through the forest, and the forest is so deep in snow there is only whiteness.

Someone took my child. The ambulance brought me to the hospital. For days I know I was still bleeding inside, and they did not expect me to live. These things I remember. I remember they did an operation on me because I know I stopped bleeding and that I lived. I remember Fr Gaunt coming in and telling me that I was going to be taken care of, that he knew where he could put me for my own safety, and that I would like the place, and that I wasn't to worry. I asked again and again about my child and each time he just said the word 'Nazareth'. I didn't know what he meant. I was so weak I think I must have done what the prisoner will do with his jailer, I looked for Fr Gaunt to help me. I may have asked him for his help. I certainly wept a great deal and I have even a memory of him holding me while I wept. Was there anyone else there? I can't remember. Soon I saw the two towers of the asylum looming above me and I was given forth to hell.

I cried out that I wanted to see my mother, but they said, 'You cannot see her, no one can see her, she is beyond seeing.'

Now memory falters. Yes. It shudders, like a motor trying to start at the turn of the crank, but failing. Phut, phut, phut. Oh, is that Old Tom and Mrs McNulty in the darkness there, in a dark room as may be, and myself there also, and are they measuring me with their linen tapes, for an asylum smock, not saying anything, except the measurements, the bust, the waist, the hips? Like they had measured all the other inmates as they came in, for a smock, and all the inmates as they went out, for a shroud?

Now memory stops. It is entirely absent. I don't even remember suffering, misery. It is not there. I remember Eneas coming in his army uniform one night, charming the staff into seeing me. He had a major's uniform on that day and I knew he was only a private soldier but he confessed to me that he had gone and borrowed his brother Jack's and very well he looked in it, with the epaulettes. He told me to dress myself quickly, that he had my baby outside and he was going to free me. We were going to go away together into another land. I had no dress to put on except the rags I had already, I knew I was filthy and lice-ridden, there was blood dried on me all over, and through the dark corridor we crept, Eneas and I, and he creaked open the great door of the asylum, and we went out under the old towers and across the gravel, me not minding the sharp stones at all, and he gathered the baby from the high pram where it had waited for us, a lovely baby boy he was, and he took the bundle in his arms, and led me on across the lawn with my bleeding feet, and we had to cross a little fresh river at the bottom of the slope. He crossed over and walked up onto a beautiful green meadow with lofty grass. The moon was speckling the water of the river, my old owl was calling, and as I stepped into the river my dress dissolved and the water cleaned me. I stepped out the other side from the rushes and Eneas looked at me, I know in my heart I was beautiful again, and he handed me my baby and I felt the milk come into my breast. And Eneas and I and our child stood in the meadow in the moonlight and there was a line of enormous green trees being stirred gently by a warm summer wind. And Eneas took off his useless uniform, it was that warm, and we stood there as content as ever people were, and we were the first and last people on the earth.

A memory so clear, so wonderful, so beyond the bounds of possibility.

I know it.

My head is as clear as a glass.

If you are reading this, then the mouse, the woodworm and the beetle must have spared these jotters.

What can I tell you further? I once lived among humankind, and found them in their generality to be cruel and cold, and yet could mention the names of three or four that were like angels.

I suppose we measure the importance of our days by those few angels we spy among us, and yet aren't like them.

If our suffering is great on account of that, yet at close of day the gift of life is something immense. Something larger than old Sligo mountains, something difficult but oddly bright, that makes equal in their fall the hammers and the feathers.

And like the impulse that drives the old maid to make a garden, with a meagre rose and a straggling daffodil, gives a hint of some coming paradise.

All that remains of me now is a rumour of beauty.

CHAPTER TWENTY-ONE

Dr Grene's Commonplace Book

Well, I finally made my trip over to Sligo, having found a gap in all these preparations for leaving the hospital. Such a short journey really, and yet I have rarely made it over the years. Beautiful spring day. Yet even on such a day, Sligo Mental Hospital looked so gloomy, with its unpromising twin towers. It is a vast building. In common parlance it is called the Leitrim Hotel, as Roseanne explained to me, since half of Leitrim is said to be in it. But that no doubt is just a regional prejudice.

Considering I was once so friendly with Percy Quinn I suppose it is strange that we have not really kept in touch, with so few miles between us. Some friendships though, even strong and interesting ones, seem to have quite a short term, and cannot be prolonged. Nevertheless Percy, with his receding hair and a new plumpness I didn't remember, was exceedingly cordial when I found his office, which occupies one of the towers. I don't know much about his reputation, how progressive he is, or to what degree he sits back and lets things take their course, as I am afraid I have often been guilty of myself, I do believe. Not that I would confess this anywhere but here, but I am sure St Peter is taking notes against me.

'I was very sorry to hear about your loss,' he said. 'I was intending to come over for the service, but I just could not make it that day.'

'Oh, that's fine, don't worry,' I said. 'Thank you.' Then I didn't know what to say. 'It went off very well.'

'I don't think I knew your wife, did I?'

'No, no, I'm sure not. After your time.'

'Well, so you're on the hunt?' he said.

'Well, I've been trying to assess the patient I wrote to you about, Roseanne Clear, for various reasons, and as she is very unforthcoming I have had to try and be a bit devious, and go round the back of the houses, as it were.'

'I've been digging a bit for you,' he said. 'Found a few things. Actually, it began to intrigue me. I suppose everyone has mysteries in their lives. Look, will I call Maggie and get her to bring us up some tea?'

'No, that's fine,' I said. 'Not for me anyway. Perhaps yourself?'

'No, no,' he said briskly. 'First thing that might interest you. There *are* RIC police records remaining. They were in the town hall, would you believe. The name you gave me was Joseph Clear, wasn't it? And yes, there was a record of that name, in the nineteen-tens or twenties I think it was.'

I was disappointed, I must confess. I think I hoped that Roseanne's denial would have proven correct. But there it was.

'I suppose that was the same man,' said Percy.

'It's not a very common name.'

'No. And then I was looking again at what we had besides the very quaint account of that Fr Gaunt fella, which I re-read. You were concerned that she had killed her child, wasn't that it?'

'Well, not concerned as such. Trying to establish the truth of it, because she denies it.'

'Oh? That's interesting. What does she say about it?'

'I asked her what became of the baby, since Fr Gaunt had mentioned it, and it was no doubt the crowning reason she was committed here, and she said the child was in Nazareth, which didn't make a whole lot of sense.'

'Yes, well, I think I know what she is trying to say. The orphanage here in Sligo was called Nazareth House. It doesn't have orphans any more, it's mostly an old persons' home now, but I try to refer people there if I can, rather than . . . You know.'

'Oh, I see, well, that fits all right.'

'Yes, it does. And, I must say, it would have been very unfair, unlawful even, of Fr Gaunt, to suggest something so terrible if he knew it to be untrue. I am searching in my mind for an interpretation of his words. I can only conclude that he meant killed it spiritually. In those days of course the illegitimate child was thought to carry the sin of his mother. This may have been what our enterprising cleric meant. Let us be generous in retrospect. That is, if it turned out she didn't kill the child of course.'

'Do you think I could go over to Nazareth House and ask them if they have any records?'

'Well, I think you could. They used to be very closed of course, about these matters, unless you knew how to prise them open. Their instinct I am sure is still to secrecy, but like many of these institutions, they have been assailed in recent times with accusations of one sort and another. There are many Nazareth Houses, and some of them have been accused of rather terrible cruelty in the past. So you may find them more helpful than you might have expected. And they're used to dealing with me. I find them always very helpful. Nuns, of course. They were a mendicant order originally. A noble concept, really.'

Then he said nothing for a bit. He was 'cogitating' as Bet used to say.

'There was another thing,' he said. 'In the interests of openness on my own part I think I can tell you. Unfortunately it was part of our confidential records. Internal inquiries, you know, that sort of thing.'

'Oh, yes?' I said, gingerly enough.

'Yes. In regard to your patient. There was a man here called Sean Keane, an orderly, a bit funny in the head himself apparently, to use layman's terms for a moment, who made a complaint against another orderly. Now, this of course is long ago, in the late fifties even, I didn't even recognise the name of the man keeping the notes, Richardson was his name. Sean Keane accused this other man Brady of menacing and I fear molesting your patient over quite a long period. She is described as a person of 'quite exceptional beauty', if you don't mind. You know, William, I could tell even from the scurry of the writing, that the notemaker was reluctant to write any of this. Not much has changed, I hear you say.'

But I had said nothing. I nodded to encourage him.

'Anyway, I think it was decided at this point to move your patient to Roscommon, and let the dust settle over the matter.'

'What happened to the alleged molester?'

'Well, that was rather tragic, because he stayed here till retirement, I could trace his presence quite plainly right to the end of the seventies. But, you know.'

'I do know. It is all very difficult.'

'Yes,' said Percy. 'The boat is always in the middle of a storm and one tries not to rock it further.'

'Yes,' I said.

'Not too surprisingly also, Sean Keane disappears with Roseanne Clear from the records, so they must have let him go. Richardson no doubt opting for peace of a sort.'

The two of us sat there then, contemplating this, maybe both of us wondering if indeed anything much had changed.

'Her mother died in here. Did you know that? 1941.'

'No.'

'Oh, yes. Severely deranged.'

'That's very interesting. I'd no idea.'

'It's funny that our hospitals are so close and we never see each other,' he said then.

'I was just thinking that as I drove over.'

'Well, such is life.'

'Such is life,' I said.

'I am very glad you came over today,' he said. 'We should try and make a habit of it.'

'Thank you for looking into this for me. I'm really grateful, Percy.'

'All right,' he said. 'Look, I'll give Nazareth House a ring and tell them to expect you, and who you are, and whatnot. All right?'

'Thank you, Percy.'

We shook hands warmly, but not all that warmly, I thought. There was a hesitation in both of us. Life, indeed.

The part of Nazareth House I was directed into was new, but still seemed to have acquired a certain institutional grimness, if not as grim as the old asylum. When I was a very young man I thought places for the sick and mad should be made very bright and attractive, given a sort of festiveness to alleviate our human miseries. But maybe these places are like animals and cannot change their spots and stripes no more than leopards and tigers. The keeper of records was a nun, like me in advanced middle age if not old age, wearing her relaxed modern gear. I had half expected wimples and robes. She said good Percy had already rung and given her details of names and dates and that she had some information for me. 'News', she called it.

'But you will have to go to England if you really want to pursue this,' she said.

'England?' I said.

'Yes,' she said, with her unplaceable country accent which I placed nonetheless as maybe Monaghan, or even further north. 'There is a reference here all right, but all the documents relating to these names are in our house in Bexhill-on-Sea.'

'What are they doing over there, Sister?'

'Well, I don't know, but as you are aware these are old matters, and you may find out more in England.'

'But is the child still alive? Was there a child that came here?'

'There is a reference against the name, and it was the particular case of one of our sisters in Bexhill, Sr Declan, who was from here of course. She is dead now, may she rest in peace. Of course, Dr Grene, she was a McNulty. Did you know old Mrs McNulty was with us here in old age? Yes. She was ninety when she died. I have her records in front of me, God rest her. God rest them both.'

'Is it possible for you to telephone them?'

'No, no, these matters are not matters for the phone.'

'It was Mrs McNulty's daughter that was a nun in England?'

'That's exactly it. She was a great friend of the order. She had a bit to leave and she left it to us. She was a very great lady and I remember her well. A tiny little woman with the kindest face you ever saw, and always trying to do the good thing by everybody.'

'Well, I am sure,' I said.

'Oh, yes. She wanted to take the veil herself but couldn't do it while her husband was alive, and then didn't he live till he was ninety-six, and then of course there were the sons. They mightn't have liked it. Do you mind me asking if you are a Catholic, Dr Grene? I think by your accent you're English.'

'I am a Catholic, yes,' I said, easily, without embarrassment.

'Then you will know how odd we are,' said the little nun.

I drove back here in a strange state of mind. I thought how curious it was how people leave a few traces as they go, that can be looked at and puzzled over, but whether ever properly understood, I doubted. It seemed Roseanne had indeed suffered greatly, as I had feared. How terrible to lose her child, however that had happened, and then to be subjected to the attentions of some miserable bastard who looked on her merely as an opportunity for his pleasure. I could suspect also that having been parted from her baby, or having lost it, or even killed it if Fr Gaunt is accurate after all, she might also have finally been parted from her wits. Such traumas might very well have brought on quite a radical psychosis. She would have been well nigh a sitting duck for any unpleasant element among the staff, with her 'exceptional beauty'. God help her. I thought of the sere old lady in the room here in Roscommon. Professional man though I am, I confess to feeling very sorry for her. And retrospectively, rather guilty. Yes. Because for one thing I would probably have been inclined to do the same as Richardson.

On the other hand, I was thinking, as I drove, it was unlikely I would find the time to go to England. And I was wondering to myself, what in the name of God are you doing anyway, William? You know you are not going to recommend putting her back in the community. She will have to be transferred somewhere (note: not Nazareth House in Sligo, and not Sligo Psychiatric Hospital, all things considered) because she is surely too old now for anything else. So why was I pursuing it? Well, the truth is, it has been a great comfort. Also, there has been something about it that I have found almost irresistible. I think I must classify the whole impulse as a form of grieving. Grieving for Bet, and for the nature of lives in general. For the lot of human creatures generally. But, I was thinking, England is a step too far, though I must say I would like to find out the truth of Roseanne's child, or no child, having come this far. But the work load at the present time is much too great (I am trying to write down a version of my active thoughts in the car, never an easy thing), and maybe, since the most crucial and important parts of life seem after all to have the characters of sleeping dogs, I should let them lie. It is all old history and what would it serve now to dig it up? And then the real thought struck me. That I have been looking at this from all the wrong angles. Because if there is a record of this child, would it not be a great comfort to Roseanne to know this, even if the person is uncontactable – to know 'before she dies' that she put someone safely into the world after all? Or would this be just further mental mayhem and trauma? Would she want to be in touch with this person, and would this person – oh, the proverbial Pandora's box. Well, well, I have no time any-way, I was thinking. But I will lay this quest down reluctantly.

Then I parked my car as usual and went into the hospital. I took an account of the day from the day nurse and among other things she told me that Roseanne Clear's breathing had worsened and they had been even afraid to move her down to the medical ward, she was so delicately balanced between life and death, but they had managed it under Dr Wynn's supervi-sion, and she was on an oxygen mask. The lungs need a 98 per cent function to have sufficient exchange of gases properly to aerate the blood, and she has only about 74 per cent, such is the congestion. Although at the end of the day she is 'just another patient' I have to say this was very worrying and discommod-ing. I hurried to the ward nearby as if she might be already per-ished and was unaccountably very relieved to find her alive, if unconscious and with an unpleasant sound to her breathing.

After a while sitting there I began to feel very idle, because there would be papers to attend to in my office. So I went in there and attacked the pile. At the bottom of the forms and let-ters was a package, a sheaf of papers in a large used envelope, in fact an envelope I had opened a few days ago and thrown in my waste-paper basket. Someone had fished it out again and put in these pages. They were written in blue biro, in a very neat small hand that required me to put my reading glasses on, something of course that I try not to do, out of mere vanity.

It didn't take long to realise that it was an account of

Roseanne's life, written it would seem by herself. I was absolutely amazed. I was instantly but rather strangely glad I had not pressed my advantage that day when she told me she had had a child. Because here was everything anyway, without the sense that I had forced her to 'betray' herself, using all the wiles and tricks of my training. I knew I wouldn't have time to read it properly until I was in my house that night (yesterday), but already I could see she offered information freely, in such strong contrast to her spoken answers to me. But also, where had it come from? And who had put it on my table, certainly not herself, surely? I was honour bound to suspect John Kane, as he was the person most usually in her room. Or one of the nurses. Of course, with all the kerfuffle today in her room, it might have been anybody. I called through to the nurses' room and asked if anyone knew anything about it. Doran, a reasonably able and pleasant man, said he would ask around. Where was John Kane? I asked. Doran said Kane was home at his little flat in the old stableyard behind the institution (also due to be knocked down shortly). He said John Kane had been feeling poorly and after a morning's work, had asked to be let go to lie down. Dr Wynn had excused him readily. John Kane of course is not a well man.

I read Roseanne's account of things like a scholar of her life, making a mental concordance of facts and events.

The first feeling I had reading it was privilege. How strange to think of her secretly writing it, like a monk in a scriptorium, all the while I was endeavouring to assess her, and getting virtually nowhere. The sense that she might be addressing it to me overwhelmed me.

It differs from Fr Gaunt's history in many ways, not least the long account of her father and his experiences. For a woman who knows no one virtually and has spent the last sixty-odd years of her life in a place like the hospital, she seems at times to me to be a surprising celebrator of life and people. Many mysteries remain. But I have tried to orchestrate the little that I know and have fallen on names I recognise with gratitude. Sean Keane who figured in Percy Quinn's records seems to have been a son of John Lavelle. Furthermore it seems he was to some degree brain-damaged. There is one person I know who I can ask about this, because my suspicion is that our John Kane is the same man. There is a story here of a strange loyalty and protection. His father asked him to look after Roseanne, and he seems to have done his utmost to do so.

Who took Roseanne's baby though is not really answered, and the fact remains that the evidence is against her about her father's work. If this is wrong, then other things she writes may also be 'wrong'. It cannot be taken at face value, but maybe no more than Fr Gaunt, who was obviously sane to such a degree it makes sanity almost undesirable.

I think I certainly can surmise that she was falsely accused in the matter of John Lavelle, unless I am reading her wrong, although I recognise that in the mores of the time, the morass, I almost wrote, just to have been seen with him in that way, just the suspicion, was crime enough. Morality has its own civil wars, with its own victims in their own time and place. But once she became pregnant she was utterly doomed. A married woman who had never been married. She could never have won that one.

I write all this, and immediately have some niggling concerns. The use of the word 'wrong' for instance. What is wrong about her account if she sincerely believes it? Is not most history written in a sort of wayward sincerity? I suspect so. In her account, she relates a very sincere and even touching account of how her father sought to show her that all things from hammers to feathers fall equally. She seems to have been about twelve when it happens (now I am forced to look again at her manuscript, because *I* may be rewriting). Yes, about twelve. And then the dire events at the graveyard, and then the rat-catching, and eventually, when she is about fifteen (blast it, must check again), her father's death. But Fr Gaunt has him being murdered by the rebels, the first attempt in the very round tower Roseanne so fondly remembers, his mouth stuffed with feathers and him beaten by mallets or hammers, which in terms of post-traumatic stress, sounds like what really happened, and suggests that Roseanne for survival's sake has sanitised it completely, even moving the event back to a time of relative innocence. But this in my experience seems an enormous and unusual transference, all things considered. Then there is the fact that the man that Fr Gaunt suggests Roseanne should marry, Joe Brady, the inheritor of her father's job at the graveyard, is presented in Roseanne's account as an attempted rapist, a passage that reads very 'strangely' to me. And not only that, but Fr Gaunt in passing mentions the name on the gravestone where the guns were buried as the same name, though he must have known. Then of course, I am thinking, Fr Gaunt, while maybe sincere in his great desire to have her committed, was also subject to mere error of memory, and he may have found the name floating in his head, and wrongly given it as the name on the grave. The one thing that is fatal in the reading of impromptu history is a wrongful desire for accuracy. There is no such thing.

So, as if to prove this, I have just gone back to Fr Gaunt's actual account, which I summarised here rather than transposed, and I find to my absolute astonishment and even shame that in his account of the events in the tower, he doesn't actually say Roseanne's father's mouth was stuffed with feathers, just that he was beaten by hammers. For some reason, in the gap between reading his account and summarising, my own brain must have supplied this detail, stealing it from Roseanne I would like to think, except at that point of course *I hadn't read her account.* At this juncture I find myself in the wildest, woolliest jungles of Laing himself. It is almost a disgusting thought to me that I might have intuited this detail out of the aether, and supplied it unconsciously, anticipating a story that I had not yet read. For this implies all sorts of horrible sixties theory about the circular and backward natures of time, and I do not subscribe to that. We have enough problems with linear narrative and true memory. Nevertheless I must conclude that to a large degree, both Roseanne and Fr Gaunt were being as truthful as they could be, given the vagaries and tricks of the human mind. Roseanne's 'sins' as a self-historian are 'sins of omission'. Her father showed her the nature of gravity at the tower, and some years later an attempt was made to kill her father in the tower, both of which events she witnessed, but would not record the second. So that my first inclination to identify her memory as a traumatic one, with details trans-posed and corrupted, and the ages changed, was even if unlike-ly, actually too simple. Then there was of course my own weird interpolation – oh dear, oh dear. Of course, of course, it is just possible that years and years ago she told me about the ham-mers and feathers as an anecdote, and I simply forgot all about it. And that reading about the tower in Fr Gaunt's deposition brought them into my mind. And indeed, even as I posit this, even as I 'invent' it, I actually seem to have a vague memory of it. Disastrous! But leaving that aside, there is something good in this conclusion. I may say before God (of all people, I hear myself say) that I believe they have written not so much wrongful histories, or even competing histories, but both in their human way quite truthful, and that from both of them can be implied useful truths above and beyond the actual ver-ity of the 'facts'. I am beginning to think there is no factual truth, although I can hear Bet say in my ear, 'Really, William?'

I have decided anyhow on the strength of reading her account to make the journey to England. She seems to have addressed her story almost to me, or at times at least to me, as her friend perhaps, and I feel it not only my duty but my great desire to follow this to the end, and see what the terminus is. I cannot imagine that I will achieve very much by this, as Dr Wynn does not expect her to regain consciousness, 'very sad news' he called it, and asked me had she any family I needed to contact. Of course I was able to say, no. I did not think so. Not a soul living that could fall under that heading, except this mysterious child. And that is a further reason to go to England, on the very unlikely chance that there is someone to notify in the event of the death of this person some might deem a nobody, but to me has assumed the proportions of a friend, and is a sort of justification of my work here, such as it has been, and my choice of this profession, such as it is.

I must never forget that in my moment of deepest travail she crossed the room and put her hand on my shoulder, an utterly simple gesture perhaps, but more graceful and helpful to me than the gift of a kingdom. By such a gesture she sought to heal me, supposedly the healer. As I do not seem able much to heal, then maybe I can simply be a responsible witness to the miracle of the ordinary soul.

I am profoundly grateful that I did not use Fr Gaunt's account to question her with, aggressively or subtly, whichever, and that I followed my own instincts. I see now it would have been an assault on her memory. Similarly her own account should not be used as an instrument of further probing.

My main thought is, let her be.

Soon I was ready to go, but before I did, I decided to write a note to John Kane, in case words written down had a better chance to penetrate him.

Dear John (I wrote), *it has come to my notice some acts of*
kindness performed by you in respect of our patient Roseanne
Clear, formerly Mrs McNulty. I think I know who your own
father was, John, I think he was the patriot John Lavelle? and
I would very much like to ask you a few questions when I
return from England, where I hope to discover more about
Roseanne Clear's child. Perhaps we can compare notes?
Sincerely, etc.

I hoped this made sense to him. I put in the word patriot to
take any possible note of threat out of it. Perhaps I was completely wrong and he would gaze at it as the work of a lunatic.

It hardly made sense to me, but off I went anyhow.

The cheapest flight was Dublin to Gatwick, so I found myself
driving the five hours eastward. But I think it would surprise
Roseanne that there is now an airport in Sligo, that I saw on a
website, right in Strandhill. But the little planes only fly to
Manchester.

I took with me my passport, naturally, also whatever documents I have in relation to Roseanne, the various histories,
and a note from the nun in Sligo. I was well aware how
famously or infamously secretive these old institutions can
be, no more than ourselves, a mixture of worry, lost power,
perhaps even concern. That the truth may not always be desirable, that one thing leads to another thing, that facts not only
lead forward to resolution, but backwards into the shadows,
and sometimes into the various little hells we make for each
other. So despite the nice nun, who anyway had not offered to
phone Bexhill, or otherwise intervene, and despite the cham-
pioning by Percy, I fully expected to be stonewalled or otherwise frustrated.

Of course, I also took with me Roseanne's copy of *Religio Medici*, just in case. Now I must confess I risked my father's turning in his grave, and on the airplane I opened the book, took out the letter boldly, and opened it, just in case it would be of some help. I don't know why I thought it might be. Perhaps there was a baser motive, mere nosiness and curiosity.

I was very surprised to find it was a letter from Jack McNulty. I looked at the date it was posted again and realised he must have been an old man himself when he wrote it. The wandering spideriness of the handwriting certainly suggested as much. The address was given as King James Hospital, Swansea. I have the letter here before me so I may as well enter it here, so as to have a copy.

Dear Roseanne,

I am lying here in hospital in Swansea and alas I am assailed by a cancer of the colon. I am writing to you because I have made enquiries about you and have been informed reliably I hope that you are still alive. I have been given my own marching orders and I suppose it is God's will but it is not likely I will be among the living much longer. I must say I have taken an interest in life and have enjoyed the visit as they say but when your number's called you must go. I do not know if you are aware I went soldiering in the war, I served in India near the Khyber Pass with the Gurkha Rifles I am proud to say, though I saw no Germans or Japanese or the like. Nevertheless if the mosquitoes had been on the German side we would have lost the war. I am writing to you because when a person is told he is going many things pass through his mind. For instance, the fact that my wife Mai after strug-gling with the alcohol died at the age of fifty-three. Though she led me a merry dance betimes I never for a moment regretted marrying her, as I adored her. Nevertheless I sup-pose she was an arrogant, wounding woman to some, to you in particular. This is why I am writing. It is greatly on my conscience what happened all those years ago, and I wanted to write and tell you that. There is no need, indeed I believe no likelihood, that you will forgive me, but I am writing to you in order to tell you that I regret it enormously, and hardly know what to make of it as an event in all our lives. I suppose it is all long long ago, but not so long ago that it does not seem like yesterday, and is often in my thoughts and in my dreams. I wanted to tell you that Tom married again and had children, but maybe you will not want to hear this. Tom died about ten years ago of a stomach complaint, he died in Roscommon General Hospital, his second wife by then also having died. We never spoke of you though we saw each other often, and yet I felt it was always there unspoken between us when we met. The truth is, it was something in his life that changed him forever, he was forever just a different man after that, never again the easy-going old Tom we knew.

Maybe you will say, proper order, I don't know. Maybe you would be right. I want to say a few words now about my mother, who as you may know was the chief instrument in all that time of difficulty. I want to tell you things about her that I could only tell you as a dying man, and maybe only like this, faceless, behind the cover of a letter. Because it is also true that she treated your – I was going to write 'case' but you know what I mean – with uncharacteristic hardness.

About twenty years ago when she was dying herself, she told me the story of her birth. It was sometimes whispered in Sligo that she was illegitimate, though you may not have heard this whisper. As it happens, she was adopted, her real mother having died young, and her family, being wealthy, and not approving the marriage in the first place, then contriving to give her away. Her mother was a Presbyterian woman called Lizzie Finn. Her real father was an army officer, and it seems she was given to his batman, a Catholic of course, to be reared as his own. It is a shadowy story, but I saw with my own eyes the marriage certificate of her parents in Christ Church some years after she died. How relieved she would have been to know they were married I can't say. Perhaps in heaven these are small matters.

Before Tom died, he also had occasion to tell me his secret, which in some ways is more pertinent to you, and may make you wonder why she did not show more compassion to you. For he confessed to me that he and I only shared a mother, his own father being other than Old Tom, though who he was he did not know, though he tried to find out, not least from my mother. My mother never shared this with anyone and brought the man's name to her grave. We must remember that my mother was only sixteen when I was born, and not much older when brother Tom came (or half-brother I should say).

Why am I telling you all this? Because of course it might explain if not excuse her enormous desire that Tom should not endure so confused a life as hers, and was a slave to her own ideas of rectitude, as only a person who thinks they have fallen can be.

Eneas? In the sixties I traced him through the War Office to an hotel on the Isle of Dogs in London. I went there one evening, was told he was out, and to come back the next day. The following morning when I approached the dosshouse, I found it a smouldering ruin. Perhaps alarmed at the news that there was someone from Sligo to see him, thinking it was his old enemies and he was to be assassinated, even after all those years, he may have burned the hotel himself, to cover his tracks. Or maybe some men had been shadowing me as I searched for him, and did the poor man in. Whatever happened, I could never pick up his trail again. He disappeared utterly. I suppose he is dead and may he rest in peace.

This is my letter and maybe it is of no good to you. It is all greatly on my conscience. Roseanne, the truth is, Tom did love

you but failed in his love. I am afraid we were all more than a
little in love with you. Forgive us if you can. Goodbye.
   Respectfully and sincerely,
   Jack

By any mark a strange and unexpected letter. There were things in it that I didn't quite understand. Suddenly of course I hoped and prayed that it was the damp had closed the letter again, and that she might once have opened it. Certainly, she had kept it, unless she had put it unopened in the book and forgotten it. Maybe it was the only letter she had ever received. Christ. I was certainly very pensive as the plane set down in Gatwick.

Bexhill is only about fifty miles from Gatwick in that part of England so English it is almost something else, unnameable. The names reek of candyfloss and old battles. Brighton, Hastings. It is on the coast that ironically holds the sites of a million childhood holidays, though I do not think the orphans of long ago would concur. Looking up flights on the internet, and directions for Bexhill, I found a discussion site, contributed to by survivors of those days. The raw pain flared up from the words. Two girls were drowned there in the sea in the fifties, the other girls trying to form a human chain to save them, while the nuns prayed bizarrely on the beach. It is like a painting stolen from the museum of inexplicable cruelty. I confess I wondered about Mrs McNulty's daughter, and confess also that for some reason I hoped she was not among those praying nuns. If Roseanne's child had ended up there in the forties . . . These were my muddled thoughts as I took the train from Victoria.

It seems I am fated to record the dismaying bleakness of institutions. It is a constant, unwaveringly. Nazareth House Bexhill was no exception. Their stories seem to be in the very mortar like those ancient seashells, the very redness of the bricks. You could never wash them out, I thought. The very silence of the place suggested other silences. I rang at the front door feeling suddenly very small and strange, as if I were myself an orphan arriving there. Soon the door was opened, I stated my business to the woman, a lay person, and I was led up the long hallway, with its darkly shining linoleum, and items of solid mahogany furniture, one of them graced by an Italian statue of St Joseph. I know it was St Joseph because his name was on the plinth. The woman stopped at a door, and smiled, I smiled, and I entered the room.

It was a sort of little dining room, at least the table had plates of sandwiches and cakes, and a setting for one, with a teacup ready. I hardly knew what to do, so sat down, wondering if I was in the right place, or the right person in the right place. But soon a tall smiling nun glided in, and filled my cup from a ceramic pot. It had I noticed a picture of the Bexhill seafront on it.

'Thank you, Sister,' I said, for I knew not what else to say.

'I'm sure you are very hungry after your journey,' she said.

'Well, I am, thank you,' I said.

'Sr Miriam will see you afterwards.'

So I ate in some bemusement and when I was finished – the nun seemed to have a sixth sense for this, because no one person could have cleared that spread – I was led deeper into the convent and shown eventually into a smaller room.

It was a room of the usual filing cabinets. I immediately had a sense of hush and history. I suspected there were some things in these cabinets that people would need lawyers to get at, if even then. And presiding over this was a neat, doughy-faced nun.

'Sr Miriam?' I said.

'Yes,' she said. 'You are Dr Grene.'

'I am,' I said.

'And you have come I believe to consult certain records?'

'Yes, I have some documents with me also, that may help us identify . . .'

'I received a call from Sligo and I've been able to make a start before you came.'

'Oh, I see, she did ring then, I thought she said . . .'

'This file has a dual reference,' she said, opening a slim folder. 'The child you are seeking did not stay with us long.'

I almost said, Thank God, but managed to keep the words in my head only.

'Although the file pertains to quite a long time ago, I understand the mother is still alive, and of course, the child himself . . .'

'So there was a child, is a child?'

'Oh yes, most certifiably,' she said, smiling broadly. Though I cannot place Irish accents, I inevitably have a go, and was thinking maybe Kerry, or certainly the west. Her slightly official use of words I supposed came from long acquaintance with these records. I must say she was an appealing person, very polite, and seemed intelligent.

'You are with me so far?' she said.

'Oh, yes.'

'There is a birth certificate,' she said. 'There is also the name of the people to whom the child was given in adoption. This latter party however would never have seen the former document, or only briefly. Enough to know the child was Irish, healthy, and Catholic.'

'That sounds sensible,' I said, rather stupidly I thought, as I heard the words come out. I was actually a little in awe of this woman, there was something formidable about her.

'The thing that gave the community a certain desire to find a good home for the child was of course its relationship to Sr Declan, God rest her. As a young woman I remember her well. She was a lovely west of Ireland person, an enormous credit to her mother and to us. She was in fact in her day the finest mendicant nun in Bexhill. That was a very great achievement. And the orphans in general loved her. Loved her.'

There was gentle but clear emphasis here.

'You might want to come out later and see her little grave?' said Sr Miriam.

'Oh, I would be delighted . . .'

'Yes. We recognise here at Bexhill that things were very different in the forties, and personally I think it is impossible to travel back in time adequately to appreciate those differences. Even Dr Who himself might find it hard.' She smiled again.

'There is a great truth in that,' I said, immediately sounding pompous even to myself. 'In the arena of mental health. God forbid. But at the same time, one must . . .'

'Do what one can?'

'Yes.'

'To make reparation and undo hurts?'

I was very surprised to hear her say so.

'Yes,' I said, flustered by her unexpected honesty.

'I agree,' she said, and like a cool-handed poker player, laid two documents before me on the desk. 'This is the birth certificate. This is the adoption paper.'

I leaned forward, taking out my reading glasses, and looked at the pages. I think for a moment my heart stopped and the blood was suspended in my body. Just for a moment those thousand rivers and streams of blood ceased to flow. Then flowed again, with an almost violent sensation of force and movement.

The child's name was William Clear, born of Roseanne Clear, waitress. The father was given as Eneas McNulty, soldier. The child was given to Mr and Mrs Grene of Padstow, Cornwall, in 1945.

I sat there before Sr Miriam in a daze.

'Well?' she said quite gently. 'So, you didn't know?'

'No, no, of course not – I am here on official – to help and aid an old lady in my care –'

'We thought you might know. We didn't know if you knew.'

'I didn't know.'

'There are other things here, notes of conversations between Sr Declan and a Sean Keane in the seventies? Do you know anything about that?'

'No.'

'Mr Keane was anxious to find you and Sr Declan was able to oblige him. Did he ever find you?'

'I don't know. No. Yes.'

'You are very confused and of course that is understandable. It is like the tsunami, no? Something sweeping over you. Carrying people and things with it.'

'Sister, excuse me, I think I am going to be sick. Those cakes . . .'

'Oh, yes, of course,' she said. 'Just go through there.'

When I was sufficiently able, there was the bizarre experience of looking at my 'aunt's' grave. Then I left that place and made my way back to London.

I wished, I wished and I longed for Bet to be still alive so I could tell her, that was my first thought.

But every subsequent thought I had, I shook my head at it. The other passengers must have thought I had Parkinson's. No, no, it was impossible. There was no door in my head where the information could go in.

That old lady, whom I had been barely aware of for years, and yet who had taken such a grip on my imagination in these recent times, that old lady, with her oddness, her histories, her disputed deeds, and yes, her friendship, was my mother.

I hurried back, hurried home as one might say. The hours of the journey didn't bring me much clarity. I was homing though, hurrying, fearful suddenly that she would be dead before I got there. I could not explain to anyone that feeling. Pure feeling, nothing else. Feeling without thought. Just to get there, to keep going and get there. I rushed across Ireland, driving I am sure with certifiable stupidity. I parked clumsily in the carpark of my hospital, and without as much as a greeting to my staff, strode on into the ward where I hoped and prayed she still was. There was a curtain drawn about her bed, although there was no one else in the room. I thought, oh, yes, of course this is the conclusion, she is dead. I looked round the curtain only to see her face quite awake and alive, turning now a few degrees, quizzically to look at me.

'Dr Grene,' she said. 'Where have you been? I'm back from the dead, apparently.'

I tried to tell her, there and then. But I hadn't the words. I will have to wait for the words, I thought.

She seemed to sense something, as I lingered at the gap in the curtain. People know more instinctively than they know in their conscious brain (perhaps medically a dubious notion but there it is).

'So, Doctor,' she said. 'Have you assessed me?'

'What?'

'Have you made your assessment?'

'Oh, yes. I think so.'

'And what is the verdict?'

'You are blameless.'

'Blameless? I hardly think that is given to any mortal being.'

'Blameless. Wrongly committed. I apologise. I apologise on behalf of my profession. I apologise on behalf of myself, as someone who did not bestir himself, and look into everything earlier. That it took the demolition of the hospital to do it. And I know my apology is useless and disgusting to you.'

Weak as she was, she laughed.

'But', she said, 'that is not true. They showed me the brochure for the new hospital. I suppose you will let me stay there for a while?'

'It is entirely your decision. You are a free woman.'

'I was not always a free woman. I thank you for my freedom.'

'It is my privilege to pronounce it,' I said, suddenly very odd and formal, but she took it in her stride.

'Can you step back to the bed?' she said.

I did so. I didn't know what she intended. But she just lifted my hand, and shook it.

'I wonder will you allow me to forgive you?' she said.

'My God, yes,' I said.

There was a short silence then, just enough of a silence for the breath of a dozen thoughts to blow through my brain.

'Well, I do,' she said.

The next morning, I went round to the old stableblock. I wanted to ask John Kane while I still could the few questions, with now all the more reason to do so. I knew it was unlikely that he would be able or even willing to answer me. I supposed at the very least I might offer him profoundest thanks, for all his strange work.

There was absolutely no sign of him. His quarters was a single room with an old-fashioned gramophone sideboard, the sort of one where you had to open the right-hand door for the sound to escape, because the door hid a simple wooden amplifier. There was a collection of 78 records in the niche supplied by the manufacturers (Shepherds, Bristol). It contained Benny Goodman, Bubber Miley, Jelly Roll Morton, Fletcher Henderson, and Billy Mayerl records. Otherwise the room was empty, except for a neat little iron bed, with a coverlet crudely sewn with flowers. I thought immediately of Mrs McNulty's work as described by Roseanne. I have no doubt that to get his way, or what he thought was the best way to serve Roseanne, he used all the pressure he could bring on the McNultys and their secret. The first wife who did not legally exist, and about whom the second family of Tom McNulty was probably never told. The mad wife who was not a wife, but nevertheless was flesh and blood. I am sure Mrs McNulty and her good daughter went as far as they humanly could to humour John Kane, even to the extent of supplying my new name, and my story up to that point. I do not know what he intended to do after he had found me, and can only suppose that having found out I had miraculously trained as a psychiatrist, he adapted himself to this, and hatched a better plan than the first, which after all, if it was a simple reunion he had in mind, might have resulted in my refusal to see Roseanne, or having seen her, my rejection of her. Because why would I not reject her, when everyone else had?

Well, I supposed all these things. It is not history. But I am beginning to wonder strongly what is the nature of history. Is it only memory in decent sentences, and if so, how reliable is it? I would suggest, not very. And that therefore most truth and fact offered by these syntactical means is treacherous and unreliable. And yet I recognise that we live our lives, and even keep our sanity, by the lights of this treachery and this unreliability, just as we build our love of country on these paper worlds of misapprehension and untruth. Perhaps this is our nature, and perhaps unaccountably it is part of our glory as a creature, that we can build our best and most permanent buildings on foundations of utter dust.

I should also memorialise a box of Cuban cigars by John

Kane's bed, which, on opening it, I discovered to be half empty. Or half full.

Otherwise nothing, except this curious and important little note on top of the gramophone:

Dear Doctor Green,

I am not no angel but I took the baby off that island. I run to the doctor with it. I would like to speke to you but I am bound to go. You will ask why I done it all for Roseanne and the anser is because I loved my father. My father was killed by Peerpoint. I got Doc Sing to right you a letter and it was a miracle he did and that you came. I am glad you came. Someday I was going to tell you the truth and now that day is come. You know the truth I am certan and plese now you do do not throw off your mother. No one among us is perfect look at me but that is not the idea. If we do not come to the gates of heaven with love averred, St Peter cannot let us in the gates. Now I say goodbye, Doc, forgive me, and God also forgive me.

Faithfully,

Seanín Keane Lavelle (John Kane)

PS. It is Doran attacked that Leitrim woman, the one that went home safely.

The other nurses and attendants did not know where he was. It wasn't as if he had packed a bag, or crept into the woodland behind us to die. There was simply no trace of him. Of course the police were informed and I am sure the gardai are keeping a weather eye out for him, and spot him everywhere and nowhere. Max Doran, the orderly referred to by John Kane, quite a young fellow and rather handsome and who has a girl-friend, confessed privately to me about the Leitrim woman, about which he is obviously ashamed and, more to the point, worried. He confessed, but then retracted. When the solicitors are ready he will go to trial, which may be some time. As the hospital and its staff are dispersed, I cannot say morale has been harmed. Perhaps something small has been gained. I would like to think it is the start of safety for our patients but alas I am not so great a fool.

CHAPTER TWENTY-TWO

Now here is the autumn and she is in good quarters. Purpose-built, state of the art, really, in truth, an asylum worthy of that ancient and desirable name. No doubt with her great age it is only a matter of time, but then, what is not? Many a good man died long before my own age. Many days she is silent, and difficult, and won't eat, and asks me brusquely why I have come. Sometimes she tells me she doesn't need me to come.

Like John Kane, I am trying to pick my moment. I see very well the difficulty he had.

One day as I was going she stood up and came the few inches towards me like a scrap of parchment, embraced me, and thanked me. Even her bones have lost weight. I was so moved I almost told her. But I still did not.

I think I fear, though she may be satisfied hopefully with me as a doctor and a friend, she may be disappointed with me as a son, as being not sufficient recompense for all her travails – a ridiculous, sober, ageing, confused English Irishman. Furthermore I am terrified of shocking her in the wrong way, medically, psychically. On this I might consult with Dr Wynn, but it might be a shock well beyond the business of medicine, beyond what he knows, and what I know. Something subtle, gentle, and fragile might be broken, beyond our clumsy fixing. The kernel of her endurance. But I believe it will keep, it will keep. The important thing is, she is safe and cared for. And she is free.

The month after I returned from England the asylum was demolished. They decided to do it by controlled explosion, so that the top four floors would collapse when the ground floor was blown away. That morning it was like going out to see my life being erased, with wires and dynamite and beautiful calculations. We all stood back on a little hill, about a quarter mile from the building. At the appointed hour the engineer pushed down on the box, and after an eternal second we heard a massive noise and saw the underside of the old building dissolve in a fiery crown of mortar and ancient stone. The huge edifice immediately headed earthward, leaving only a hanging memory of its old positions against the sky line. Behind it was an angel, a great man of fire the height of the asylum, with wings spread from east to west. It was evidently John Kane. I looked about me at my companions and asked them if they saw what I saw. They looked at me as if I was mad, and I suppose, having lost my asylum and now being only the superintendent of an enormous absence, filled by an unlikely angel, I suppose I was.

It was of course grief that saw the angel. I know that now. I was thinking I was quite over Bet, Bet was a safe memory, but it was only just beginning. Grief is about two years long, they say, it is a platitude out of manuals for grievers. But we are in mourning for our mothers before even we are born.

I will tell her. Just as soon as I can find the words. Just as soon as we reach that part of the story.

Today I drove back to Sligo. At the top of the town I passed the municipal graveyard, and wondered what time had done to the concrete temple and the acres of graves. I dropped in on Percy after all, and thanked him for helping me. I don't know if he was surprised. When I told him what had happened he certainly looked at me gobsmacked for a few moments. Then he got up from behind his desk. I was standing by the door, not having been sure whether fully to enter, or half to stay outside, so as not to disturb him.

'My dear man,' he said.

I don't know, I thought he was going to embrace me. I smiled like a boy, that's what it felt like, and I gave a laugh of happiness. It was only then really that it hit me. I am content to report that at the centre of it all, given everything, the nature of her history and mine, there was a very simple emotion.

I wanted to tell him that I thought it wasn't so much a question of whether she had written the truth about herself, or told the truth, or believed what she wrote and said was true, or even whether they were true things in themselves. The important thing seemed to me that the person who wrote and spoke was admirable, living, and complete. I wanted to tell him, to confess in a way, that from a psychiatric point of view I had totally failed to 'help' her, to prise open the locked lids of the past. But then, my original intention was not to help, but to assess her. All the time I might have helped her, all those years she was here, I had more or less left her alone. I wanted to tell him, she has helped herself, she has spoken to, listened to, herself. It is a victory. And that, in the matter of her father, in the upshot I preferred Roseanne's untruth to Fr Gaunt's truth, because the former radiated health. That moreover I believed that if the wonderful Amurdat Singh had not summoned me, I probably would never have practised psychiatry, and did not believe that I had ever been a good psychiatrist, whatever about a good man. That Roseanne had instructed me in the mystery of human silence and the efficacy of a withdrawal from the task of questioning. But I wasn't able to say these things.

Then he made a remark that might have been offensive, but actually I think represented an aperçu on his part, of which he was quite proud, and for which I was quite grateful, in the circumstances.

'You will be retiring soon,' he said, 'and yet, in many ways, you are just starting out.'

Then I thanked Percy again and went back to the car and drove out to Strandhill. I sort of knew the road from

Roseanne's account, and went there as if I had been before. When I reached the C-of-I church, obediently where it was supposed to be, I got out and looked about me. There was Knocknarea as she had often described it, rearing up as if fleeing away into the past, the remote and unknowable past. Below was Sligo Bay, with Rosses over to the right, and Ben Bulben where Willie Lavelle was killed, and I saw the bollards still on the strand leading out to Coney island. It was just a little place heaped up, a few fields and houses. I almost couldn't say it in my mind, *that is where I was born*. Somewhere there at the edge of things, appropriately enough, as Roseanne had always lived on the edges of our known world, and John Kane too. I was born on the edges of things, and even now, as the guardian of the mentally ill, I have by instinct pitched my tent in a similar place. Beyond the island, distantly, was the faithful figure of the Metal Man, eternally pointing.

To my left was the little village, I would say not much changed, but there are of course many more houses in Strandhill than there would have been in Roseanne's day. Nevertheless I could make out below the facade of an old hotel near the beach, and the great mound of sand that gave this place its simple name, and even I fancied the front of what looked like a humble dancehall.

It seems it was a well-chosen day, because as I drove down to the seaside, noting the cannon and the innocuous water, I saw there were men at work on the dancehall. It looked like they were readying it for demolition. There was an architect's sign that said there were going to be apartments built in due course. The hall itself looked almost ridiculously small, the hump of corrugated iron behind, the front itself that must indeed have once been a seaside dwelling. The flag was gone that once would have said the name, but in later years someone had affixed five iron letters to the front, now all greyed and rusted: P-L-A-Z-A. It was extraordinary for me to think of all the vanished history of this place. To think of Eneas McNulty walking here in his burned uniform, of Tom going in with his instruments, of the cars coming out from Sligo along the glistening strand, and the strains of music leaking out into the untrustworthy Irish summer air, and maybe straying even as far as the ancient ears of Queen Maeve. Certainly the ears of listening Roseanne, in her own buried exile.

It was more difficult to locate her hut. I found I had already passed the spot where it must have been, because I was able to find the fine wall of the big house across from it, and the gate where Jack's wife had humiliated Roseanne. At first I thought it was all just brambles and ruin, but the old stone chimney was still almost intact, though covered in lichen and climbing weeds. The rooms where Roseanne had lived out her sentence of living death were no more.

I walked in the ruined gap of the little gate and stood on the scruffy grass. There was nothing to see but in my mind's eye I could see everything, because she had supplied the ancient cinema of this place. Nothing except a neglected rose bush among the brambles, with a few last vivid blooms. Despite my reading of Bet's books, I found that I didn't know the name of it. But hadn't Roseanne mentioned it? Something, something . . . For the life of me, I couldn't remember what she had written. But I pushed forward through the thorns and weeds, thinking I might take a few blooms of it back to Roscommon as a souvenir. All the blooms were uniform, a neat tight-curled rose, except on one branch, whose roses were different, bright and open. I could feel the brambles tearing at my legs, and pulling at my jacket like beggars, but suddenly I knew what I was doing. I carefully peeled off a sprig as recommended in the books in the chapters on propagation, and slipped it in my pocket, feeling almost guilty, as if I were stealing something that didn't belong to me.